MW01639721

A Lady Crowned with Fleurs-de-lys

An Historical Novel

Amelia V. Rogers

WingSpan Press

This is a historical work of fiction based on actual events. Apart from the well-known places, people and incidents incorporated into the story, all names, places, characters, and event are derived from the author's imagination or have been used fictitiously. Any resemblance to actual events, locals or to any living person is entirely coincidental.

Published in the United States and the United Kingdom by WingSpan Press, Livermore, CA

The WingSpan name, logo and colophon are the trademarks of WingSpan Publishing

ISBN: 978-1-59594-525-9 (pbk.)
ISBN: 978-1-59594-864-9 (ebk.)

First edition 2014

Printed in the United States of America

Library of Congress Control Number 2014938534

www.wingspanpress.com

1 2 3 4 5 6 7 8 9 10

Table Of Contents

A Lady Crowned

A Lady Crowned with Fleur de Lys
Essential Genealogy

Charles V = Jeanne of Bourbon
1364-1380

Philip of Burgundy = Margaret of Flanders
John the Fearless

Charles VI = Isabella of Bavaria
1380-1422
Isabella = Richard II of England
= Charles of Orleans
Catherine = Henry V of England
= Owen Tudor
Charles VII = Mary of Anjou
1422-1461
9 more children

Louis = Valentina Visconti
Charles = Isabella of France
= Bonne of Armagnac

Between 1337 and 1453 France and England were involved in a succession of wars, truces, invasions, and armistices that go under the name of Hundred Years' Wars. The most recent cause for this turmoil was the inheritance of the French throne, which the English claimed as their king was the direct descendant of the king of France, but the French rejected because they recognized only male lineage and the English claim was based on a French Princess.

France was devastated by the wars because the battles were all fought on its territory and eventually a civil war ensued that led to the coronation of an English king. The country was saved and the rightful French king crowned thanks to that famous French heroine that the Church considers a saint: Joan of Arc.

Prologue

The King Is Dead

The bells of Paris filled the luminous October air with a slow, sorrowful sound. Charles of Valois, the mad King was dead and his people, in Paris and in the most remote corners of his country mourned for him. They loved their sovereign, even if his long malady had precipitated France into an abyss of war, famine and destruction. In him they had seen their last frail bulwark against the English; with his death the infamous Treaty of Troyes became a reality and a foreign Prince would sit on the throne of the fleurs-de-lis. More ruin loomed on the horizon of the unhappy country because the foreign Prince was only an infant and his uncle, the rightful heir of the dead King, would certainly not renounce what he considered his sacred inheritance.

Once again the Queen's name came to the people's lips and the tone of their voices was angry, contemptuous. "It's Isabeau's fault ....," they would say. "It's her, the German woman....God is punishing us for her sins. We bore too long with her greediness, her lust, her lewdness; God will bear with us no more..."

The sad tolling of the bells seemed to underline the magnificent yet gloomy funeral procession. Slowly dusk was descending both on it and on the whole of France and soon the shadows would cover that world completely.

Forgotten and perhaps forgiven, villains and heroes would become only names indifferent to the listeners, but while the sun still lingered on the glass windows of Notre Dame de Paris the ghosts from the past would crowd on the scene, eager to talk, justify, explain. Once again, yet briefly, the stage is occupied by the main actors that convulsed France and England for one hundred years: King Charles, Queen Isabelle, the Duke of Orleans, Valentina Visconti, and Henry of England. Minor characters appear as well —they too want to be heard, they too have their insignificant lines to read.

Frozen for eternity, all the actors wear the smiles and colors of their youth, when the drama started and their lives changed forever.

Chapter I

A Princess From Germany

The castle of Ludwigsburg was large, imposing and gloomy. It had been built by Elizabeth's great-grandfather and every room, tower, gallery still seemed to bear the mark of that brave, illustrious man. Its halls were huge, with long narrow windows and cool stone floors. Everywhere armors, trophies, shields, hanging on the walls, bore testimony to the valor and love of war of the Wittelsbach.

Catherine loved the old castle, its high vaults and ceilings, the vast halls that her imagination filled with the heroes of the chansons-de-geste that the troubadours narrated in the long winter nights. It was the only home she could remember as her father, one of the noblemen in Duke Stephen's retinue, had brought Catherine there when the death of her mother had left her the only member of his family. Little Princess Elizabeth was Catherine's age and she joined her household, sharing her nurses, her dolls, her life.

Catherine's father was absent from Munich most of the time, as he followed his lord everywhere the Duke's expeditions took him and his little army of two-hundred knights. They would go from Alsace to Italy, from Germany to Poland, wherever there was a war or a skirmish, wherever the Pope or a Prince needed the services of the Bavarian troop to quell an insurrection or start a war on a neighbor country. Stephen, Duke of Bavaria, loved adventure, but he also loved and needed money, as he was extremely generous, extravagant, and his coffers were permanently empty. He was tall, fair and very handsome, he loved hunting and drinking with his comrades and was never at a loss to find a word or compliment for a lady. The Duke's brothers, John and Frederick, took part in his campaigns, and that very often left the Duchess to preside over Ludwigsburg alone, helped by her sisters-in-law, Anne and Catherine.

Elizabeth's mother, Taddea Visconti, was a small thin woman with olive skin and very dark piercing eyes. She came from Milan, an Italian city renowned for its beautiful churches, palaces, and the refined life that Taddea's father, Barnabo, led among the artists and poets that gathered at his court.

The coat-of-arms of the Visconti, a viper with a naked child in its open jaws, seemed very appropriate to the fame of cruelty and despotism that surrounded the family, and especially the redoubtable Barnabo. At Ludwigsburg it was whispered that he was deeply irreligious and scorned any civil law to which he did not consider himself bound. The list of his murders was apparently endless, as was that of his mistresses and bastards.

Catherine learned these things only many years later because every time Elizabeth's grandfather's name was pronounced aloud, it was done so with the respect that the Duchess demanded for a beloved father. The Lady Taddea herself, like the rooms she inhabited, had a great charm and attraction for Catherine. The dresses she wore were different from those of her sisters-in-law, simpler, but more refined, richer in their hues, softer in their textures. She was often cold and wrapped herself up in warm fur capes of beaver and ermine trimmed with gold braids, hid her hands in muffs and gloves. A heavy, heady scent of jasmine and roses perfumed her dresses and permeated her apartment. The cold flagstones were covered with soft carpets woven with threads of gold and silver, the rough drafty walls disappeared under precious Flemish tapestries depicting scenes of falcon hunting, where pretty flowers, charming rabbits and birds enlivened the brown background with their bright colors.

It was a thrill for Catherine to be asked to join Elizabeth in her visits to her mother, and the smiling lady, on whose lips German sounded so soft and different, always had a kind word or an interested question for the little girl.

On a warm June day, when Catherine and Elizabeth were still adolescent, the palace had been in a flurry of activities from dawn. The Duke Stephen and his knights had returned a few days previously from a successful campaign in Northern Italy and a banquet had been planned in his honor for that evening in the great hall of the castle. A poet had been asked to the festivities to entertain the noble company playing the flute and singing poems of love and war for them.

The servants were working hard, slaughtering the animals to be roasted and stuffed for the banquet, carrying vats of ale and cider from the depths of the cellars, setting up trestle-tables, filling sconces and candelabra with sweet-scented candles.

The first rays of the sun streaming through the windows had stirred the girls awake, and soon Elizabeth, her cousins Margaret, Jacqueline, and Catherine, her friend, donned light summer dresses and ran outdoors. The park of red-barked fir trees that surrounded Ludwigsburg was dark and cool, but the green grass of the garden, with bright spots of red roses and orange marigolds, yellow honeysuckle climbing over the dove-cotes where Elizabeth's favorite birds cooed, was more inviting. The four girls sat under the shade of a tree and chatted merrily of the night festivities, the dresses they would be wearing, the food the servants were preparing, the guests attending the banquet.

Even when the Duke, his brothers and his men were away, Ludwigsburg was hardly deserted, because a multitude of pages, equerries, servants, ladies-in-waiting, maids, were left behind to minister to the princes' families. Young children were numerous too—besides her older brother, Ludwig, Elizabeth had several cousins, boys and girls her age, who were her best companions. The young princes and princesses shared many of their daily activities, including the study of Latin, the language of their prayer books and a hateful task that the strictness of the Duchess would not allow them to avoid. But today was a day of celebration; their teacher would not make his appearance until the morrow, and that enhanced the carefree mood pervading the young people.

Later, Catherine accompanied Elizabeth to her mother's rooms. They found the Lady Taddea intently observing a small painting framed in gilded wood that hung over her carved prie-dieu. She looked up when they entered and smiled fondly at Elizabeth.

"I am glad you came, my dear, and you too, Catherine," she said, "because I want you to admire this pretty picture my father gave to the Duke for me. Is it not beautiful?" The oval painting represented the Annunciation, set in a white-columned porch opening onto a green garden. The divine messenger was kneeling, in front of a blond Virgin absorbed in her prayers. The splendor of his variegated wings, shimmering with hues of blue, pink, green, made him similar to a beautiful bird ready to fly up and contrasted with the simplicity of Mary's plain attire. The scene had a charm end freshness the girls-loved and they agreed with the Duchess on the beauty of the gift.

Elizabeth was standing next to her mother and though she was barely- twelve, she was as tall as Taddea. The two women looked a lot like each other, but if Elizabeth had inherited the Visconti dark hair and eyes, she resembled the Wittelsbach in her more robust figure and creamy complexion. Her face was round, her mouth large and fleshy, her nose too wide to make her beautiful, but there was mischievousness in her eyes, warmth in her smile that added attraction to her features. The way she bore herself, too, very erect and proud, made her look taller than she was.

The little Annunciation that an unknown Italian artist had painted for her grandfather later became one of Elizabeth's favorite possessions, forever linked with memories of a beloved mother.

* * *

The Duke of Bavaria and his lady were sitting together at the table of honor under a red canopy, his handsome fairness contrasting with her dark colors, the light blue of his gown set off by the soft waves of her red dress. Her dark hair was held tightly against her head by a gold circlet encrusted with hanging pearls, and her laughter was merry and infectious. At the same table set Elizabeth's uncles, the noble, gregarious Frederick with his wife Anne, and the more solemn, grave John, whose wife, Catherine, was the most beautiful woman in Bavaria.

Catherine of Fastavarin's place was at the end of the hall, with the younger members of the Wittelsbach clan, and there she sat, too thrilled by the noise, music, laughter, drinking, to do more than nibble at the different dishes displayed in front of her. Something else was adding to her excitement, something she had never experienced before and did not know how to define. All through the evening, Elizabeth's brother, Prince Ludwig, had been looking at her with soft admiring eyes that held no reflection of the arrogance that was so much part of his personality. Catherine had felt her cheeks blush and there was a new confusion in her heart.

Ludwig was a couple of years older than Catherine. A tall, thin boy with a shock of blond hair and bright blue eyes, he decide favored the German part of the family. He had never shown interest in any of the numerous girls in the Wittelsbach household; his passionate love went to horse-riding, weapons, hunting. Ludwig hero-worshipped his father, whom he imitated in the proud bearing and arrogance, and seemed fond enough of his mother end only sister.

His cousins and their friends had given signs aplenty of their admiration for the handsome heir to the Duchy, but Ludwig had seemed to ignore all the girls with perfect equanimity and they soon directed their attentions elsewhere. Good looking polite pages were not lacking at the court of Munich and flirting was one of the most enjoyable pastimes.

Catherine could not understand her excitement—she was not one of the silly girls that talked nothing but boys and blushed end squirmed every time a page addressed them. After all, boys were just the boisterous companions of your games—were they not?

If Ludwig had never exactly been a companion, it was because he considered girls, all girls, uninteresting and was too dignified a young man to take part in the childish pastimes of Elizabeth and her young friends.

Still, she was confused. In the depths of her pocket lay a crumpled piece of paper. It was a note, the third one, that a page, an intense looking youth with passionate eyes and curly hair had sent her. He begged Catherine to meet him secretly that night. He wanted to talk to her, confess his longing and desire for the prettiest girl in Bavaria.

The-prettiest girl in Bavaria...Catherine liked the words, and this added to her confusion. Was she going to meet him? What would she say to him, what if he tried to kiss her?

She lifted her eyes to the table where the Duke and his family were seated. Christian stood behind the Duchess' chair, a dutiful page ready to obey his mistress' command, but Catherine knew how often his gaze had wandered to where she sat, and their eyes had met.

The stewards removing the tables and making room for the minstrel that was going to entertain the company, distracted Catherine from her reverie and, together with the other young people, she sat on one side of the hall where soft goat skins and pillows had been piled up.

The poet took his stand in the center of the room, strumming on a lute. He was a tall, thin man, with a short blond beard and hair the color of ripe wheat. He wore a short violet doublet, and tight green hose. His eyes were sad, the voice as sweet and gentle as the words of the love songs that filled the hall.

The Minnesanger were a hymn to love; they spoke of unhappiness and solitude without the loved one, they exalted a noble and courteous woman who was God's masterpiece and whose love was not sinful. Catherine looked around her. The minstrel's words seemed to find an echo in everyone's heat; the men's eyes became ardent, the smile on the ladies' lips soft and yielding.

All of a sudden a hand touched hers, eager fingers, a strong palm. Instinctively she returned the pressure. She knew it was not Christian—the young page was still attending the Duchess, Catherine could see his tall figure half-hidden by a column. The pressure on her hand became stronger, more demanding. She had to turn her head and meet the eyes of the boy that had come behind her and whose strong, body leaned so close and warm next to hers.

It was Ludwig. He was staring at her and smiled when she returned his look. An all-encompassing wave of happiness rushed through her, leaving her languid and exhausted.

The hall end its inhabitants blurred in front of her eyes, the sound of the poet's voice became as indistinct as the far-away barking of the Duke's hounds.

Perhaps aware of her confusion and wanting to reassure her, Ludwig held her nearer to his body.

Catherine felt everybody's eyes on them. Certainly Elizabeth had noticed her brother's movement; surely Christian had seen how willingly her body had yielded to Ludwig's pressure....

Just then though, the minstrel started the first lines of "The Hunt" en epic poem that celebrated the joys of that manly sport, and the mood in the hall seemed to change, become merry and carefree. The Duke and his gentlemen joined in the refrain; their voices were loud and fierce, their faces flushed, their eyes exalted.

Ludwig let go of Catherine's hand and stood up. He was not a boy any longer, but a young man, a hunter, a killer of the wild boar that roamed through the woods, and the spear he carried was red with the blood of the slain animal.

But he had not forgotten her.

"I want to see you, Catherine," he said. "Meet me later, when the celebrations are over, in that corner of the garden where my sister keeps her dovecotes."

"But what shall I tell Elizabeth? And your cousins? You know we share the same room."

"Catherine," he smiled ironically, "You are no longer a child. No doubt you know how you can leave your room without Elizabeth and my cousins noticing it. Besides," he added imperiously, "what if they do notice? Jacqueline, Margaret and my sister as well, no doubt meet their friends secretly. So, you do not have to worry, my pretty Catherine. But, please, do not keep me waiting too long," he added more gently and was quickly gone, without giving her time to protest his assertion.

Catherine knew that Elizabeth never met anybody secretly. They were so close that Elizabeth would have confided in her, as now she herself had the urge to do the same with her friend.

For the remainder of the evening Catherine did her best to avoid both Elizabeth and Christian. Fortunately, the page was in continuous attendance on the Duchess and could only follow her with longing eyes.

Elizabeth did not seem eager to be with her friend that night. Her cousin Johann was constantly at her side—a tall, strapping boy with hazel eyes and brown hair, who had just returned from the Italian expedition with the Duke his uncle.

The June evening seemed to linger forever and when at last night a fell over the castle of Ludwigsburg, and Catherine joined the other girls in their room; she found them quiet and sleepy. They undressed quickly, commenting briefly on the night's festivities, and crept silently into the canopied bed they shared.

Soon their regular breathing convinced Catherine that her friends were asleep. She stole quietly out of bed and reached for her dress. The room was dark but for the rays of the half-moon streaming through the window.

"Where are you going?" The voice startled Catherine, and she had to suppress a cry of fear.

"Oh, Elizabeth," she whispered, approaching the bed, "You scared me out of my wits. I thought you were asleep."

'Elizabeth chuckled. "How can you think you can deceive me, Catherine? Both you and my brother think you are so clever, do you not? Well, you are not. I kept my eyes on you, and sew all of Ludwig's sly maneuvering while that poor minstrel was pouring his heart out."

"You did?' Catherine marveled. "You seemed so engrossed in Johann that I am surprised that you had eyes for somebody else."

Elizabeth seemed to hesitate. "You know, my friend," she confided breathlessly, "Johann says that he loves me, and he gave me an enamel cross he bought for me in Italy. I will show it to you tomorrow. But you have not answered my question. Where are you going?" she repeated.

"Ludwig wants to see me, Elizabeth. Put, please, do not tell Margaret, or Jacqueline, or anybody else, will you?"

"I will not, I promise. Besides, you are so fickle, Catherine, that in two days my poor brother will have been forgotten and your faith pledged to somebody else."

"You are wrong, you are wrong, Elizabeth, sang, Catherine's heart, as she found her way in the maze of corridors, halls, staircases, that led from her room to a little door opening onto the garden. I love Ludwig, I know it now, and I always will.

"Here you are, at last!" he said impatiently. It was dark under the leafy oak tree, and Catherine could hardly make out his figure leaning against the trunk. "I was almost despairing of your coming tonight, Catherine, and yet you must know how anxious I am to talk to you alone."

"Anxious, Ludwig?" she said. "Until tonight you paid no attention to me, you always made me feel that neither you nor your friends had any interest for the girls at court, and now it is hard for me to believe your words."

"Perhaps I have changed, Catherine. You certainly have, you have become the prettiest girl I have ever seen and I have been thinking about you constantly." He pulled her to him and lifted her face to his.

The moon was high above the trees, and its beams, filtering through the leaves, lent a pale glow to the trunk end the thick grass underneath.

She could see Ludwig's face more clearly—he seemed in earnest, and on his white face his eyes stood out like dark mysterious pools.

Catherine was light-headed and confused, yet strangely aware of her power—his happiness depended upon her. She could make smile, tremble with desire or, if she rejected him, she would sadden and upset him. She was the stronger.

Or was she? When he kissed her, she felt instinctively that she depended on him as much as he on her. If it was a game that they were playing, they were equal partners at it.

His lips were soft and strong on hers, his arms held her tightly to his chest—Catherine could smell the different scent of his skin, feel the smooth silk of his shirt. He made her lie on the grass and lay down beside her, one arm around her waist.

In the stillness of the night, the perfume of the flowers was intoxicating. No sound to be heard but the hesitant cooing of a dove or the faraway neigh of a horse.

"I could stay here forever," she murmured. "I do not want to think that in a few hours the sun will be up and everybody will be stirring about and destroy this marvelous quiet and solitude."

"But later the moon will rise in the sky, again, my darling. I will meet you here and the night will belong to us once more."

"Will you always love me, Ludwig, and be faithful to me?"

"Oh, Catherine, how many love songs have you ever read? You do believe that love is eternal and everlasting happiness is sealed by a kiss, do you not" he laughed. "Remember, my dear, that the words of the love poems have no bearing to reality. You are beautiful: Catherine, end mine is not the only heart you will break. As for me, I can only promise you that "now" my heart is yours, green-eyed witch, and that is what matters."

He leaned over and started kissing her again, covering her lips, eyes, cheeks with long passionate kisses that left her weak and trembling.

I will make you love me forever, she silently promised herself, trying to dispel the pain that his words had given her. Then her fears, dreams, anxieties were silenced as she was swept away by the intensity of her passion.

* * *

A couple of months after the festivities that had celebrated her husband's homecoming, the Duchess died suddenly.

A long, black-clad procession accompanied her to her last rest in the church of Our Lady. She was buried in the ornate Wittelsbach tomb, near the altar the proud ancestor of the family, the Emperor Ludwig, had built in honor of the Virgin and the Holy Cross.

Elizabeth went back to the silent rooms that had been her mother's, trying to find her among the silks and brocades that had wrapped her body, in the polished mirrors that had reflected her beloved features. But it was in vain. The Lady Taddea was no more; the perfume of roses and jasmine that still floated in the air was the last ephemeral trace of her existence.

Elizabeth mourned her for a long, time and became more fiercely possessive of her father than she had ever been before. Then, her Aunt Anne died a few months after the Lady Taddea, and not long afterwards, her uncle, Prince Frederick, brought a new bride to Ludwigsburg.

Elizabeth was shattered. "He seemed to love his wife so dearly. How could he replace her with another woman, how could he? Tell me, Catherine, you must know: is love like this then? Is it so frail that it can only last as long as the person we love is with us? Vows do not count—separation and death are more powerful than any pledge of love. It *is* not true, though, is it? Certainly you will love Ludwig forever, will you not?"

"How can I answer these questions, Elizabeth? I know that I will love him as long as I live, but he is not pledged to me, he has never promised me that he will be faithful to our love. He never says that he loves me," she added quietly, as if to herself.

Elizabeth was silent for en instant. "I must admit that I have often noticed the way Ludwig behaves with you, Catherine," she went on, "and I assure you that I would not let Johann or any other boy treat me in such a fashion. Why, he even kissed Jacqueline in front of you once, and you did not say a word but just ran away."

Catherine blushed. "Ludwig is the heir to the Duchy, Elizabeth. Do you think he will be allowed to marry a poor courtier's daughter, when he can choose among the noblest and richest princesses in Europe? I have no claims on him; he has told me this from the beginning."

"Poor Catherine," sighed her friend, "but do not despair. Perhaps

I will marry a very wealthy prince, you know. This is highly possible, there are so many powerful and rich lords ruling over the lands of Germany who would he overjoyed at an alliance with the Wittelsbach. Then I would ask my husband, to grant you a most generous dowry, and Ludwig would have no objections to marrying you."

Catherine smiled sadly. "I do not think that wealth is the main obstacle to my marrying your brother, Elizabeth, but T thank you for your thoughtfulness. But does this mean that you do not intend to marry Johann, after all? I thought you were devoted to each other!"

"If truth be known, my friend," she frowned, "I think that Johann is slightly uninspiring and dull. Soldiering and horses, that is all he talks about when we are together!"

That cannot be all, if I have to judge from the way you look when you come back from your walks with him, Elizabeth, Catherine thought mischievously. Why you are always breathless and disheveled, and so lost in your daydreaming that it is no use for me or anybody to address you and wait for an answer! Put she did not say anything and let her friend continue.

"Besides, I have been told from infancy that I am destined to marry a great German sovereign, and my cousin is not the heir to any important lands or holdings. No, I consider Johann as an... experiment, you know. Perhaps the man I marry will be a plain, sluggish prince, a fat, unattractive man that I cannot love, but I wanted to see what love is all about, if one really feels the ecstasies and torments of which poems and books talk."

"And what have you found out?" Catherine inquired ironically.

Elizabeth did not notice her tone. "To tell you the truth, I do not know, Catherine. At the beginning it was as beautiful as the poets say it is. I would look for Johann every time I entered a room where he might be, start and blush if he approached me unaware, daydream about him and a future together. Do you remember the cross that he brought back from Italy for me? I would touch it a hundred times a day, because he had touched it, and put it; under my pillow at night as I hoped to dream about him. But all this is changing now. I still think he is handsome and courteous, but his conversation is so boring I sometimes think I will fall asleep just listening to him."

"Just as well you will not have to marry him, then," her friend said.

"Perhaps you will be lucky and marry a handsome and generous Prince end then your 'experiment' will be successful!" teased Catherine.

"As lucky as my mother was when she married my father," said Elizabeth. "Theirs was true love, I know. That is why I am sure that my father will never marry again, he will never forget my mother as my uncle forgot his poor deceased wife."

"But, my dear, do you not remember that a month ago even your brother assumed that the Duke was going to marry that princess of Flanders that was visiting in Ludwigsburg?"

"But then he did not, did he, Catherine?" she replied triumphantly. "No, it is as I tell you. My father will always remain faithful to my mother's memory. Besides, he loves me too much to give me a step-mother. He knows I would hate to have to curtsy before another Duchess of Bavaria!"

"I hope you are right, Elizabeth," said Catherine. She felt dejected and hopeless. Her friend's words had made her realize, if not for the first time, how little she meant to Ludwig. She could hardly blame him of heartlessness—he had never promised her a thing but tried, in vain alas, to persuade her to regard their love as a pleasant, light flirtation. Hard as she tried, Catherine did not succeed. Her love for Ludwig was as deep and strong as his seemed to be lighthearted and nonchalant.

As the Duke continued his expeditions abroad, Ludwig and his cousins were often away. Their homecomings were welcomed with joy by all and the younger boys and girls that had been left behind listened eagerly to the tales of the fascinating worlds they had visited.

Sometimes Elizabeth and Catherine wished they were boys. Then they could accompany the men in their campaigns, and see the gold-domed cathedrals, the shining mosaics, the tall spires of mysterious cities, the shimmering blue oceans, the dark forests where bears and wolves hid, the brilliant courts of the great lords of the world.

"The people that live far away, across the mountains, seem .to have so much more excitement in their lives, do not they, Catherine?" the young princess would wonder. "The dresses that those ladies wear are so different end refined that I am sure my father and his knights must compare us very unfavorably with them. And the pretty, extravagant jewels with which they adorn themselves! I am glad that my father brought me these gold beads from Italy. Look, Catherine!"

She showed her friends the shining globes that glittered in the sun and carefully pushed an invisible spring on the largest bead. The round object opened up as if by magic to reveal an exquisitely carved Virgin of white ivory on one side and a delicate blue enamel angel carrying a wreath of flowers on the other.

Grandfather Barnabo gave it to *my* Father for me," Elizabeth said. "My father says that the best goldsmiths and artists work for him and that his court is the most splendid in Italy. He might even try to arrange my marriage to a great prince of Italy and my father thinks that such a match might be more advantageous for Bavaria than a German alliance. What do you think, Catherine, how would you like to accompany me to the country of myrtle and oranges?"

"That would be splendid indeed, Elizabeth," and for an instant the image of the Lady Taddea was in front of her, and she could almost smell the scent of exotic flowers. "Besides, do you not have a cousin in Italy, a girl of your age, whose father has a splendid court near Milan?"

"You mean Valentina Visconti? Well that is another branch of the family, and their court at Pavia is very modest in comparison to my grandfather's in Milan. I do not know much about "those" Visconti, but perhaps I will meet my cousin Valentina, if I marry an Italian prince."

* * *

The seasons rolled by slowly and almost uneventfully for the girls of Ludwigsburg Castle.

Elizabeth soon lost all interest in Johann and embarked on light-hearted flirtations with equerries and young knights of the Duke's retinue.

From time to time the rumor of her oncoming marriage to a German or Flemish prince would reach Elizabeth in the sheltered wing of the palace where she lived surrounded by her cousins, friends, pets and birds. As no result ever came out of the Duke's negotiations, the princess soon learned to treat those rumors with great indifference—when he reached an agreement, no doubt her father would call her and announce it to her personally; until then she would neither worry nor fantasize about the man with whom she was to Trend her life.

The seasons were not as kind to Catherine.

Ludwig was often away from Munich, either accompanying his father in his campaigns or visiting other sovereigns' courts. When he was in Ludwigsburg, his behavior towards Catherine was marked by the same mixture of ardor and indifference that had characterized the first days of their relationship. If she was unhappy when he was at the castle, she was even more unhappy when he was away—then her mind tormented her with visions of the splendid courts he was visiting and the ravishing princesses that would gather around him and listen to his deeds of war and valor. Certainly the Duke would soon arrange a grand match for him—an unknown girl would come to Munich as his bride and Ludwig would be lost to her forever.

But no marriage had been decided either for Elizabeth or Ludwig when, in the spring of the year 1385, the Duke announced that his daughter was going to Amiens, in the kingdom of France, on a pilgrimage to the relics of St. John the Baptist, and that her friend Catherine of Fastaverin was to accompany her.

Chapter II

"... I Have A Niece..."

The Duke of Burgundy asks to be received by your Highness," announced a page.

Frederick of Bavaria got up quickly and met his guest at the opening of the pavilion. "My dear cousin," he said eagerly, "I am enchanted to see you. I hope you will do me the honor of sharing a drink of cool spiced wine." Philip of Burgundy smiled genially and accepted the silver tankard that the page offered him.

It was a hot summer day and the countryside was still and yellow under the mid-afternoon sun. The sea was too far away to mitigate the heat and the countless tents and pavilions that dotted the plain with their bright colors looked empty end abandoned as if en army of ghosts inhabited them.

It was cooler under Frederick's silver-colored tent, where silk cushions were scattered on the oriental carpets of the floor and multi-colored birds chirped in delicately carved cages.

The two men sipped slowly from their cups.

Philip broke the silence first. "Dear Frederick, it was generous of you to leave Munich to answer my nephew's call for help in his struggle against the English and their allies. We are grateful to you and your Bavarian knights for the valor you showed in our behalf when Bruges was captured." A kind smile lighted his face and made his coarse features look gentler.

There was a great contrast between the two princes and all to the advantage of Frederick of Wittelsbach, a tall, blond man with strong yet fine traits and, like his cousin, magnificently attired. They both sported colorful wraps with long wide sleeves and padded shoulders, long tight hose and pointed shoes. The Duke Philip's head was covered with a red draped turban of the same hue as his hose, which emphasized his strong beaked nose and round dark eyes.

"Cousin, my honor is very dear to me and nowhere as in France, in the service of the noble Charles, could I have hoped to enhance it, as France is the land of all honor and chivalry."

"Thank you, Cousin." said the Duke of Burgundy. "The links between France and Bavaria have always been close, as you know, and it would be to our mutual benefit if we could make them closer still. My nephew is a young ardent man; he loves women as much as he loves war and honor and we, his uncles, who are so much older and, should I say, wiser than he, would see with great favor a marriage between him and a young German princess."

"I can not think of anything that would make me happier, Philip," replied Frederick. "My admiration for your country is without limit, and I only wish I had a daughter of my own, whose quality of body and spirit would attract the king of France. Such a union would further the ties between our two Houses and countries. Alas, my beloved only daughter Elizabeth has been dead these past two years, carried away by the plague that swept Milan and killed her husband Marco Visconti also. But my brother Stephen does have a daughter of the right age, and she is ravishing."

"That is exactly the young lady we want for our nephew, who loves all beautiful women but is ready to bestow the ardor and generosity of his heart on his own beloved bride. It would be good of you if you could relate our interview to your brother. I do not have to emphasize to you the great state and magnificence that are the lot of a Queen of France and the honors she can grant her family and country of birth."

You are not mentioning, of course, that a German marriage would mean an important ally in the war that France has been waging against England for so many years, thought Frederick shrewdly. Besides, a branch of the Wittelsbach family is ruling Hainault and a friendly power there would give France a useful wedge in Flanders to use against its enemy across the Channel. But of course Philip was right. What an exalted fate for a Bavarian princess to become Queen of France! Surely Stephen would be overjoyed at the prospect. He tried to sound cautious: "My brother is very jealous of his honor and extremely fond of his daughter," he said. "What assurance can I give him that such a marriage will take place?"

"Cousin, Cousin," laughed Philip of Burgundy, "How can we talk of assurance for something as ephemeral as love? This is what I suggest we do. Let the princess come to France as if on a pilgrimage; let the two young people meet as if by accident. Then, I am sure, the beauty of your niece end the ardor of our nephew will achieve what our interview has just started. I trust your niece is as healthy as she is pretty, and apt to bear children. Of course, we need a Dauphin and a lot of little princes at the court of France. But then, ladies of great virtue and sagacity will examine her, and give their opinions on this fundamental matter."

Frederick shivered inwardly. This marriage will never take niece, he thought. Stephen will never allow himself and his daughter to be humiliated by a refusal and become the laughing stock of the courts of Europe.

He knew his impulsive, headstrong brother only too well. Stephen was flattered by the proposal, but he was too proud to run the risk of having his beloved daughter declared sterile in front of all of Europe. He loved her too much to want her to leave him so soon and for that far away country.

"Brother, I thank you for the loyalty and love you have shown to me and our family," he said to Frederick, "but I'd rather have Elizabeth marry a German prince then the king of France."

A disappointed Frederick transmitted the negative answer to the Duke of Burgundy.

Princess Elizabeth, meanwhile, continued her placid life in the castle of Ludwigsburg, unaware of the brilliant prospects that had been shattered for her by her obstinate father.

* * *

Joanne, Duchess of Brabant, sighed a deep sigh of relief and eased herself on the velvet cushions of her chair. "What a triumph the whole day has been," she murmured to herself, excitement still lingering and making her restless.

The double wedding between the children of her cousins of Burgundy and Hainault had gathered the most illustrious personages of France, Burgundy, Hainault, and Brabant, and had made Cambrai the center of the Western world for a few glorious days. Margaret of Hainault was not too pretty, of course, but certainly the richness of her dowry and the splendor of her wedding attire must have made her attractive in the eyes of her intelligent, ugly, passionate bridegroom, John of Burgundy.

Her thoughts strayed to another wedding day, many years before, when a younger, vibrant Joanna had seen her niece, plain, dour-looking Margaret of Male become the bride of Philip of Burgundy and had danced at the hall following the nuptials.

Philip had married one of the great heiresses of Europe and the dowry his bride handed him was dazzling: the prosperous towns of Flanders, hustling with trade and activities, inhabited by wealthy burghers who vied with the nobility in riches and ostentation. Perhaps Philip did not love Margaret, but he had been a faithful and considerate husband.

Joanna of Brabant liked the Duke of Burgundy. She knew he was shrewd and desirous of furthering the power of his House, but she had no doubts about his loyalty to France and his nephew, the young King.

She was partial to France. She had joyous memories of the long months spent at the court of Paris, when King Charles and his Queen, Joanna the Good, were young and the country at peace.

Charles the Wise had reconquered the lands that his father had lost to the English, and when Philip had married Margaret and added Flanders to his Burgundian possessions, it had been a most welcome event. That acquisition meant that France would have a powerful ally against England, if the horrible war should ever start again. But then, if such an occurrence came to pass, an ally in Germany would also be of considerable importance to France.

How unfortunate that insignificant prince Stephen of Wittelsbach, had failed to see the advantages accruing to Bavaria if his daughter married the King of France. Not to mention the honor that such a proposal carried with it. Stephen's brother, Frederick, an intelligent, shrewd politician, had understood only too well that a similar chance would never present itself to his family again, and tried in vain to persuade the Duke to give his assent.

She had liked Frederick when she had met him two years before. Wes it already two years ago that Prince Frederick had taken part in that already forgotten campaign and the Duke of Bavaria had refused the King of France as a son-in-law? Now, she had not heard of any great match for that German princess, what was her name, Elizabeth... She wondered, if she contacted the King's uncles, reminded them that there was still a young unmarried princess in Munich. ..At the same time, if she wrote to Frederick, perhaps he could insist with his brother again and make him see the advantage of such a union.

Joanna's great passion was diplomacy, arranging matches, suggesting alliances, weaving intrigues. She got up slowly and went to her writing table. A letter was already taking shape in her head: Dear Cousin Frederick.... She must make sure to see Philip privately tomorrow, and also John of Berry, the other influential uncle of King Charles of France.

She was tired; the banquet that had followed the double wedding ceremony had been endless. Through her windows, open to let in the mild April night, the Duchess could hear the laughter and clamoring of the good people of Cambrai, still celebrating the great events of the day.

Joanna of Brabant sat at her desk, picked up a quill and started to write.

Chapter III

A Pilgrimage To Amiens

Will ye ever reach Amiens, Catherine? This trip seems endless and I start wondering whether we will ever be able to kneel in front of the relics of the Blessed John the Baptist."

"We have been on the road en awfully long time," agreed her companion, "but the Duke Frederick promised we will be in Brussels in a few days now. That should be pleasant, do you not think, a visit at court of your Aunt of Brabant."

Elizabeth of Wittelsbach nodded end started getting undressed.

The two girls were in the little bedroom that the hospitality of a German nobleman had put to their disposal. All over Germany Duke Stephen's friends and vassals had been happy to offer shelter to the Duke Frederick, his niece and their retinues, but often the little group of pilgrims had had to content themselves with bed accommodations in remote hostels and convents because darkness fell before they could reach an hospitable castle.

They were traveling on horseback, and the stops to rest the horses were innumerable. Fatigue and boredom were taking their toll on the girls, as the excitement of the first day after their departure was waning sway, and the road stretched endlessly in front of them.

"I miss Ludwigsburg and my father," murmured Elizabeth, nestling dejectedly under her eiderdown.

"Do you not remember how happy and excited you were when the Duke announced you the pilgrimage to Amiens? You could not wait to get started, and you insisted that he let you visit your relatives of Brabant and Hainault."

Elizabeth was annoyed. "It is so much like you never to forget any details, Catherine. Of course I was happy. France is supposed to be the greatest Kingdom on earth and I probably will never have another chance to go there. And as we were traveling so far I thought it would be enjoyable to stop at the courts of our relatives. My father was very agreeable to the suggestion, if you remember, end my uncle Frederick said it was a splendid idea."

"Please do not get upset, Elizabeth. Of course I was not criticizing you; I share your fatigue and weariness, and only wish we were in Amiens tomorrow."

"And miss the splendors of Brussels and the visit with Aunt and Uncle of Hainault? No, Catherine, I would not want this. Promise me you will forget how tired you are, and make me forget it too. Think, my friend, perhaps in France we will see Charles. My uncle Frederick met him when he was fighting for him at Bourbourg and says he is without comparison the handsomest and kindest prince in all Christendom."

"I remember hearing him say also that the splendor and pomp of his court in Paris were without rivals and the ladies there the prettiest and most elegant he had ever seen."

"Yes, Uncle Frederick is most enthusiastic about France and her King," laughed Elizabeth. "I am sure that he is the one that suggested the pilgrimage to my father; he knew I would love to visit this enchanted kingdom."

"Your uncle is a most agreeable gentleman," Catherine agreed. "And he is so fond of you that your father knew that you could not have a better protector in your pilgrimage."

"My poor father! Did you not think that he was terribly moved when he kissed me goodbye?"

With a shiver of happiness, Catherine remembered that Ludwig too had seemed very upset to see her leave. Perhaps my absence will make him realize that he does love me after all, she hoped against hope—how often had they been separated during the last three years and how little had absence influenced their relationship!

The thought of her father had made Elizabeth pensive. She had seen tears in his eyes when he had bidden her farewell, she had felt the warmth of his embrace when he had kissed her, she remembered the words he had spoken to his brother, pressing his hands over and over again. "I entrust my precious Elizabeth to you, Frederick. I knew I can count on your loyalty and affection."

To dispel the emotion of the moment, Elizabeth had laughed at her father. "We are coming back in a few months, Father! And is certainly not the first time you are away from me!"

Ludwig too had kissed her warmly. "Why do you not come with us?" she had pleaded. "Uncle Frederick would love to have another man in his party." But Ludwig had begged off.

"Father is planning to send me on a mission to the court of Trier," he had explained, "and frankly a pilgrimage to the holy relics of St. John does not sound too inviting!"

Elizabeth had frowned at his words. Sometimes Ludwig sounded almost as godless as rumors said their grandfather Barnabo had been. St. John the Baptist was a powerful saint, who had worked innumerable miracles. His place was close to the gold throne where Jesus sat surrounded by His angels and archangels, and all knew that God listened to his words of intercession.

The little group of German pilgrims had left the castle of Ludwigsburg on a cool spring morning. The Duke Frederick was accompanied by two of his equerries, while a page and Elizabeth's nurse and lady-in-waiting, Catherine, were all her suite.

The horses were laden with innumerable packs and bundles. The pilgrimage included a visit to the courts of Brussels and Hainault, and Elizabeth had begged her father for a rich wardrobe to go with her.

"Those courts are so brilliant, Father, that I am afraid they will think me plain and simple, if I do not dress as elegantly as they do. What if they stare at us, and laugh at the way we dress?"

Her father had readily given in—his daughter must cut a figure worthy of him and the ancient house of Wittelsbach.

Elizabeth and Catherine had been allowed to choose fine damasks, velvets and silks, and the castle seamstress had sewn new dresses, tunics, capes, they had embroidered belts and shirts, starched lawns for caps and bonnets, stitched gowns and shoes.

So far, though their attires had been of the simplest and most practical kind—gray-colored dresses of sturdy cloth, warm capes against the morning and evening chills, strong leather boots.

Soon they would reach Brussels, the Duke Frederick had announced, and the two weary pilgrims fell asleep with dreams of a glittering court, dashing young men and lovely ladies in their minds.

* * *

The Duchess of Brabant received her relatives from Munich with great amiability and friendship.

"My dear Frederick, it is good to see you. And this pretty girl is your niece, then, Elizabeth. Come my dear, let me kiss you." She looked kindly, but with sharp inquiring eyes at the blushing princess.

"What pretty colors you have, Elizabeth! Remarkably un-German, is she not, Frederick, with those big dark eyes and lustrous hair!"

"My deceased sister-in-law had the same eyes and hair," said the Duke. "But Elizabeth is taller and more robust then her mother, Cousin. She is a Wittelsbach, after all, and we are a sturdy family!"

"A most important quality for a princess, I am sure you agree, Frederick. Have you learned any French, Elizabeth?"

"Unfortunately I have not, Cousin. Our teacher thought that Latin is the most important language for anyone to learn, as our books of prayer are in Latin, end this is the language of the Holy Church."

"Quite so. But French is a most pleasing language, my dear, and it would give you pleasure to read the Chansons de geste in the original, I am sure."

Joanne of Brabant was an elderly woman, with white hair elaborately dressed under a jeweled cap, pale blue eyes and a snub nose. She seemed to be very energetic and curious, too, as she asked countless questions of Frederick and Elizabeth concerning the Wittelsbach court and their pilgrimage to Amiens.

The Duke answered her with solicitude, while Elizabeth soon lost interest in the conversation and let her mind wander.

That did not escape Joanna of Brabant. "My dear, Elizabeth, you do lock tired after your long journey. You must be looking forward to a long, nice rest in your apartment. I hope you will forgive me if I keep our uncle with me a while longer. I do not often get e chance to see my relatives from Germany and your uncle has always been a great favorite with me!"

The Duke bowed at the compliment and the Duchess of Brabant continued: “We are very proud of our city of Brussels, and once you are rested, I feel confident that a visit to the Grandplace, will make you share our enthusiasm.”

The Duchess was right. From the moment Elizabeth and Catherine saw the “Grandplace” from the windows of their apartment that looked over that beautiful square, they fell in love with the city.

It seemed that the whole population of the city gathered there at all tires to meet, transact business, shout, laugh.

The girls loved to mingle with the crowd in the “Grandplace”, and browse along the endless rows of shops that lined the square. Beautiful cloths were sold, woven with silver and gold, precious furs, gowns, capes, mirrors, gloves, combs. It was different from Munich, more lively and noisy, and they felt at home there, even if they knew only a few words of French, also because German was spoken and understood by all.

Receptions and banquets were given in honor of the German guests and Elizabeth and Catherine found all their expectations fulfilled—the men at the court of Brussels were indeed charming, the ladies glamorous, life there refined and splendid.

The night before their departure from Brussels, Elizabeth returned from a visit to the Duchess’ rooms looking puzzled but pleased.

“You were with your cousin a long time,” commented Catherine, busy arranging the gowns and jewels they were going to wear for the evening.

Elizabeth agreed. “You are right, Catherine. And it was a strange conversation, I could not quite understand what she had in mind. She really seems to think that it is very important for me to learn some French by the time we reach Amiens. Apparently in Hainault too the main language is French and she is concerned that I might find myself at a disadvantage there if I do not speak that language. Anyway, at the end of our interview, she summoned one of her ladies to the room, her name is Marguerite de Gremonville, and she announced that this young woman, who is French, is being added to our party so that I can practice French with her end master a few words as soon as possible.”

“Marguerite de Gremonville? What is she like?”

There was a note of anxiety in Catherine's voice, and her friend noticed it.

"Do not worry, Catherine. Mademoiselle de Gremonville is a girl our age, quite pretty and nice, but you are my one real friend, the sister I chose, and I will never forsake you. She will be with us for a few weeks only; we are going back to Munich, remember, and we will not need French there!"

Catherine smiled gratefully at her friend.

"One more thing," added Elizabeth, "the Duchess said she will judge on my progress in French personally, as she too will be in Amiens in July."

The following day, their journey continued towards Le Quesnoy where the Wittelsbach of Hainault had their court.

* * *

"My dear Isabelle, Margaret tells me you have brought with you the loveliest gowns ever, all terribly rich and elaborate and I am anxious to admire them."

The Duchess of Hainault was all smiles and polite words, but her grey eyes were cold and appraising. She spoke in French, and too fast for Elizabeth to understand more than the general meaning—Marguerite de Gremonville had not been with her vary long and her advance in that language had not been too rapid.

Still Elizabeth, or Isabelle, as they called her at Le Quesnoy in the French way, understood her words and blushed. There was condescension in the Duchess's voice, unmistakably, and the princess's eyes looked darker and very determined when she beckoned her ladies to open her trunks.

They took out her lovely robes, the brightly colored under-dresses, a few stoles, embroidered undergarments, stiffly starched headdresses, and lay them on the vast bed. The Duchess didn't miss a single detail. Her eyes were seldom approving, her lips tightly pursed. At last, she could not contain herself, "And, pray, niece, what is this?" she asked lifting a two horned headdress.

"We call it escoffion, and I think it is very becoming."

Elizabeth was very fond of that fashion and had a few of them, all of the finest lawn and most delicate colors—white, violet, blue. She thought the made her look taller and her forehead higher, too. "Well, I must say, they are not too popular here, niece, or in France either. You might like to try on some of my daughter-in-law's hennins, and perhaps you will allow your Uncle Albert and myself to present you with a dress or two made in the French fashion."

Elizabeth's aunt of Hainault could be nice and tactful when she wanted to, and her new daughter-in-law, another Margaret, had been very amiable and had admired Elizabeth's things.

The palace of Hainault, smaller and more modest that the one in Brussels, still seemed very worldly to the travelers and, even if she knew that her own robes and caps were just as beautiful as those worn at her relatives' court, Elizabeth sometimes could not help wondering whether she, a German princess of the Wittelsbach family, was being slighted and considered plain and unsophisticated.

Later that day, her nurse and Catherine were helping the princess to get ready for the banquet, when Marguerite de Gremonville came in carrying a heap of shimmering blue and gold.

She gently spread it on the bed and they could admire a beautiful dress of light blue brocade, embroidered all over with gold flowers and birds. The bodice was tight-fitting with a deep U-shaped neck lined with white fur, the skirt very voluminous. A wide belt embroidered with the same motif of flowers and birds, accompanied it, and a heart-shaped cap of white lawn adorned with turquoises.

"The Duchess hopes you will like this outfit," said Marguerite, "and will do her the honor of wearing it tonight."

Elizabeth looked ecstatic, her eyes shining—she couldn't wait to put it on. How more stylish and refined that gown looked than any of the dresses that they had brought from Munich!

When Elizabeth had it on, she looked beautiful—the short, small waistline accentuated the curve of her bosom and made it look higher end softer, the folds of the skirt hid her round hips and made her look slender, and the white cap accentuated her bright colors, the dark brown of her eyes end hair, her glowing complexion.

When Elizabeth went to the great hall where the tables had been set for the dinner, she could notice a look of admiration and satisfaction in the eyes of the Duchess, her husband, and even the Duke Frederick.

"Niece, you look wonderful tonight," he said. "I am sure it is to your advantage to follow the food advice of your aunt of Hainault. We are proud of our customs of Bavaria, are we not, but sometimes we may find out there are areas that can he improved without our pride suffering because of it!"

The German guests remained in Hainault for four weeks, and their way did improve. They learned to curtsy in the French way, very deeply and bowing their heads, walk gracefully, shave their hair at the temples to make their foreheads look higher, put rouge on their cheeks, choose the appropriate jewels and shoes.

The dukes were very generous to their niece and lavished presents, compliments, blandishments on her.

Elizabeth came to admire them greatly and was eager for their approval. Her French improved considerably and she was overjoyed to know, when the time came for her to leave Le Quesnoy at the beginning of July, that the Duke Albert, the Duchess, and their son were going to Amiens with her.

* * *

Elizabeth was going to meet the King of France! The palace in Amiens where the princess, the Duke Frederick, the sovereigns of Hainault and their retinues were staying was in a state of commotion. Messages were endlessly being sent to the palace where the Duchess of Brabant was staying, others received by an impatient Duke and communicated to nobody and the happy suspicion was insinuating itself among Elizabeth's people that there was something more to the meeting than it was avowed.

The King had his lodgings in the Bishop's palace from where rumors and gossips had escaped and reached the eager ears of the Wittelsbach people and the burghers of the town.

The impatience and excitement that were gripping everybody had certainly not escaped Elizabeth

She had confusedly felt for a while now that the pilgrimage to St.

John the Baptist had been only a pretext and that at the end of her journey her very destiny was going to be decided.

Her sojourn in Hainault, where the court had been almost sycophantic in their blandishments and flatteries had made her wonder and she had noticed that emphasis was laid on anything "French", that they were trying to conceal her most pronounced German characteristics and make a French princess out of her.

She loved the attention, as she loved pretty dresses, jewels, presents, but she was shrewd, or humble, enough to know that her condition of Wittelsbach princess did not warrant so much solicitude. Besides, her uncle of Bavaria and relatives of Hainault had been extolling the King, the court of France and its magnificence at any chance they had, and this insistence had, not been lost on Elizabeth.

She shared some of her growing excitement and, impatience with Catherine, but both in Hainault and during the trip from Le Quesnoy to Amiens, she had been almost constantly in the company of her relatives, had shared her carriage with them and only in the evenings, when banquets and festivities were over, had she been able to make her friend part of her dreams and expectations.

"Do you think it is possible that I came here to meet the King of France, that he may fall for me and marry me? But then my father did not say a word about it and he should have, should he not? And where are my trousseau, and my dowry? Princesses do not marry Kings without bringing a dowry, gold, lands. And what if Charles does not like me? Will I be sent back in disgrace? And my father? Why did he not confide in me if a wedding not a pilgrimage, was at stake? Could I really become Queen of France? One of the greatest ladies in the world? What do you think Catherine?"

The premonition was growing in Catherine too that something extraordinary was expecting her friend once they reached Amiens. The lives then had been living until a few months before were starting to assume the blurred, half-remembered lines of dreams, while the landscape surrounding them, the people traveling with them, strangers but a few weeks before, seemed the only realty.

Just before they reached Amiens, two gentlemen were seen galloping towards the group.

They halted their horses in front of the litter carrying Elizabeth and her aunt of Hainault, took off their wide-brimmed hats, and after introducing themselves as Bureau de la Riviere and Guy de la Tremoille, counselors of the King, welcomed the noble travelers to the Kingdom of France, and assured them the king was impatiently waiting for them in Amiens. They asked the honor of escorting the ladies and their party to the palaces that the King had put to their disposal in that town.

That night Elizabeth could not fall asleep, she was living in a dream, but at the same time she had premonitions of disaster, was afraid that her 'multi-colored beautiful' bubble would burst.

"I have been told so often that Charles is the most handsome man in the realm, that he loves the ladies to indiscretion, that it is easy to kindle his passion but hard to hold it. Will he like me, and my dark hair and eyes, my shyness and lack of polishing? How can I excite his interest and love when my French is broken at best, and I do not know the uses of the court of France?"

"You are beautiful, Elizabeth, and so different from the women he usually sees. I'm sure your shyness will charm him; your accent will make your most common words sound enchanting to him. They would not have had you come and meet him if they had not been assured of the result before hand."

Catherine didn't know who "they" were, but she had heard of the powerful uncles of the King, and she felt that the Duchess of Brabant, the Duke of Hainault and the Duke Frederick, must have had a part in the "scheme."

"They know the King and are aware that an informal interview with an unknown princess must be more appealing to him than any negotiations between the ambassadors and counselors of two countries."

If Catherine was obviously totally without experience in the game of politics, she was sentimental enough to feel the charm that a meeting under such strange circumstances would hold for a passionate, exuberant young man. And Elizabeth was only too happy to believe her words.

On the eve of the meeting between Elisabeth and the King, her uncle Frederick summoned her to his rooms. He looked nervous and impatient, but the embrace with which he received his niece was as warm and loving as ever. "My dearest Elizabeth, or shall I call you

Isabelle, "a la francaise," he said jokingly, "I am sure you appreciate what a great honor it is both for you and our family to be welcomed to France by the King himself."

"Dear Uncle, I am sure that his Majesty had other reasons to come to this part of his Kingdom then my humble person."

"Allow me to contradict you, Elizabeth. I had the honor of being received by the King, and he assured me that the fame of your beauty and refinement had reached him and he was most anxious to meet you."

"Was my father aware of the fact that I might meet the King of France in the course of my pilgrimage?"

The Duke hesitated. "I think I did mention this possibility to my brother, yes, Elizabeth.

"Why did he not tell me then?"

"Elizabeth, nothing firm had been arranged, at that time. Not that it has now, mind you, Niece," he hastened to add.

Elizabeth felt instinctively that the Duke would not, could not, be more, explicit.

When she left her uncle's room she was less buoyant than she had been. She knew that so much was at stake, yet she had not been given any weapon to fight with.

"I can hardly believe that a matter as momentous as the marriage Of the King of France can depend solely on his falling in love," she confided to Catherine. "Why, even my brother's marriage, as you well know my dear, is subject to other considerations. And Ludwig is merely the heir to the Duchy of Bavaria!"

Sadly, Catherine had to agree with her, "What did your uncle exactly tell you?"

"Nothing, really, when you come down to it. He asked me to be my most charming when I see Charles, hinted at some obscure advantage that France could gain from close ties with Bavaria, inquired about my progress in French. Perhaps we have been too hasty in believing the rumors floating about this town; perhaps my relatives really liked me for myself, not because I will marry the King of France!"

The anxiety they both felt kept the two girls awake for long hours.

The following morning, when the ladies of Brabant and Hainault entered Elizabeth's room to supervise the preparations for the interview with the King, they commented on the dark shadows under her eyes.

"You look pale and tired, Isabelle," said her Aunt of Hainault, "This will not do. Do apply more rouge to your cheeks."

"Here, I think this almond paste diluted in milk will work for those dark spots under your eyes," said her cousin of Brabant.

A red velvet dress had been chosen for the occasion, as red was the color that best suited Elizabeth's dark eyes and hair. The robe was very simple, but its large scalloped slashes showed the beautiful gold of the brocade underneath, and a belt of linked gold plaques decorated with blue enamel was worn high to emphasize her breasts. Her hair was almost completely hidden by a short 'cone—shaped "hennin" from which a veil of white gauze fell over her shoulders.

At the palace entrance a litter was waiting for Elizabeth. An older lady, Margaret of Burgundy, who was the King's aunt, was sitting there, and she smiled graciously when she saw Elizabeth, and invited her to sit next to her.

Other litter carried Catherine, Marguerite de Gremonville, and the ladies of Brabant and Hainault to the Bishop's palace, the King's residence in Amiens.

It was an imposing building adjacent to the cathedral, of which it matched the gray stone, profusions of pinnacles, narrow tall windows, multitude of gargoyles and decorative carvings.

The ladies and their retinues were led up a gently-inclined staircase to a vast hall dominated by a huge elaborately carved fireplace.

A group of magnificently dressed gentlemen was standing in the middle of the hall.

Her heart beating hard, Elizabeth advanced towards the men. Her aunt and cousins were at her sides and, with a sigh of relief, she recognized her uncle among the strangers watching her.

The Duke smiled warmly and took her hand. "Your majesty," he said, "allow me to present my niece, Elizabeth of Bavaria, to your Highness."

Then Elizabeth saw Charles for the first time and, knew that, even without her uncle's words, she would have recognized him among all.

He was tall and slim, with blond curly hair escaping from a violet hood in the form of a cock's comb. The doublet he was wearing was short and snug at the belt, of a cloth of gold embroidered with threads of different colors, the green hose were tight and laced at the waist, his shoes terminated in slender points.

Elizabeth curtsied deeply, the way she had been shown in Hainault, but the King quickly took her hand and helped her to rise, whispering something she could not understand.

What a waste my French lessons have been, she thought. Here I am, in front of the King of France, and I cannot make out what he is saying to me! And my relatives, who have schooled me for this, very day so carefully! How upset they must be!

She stole a glance at her uncle, sensed his nervousness. She felt completely inadequate, and her confusion brought blushes to her cheeks.

The King smiled kindly at her and led her to an armchair, near the fireplace.

"What do you think of my Kingdom of France?" he inquired.

"Amiens looks like a pretty town," she replied haltingly in the foreign language.

"Your French is very good," he complimented her. "Do you know our poems and chansons de geste?"

"I regret to say I do not."

"Then you must allow me to send you a copy of my favorite ones."

"That is very kind of your Majesty."

"It is my most fervent wish to make your stay in my country as pleasant as possible, my lady," he said. His voice was gentle; his eyes looked lovingly at her.

Elizabeth lowered hers. He was extraordinarily handsome and charming; he could not possibly be attracted to her. And even if he were, that was not the way a King of France chose his bride! The previous night's doubts and anxieties started tormenting her again. She could not understand his words anymore; they became meaningless sounds, which, she hoped, did not require an answer.

After what seemed like an eternity, the Duke Frederick approached them, and she understood that her interview with Charles of France was over.

* * *

Elizabeth went back to her lodgings in a state of complete agitation. Her meeting with Charles had been so unsatisfactory, she was sure he had found her unattractive and dull.

"It was so hard to find the right words in French, Catherine. And he kept looking at me so intently that I lost my head completely and I did not answer him at all! He must think me a perfect fool!"

"I was certainly too far away to hear his words, Elizabeth, but his expression was so full of love and admiration that I am sure he found you absolutely charming."

"Do you really think so? Oh, I hope it is true because I already love him, Catherine, I will never be able to love another man."

A few hours after the fateful meeting, the Duke Frederick and the Duchess of Hainault entered Elizabeth's room.

She looked at their faces and knew that the dream had come true; the unbelievable had happened and she was to be Queen of France.

"Yes, my dearest," said the Duke embracing her, "the Duke of Burgundy, the King's uncle, has just left me. He brought a message from his nephew—the King wants you as his bride. The Duke of Burgundy quoted the King's very words: 'It must be Isabelle or no one else, and please hurry up with the wedding." Charles is enchanted with you and has resolved not to ask your father for your dowry. Again, let me quote his words: 'The great qualities and virtues of Isabelle are enough for me.' My dear, it seems that you cast a spell on him," laughed the delighted Duke.

"Oh, my dear niece, I am so happy for you and your family," said the Duchess of Hainault, opening her arms to Elizabeth. "The Duke of Burgundy would have loved to have your wedding celebrated in his town of Arras, but the King will hear of no delay. Your uncle is right, you must have cast a spell on him—he thinks of you constantly and wants the wedding to be here in Amiens next Monday, July the seventeenth."

"I will marry the King next Monday? And my father, Uncle? Will he give me his blessing? Did he know when I left Munich that I was not going back?"

"Your father will be delighted with this match, niece. If he did not say a word to you about it—and he was aware of this possibility when he bid you farewell—it is because it was the King's desire that the marriage would only come about if he loved you. He does, he is love sick for you, and we are anxious to heal him as quickly as possible, are we not, Margaret?" he said laughing at the Duchess of Hainault.

The new few days were hectic, but with a quality of fairytale in them of which Elizabeth and her relatives and friends were keenly aware—her dreams of power and beauty were coming true as if by magic. It had been enough for Charles to look at her and the little German princess of no much consequence had become a powerful, sought-after lady, one of the greatest of Christianity.

A crown to wear on her wedding day was presented to Elizabeth. It was worth a French province, a cousin whispered to her, and was set with beautiful pearls, diamonds and all kinds of precious stones.

Cutters and seamstresses, shoemakers and goldsmiths worked day and night to prepare her weeding attire and trousseau.

Everything was a gift from the King. He had refused a dowry; he had refused the money that Frederick of Bavaria wanted to donate as a wedding present. He only wanted Elizabeth's love and loyalty.

He also wanted a new name for his bride, a name that his subjects would prefer to her German one, the French form of Elizabeth- Isabelle.

CHAPTER IV

THE WEDDING

The beautifully painted and upholstered open carriages where Isabelle and her suite had taken seat stopped in front of the Cathedral of Notre Dame, and the noble knights who had accompanied them on horseback helped the ladies to descend.

A huge crowd had been gathering from the early morning in the square facing the church and the good citizens of Amiens were excited and vociferous, as never before had an event of such magnitude and splendor graced their town. Mimes, jongleurs, minstrels, singers from all over Flanders had been entertaining the crowds with their skills; sellers of all kinds of goods had erected their stalls next to the cathedral walls.

It was a hot, sweltering, July day and the merchants were doing booming business selling fruits, ale and cold drinks, multicolored ribbons, poorly executed miniatures of the main actors of that day's events: the King, his bride, the royal uncles and aunts.

Silence fell over the crowd when Isabelle stepped out of her carriage. She was a beautiful vision. Her face was aglow with the triumph of that day, her eyes shone with pride, her carriage was erect and dignified.

She was dressed in a green gown woven with gold threads and fleurs-de-lis embroidered in sapphires along the neck and hem. The skirt was gathered full from the hips and fell along in the back forming a short train. A mantle of silk, edged with ermine, completed the outfit, and a headdress of gold netting held her hair tightly against her head.

Above these side pieces was the magnificent crown, all aglitter with hundred of stones.

She leaned for a moment on the Duke of Hainault's arm, as he was gallantly helping her to alight, and lowered her head out of the carriage.

A ray of the mid-day sun hit the gold and stones of her crown, and, as if by magic, her head was surrounded by a halo of luminous splendor.

A cry burst out of the multitude: "Noel! Noel! Long live our Queen Isabelle!"

She turned around slowly, facing the people, her people, for the first time. The haughty expression of her face softened and a quick smile appeared on her mouth. She lifted a hand to acknowledge their admiration and devotion, then took the Duke's arm and entered the cathedral.

Catherine followed her, holding her brief train, and the darkness of the church blinded her for an instant, after the brilliant sunshine outside.

Hundreds of candles glowed in the cathedral and their flickering lights played on the carvings of the stalls, on the choir screen, shone on the statues of the Virgin Mary and St. Firmin, who smiled benignly behind the grills of their chapels, were lost in the breathtaking height of the columns and vaults.

The procession walked slowly to the Chapel of St. John the Baptist, where the Bishop of Amiens, Jean Roland, was waiting to celebrate the wedding ceremony. The shouts of the crowd outside announced that the King was on his way from the Bishop's Palace and a few minutes later Charles appeared in the chapel, accompanied by his uncle of Burgundy and a host of magnificent gentlemen.

His countenance was gentle and smiling, his eyes searched his bride's face, but Isabelle kept her head lowered during the entire brief ceremony.

When this was over, Charles took his Queen's hand, kissed her on both cheeks and invited her to kneel next to him on a prie-dieu covered with blue cloth adorned with gold fleurs-de-lis.

The Archbishop then celebrated High Mass.

Isabelle followed very devotedly, raising her eyes from her prayer book only to look intently at the statue of St. John the Baptist that adorned the chapel.

Once more the power and goodness of that great saint had manifested themselves and she, an obscure German princess, had been deemed worthy of a miracle and become Queen of France. Her love and gratitude for St. John were overflowing; she desperately hoped that the tears coming to her eyes would not fall down and add to her confusion.

She stole a quick glance at the young man at her side. He was so handsome and exciting! His eyes were always trying to meet hers, they were tender and passionate. She felt she was blushing; her mind was straying from the Mass. Her heart was pounding at the thought of the long day ahead, her first as Queen of France, of the long warm night, her first as bride of Charles of Valois.

When the Mass was finished, Charles and Isabelle knelt in front of the Archbishop, kissed his pastoral ring and, hand-in-hand, walked the long nave of the cathedral to the central portal. The sun illuminated the rose-window of the facade and played with the reds, blues, greens of the stained glass, reflecting them on the grey stones of the floor, the pillars and statues of the aisles.

* * *

It was a slow summer evening; the sun had set but a red glimmer still lingered in the sky. All the scents of a full summer night penetrated through the high windows of the Bishop's palace into the big hall where the festivities for the royal wedding were reaching their end.

The walls were hung with tapestries depicting hunting scenes, the tall pillars festooned with branches adorned with fruits and ribbons. Canopies of cloth of gold embroidered with fleurs-de-lis were placed over the two tables, raised above the others, covered with damask cloths and set with precious plates, platters, saltcellars, at which the King and Queen sat with their ladies and gentlemen.

Musicians and singers had been playing lutes and "vieilles", singing their songs of love and war; the noble guests from France, Flanders and Germany had been dancing slow complex dances charged with amorous symbols, sipping cold wine and beer, nibbling fruits and sweetmeats.

The noise of the crowds outside, celebrating the wedding of their King, had subsided and only from time to time the quietness of the night was broken by a burst of laughter or the distant echo of a quarrel among drunkards.

The vast hall too was growing quieter. The food had been delicious and very rich, the silver and gold goblets and tankards had been kept full with wine and beer by busy cupbearers, the musical entertainment and the dancing had been enjoyed by most of the people present.

The King was growing impatient. His face was flushed, his eyes excited. He kept turning his head towards the table where Isabelle was sitting with her ladies and paid poor attention to whatever his uncles and cousins were whispering to him.

Then the Duchess of Brabant said something to Isabelle, who blushed deeply and got up. She looked at Catherine, silently asking her to accompany her. She curtsied before the King, not daring to look at him, and left the hall followed by the Duchess of Hainault, Marguerite de Gremonville and Catherine.

The room that had been prepared for the wedding night of the sovereigns of France was small and elegantly decorated with tapestries, carved chests and chairs, an ample bed hung with blue curtains, Arras carpets on the floor.

The high mullioned windows opened on a garden and the intoxicating perfume of the linden-trees mixed with that of a bouquet of lilies filling a white and blue Faience vase.

Her nurse, Marguerite and Catherine helped Isabelle to undress. The silk of her mantle and dress felt smooth and fresh; they were given to one of the maids, who carried them to an adjacent room.

Isabelle was standing near the bed, naked but for her crown. The beautiful tiara and the gold netting were removed

And fell on her shoulders, dark and wavy.

Margaret of Hainault handed her a white linen chemise and the nurse slipped it over her head. Without her crown and sumptuous dress, Isabelle looked small and young, with an anxious face and shy eyes.

"Catherine, do not go away, stay a bit longer!" she whispered in panic. But that was silly, of course, and too late also, as the voices of the King and his friends could just then be heard near the door.

Catherine curtsied to her Queen, took the nurse's hand and Marguerite's, and they left the room quietly, just as the other door opened and the King appeared, smiling and eager.

He bowed lightly to the Duchess of Hainault, kissed her hand, thanked her and escorted the older lady out of the chamber.

* * *

Isabelle's heart was beating so hard she was afraid that Charles would hear it. The excitement of the day, the copious eating and drinking, the voices and sounds that had surrounded her ceaselessly, the heady perfumes of the night, the presence of her bridegroom, the handsome stranger who had made her Queen of France three days after their meeting, all made her head spin. She just wanted to lie down on the soft mattress and close her eyes.

But already Charles was at her side, his hot hands touching her face, moving a curl away from her forehead. He too had discarded his ceremonial costume and was wearing only a short chemise, his long light brown hair was free of ornament, his legs were naked and shapely.

His voice sounded sweet and passionate. Isabelle's poor knowledge of French almost completely abandoned her and she let herself be carried by the music of the strange language, by the emotions that the unknown words stirred in her.

I will love this man and be a good wife to him, she silently promised herself. I owe him everything I have, by choosing me as his Queen, he has made all my dreams possible. Nothing will ever be beyond reach for me after tonight.

She did not feel any passion or desire; the events of the past days had been too quick. She had been living in a daze that had dulled all deep feelings.

Passively she let Charles remove her chemise, felt his eyes linger over her breasts, hips, thighs. Gently he made her lie on the silk sheets and started exploring her body, touching her hips, kissing her breasts, caressing her pubic hair.

Excitement started mounting in her when she heard him breathing heavily, his words of endearment getting more and more confused, when she felt his hands becoming more and more audacious.

She forgot her shyness, the dreamy state in which she had been living and let her instincts take over. She pulled away his chemise, and her hands too started touching, exploring the handsome body of the man. She wondered at the toughness of his muscles, slenderness of his waist, hardness of his sex. She responded to his passionate kisses with hers, she matched his ardor with her own.

When he entered her, the pleasure of her orgasm left her weak and shivering. She held on to him more tightly, wanting it to last forever and knowing, while she was enjoying it, that the ecstasy was already over.

Chapter V

A Ride In The Forest

The month of September in the year 1386 had been unusually hot. Storms and torrential rains had intermittently broken the heat, but the hail that accompanied them had made havoc of the countryside and now the long rows of vines showed dried-up and crushed grapes instead of the plump, golden ones they usually carried at that time of the year. The wind had added another note of destruction, and it had been so violent as to pull ancient trees off their roots, raze huts to the ground, and take the roof off houses.

Queen Isabelle and her household had taken up residence at the castle of Vincennes, which stood in the middle of the forest that bore the same name. It was a somber building with brick walls, high turrets and an enormous dungeon, the construction of which Charles V, the King's father, had initiated. It was surrounded by a park and a forest of oaks and elm trees that terminated on the banks of the Marne. The formidable outlook of the fortress contrasted sharply with the splendor and glitter of the royal quarters. Gold and precious stones shone on the sacred images of the chapel, carpets woven with gold lions and flowers covered the floors, tapestries and paintings, ivory carvings, hung on the walls.

An enamored King had added precious tokens of his love for his young bride, and now a silver clock that had belonged to Philip the Fair stood near the massive door of the Queen's oratory, a mirror framed in gold and enamel reflected her smiling face, a St. Margaret chiseled in silver, demurely facing a fierce dragon adorned with emeralds, graced a chest in her room.

In the dungeon itself, a small round room held countless bolts of precious cloths—silk, velvet, transparent gauzes and rich damasks. The fabulous treasure of the royal family was also housed there, in a secret retreat Isabelle had visited once accompanied by the Count d'Eu, that noble and wise gentleman who had been a companion of Charles V and whom the royal uncles had deemed to be the fittest mentor for the young Queen.

That sultry September afternoon, Isabelle was sitting languidly on a couch piled high with soft cushions. Her pregnancy was very advanced and she tired easily. Her state had made her look less attractive, because not only had her body got heavy and shapeless, but her hair had lost its luster and her features become coarser. She was aware of it, and had grown irritable and short-tempered.

Most of her women were with her when Catherine entered the room. She had a very large household and some of the noblest ladies of the country had vied for the honor of being part of her retinue. Isabelle of Melun, Countess of Eu, was sitting near the Queen, and next to her was Marie of Savoisy, who was reading from a volume that rested on a. high book-stand:

"Je cuidoie que plus loiaus me fussiez, si Dieu me consent, que ne fu Tristan a Yseult..." (I thought you were more faithful to me, so God help me, than Tristan was to Isolde...)

She was reading slowly from one of Isabelle's favorite poems—"La Chatelaine de Vergi" and her voice sounded harmonious and gentle as the words of love and longing of the lady of the manor betrayed by her lover filled the room.

Isabelle interrupted her brusquely when she heard Catherine enter.

"Here you are, Catherine! And pray, where have you been all this time, when you know full well I need you and this horrible weather makes me feel so hot and uncomfortable?"

Her friend blushed at the reproach and was thankful that she had spoken in German, which she did with her most of the time, even if her French had become very fluent and elegant.

Isabelle didn't wait for an answer, had not wanted one, and went on plaintively: "I do wish Nurse had not left me to go back to Germany; and a fine time she chose too, when I needed her most!"

Silently Catherine agreed with her. Nurse could have waited a couple of months at least. Isabelle was very fond of her and even as disappointed as she was by her departure, had wanted her nurse to return to her native land with great pomp. She had been supplied with a magnificently painted carriage drawn by four horses, and entrusted with precious gifts for Isabelle's German family.

"You are the only person that is left to me from my past, my dear friend," she had told Catherine emotionally after bidding farewell to her nurse, and when she had embraced the old woman, her tears were running down her cheeks.

Yet Isabelle was happy in France. She was impressed by the wealth and magnificence of the innumerable castles and manors that belonged to the Valois, the richness and quality of jewels and gifts that were presented to her. She was flattered by the deference that everyone showed to her, and touched by the love her husband surrounded her with.

Isabelle loved Charles immensely too; she thought him the handsomest man alive and Catherine knew very well that part of today's discomfort and petulance was due to Charles' absence, to his departure for yet another expedition against England.

"And Charles too, always following his uncle of Burgundy's advice and getting entangled in this endless series of expeditions against those awful English."

She was very bitter about the Duke of Burgundy and his influence over her husband. She remembered only too well how Charles had left her barely a week after their wedding for a campaign in Flanders that the Duke had wanted.

And again, few weeks before, Charles, who loved war and martial enterprises, had started with great enthusiasm on an expedition to Sluys in Flanders where a huge French fleet had been gathered. His wife's advanced pregnancy had not deterred Charles and he had sworn he would come back only when the invasion of England was completed successfully. His younger brother, Louis, Duke of Touraine, had accompanied him.

Silence fell in the room at the Queen's outburst. The French ladies did not understand her words, obviously, but her tone did not leave any doubt about her feelings. Isabelle was a moody woman, given to extremes of both happiness and despondency, but she was popular with her ladies because she was very generous with gifts and praise, and would always stand by and protect even the humblest of her servants.

Perhaps she felt reproach in their silence or she had grown restless. She beckoned to her maid, Femmette, to help her and rose slowly from her couch.

"Ladies," she said in French, "I think it would be pleasant to go for a ride through the forest to Beaute."

True to its name, "Beauty", this was a beautiful manor at the edge of the forest of Vincennes, planned and built by King Charles V, who had wanted to relax there and enjoy the beautiful view of the river and the lush countryside.

Ordinarily, it was a picturesque ride to Beaute which all the ladies loved and, once there, they would visit the park where nightingales were kept in aviaries, white doves flew freely and nested among the trees and bushes. A light repast would be served on the grass, after which they would play ball, gather flowers, flirt with the pages and equerries that accompanied them.

But the afternoon looked overcast and menacing rain any time.

The Countess of Eu tried to sound a note of caution: "But your Majesty, do you think it is advisable to start for such a long ride now? I think I hear the rumble of thunder already and these grey clouds look ready to burst into rain before we are out of the castle."

"Countess, I do appreciate your concern, but I am growing impatient with your omens of doom. You know how apprehensive I am for the King's safety, how jealous of his honor, yet you had to suggest that this campaign is destined to disaster, as people have seen crows carrying hot coals and dropping them onto thatched-roofed barns and have drawn the worst auspices for the King and the French army from such a portent. Now, you are worried about the weather, the distance, and I not know what else....You do not have to come if you think the ride is too long for you. I am sure that I will not want your company."

Her ladies all declared themselves delighted to go on such an expedition and break the monotony of the day, and certain it would not rain until the morrow.

The Countess of Eu pursed her lips and did not add another word but gave quiet orders to Femmette.

Isabelle d'Eu was an older woman and the highest ranking among Isabelle's ladies. She was also very sensible and cautious, a kind of mother figure among the young, pleasure-loving ladies of the Court.

Jeanne de Dreux, Marguerite de Gremonville, Catherine de Villiers, Marie d'Harcourt, Jeanne de Luxembourg—all young, pretty, laughing, dressed in bright colors—followed the Queen down the staircase that led to the main courtyard.

Catherine was going too, when the Countess of Eu called her back.

"Catherine, I will have a litter follow your group, but I hope the Queen will not notice it. She is at too advanced a stage of pregnancy to run the risk of being caught by pains in the middle of the forest without means of coming back to the castle. I know you share my concern, Mademoiselle, and I beg of you to ride slowly with her and, if at all possible, persuade her to desist from her purpose."

Catherine smiled at the good lady. She knew she felt very keenly her responsibility as the head of the Queen's household and that the King had entrusted the safety of his wife and child to her devotion and common sense.

Catherine shared her anxiety about that silly ride; the distance between the two castles was of some miles, the bridle path they were to follow was very narrow, and the grey sky uninviting.

But Isabelle was obstinate, as Catherine well knew, and all she could do was to ride by her side and hope that the expedition would have a happy ending.

A few pages would come with them, as usual, but Catherine too had misgivings.

The horses were waiting for the ladies in the courtyard. They were pretty, docile animals that had carried them before, elegantly harnessed in silver and velvet, bearing soft leather saddles adorned with silk ribbons.

The Queen and her suite were helped to mount by solicitous footmen and a few minutes later their little group was on its way among the century-old trees, followed at a distance by some equerries of Isabelle's household carrying a painted wood litter curtained in blue.

The air was still, the birds were flying low and little animals scurried to-and-fro among the bushes and the yellow patches of marigolds that brightened the dark greens of the forest.

Catherine was riding with Marguerite de Gremonville, whom she had known since the days of Brussels and with whom she had become very friendly, when Isabelle, at the head of the group, beckoned her to join her.

"My friend, you too seem to think that it is foolish to take this ride; but I ail bored and restless, Catherine! I cannot sit another minute in that room, listening to that monotonous voice of Madame de Savoisy reading that silly poem. Love, loyalty, broken hearts — that is all those poems are about. And love always brings unhappiness and betrayal. I know that is not true. Love is being happy and being loved in return."

She smiled mischievously and went on, "Sometimes love can also bring you a crown. I do miss Charles, though, and all the fun we have when he is with me. I think that the parties that are being held at court are getting more splendid each time."

"It must be thanks to you, your Majesty," Catherine answered truly, "and to the beauty and 'joie de vivre' you have brought with you. Did you notice too that the French ladies have started adopting the headdress you favor, the two-horned hennin?"

"Yes, and it does not suit some of those old stuffed ladies, either," she said contemptuously, "but of course, they will follow the fashion and the Queen is the fashion at the French court. I wish this child would be born soon. I am so tired of these shapeless outfits I have to wear and of my corsets being forever let out."

"It will be a boy, Your Majesty, the Dauphin that the King and the country are waiting for," Catherine replied soothingly. "Then you will be thin again and able to enjoy the great festivities the King will hold to celebrate the events, and wear the most dazzling costumes and jewels."

"I do hope so, Catherine. The King has promised me the grandest entry into Paris and a coronation such as never was held for any queen before. He tells me the people of Paris are anxious to receive me officially in their capital. But all this has to wait. The King is so desirous for the English campaign to be a success. The Duke of Burgundy is behind the expedition, wholeheartedly, as you know, but his uncle of Berry continues delaying his arrival at Sluys—I am afraid this will only put off the crossing of the Channel until the Fall, when the sea gets rougher and the days shorter and colder. But I am getting a little bit tired after all, my good Catherine. Let's dismount and sit down on the grass for a few minutes' rest."

There was a small clearing behind a clump of tall oak trees. They directed themselves there and the ladies of the escort followed them.

The leaves had started changing colors—bright reds and yellows were showing among the foliage. A breeze had arisen and was playing with the veils in their hair, the tall grass they were sitting on, a few leaves lying on the ground.

The pages carrying the litter were nowhere to be seen, but a valet approached the Queen and brought her a goblet of cool wine. She drank it greedily; small drops of perspiration were on her forehead.

She was leaning against the trunk of a tree, a few cushions behind her back and shoulders. She let her eyes wander around her, taking in the group of ladies talking quietly to one another, the valets and pages serving wine and sweetmeats. The white and black horses were grazing nearby.

She turned to Catherine gently: "Are you happy here? Do you miss Germany; your family?"

"I do not miss my family, your Majesty. I never liked my stepmother too well and my father was seldom at court. I have been with you so long, your Majesty, that you are my family, if I may dare say so."

She smiled: "You are my chosen sister, Catherine, as I have told you before, and I would be only too happy if you became my brother's bride. No marriage has been arranged for Ludwig, my father assures me. Why are you blushing so deeply? You have confided in me so often, cried so many tears for him that I should love you very little indeed if I did not hope with all my heart that your fondest wish may come true. I know what a cruel, indifferent lover Ludwig has been, Catherine, but I have always felt that he is fonder of you than he has chosen to show. Perhaps he feels that his position requires a rich marriage of him but if a dowry is to be the major obstacle to your happiness, the King no doubt will grant a magnificent one to the girl that his Queen loves above others."

Dear mistress and friend. Catherine felt so shy and ashamed at having to reveal Isabelle her secret, tell her that a marriage to Ludwig, which had been an impossible dream for as long as she could remember, did not appeal to her anymore, that she started stammering, could not find the right words.

She needn't have worried; Isabelle was not going to listen to her answer. With a cry, she put her hands on her stomach and almost bent over, moaning with pain.

Oh my God! Not now! Catherine thought desperately.

The same thought must have been in all the ladies' minds, as they rushed to the Queen, eager to help but not knowing what to do.

Then Guyot de Fresnoy, Femmette's husband and one of the valets that were carrying the litter, stepped out. He bowed to the Queen end begged her to take his arm and lie down in the litter so that they could rush her back to the castle. Isabelle agreed without question, fear showing in her eyes. Then the pain subsided and she was able to walk to the litter, holding onto Catherine and Marie d'Harcourt.

They got on their horses again and were just starting back when the storm broke loose.

The light breeze became a wind that seemed to gather strength as it kept on, scattering branches and twigs around, pulling bushes and even trees off their roots. The young ladies were terrified, the leaves and dust blinded them, the howling wind made their words—their shouts—incomprehensible. The lead-grey sky was broken by the zigzags of hundred bolts of lightening; the thunders were booming mercilessly, the rain started to pour down in huge drops.

The men laid the litter under a tree, then helped the other ladies to dismount and take shelter.

Catherine hurried to Isabelle's side, entered the litter where she was, and they remained there huddling together in terror while the storm raged around them.

Trees were coming down; the rain became hail stones, adding another noise to the incessant din made by the howling winds and rumbling thunders.

From time to time, Isabelle would moan and Catherine could feel her body stiffen with pain, then relax again. She could do nothing but whisper soothing words that could not be heard and hug her tightly. They were drenched through, as the wood and cloth of the litter were but a frail bulwark against the fury of the elements.

The nightmare lasted what seemed to be an eternity. At last, the intervals between thunders became longer, the lightening less frequent, the howling of the wind lost strength, and the pouring rain had less intensity.

Guyot's haggard, scared face appeared as he drew aside one of the litter curtains. "Your Majesty, I think we should try to head back now. The storm seems to have let out a bit, and we are not very far from the castle."

Isabelle did not answer. Pain was racking her body again; she was holding her friend's hands, squeezing the, desperately.

"You are right, Guyot," Catherine said. "Let us start back: I think her Majesty should have the midwife and the doctor attend to her as soon as possible. Ask the other men to try not to jolt the litter too much. Her Majesty is in pain and her progress should be as free of bumps as possible. I will walk with the other ladies, too."

"Cheer up, Elizabeth," she murmured, wiping her mistress's forehead. We will be hack before long. Master Guillaume will help you with one of his soothing potions and you will feel much better. I have to leave you now, dear, and walk with the other ladies."

She stepped out of the litter and gazed in horror at the havoc caused by the storm.

The bridle-path they had followed had disappeared under torrents of rain and mud, huge tree trunks had been pulled off the ground and flung around as if by the hand of a mad giant.

Slowly and painfully Catherine and her companions started out for the castle, holding the bridles of the horses that had not been killed or run away. The servants led the way carrying the litter that swayed continuously, as they tried to make their way among slimy mud, avoiding huge potholes filled with water, climbing on their knees over the trunks of the trees scattered around them.

They kept getting lost as the storm seemed to have changed the geography of the forest and the rain that continued to fall confused all sense of direction.

The hope of finding the castle before dark had abandoned them, and they were getting frantic with fear, when, all of a sudden, the huge bulk of Vincennes with its towers and dungeon loomed in front of them. A cry of relief escaped from all of them, and they almost ran the last hundred yards, indifferent to the mud and the rain, only anxious to leave the hell behind them and have the Queen taken care of promptly.

The castle was in a turmoil—anxious pages, valets, servants, the ladies who had remained behind, were all consulting on what to do. Search parties had gone and come back, and the Countess of Eu, who felt responsible for the Queen, was beyond herself with concern.

When their group was sighted at last, not a minute was lost in helping Isabelle out of the litter, taking her to her room, changing her soaked clothes, summoning Master Guillaume de la Chambre and the midwives.

Charles, the first Dauphin of Charles and Isabelle, was born the following morning—September 25. He was small and puny and seemed to breathe with difficulty.

Bad omens accompanied his birth: the storm that had caught them in the forest was the worst in the region within living memory; the church of Plaisance on the river Marne, near Vincennes, was hit by a lightning and burnt to ashes.

Charles was informed immediately that the Valois line had added another leaf to its ancient tree, but he could not leave Flanders and his army. They were still waiting for the Duke of Berry's arrival, and things were not going smoothly either.

Just a few days before the Dauphin's birth, some of the French ships carrying parts of the movable town that had been built to shelter the invading forces when they landed in England, had been attacked by the English and towed away to their coast.

No festivities accompanied the birth of the Dauphin, although "Te Deums" of Thanksgiving were sung in all the churches of the Kingdom and bright bonfires lit up the darkness of the Fall evening.

The King was not present when the infant was baptized by the Archbishop of Rouen. His godfather was Charles, Count of Danmartin, who had been a friend of the late sovereign and stood godfather to Charles VI, too.

But the little Dauphin remained very small and sickly; he had a fuzz of dark hair and very yellow skin. His nurse, a buxom peasant girl, was desperate, as he would not eat and cried endlessly.

* * *

The Queen and her suite remained at Vincennes. Isabelle loved her beautiful apartments and would pray for hours in the chapel which Charles V had built and where her religious feelings and her love of beauty and elegance were gratified by the harmonious proportions of the building, the precious colors of the stained glass and the exquisite statues and carvings of Jesus, Mary, saints and angels.

One afternoon in November, when she had just come from the chapel, where her prayers to the Blessed Virgin had been more earnest than ever as little Charles had spent a very bad night and had been strangely quiet all day, Marie d'Harcourt approached the Queen and announced her that a gentleman from Florence requested to be admitted to her presence.

Excitement swept through Isabelle at those words end she told Marie that she would receive the stranger in the study. She then hurried to her room and dismissed the ladies who were there.

"I wonder who it can be? "Why from F1orence? Perhaps he is just a merchant who wants to sell me some particularly expensive jewel or trinket. Hand me on Catherine, I hope I do not look too dreadful."

She made a face at her reflection, pinched her cheeks, smoothed her eyebrows. "Give me my blue hennin, my good friend, and perhaps the-pearl necklace with the sapphire pendant."

Catherine did as she was asked and helped her to put on the cone-shaped hat, tied the pearls around her neck. Her recent maternity had left her plump and buxom, but had added a radiance to her skin that suited her and made her neck soft and smooth.

A few moments later, a swarthy looking man was bowing deeply to the Queen, removing his black velvet hat.

"I am Filippo Corsini," he started, "en envoy of the Republic of Florence. I am grateful for the privilege of this interview, your Majesty."

"Please be seated, Messer Corsini," she said in her guttural Italian.

Her mother had taught her that language and her Uncle Frederick's second wife was from Milan, too, but Isabelle had never mastered it. She beckoned him to a chair near hers and continued in French: "Why is Florence interested in the Queen of France?"

The man stretched his long legs covered in hi-color hose.

"We feel that the Queen of France has not forgotten she is also a princess of Bavaria, and the granddaughter of Barnabo Visconti."

Catherine was standing behind her Queen, and saw her stiffen at those words. In a flash she understood the man's mission and knew that he could not have found more favorable ears at the French court than the Queen's.

"Your Majesty," he continued, "I do not have to remind you what a menace Giangaleazzo Visconti represents to the Wittelsbach and to all those who oppose his policy of invasion and expansion."

Isabelle got up, toying nervously with the gold belt at her waist.

"The activities of my cousin Visconti are well—known in this court, Sir," she said, "and I am not aware that he has plans to invade France or Bavaria," she ended with a smile.

Catherine could see that she was nervous, though, as she had been taught as a child not to trust the Pavia branch of her mother's family and the lesson of distrust and diffidence towards them had proven only too real a few months before her trip to Amiens.

Her grandfather, Barnabo, who was Lord of Milan, shared his power with his nephew Giangaleazzo, whose rule was over the western part of Lombardy. One of Barnabo's many daughters had married Giangaleezzo, whose first wife, Isabelle of France, had died leaving one daughter, Valentina. Barnabo, though getting old and more dictatorial than ever, had no suspicion of his intelligent but pious and timid nephew.

One day in May 1385, Barnabo accompanied by two of his sons and a small escort, rode out of Milan to meet Giangaleazzo who was on his way to a shrine in Varese. Instead of being greeted by an affectionate nephew, he fell into the ambush laid by Giangeleazzo, was arrested, disarmed, and thrown in the castle of Trezzo's dungeons. There he died a few months later, while Giangaleazzo made himself Lord of Milan. Barnabo's sons either died in prison or fled abroad. The Wittelsbach had sworn Giangaleazzo implacable hatred and Isabelle shared their feelings.

"Indeed he has no such plans, your Majesty," replied the Florentine, "and I may add, he does not need to use force when he can reach his objectives by peaceful means."

"Messer Corsini, I am afraid I do not understand your words. I do understand your concern, though, as Florence is very close to Milan and the ambition of Galeazzo is such that he may be tempted to add your city to the many he has under his rule."

"And an alliance with the Kingdom of France will give him the strength and authority he needs to carry out his expansionism."

"An alliance with France?" Isabelle was too surprised to be able to react to the news with indifference.

"Your Majesty has been so busy with her maternal duties, that I am sure she was not able to heed the negotiations that are being carried on for a marriage between Valentina, only daughter and heiress of Pavia and Milan, and Louis of Touraine, the King's brother."

"A marriage between Valentina Visconti and Louis?" Isabelle's voice became shrill with rage. "I am sure you are wrong, Messer Corsini. Why would the King of France look for an alliance with that branch of the family again? His aunt Isabelle married Giangaleazzo because her father, King John, needed money to pay the exorbitant ransom the English had put on him, but now France does not have to pay to have the King back, the country is prosperous and victorious. We do not need the Visconti money."

"Of course, your Majesty," Corsini agreed, "France and the King do not need the Milanese's help, but the Duke of Burgundy has been borrowing money from Visconti and he is said to be favorable to the match, in fact, its very promoter."

"The Duke of Burgundy! I am sure you over estimate his influence over the King, Sir. His Majesty will always act in France's interest, and the Duke's advice will only be requested and listened to if such interest is kept paramount." Isabelle was very disturbed, her face was flushed, her eyes anxious.

Filippo Corsini got up from his seat and bowed to her deeply. "Your Majesty, I am profoundly grateful for the interview you have granted me. Florence shares France's joy for the birth of the Dauphin and I have been entrusted by my government and the citizens of Florence with this modest token of our admiration."

From the folds of his sky-blue mantle he took a velvet case and he handed it to Isabelle. She accepted it smilingly and when she opened the bejeweled box, she could not repress a cry of appreciation and joy.

On the red velvet shone a gold reliquary pendant. Two small doors adorned with sapphires opened to show a scene from the Nativity—the Virgin Mary was carved in gold and white enamel, Joseph was in blue enamel, the Holy Infant in smooth ivory. The scene was complete with an ox and a donkey, the three Kings glistening with precious stones, and two angels blowing gold trumpets. It was a masterpiece of miniature, each tiny figure perfect in every detail, and a gift that would please Isabelle immensely, as her piety was very profound.

She closed the box and handed it to Catherine. She then turned to the ambassador and took both his hands.

"I am grateful for this beautiful gift, Filippo Corsini, and I ask you to convey my thanks and the King's to your government. I am sure that the information that you have brought me is unfounded, but I appreciate Florence's concern for my native country. Rest assured you have a friend in me, Messer Corsini."

He bowed and kissed her hand, his lips lingering for a second on the plump perfumed fingers of the Queen. Then he left the room.

Once alone, Isabelle gave vent to the surprise and ire that she had had to contain in front of the Florentine ambassador.

"How dare that murderer, that Giangaleazzo, even think of having the King's brother, my brother-in-law, marry his daughter! It will never come about, I promise you this, Catherine! Never will I have that girl share the honors and pomp that are my due and be the second highest-ranking lady of the Kingdom! My father and my uncle have sworn revenge against that traitor and I know that they will carry out their promise. I do loathe the Duke of Burgundy, though. The King should send him back to his province and escape from his influence. Only harm can come from that ambitious man. This expedition against England is going nowhere, I hear, and am sure that once this folly is over, he will persuade the King to embark on another, and all for the glory and increase of the house of Burgundy! I must confess that the ambassador's visit has disturbed me, though, and I will try to find out if there is any truth in what he said—Valentina Visconti, Duchess of Touraine, at my court!"

Two months later the engagement was announced between Valentina Visconti and Louis of Turaine.

The event did not upset Isabelle as much as her friend was afraid it would—she was still prostrate with grief for the death of little Charles, which had taken place a few days before Christmas.

The King had come back from the unsuccessful expedition against

England at the beginning of December, just in time to see his son and accompany him to his rest in a chapel of the Abbey of St. Denis.

The visit of the Florentine envoy had no practical results: Isabelle found herself powerless in thwarting a plan she strongly opposed. The interview with Filippo Corsini awakened a new ambition, though, a desire for political influence, a love for scheming and plotting that she was going to fulfill in the tragic years to come.

Chapter VI

A Princess In Pavia

The hand that took the miniature trembled and a slight blush covered her pearly skin with hues of pink.

"My cousin looks like a serious and honest gentleman, Father," she murmured, lifting her eyes to the man that was observing her affectionately.

Giangaleazzo Visconti laughed aloud, a deep raucous laughter that shook his thin frame and contrasted with the melancholy of his expression.

He was a man of medium height, with sallow skin and thick-lidded prey eyes, a large thin mouth with pale lips that curved irreconcilably downwards and gave his face a perpetual look of sadness. He wore a short, pointed beard which had the same gold color as his hair.

"My dear Valentina," he said, laying a hand on his daughter's shoulders, "I am not sure whether Louis of Touraine would appreciate your remarks. They say that he is the handsomest man at the court of France, and one that enjoys more favor with the ladies than even the King, his brother."

A quick light of annoyance crossed Valentina's face at his words and she looked at the miniature again.

It represented the face and bust of a young man, superbly attired in a multi-colored doublet and a red turban terminating in a bejeweled ribbon at his right temple. The man's features were handsome—almond-shaped eyes, a finely shaped mouth, and high cheekbones. But the main characteristic of that face was its nose, which was long, down-turning and added interest to a face which would otherwise have been only handsome. The prince's lips were curved in a gay smile, while his eyes retained the dark, languid look that had prompted Valentina's comment.

"You must admit, Father," she said, "that his popularity with the ladies can hardly recommend my cousin as the husband that I am prepared to love and recognize as my lord."

"My inflexible Valentina," smiled the man. "But he has not yet met you," he added, looking at her proudly. "He does not know what a lovely, perfect bride the Lord of Pavia has prepared for him! When he beholds you for the first time, all the other ladies, if he has any dear to him, will forever disappear from his mind and heart."

"Oh, Father," she sighed, as if amused end yet exasperated by the man's confidence, "you always believe that everything you own, be it a horse, a miniature or...a daughter is a paragon."

Giangaleazzo sat on the heavily carved chair next to his daughter. His face had become serious once again; his eyes lost the playful expression of a few instants before.

"I have schemed and fought for everything I have, Valentina, because I was given nothing. My heirs will inherit a great dominion, wealth and power, but only I know how much every bit of land, every town of my dukedom cost me. When you were born, my dearest, and your Mother left me, I took a sacred oath in front of her body. I promised her that I would raise you in a way worthy of your heritage because you are a princess of Valois, the granddaughter of King John, a descendent of Charles the Great. I hope I have fulfilled my promise. I gave you the best teachers, the most accomplished musicians and poets to teach you to love art and music, I surrounded you with beautiful end precious things, I made my court the most liberal and splendid in Italy. It was an easy task, Valentina—your soul is as gentle and beautiful as your face!"

His words moved his daughter. She took his hand and brought it to her cheek in a caressing gesture. "You have made my life beautiful, Father, and I am grateful to you. But sometimes, when I pray in my chapel and all is quiet and serene, I think I hear the voices of Barnabo and his sons. They shout at you, they scream in pain, they curse our family."

Giangaleazzo paled. "Do not talk like this, Daughter," he said, taking her hands in his. "I know that in Milan they consider me a tyrant, an usurper. But I also know that if I had not imprisoned my uncle and his sons, either Barnabo or my cousins would have plotted against me and robbed me of my inheritance. Barnabo was a cruel despot, a murderer, and his very daughter, that Catherine that is now my beloved wife and your mother, was afraid of him and could not cry when he died."

Valentina stood up. She was a fairly tall, slender girl of sixteen, with thick gold braids and large, pensive amber eyes. Her nose was short and straight, her mouth small, and when she smiled two dimples danced merrily in her cheeks.

She was not smiling now. Engrossed in her thoughts she seemed to have forgotten her father's presence. She walked slowly to one of the mullioned windows overlooking the courtyard and stared absent-mindedly into the distance.

Giangaleazzo followed her and touched her arm impatiently.

"What is troubling you now, Valentina? Barnabo has been dead for many months, and so have two of his sons. As for Carlo, the one who fled to Germany, why he has not been able to carry out his plans of revenge against me, and he has tried hard enough, plotting now with the Germans, now with the Florentines, to raise my subjects against me."

"But Barnabo's granddaughter, Isabelle of Bavaria, now reigns as Queen of France," she murmured.

"That's what worries you!" Giangaleazzo exclaimed triumphantly, he could understand his daughter's misgivings and knew how to allay her fears. His practical mind did not like to dwell on ghosts and mysterious voices.

"Isabelle of Bavaria is indeed Queen of France," he said soothingly, "but her role in that court is limited to bearing the King's children and setting the pace for fashion. She has no voice in politics; neither does the King, for that matter. The King's uncles, and especially the Duke of Burgundy, are the real masters of France. They wanted an alliance with our family; they will see to it that your position at the court is beyond the reach of the Queen's hostility."

"You do think, then, that Isabelle will be my enemy?"

"That is possible, yes. You know that I value your intelligence and judgment too much to try to lie to you. Bur your husband's protection, and his uncles' are very powerful, Valentina, and no harm will ever come to you."

"They say that the King is deeply in love with his wife, Father. He married her in three days, and refused her dowry. I know that my marriage is costing you a fortune, and that I will not be received in France until most of my dowry has been paid."

"The French can be obstinate and self-conceited, I am afraid. They hate to admit that; they need an alliance with our family, seem to forget that your mother was a French princess but remember that our dynasty dates back only a few generations. They need our wealth; we need the prestige that an alliance with France will bring..."

"And I will be the pawn," she finished for him. But there was no bitterness in her words. She had known for a long time where the duty of a princess lay, and her love for her father made her burden light to carry. Was it really a burden? Valentina closed her eyes for an instant and the good-looking face of the prince she was to marry beckoned to her. A current of joy ran through her and she smiled at her father. "If I am to be the pawn, Father, I am a willing one," she said.

* * *

The countryside stretched flat and sandy on either side or the river. It was a marshy land, the home of wild birds and geese that found temporary refuge in the reeds and water plants that grew along the river banks. Farther away from the muddy river, the plain became green and fertile, and the elegant silhouettes of silver poplars stood out against the pale turquoise sky.

On a windy April day, two figures of women astride their horses could be seen making their slow way along a bridle path that cut across the meadow.

They were coming from the beautiful city of Pavia, where countless towers and church steeples pierced the sky like sharp needles and red and gray roofs shone under a sun that the recent rain had washed bright and gold.

They wore light capes that the wind made billow around their bodies in soft folds, and carried wicker baskets of food and clothing on the back of their mounts. They were riding gracefully, obviously enjoying the exercise and the morning air, towards a group of poor huts that stood near a cluster of poplars.

It was Valentina Visconti, accompanied by one of her ladies-in-waiting. It was the young princess's custom to visit the poorest families of the Dukedom and bring them what little relief she could— bread, meat, clothing, dolls and toys for the children.

She felt particularly compassionate towards the people who depended on the river for their livelihood—the fish were scarce and bony, the soil they tilled might be washed away by a sudden flood, the insects that infested the area brought disease and death.

Her father had encouraged this side of her personality since her childhood and for many years now the citizens of Pavia, and the inhabitants of the most distant villages of the Dukedom, had been accustomed to seeing their princess enter their poor dwellings and hand them whatever goods she was bringing with a kind smile and caring words.

Riding at Valentina's side was Mariette d'Enghien, a French girl who had joined her household a few months before and become her closest companion.

Almost two years had gone by since the day when Valentina had married Louis of Touraine by proxy, but the princess still lived at her father's court.

Questions had arisen about the payment of the fabulous dowry that Giangaleazzo Visconti had had to promise to have his daughter married to the king of France's brother, and the birth of a male heir to Giangaleazzo and his second wife had made him regret giving away parts of his dominions to his son-in-law, and ask for the revision of certain clauses of the marriage contract.

Valentina Visconti had been Valentina of Touraine for a while now, but her bridegroom remained for her the man of the miniature, the unknown writer of tender love letters—she had never met him.

A few months before, Mariette d'Enghien had arrived in Pavia. She had been chosen to be one of the ladies of Valentina's suite, and Louis of Touraine had wanted her at his bride's side, as if to start, preparing Valentina for the life that expected her' in Paris.

Mariette d'Enghien had brought a breath of freshness and difference to Valentina's days.

She was slightly younger than her mistress, with a heart-shaped face framed by dark curls and grey-green eyes as changeable as the sea. She was a lively and fun-loving girl, and that had charmed Valentina, who was by nature serious and quiet.

But above anything else, Mariette had brought with her echoes of Paris, the French court, the King, the Queen, Louis.

"The Duke of Touraine is the most fascinating man at court, your Highness," she would tell Valentina. "Why, there is no lady there that is not a little in love with him."

She would note the frown on Valentina's face and add quickly: "He is also a writer and poet, and Eustache des Champs, our greatest poet, says that the Duke is his most formidable rival."

She would see the smile on Valentina's lips, that sly Mariette, and continue to list his accomplishments in music, his love for books and paintings, his skill with horses and weapons.

"What is the Queen like, Mariette?"

"She is not as beautiful as you, my lady, but dresses in the most elegant fashion and wears the most extraordinary jewels."

"The King must love her dearly."

"He certainly does, your Highness, even if..."

"Mariette, Mariette, one should not listen to rumors, you know."

"But some are not rumors, I assure you. I myself have seen some of the Queen's ladies enter or leave his apartments at the most inappropriate times of day and night and it is well known that he again calls on Floriane, a beautiful lady of pleasure whose house he used to patronize before he got married...'"

"I will have no more of these gossips, Mariette. I know only too well that no royal person is immune to rumors and innuendoes."

"Why, Your Highness, nobody will ever gossip about you!"

"I am not too sure about that, Mariette. But tell me, what musical instrument does my husband favor? Does he care for the harp?"

More and more questions about Prince Louis, Valentina's loving curiosity was never satisfied, and her companion was glad to answer her questions—she too, was partial to the charming duke.

They had arrived at one of the huts. It was a very poor dwelling made of reeds and dried mud, and their arrival was noisily saluted by a swarm of children playing nearby.

The rain had left big puddles everywhere and made the sandy soil soggy and slimy. Dirty mud clung to the children's rags, their bare feet looked blistery and filthy, yet they seemed happy enough, romping in the mud, chasing each other and a few scrawny pigs with sticks, scaring a couple of flapping hens away, running after a miserable-looking old dog.

The noise made by the visitors' horses brought a woman to the hut door, a poor, emaciated creature with pendulous breasts which an infant was sucking.

A smile of joy crossed the creature's face when she saw the two girls and she dropped the clumsy version of a curtsy to Valentina.

The princess and her lady had dismounted and were busy taking food and clothing out of the baskets. The children had stopped their playing and were surrounding the visitors with expecting feces and ready hands.

Some of them, the woman's children no doubt, accompanied Valentina, Mariette and their mother inside the hut, hovering about the princess until she smilingly acknowledged their presence and handed out the gifts she had brought them—a few rag dolls, wooden horses and carriages, a small, hard leather ball.

Squealing with delight, the urchins swarmed outside once again, and Valentina sat on a stool near the fireplace and looked around.

She had been in that hut before— and this particular one was in no way different from hundreds of others she had visited during the years—but its squalor and dinginess struck her anew as if it had been the first time.

An acrid smell floated about the room—old straw rotted on the mud floor, a few embers in the hearth gave out a trail of smoke— a wood table stood in the middle, one leg shorter than the others and propped up with a stone, a couple of rickety chairs leaned against the bare walls, and, in the darkest corner of the room, a bundle of old blankets and rags thrown on the floor showed that that was the sleeping area of the family

"How do you feel, Bella?" Valentina asked of the woman.

"Still weak, my lady, and this baby seems to suck my blood away with my milk."

"I brought you some meat. Make a soup with it and drink as much of the broth as you can. The doctors say that it is the best medicine, when one feels weak."

The woman sighed. "I'll do that, my lady, but Rico and the children are always so hungry; it is a miracle if I can get a bite myself; they steal whatever I keep in the cupboard, even the eggs the hens lay, if I do not get there first!"

"Where is your husband, Bella?"

"Rico went to the river, to try to find some fish. It will be hard today, after all the rain we had last night. The river is a big sheet of mud, in days like today."

Wherever Valentina and Mariette went, they heard a similar story of grief and despair—here a father had been thrown to jail for poaching, there a child had died of a strange disease, or a boat had been stolen, which was the family's livelihood.

Her charity was greedily accepted, her presence welcomed everywhere. Valentina knew that the poor people of the Dukedom loved her and that none of her father's unpopularity touched her. She wished she could do more for them, but at times she was bothered by the resignation and indifference with which they seemed to accept their lots.

They were now approaching the last house they were to visit, one that stood under the shelter of a few trees at the edge of a cluster of poplars.

That women that lived there was an old widow without children. She owned a cow, and milk and cheese she obtained from the animal were her only rears of subsistence. Valentina's charity was most necessary to old Nina and the princess was therefore surprised when nobody answered her knocking.

Had the old woman died in her sleep? None of the other villagers had said anything about Nina. Valentina pushed the door open.

The room looked deserted. The sun coming through a small opening created bright patches on the walls hut let most of the room in shadow. A fresh scent of clean hay filled the room and a pottery vase with three pink roses in it stood in the middle of a little table.

Surprised, Valentina turned to Mariette, only to see her companion disappear quickly behind the closing door.

"Do not be afraid, Valentina of Touraine," said a voice, and a young man stepped towards her and took her hand.

She freed her hand, and leaned against the table. "Who are you?" she asked, trying to control the tremor of her voice. But she knew the answer as she had looked at his portrait too many times not to recognize him.

"I am Louis of Touraine, your husband," he said, and his voice was daring end yet respectful. "I have come to see my bride, at last, to kiss you as I have wanted to do since I saw your portrait, to whisper to you the words of love that I could not write."

Valentina was shaking with emotion. She was grateful for the hard surface against -which she was leaning, but he took her hand again and led her away to the little window.

"You are so much more beautiful than your portrait, " he murmured. "Your eyes are not brown, they have gold and emerald flakes in them, and there are threads of copper in the gold of your hair. Smile at me, Valentina, I want to kiss your dimples."

He did not wait for her smile but took her in his arms and kissed her on her cheeks. Then his mouth found hers, and his lips were like fire on hers. His arms were crushing her against his chest, she felt breathless and fainting.

Louis felt her weakness and slowly let her go. "You must forgive my ardor, Valentina," he said, "but I have dreamed of you for so long that I could not control my feelings once I had you in my arms."

It was her turn to gaze into his face, and she recognized the dark, languid eyes of the portrait, the high cheekbones, long nose, shapely mouth. But the miniature had not captured the lighthearted, amused expression of his face, the healthy glow of his skin, the sensuality of his lips. The man in front of her was young, daring, pleasure loving and self-confident.

Her heart went to him and when he took her in his arms again she returned his kisses passionately.

"I want you in France with me," he murmured, cradling her in his arms. "We have waited so long."

"I know, Louis, and the end is not in sight, yet. There seems to be more and more details to be ironed out; both my father and your uncles are hard to please and will not give up what they consider their rights."

"Yes, my uncles of Burgundy and Berry rule in France, and my brother only executes their orders, I am afraid. But still it will not always be like that, I hope. One day Charles will become aware of his responsibilities, duties and find the courage and energy to exile our uncles to their provinces. Right now, I am afraid my brother is too interested in playing war and organizing pastimes for his Queen to mind their interference. But I did not come to Pavia to talk politics with you, my beloved."

"How did you come here?"

"That was easy enough to organize. France has friends at your court, and I have a. very powerful one, who is also very partial to you."

"Do you mean Mariette d'Enghien?"

"Of course. She has been writing to me about you all these months. Her words depicted you as the loveliest, most charitable, accomplished princess in the world—I could not believe such perfection, I had to come and see for myself! Well, she was right, my Valentina, and I am the luckiest of men because you are mine, even if only in name, alas," he ended with a sigh.

She blushed. "I am sure that both you and Mariette are too kind to me, Louis. But tell me, how long will you be here? Is my father to know of your visit?"

"Not a word to your father, my angel. This is not an official visit of the Duke of Touraine to the Duchess and her father. It is Louis's visit to Valentina, a bridegroom visit to his beloved. Nobody has to know of your meeting but Mariette and the friends I have in Pavia."

"Whatever happened to old Nina, the woman that lives in this place?"

"She will live with my friends, I think. The seemed to need another servant and glad to take her in," he answered nonchalantly. "I cannot stay in Italy long, Valentina, and I want to see you every hour of these days."

"I want that too, Louis," she murmured. "I will come tomorrow again, I promise."

"Do not go yet. I brought something for you. Promise you will always wear it, Valentina."

He took something out of his doublet pocket and handed it to Valentina. It was a gold ring on which a perfect pearl shone in solitary pink splendor.

"It is beautiful," she exclaimed delighted. But she could not help a pang in her heart—pearls bore bad luck to the bride that wore them.

"With this ring I marry thee," he murmured, slipping the ring, on her finger and kissing it. "Remember, this is our real wedding ring, the one that Louis gives Valentina, the pledge of the eternal love of this man f r this woman."

* * *

Louis and Valentina met three more -times before the prince had to return to France.

Louis was Valentina's first love, and one that marriage vows had made sacred. She could let herself be swept away by her passion for her husband; it was no sin but a holy duty that God and his church praised.

If Giangaleazzo Visconti knew of the secret visit of his son-in-law —and nothing ever escaped his police and informers- he chose to ignore it and let his beloved daughter enjoy those few days of togetherness with her husband.

But the story of the meetings between the mysterious knight and the good princess, their solitary walks among the poplars, their kisses along the river banks, spread quickly among the villagers of the plain, and, like a fairy tale told at night, near the warmth of the hearth, remained among them long after Valentina had left for her new country

Chapter VII

A Damsel In Distress

It was January and Northern France lay under a heavy blanket of snow and ice, but there was so much happiness and expectations in Catherine's heart that everything looked bright and cheerful to her.

They woke up early; it was still dark outside and the few noises that reached her were muffled by the distance and the thick walls of the rooms. Once again they were in Vincennes, the castle the Queen favored above the others and where she would spend long periods.

It was lovely to linger under the soft eiderdown and daydream about the past few months. She slowly passed in review the events that were culminating in the he wedding-day —the day she had met Michel de Campremy, the immediate mutual attraction, the opposition of his parents to their union, the generosity of the King, the tender friendship of Queen Isabelle.

Two chests at the foot of her bed, one of wood, the other of tan leather, were filled un with the magnificent trousseau that Isabelle had presented Catherine and she still could hardly believe that those soft silks, shiny cloths-of-gold, pretty dresses embroidered with birds end roses, branches and does, really belonged to her.

Dawn was creeping in through the high narrow windows. This was the last night she spent in the room that had been her own every time they came to Vincennes. A new room, all bedecked with tapestries, carpets, ribbons, braids, awaited Michel and Catherine. From today she ceased t he Catherine of Fastavarin, the German, to become Madame de Campremy, the bride of one of the young knights that formed the King's escort.

Their first meeting had taken place over a year ago, just before the King's ill-fated incursion into England.

The court was staying at the fortified castle of Creil, which stood in a picturesque island in the middle of the river Oise and was one of the countless royal residences around Paris.

Isabelle was only a couple of months away from her first confinement, and was haunted by nightmares. She was superstitious by nature and her state intensified her terrors.

That morning, frantic with anxiety, because the night had brought her omens of pain and death, she had wanted Catherine to go end ask the King to join her immediately.

It was the first time Catherine went on such an errand, which was usually the duty of the pages to perform, and she was confused in that labyrinth of corridors and halls, galleries and staircases.

The King's apartment was removed from the one occupied by the Queen, and after getting lost a few times and finding, her way again, Catherine was standing on a landing deciding where to direct herself, when a voice from behind startled her: "Can I help a damsel in distress?"

She turned around and found herself gazing into bright blue eyes, staring at the smiling face of a blond man elegantly attired in green velvet.

She blushed ant diverted her eyes from his. "I am charged by the Queen to inform the King that her Majesty requires his presence in her rooms, Sir she stammered, her French sounding coarse and incorrect to her own ears, "but I do not seem to be able to find his Majesty's apartment."

He smiled and bowed graciously: "Then do allow me to be your guide, Madame."

She followed him in confusion, wanting to know who he was, wondering why she had never seen him before, but he did not say a word and left her at the door of the King's apartment, once again smiling and bowing.

A page took Catherine to his Majesty's room, richly furnished and paneled in blue and gold fleurs-de-lis, where the King was sitting consulting maps. He immediately agreed to visit his wife and thanked Catherine kindly for bringing him the message.

King Charles was unfailingly polite, one of the many charms that made him popular and beloved by his court and subjects.

When she was ushered out, her heart missed a beat, but at the same time she was not really surprised: a figure stepped out from a window alcove nearby and once again she found herself gazing, into those blue eyes.

He took her hand end said, "I would like to escort you to the Queen's apartment, Madame. I am Michel de Campremy."

She nodded her head in agreement; her emotions were too strong her to utter a word.

He broke the silence again: "May I ask your name?"

"I am Catherine of Fastavarin, she answered softly.

"Oh, the Queen's friend," he said "Catherine the German."

She hated when they added the adjective to her name but on his lips it sounded all right; there was no scorn or condescension in his tone.

Then Michel told her that he had recently joined the King's escort, leaving his parents in their castle near Bourges. He was their only son and they had tried to retain him in Berry, to lead the life of a country gentleman, but he was ambitious and desirous of gathering laurels of glory accompanying the King in his campaigns.

"The King is eager to follow in the footsteps of his ancestors, Mademoiselle, to repeat the glorious deeds of Charles the Great, to drive the English out of Calais, to attack them in their own country. He will not suffer to have the honor of France and his army slighted; he will not have his authority defied, either by the burghers of Flanders or the rulers of states bordering France. It is such a King I came to serve."

His tone of voice was enthusiastic, his face flushed with eagerness. She was only half–listening to his words though, it was enough to walk besides him and know that he was sharing with her, a stranger half an hour before, some of his dreams.

"But I do not want to bother you with the story of my life, Catherine. Do tell me about you, ifyou are happy in France, what plans the Queen has for you."

"Her Majesty has no plans for me." she laughed. "She is gracious enough to say that I am her best friend, her sister, and she has always treated me with love and generosity. I love her too, Sir. We have lived together since we were very young; she is my only real family. My mother died many years ago, my father is remarried and has sons. My life is here, in France, with Queen Isabelle. Everything is so magnificent at the court of France, and I am being treated so kindly, that I cannot help being happy here."

She stopped abruptly, checking herself. Why was she telling all this to this knight, to this Michel de Campremy, that she had just met and probably would never see again?

By then they had reached the wing of the castle where the Queen had her lodgings. Catherine stopped. She did not want to be seen by the other ladies talking to this stranger. She was not the most popular of Isabelle's ladies—they resented the love the Queen had for her, the preferential treatment she was accorded, whenever Isabelle had a chance of favoring her.

The Queen was very generous with all her ladies, but very often only with Catherine would she share particularly fine pieces of cloth, gold trinkets, satin slippers.

The French court was very worldly—luxury and extravagance reigned, and costumes were loose. Yet, Catherine had kept herself aloof from the whirl of lovers, affairs, secret meetings that made up much of the courtiers' life.

She had not forgotten Ludwig and the love that had filled her heart for so long. But the young man had never written to her, sent her a message that would tell her that she was on his mind. Catherine's love for him had to feed itself on memories, echoes of words whispered long ago, kisses that her lips could no longer feel.

She knew that he was not married yet—Isabelle received frequent messages from Germany— and with that knowledge the lingering hope that one day he might come to France and claim her as his bride was still kept alive.

With Ludwig's image in her heart, it had been easy for Catherine to ignore the young men that lived at court. None of them had the qualities that she found attractive in her German love—they were slightly effeminate, cynical men, whose impeccable manners hid a supreme indifference for love, loyalty, pledges. They fawned on the King and Queen, to whom they owed everything, and thrived on intrigue and gossip.

Michel de Campremv looked different. His handsome face and

blue eves reminded her vaguely of Ludwig's, but his nose had a more delicate curve, his chin a roundness that Ludwig's sharper features lacked. None of Ludwig's arrogance was in his eager manners and when he took Catherine's hands in his, his touch was gentle and caressing.

"Could I see you again, Catherine?" he asked, looking at her intently, a smile on his lips and in his eyes. "I will not be at court too long; the King has announced that we are to leave for England in a few days, and it will be a while before we are back."

"The chances are that we will be meeting very often, as the castle is not very big and the King and Queen spend most of her time together," she answered, evasively.

A look of disappointment crossed his face. "Are you already promised, Mademoiselle on Fastavarin?" he asked, and for some reason the pain in his voice made her happy.

"I am surprised you do not have already an answer to this question, Sir. There are not many secrets at the court of France, and none about the German retinue of the Queen."

Her light-hearted tone gave away her answer. The smile came back to his face and he became more insistent. "I would like to talk to you alone, Catherine. I feel I have so much I want to tell you, and so little time."

"I will see you tonight in the Great Hall," she said. "Perhaps we will find some time to be alone there. I must go now, Michel. Thank you for your help."

He followed with longing eyes and saw her disappear behind the massive door that opened into the Queen's apartments.

Catherine spent the rest of the day lost in her thoughts and memories, but when the evening cane she instinctively chose to wear her prettiest dress, flimsiest headdress. Her hair was her greatest ornament, very blonde with long soft curls, and she brushed it long and carefully, and let a few ringlets escape from under her heart-shaped bonnet, and dance freely on her forehead.

The look with which Michel welcomed her made her feel beautiful, and she followed him silently to a hidden, quiet corner of the Great Hall.

"Have you thought about me, Catherine?" he asked anxiously. "You have been on my mind all day, I could not think of anything else."

The lifted her eyes. "I have had a man in my heart for many years," she confessed. "I do not know any more what my feelings for him are, but I still think about him."

"I will make you forget him," he promised. "A man lucky enough to be in your heart should not leave you and make you unhappy."

"Unhappy, Michel? Why do you say that?"

"The first moment I saw you, Catherine, I thought to myself: here is a damsel in distress, I will help her.'"

"A damsel in distress," she repeated. "Why, that was the way in which you addressed me, was it not?"

He nodded. "I did not simply mean that you were lost, Catherine. I immediately felt that you were unhappy and uncertain and thought that to see you smile at me would be the greatest reward I could dream of."

His words moved the girl. "You see, Michel," she said softly, I am smiling now."

Swiftly he took her in his arms and kissed her on her lips. It all happened so quickly—his arms around her, his hot lips, hers parting to receive his kiss—but the sweetness of that instant lingered in Catherine's heart after it was over.

She felt that she could let herself go and love this man.

There was no arrogance in Michel, no selfishness where she was concerned. After years when she had felt rejected and slighted, it felt good to know that somebody really cared for her. Was that the beginning of another love?

Michel de Campremy left shortly afterwards for the campaign against England, and when he came back Catherine was ready to confess that she returned his love. The long days without Michel, the hours spent thinking about her life, the future that it held for her without the protection of a husband had persuaded Catherine that waiting for an indifferent Ludwig was foolish. When she saw Michel again, and was held in his strong arms, and whispered words of endearment, she also knew that she loved that man and that Ludwig and the tears she had wept for him belonged to the past.

But Michel's parents were strongly opposed to the marriage of their son to a penniless German lady. Their revenues were minimal, they were in debt and their son had to marry a rich heiress to raise the family's lot.

"What can I do, Catherine? Their plight is quite desperate, I assure you. Our lands can be taken away from us, if we do not come up with a lot of money, and soon too. But I cannot live without you, I told that to my parents, and they are miserable seeing my unhappiness."

"I will ask for the Queen's help," she said. "I know that she loves me, and I will tell her how much my happiness depends on my marrying you, how desperate we are. Do not worry, Michel, I know my friend and her generosity too well."

She smiled at her unhappy lover, and rushed to seek an interview with Isabelle.

"Catherine of Fastevarin, said the Queen, mockingly solemn, "you do not deserve my help, as you did not trust me enough to let me share in your secret, but I will forgive you. But I am surprised, Catherine. I really thought that your love for Ludwig would last forever, and I had already broached the subject with the King, enlisting his help to persuade my father to give his consent to a match between you and Ludwig."

Catherine knew from her tone that Isabelle was in a happy mood, and enjoying the role of her friend's benefactress. Perhaps she was also secretly relieved not to have to keep her promise—- Stephen of Wittelsbach had had to be prevailed upon to give his daughter to the King of France, the greatest lord on earth, how could he let his son and heir marry the daughter of one of his poorest and least important vassals?

Not for the first time, the realization came upon Catherine that she was totally dependent on the Queen's favor for her happiness, for her existence, almost. She had neither wealth nor political connections; in a place like the French court she was completely negligible.

Following his wife's suggestion, the King presented Catherine with a very generous dowry, part of which went to pay the family of Campremy's debts. Their lands lay in Berry, a province that was the appanage of Duke John, one of the King's powerful uncles.

Unlike his brother, Philip of Burgundy, Berry's interest in the politics of the realm was limited. His all-consuming passion was collecting works of art of all kinds and having spectacular Palaces end castles erected both in Paris and wherever his fancy suggested. To do so, he needed a fortune and he never hesitated to bleed dry the unfortunate provinces that lay under his rule.

Most of Catherine's dowry, though, was to be put aside in her name and with that money she eventually purchased fertile lands and pastures adjoining the possessions of her bridegroom's family.

In that cold January morning, thoughts of wealth and properties did not occupy her mind. All her being was pervaded by her love for Michel and gratitude for Isabelle who had made her wedding possible.

Dressed in a gown of green silk, with peacock feathers embroidered in multicolored threads, her golden hair cascading; around her face in shining locks, her green eyes like bright emeralds in her rosy face, Catherine of Fastavarin pledged her faith to Michel of Campremy.

The King himself danced at the festivities that followed the wedding ceremony, and so did the Queen and all the great personages of the court. They toasted the bride and the groom and wished them everlasting happiness.

That night, nestled in her husband's embrace, exhausted and content after their act of love, Catherine savored her happiness. She looked at Michel's face, calm and relaxed in the abandonment of sleep, and thought with relish of the countless nights when she would fall asleep in his arms, mornings when she would wake up at his side.

Nine months later, Michel de Campremy followed his King an expedition against a rebellious German Duke.

The King's uncle of Burgundy once more exploited his nephew's desire for war and glory and engaged him in an adventure where nothing more was obtained then a promise of submission by the young, reckless Duke of Guelders.

Heavy rains had been falling since the summer and the countryside had become an immense marshland.

Michel, brave knight of his Majesty's army, drowned while fording, a flooded river.

His body was not found. The swift, powerful current of the swollen river Meuse seized the body that the armor and shield made heavy, twirled it around, drifted it aimlessly among weeds and twigs, fish and mud, and deposited it in the cold waters of the North Sea.

In the years to come, when loneliness, fright, memories became unbearable, Catherine would kneel in front of the wood chest that had stood at the foot of her bed on her wedding day. She would open the lid that the years had rendered smooth and shiny, pick up her pretty wedding dress, put it to her cheeks, and let that happy period of her life rush back to her from the fog of the past.

Expect Nine months of happiness—perhaps that is all one can from life—and no more.

Chapter VIII

A Golden Summer

The court was in an uproar. The old Duke of Berry, the King's uncle, who was almost fifty years of age, had married a child of twelve—Jeanne of Boulogne—and paid very dearly for her, too.

The Duke had wanted Jeanne for his son but, during the negotiations, he had met her. The young girl, with her slender, dark prettiness, had awakened his interest and so quickened his dormant senses that he had had no peace until his nephew, the King, had consented to the match.

"But, Uncle," had laughed Charles, "what would you do with a child of twelve? My faith, this is pure madness!"

"My Lord," the Duke had answered, "if Jeanne of Boulogne is young, I will spare her for three or four years, until she is woman enough!"

"Then she will not spare you, Uncle!" had joked the King, "but if you insist, we gladly consent to your desire."

The King's intervention had not persuaded the Count of Foix, Jeanne's warden, to look favorably on the old suitor. He had permitted the wedding only when the Duke of Berry had paid the vast amount that he had pledged.

As an ardent lover, the Duke-of Berry cut a somewhat ludicrous figure. His appearance was not imposing: dark, protuberant eyes and a snub nose were the most noticeable features of his small round face. His magnificent apparel and priceless jewels could not hide his short and corpulent body and he always wore hats with high crowns to appear taller and more regal. The opulence and elegance of his palaces were unrivaled and his collections of precious things of every description aroused the admiration and envy of all. He had been long and happily married to Jeanne d'Armagnac and, the court strongly suspected, he had been a faithful husband, notwithstanding the wounded swans and bears on his heraldic motifs that alluded to a great passion for a mysterious lady called Ursine.

The wedding between December and May was the first of the great events and celebrations that took place in the Spring and Summer of that year. The splendor of those festivities was never surpassed, as the courtiers vied with each other in the magnificence of clothing, extravagance of hats and shoes, brilliancy of jewels, richness and elaborateness of tables, daring of tournaments.

On a sunny April day, Isabelle summoned Catherine to her room.

Michel had been dead for many months, but the young woman still held his memory precious in her heart and only recently had started taking part again in the social activities of the court.

When Catherine entered the Queen's room, she saw a tall stranger standing by Isabelle, his hands clasping hers, her face radiant with happiness.

"Is this little Catherine von Fastavarin, Sister?" asked a deep German voice.

She recognized that voice instantly, her heart skipped a beat, and she felt her face flush up. It was Ludwig.

The man took a few steps towards Catherine, lifted her hands and kissed her on the cheek. His soft lips lingered for a second, then he pulled her away from him and let his eyes wander all over her, an expression of surprise and admiration on his face.

"Christ's nails, Catherine! You were a pretty girl, but I never thought you would grow into such a beauty!" he exclaimed.

"Do not tease her now, Ludwig," Isabelle scolded him lightly. "Catherine is in mourning and has no ears for compliments."

He kept looking at Catherine appraisingly.

"A thousand pardons, Catherine, and my condolences," he said. "As we have not met in over six years, I could not help expressing my surprise at how changed I find you. My sister tells me you are still her best friend, and a faithful one. I am grateful to you for this. But here, I did not forget you, Catherine; here is a brooch I had one of our goldsmiths make especially for you. I hope it will remind you of the country of your birth."

He handed her a massive gold pin, on one side of which blue forget-me-nots had been enameled. A pang of homesickness swept over Catherine, and in a flash she saw a green meadow, and a carpet of pale blue little flowers waving in the breeze. A handsome blonde boy was sitting next to her, his hand was caressing her cheek and his voice was saying lightly, "You are a pretty, girl, little Catherine."

When her eyes met Ludwig's, she saw from his expression that he was sharing the same thoughts.

Isabelle's voice broke the spell. "I am delighted to notice that you approve of my 'little surprise' for you, Catherine, Ludwig tells me that he will be at court indefinitely, will you not, Brother?"

"That is right, Elizabeth. As you know, our father and his brothers decided to divide the dukedom. It was all quite sudden, and left me with too confining a share of my father's heredity to be happy in Germany at this time. Besides, I was longing to see you again, after so many years, and rejoice with you in the splendor and glory of your position, dear Sister."

"You could not be more welcome in France, I assure you, Ludwig. I only hope that your quarrel with Father will be short-lived. I cannot stand the thought of a rift between two people I love so dearly."

He kissed Isabelle's hand. "Dearest Sister, I expect that my absence will bring about a change in Father's attitude. He has always teen too generous with his brothers, seeming to forget that he is the first-born, and the Dukedom was never divided among brothers before."

"Let's hope so, Ludwig. Some good has already come from this, after all, because here you are at last."

"I am afraid my German habits will look quite wild and out of fashion in your court, Elizabeth. I will need a guide to direct me in the maze of strange customs and laws that surround you, Sister. Will you help me, Catherine and be my teacher in these days of apprenticeship?"

"I am sure that you could find many and better teachers than me, Ludwig."

"But none more charming, I assure you, Catherine."

She knew that he was making fun of her—had that not always been his wont?—but she could not resist the challenge that his request implied. She saw an expression of amused self-assurance in his eyes—of course, you still love me, Catherine!—and impulsively accepted the challenge.

"I owe you for the pretty brooch you brought me, Ludwig,

If I can help you, it will be my way to thank you for your gift."

His eyes lingered on her face, and Catherine returned his stare.

The handsome boy of Munich had become a handsome man. He was tall and blond, with the same cold blue eyes she remembered, a full mouth and chin now adorned with a short golden beard. He had discarded his mantle and stood tall and erect in tight hose and doublet. How different he looked from the other men at court, who strutted like peacocks in their magnificent costumes, whiling the time away in balls and banquets, languidly preparing for expeditions that never materialized! Here was a man full of vigor, exuberance, high spirits.

Catherine felt the old magic start working on her again and she promised herself that she was going to resist the charmer, at all costs.

"It will be good for Catherine to come back fully to the life of the court," said Isabelle. "You both have missed the wedding between the Duke of Berry and Jeanne of Boulogne, but there will be other and much grander celebrations ahead in the months to come, and of course my brother and my favorite lady have to be part of them!"

"I have heard that the King's cousins of Anjou will be conferred their knighthood among great pomp and splendor," said Ludwig.

"Yes. The King wants to honor them and their mother particularly," said Isabelle. "My husband thinks that his Uncles of Burgundy and Berry have considered themselves the masters of the Kingdom for too long, and he wants them to realize-that that period is over and done with and the sons of his late Uncle of Anjou stand as high as Burgundy's and Berry's."

"Sister, do not tell me that Charles has at last decided to take the reins of power in his hands! What a blow to that intriguer, the Duke of Burgundy!"

The Queen laughed. "Not only that, but his father's old counselors, whom his uncles persuaded Charles to dismiss, have come back to help him in his task."

"The ones that the people call Marmosets?"

"The very ones. They are old and of humble origins, and our

subjects liken them to the gargoyles that they see on the cathedral walls. Not very flattering, I admit, and also unjust, because they are the best advisers a King ever had, and they relieve Charles of the great burden that he would otherwise carry by himself."

"It must be very hard for my brother-in-law to immerse himself in affairs of state at a time like this, when everybody is eager for the celebrations that lie ahead and of which the King himself is the very promoter."

"Fortunately, Charles knows that he can rely on his Marmosets, Ludwig. As you know, he is terribly busy arranging for my solemn entry into Paris in August and can hardly worry himself with problems of finance or alliances."

"Your entry into Paris, your Majesty?" interjected Catherine.

"Yes, my friend. The King has also announced me that I will be crowned Queen in St. Denis after my official visit to the capital. He feels that our wedding was not adequately solemnized with the ceremonies, jousts, tournaments that customarily take place in such occasions, and he wants me to have all the privileges of which he thinks I was deprived."

Catherine and Ludwig exchanged a secret, incredulous look. Isabelle deprived of fun and luxury? It was enough to look at the young Queen, in the full bloom of her youth and beauty, covered with precious stones, surrounded by precious objects, to know that she had been hardly deprived of anything!

Ludwig accompanied Catherine out of the Queen's room.

"My sister delights in the glamor of her position, does she not, Catherine?"

"She has always loved splendor and luxury, if you remember, Ludwig, and this coronation ceremony, and her entry into Paris seem to be just more dazzling chapters that are going to be added to her fairy tale-like life."

He nodded. "Their life seems indeed to be a succession of magnificent pageantry. My sister is very fortunate."

"This is true, but pain and sorrow too have visited her. She suffered so much when little Charles died, and her daughter Jeanne's health is so frail that the Queen is afraid she will never improve."

They had reached the castle courtyard and Ludwig seemed in no hurry to leave her.

“I have been thinking about you all these years,” he whispered, and his voice had a ring of sincerity in it.

“I do not believe you, and I do not care, Ludwig. I am a woman mourning a beloved husband, not the naive maid you could make smile or cry at will in the castle of Ludwigsburg. I promised the Queen I will help you and show your way around at court—even if I can hardly believe that you need a teacher—in anything—but that is where our relationship ends.”

“Have you become hard-hearted, too, Catherine? This I do not believe. Not when a woman is as beautiful as you are, not when her body is as soft and pliant as yours...”

She did not let him finish and ran away from him, his caressing voice, his admiring eyes.

Michel, she prayed, stay by me. Do not let me fall into his trap once again. Make me strong; keep me faithful to your memory. You loved me; you have to protect me still!

Soon afterwards, the ceremonies for the knighthood of the princes of Anjou took place—a dazzle of gold, blue, noble horses, shining armors, in which the figures of the two young men and the religious meaning of the festivities were soon forgotten. They had only been a pretext needed by the King and his court to devote themselves completely to their love for pleasures and revelry.

Catherine and Ludwig became constant companions. They danced together, rode together, sat side by side at banquets and ceremonies.

Catherine was taking full part in the pageantry that marked every stage of the celebrations. Like the other ladies, she wore magnificent costumes and rode on richly caparisoned horses, entered the lists to bestow prizes to the winners of jousts and tournaments, danced to the music of harps and flutes.

Ludwig was never far from her and in his eyes she could read the admiration that her beauty excited in him, the passion that she was stirring up in his heart. But she had steeled herself to resist, end she would only smile at him and listen with pretended indifference to his words of love.

* * *

The ceremonial entry into Paris of Isabelle had been decided for the twenty-second of August, with her coronation to follow the next day. Preparations had been going on for months, as both Paris and the court readied themselves for yet another show of magnificence.

The King had consulted the dowager Queen, Blanche, widow of Philip VI of Valois, who was considered the guardian of the noblest traditions of the Kingdom, on the ceremonial to follow. Even the jewels of the crowns kept in Vincennes were considered inadequate for such an event and therefore, crowns and necklaces, crosses and rings were put into pieces and their gems given a more modern setting or employed to embroider the dresses of the Queen and the ladies of her escort.

The procession was to leave St. Denis and reach Notre Dame following the rue St. Denis, which was one of the longest and most crowded of the capital. The people of Paris were busy getting their city ready for the official welcome to Isabelle. Houses were being painted, streets cleaned of the garbage and trash that accumulated there daily, and gutters that ran along the streets were drained into the Seine and its Parisian branches, the Menilmontant and the Bievre. Carpenters and artisans were erecting galleries and platforms from where the citizens could watch the royal progress, scaffolding and stands where "miracles" and religious scenes were going to be enacted in honor of the sovereign.

Catherine spent long hours with the Queen and the other ladies selecting materials and jewels, hats and shoes, deciding on patterns and designs. Isabelle was once again pregnant, and she was afraid that her thickened body and sallow skin would detract from her looks and mar those days of triumph. The ladies of her retinue were renewing their wardrobes, too, selecting the most becoming silks and furs, the most precious stones.

The King was taking an active part in deciding what costumes his lords would wear, their colors, what litters, carriages, horses were going to be used. He was the producer of a show that had to surpass anything seen until then; thanks to the assistance of the people of Paris, his desire was fulfilled.

Just a few days before the beginning of the festivities, a wedding took place at the Castle of Melun that filled Isabelle with spite and indeed cast a shadow on those radiant days. Her cousin, Valentina

Visconti, finally arrived from Italy, two years after her marriage by proxy to Louis of Touraine.

At the court, the curiosity about the new princess was great. The French gentlemen that had visited Pavia when the marriage contract was discussed and later at the time of the marriage by proxy, had brought back news of a different, more refined country. Unlike the gloomy French castles and manors, the Italian palaces were of light-colored marble, with wide windows and ornate columns; the walls were painted with scenes of hunts and mythological subjects, and art objects, mosaics, statues filled tables and rooms. There were books everywhere because Giangaleazzo, her father, delighted in poetry and painting, and artists and men of letters were welcomed at his court. The ladies wore simpler dresses, they let their hair fall in ringlets on their shoulders and to protect their fingers when eating, men and women alike used "forks" imported from the East.

The King's envoys had been unanimous in their admiration for the accomplishments of the princess, her pious disposition, her love for books and music. She spoke French beautifully, they had reported, and played the harp enchantingly.

Obviously, this glowing portrait of the daughter of the man that had caused her grandfather's death and the ruin of his family was not one to impress Isabelle. Her cousin's beauty too had been highly praised and having to meet Valentina when she herself was heavy and slow added to Isabelle's displeasure.

"Your Majesty, I think you are being absurd!" Catherine would tell her to appease her rage. "The Duchess of Touraine will always be the one that bows to you. She may be attractive, but her looks did not win her Louis of Touraine, her dowry did." They would laugh together at that because Valentina's dowry was indeed immense and it had taken her father two years to amass it.

"It was your beauty, your charm that conquered the King. His Majesty wanted you, my Lady, and your dowry did not interest him. Valentina Visconti cannot boast of such a 'coup de foudre' on the part of her bridegroom."

But when Catherine saw Valentina, she did wonder whether Louis would not have had her even if she had been penniless. She was lovely, tall, and graceful, with blonde hair and brown eyes. Her long slim neck supported a small head adorned with thick braids of burnished gold, her finely chiseled features were delicate and harmonious.

She wore a dress of turquoise silk, embroidered in gold and tightened at the waist by a sapphire belt. Its square neckline was adorned with little pearls, and revealed her high soft breasts. The man at her side, her husband Louis could not keep his eyes off her.

"She is pretty, I will grant this," Ludwig's voice whispered in Catherine's ears. "I wonder whether Louis may not abandon his womanizing, for a while at least; she is such a lovely creature."

Catherine glanced at Louis standing next to his Duchess. Once more, she wondered why he was considered so attractive, even more so than his handsome brother. His nose was so long, and down-turned, his skin pale.

She turned to Ludwig. "I am sure that his so-called 'womanizing' is grossly exaggerated, Ludwig. The court is such a hot bed of gossip and rumors, as you have immediately found out, and without my help, I may add, that no man or woman is immune from them. Why, they even say that the King and his brother share the favors of the same 'fille de joie', and the Queen is in love with her brother-in-law!"

Her last words annoyed him: "My sister is in love with her husband, as you well know Catherine, and I dare anyone to repeat such a calumny in my presence!"

"But you will say that the Duke of Touraine is a womanizer; that is not a slander, is it, as it does not touch your sister or family. How unfair, Ludwig!"

"My darling Catherine, you have indeed become much harsher than you used to be. But as I am your captive, I will suffer your hardness in silence."

His tone was light-hearted and amused. She looked at him and could not help noticing the soft expression of his eyes, the softened curve of his mouth. Was he in truth her captive?

On the triumphant day of her official entry to Paris, Isabelle wore a mantle of blue velvet strewn with gold fleurs-de-lis; her hair was hidden under a high "hennin" of gold damask on which was placed a crown of pearls, turquoises, and sapphires. Her litter was gilded and painted with the emblems of the Houses of France and Bavaria, fleurs-de-lis and twenty-one silver diamonds. It was covered with thin gauze, and it was drawn by two beautiful horses, one black and one white. A long procession of carriages and litters followed the Queen's, all ablaze with gold and precious materials.

The greatest lords of France—the Duke of Touraine, the Dukes of Bourbon, Berry, Burgundy—on horseback escorted the Queen and her noblest ladies. Behind Isabelle's litter advanced those of her aunts and relatives, followed in turn by the carriages of the ladies of the lesser nobility.

Before reaching Paris, the procession was continually being stopped: just now it was a group of knights asking leave to introduce foreign lords, then a crowd of Parisian bourgeois in green or crimson gowns led by the Prevost of Merchants reading a welcoming address. Eventually the veil that covered the Queen's litter was removed, the princes got off their horses and placed themselves behind her litter according to their ranks.

The rue de St. Denis was the main thoroughfare the cortege was to follow and there the citizens of Paris had lavished treasures of ingenuity and extravagance to honor their Queen. From the windows and balconies of the houses facing that boulevard hung precious cloths and carpets, wreaths of leaves and flowers, and even the humblest lodgings displayed what their households contained of most valuable and cherished, perhaps a vase, a silk cloth, a thin scarf. Curious and smiling faces also appeared at the windows, hands ready to clap, mouths ready to shout joyous Noels.

Shops and taverns were open and doing booming business with both Parisians and the hundreds of visitors that the ceremonies had attracted to the capital. The hot weather made beer and wine flow aplenty, and the immense crowd, milling around purposelessly secured a hefty boot to the pickpockets come to Paris from all over the Kingdom.

Students, clerics, bourgeois, beggars, children, artisans, vendors, all dressed in their finery, formed an ever-changing and moving background to the procession. From time to time, Isabelle would glance at the throngs, notice an unusually pretty face, a running child, a handsome student, the shining brass sign of a tavern, a preciously embroidered cloth hanging from a window, colorful pot of geraniums.

The wonders that the city was offering to the Queen were such and so many that Isabelle, enchanted, would ask her escort to stop her litter to admire some of the most striking: a fountain draped in blue and gold fleurs-de-lis spouting red and white wines that beautifully singing girls would serve in golden cups; a drama of the third Crusade performed on a stage and representing a battle between twelve Christian lords led by Richard Coeur-de-Lion and the Saladin with a group of Saracens. A cloth of blue and white represented the heavenly sky with the figures of the Trinity and a chorus of angels. It opened up and two cherubs descended, who crowned the Queen with a crown of gold and gems, while sweetly singing:

"Dame enclose entre fleurs-de-lis
Reine etes-vous de Paris
De France et de tout le pays.
Nous en rallons en Paradis."
(Lady enclosed among fleurs-de-lis, you are Queen of Paris, France and the whole country. We are going back to Paradise.)

The noise, shouts, applause, and cheers of the crowd were deafening, but that enthusiasm pleased Isabelle. She hardly knew Paris, even if she had resided at the royal palace of St. Pol a few times, and the excitement and enthusiasm that her official entry seemed to arouse gave her pride and a sense of power.

Wonders followed one upon the other. Near the grim fortress serving as prison called the Chatelet, an allegory dramatizing the Bed of Justice was performed: St. Anne, representing Justice, was lying on a bed of blue cloth strewn with gold fleurs-de-lis. A white hart with gold antlers and a gold collar chased by a lion and an eagle, ran out from a wood nearby. Would the deer be caught and mauled by those fierce predators? No, because twelve maidens with naked swords rushed from the woods and shielded the white hart.

The Queen enjoyed that play and admired the prettiness of St. Anne, the noble shape of the deer, the way he could move his eyes, head, legs, and even hold the sword of justice.

The procession was starting off again, when a great commotion on one side of the avenue attracted everybody's attention: a young man and an older one, riding on the same horse, were trying to force their way to the front row of spectators; they too wanted to see the Queen close by, they shouted. But the sergeants-at-arms, who were hard at work to keep some kind of order in the huge crowd, pushed them back and hit them with their thick sticks.

Once the order was reestablished, the cortege crossed the Seine on the Pont-au-Change. By then it was late afternoon. Isabelle felt tired, hot, hungry, but the climax of the day, her coronation, had not yet been reached, and only then were they slowly approaching Notre Dame, where the ceremony was to take place.

The huge mass of the cathedral was looming ahead, its two towers standing out against the darkening sky, when the people's attention was attracted by two faint lights moving up in the sky, and they gasped with wonder. A tight rope linked one of the towers to the tallest roof on the Pont-St. Michel and on it an acrobat was walking, holding two flaming candles in his hands and singing a song praising the Queen.

The crowd gathered around the church fell silent, the procession stopped, and all the eyes were fixed on the tiny figure perched in mid-air, on the two flames that waved and shimmered. When at last, the man reached the other end of the rope, the throng roared with enthusiasm and relief. It was like an act of magic, a feat nobody had accomplished before.

The beautiful cathedral was ablaze with candles and torches, their flames flickering on the golden robes of the Bishop and high prelates, on the jewels of the Queen and her train. An invisible choir was singing in praise of God and his Blessed Mother.

Isabelle knelt in front of the statue of the Virgin Mary, then offered her the crown that she had been given by the angels that afternoon and two magnificent cloths of gold. A shiny new crown sparkling with jewels, was placed on the Queen's head by the Bishop and the four royal dukes.

It was very dark when the Queen and her suite left the cathedral, and the night was pierced by a thousand candles. Their lights accompanied the procession to the Palais Royal, where the court was to be lodged.

Excited and moved beyond measure, Isabelle went through the last hours of that day as if she were in a dream. She was exhausted and at the same time exhilarated by the show that had been staged for her. She had become one of the greatest ladies on earth, Queen of a man who cherished her, Queen of a country of immeasurable wealth and splendor, and a people who delighted in making her happy and prosperous.

Afterwards, she had a dim recollection of that night—-the banquet held in the Great Hall of the Palais, the ball following it. But she remembered one detail with a vague sense of inquietude. Charles went to her, kissed her warmly, and laughingly showed her bruises on his arms and shoulders.

"I know that you did not recognize us, Savoisy and me, riding on the same horse and shouting that we wanted to see the Queen! The soldiers did not either, and these are the blows we received for our audacity. But it was fun, was it not, Savoisy? "Mysteries" and official addresses to tend to become slightly boring after a while, and we had to enliven things a bit!"

"But you could have been seriously injured," she protested, disturbed by his odd and childish behavior.

Charles shrugged off her comment. "The soldiers were too busy trying to keep the order to concentrate on a single incident," he replied. "And our horse was swift, and we could make a fast escape."

Isabelle's crowning in Notre Dame had been a symbol of the welcome that the city of Paris offered to the Queen, but the real holy ceremony of the coronation had to take place the following day, and the people of Paris were excluded from it.

The Sainte Chapelle, built by St. Louis next to the Palais Royal, was the place appointed for the anointment of Isabelle. The beautiful glass windows, the gilt carving of the choir, and the precious statues of the saints, shone more brightly than ever in the August sun, while the chapel filled with the noblest personages of the Kingdom. Dressed in their most precious robes and adorned with priceless jewels, they had all gathered there to salute in their Queen the dawning of a new reign that they wished prosperous and glorious.

Charles VI reached the chapel before his wife. He was attired in the full regalia of his state, a gold crown on his fair hair, a "surcoat" of scarlet furred with ermine and tied with gold ribbons on his shoulders.

When the Queen appeared, the simplicity of her red silk costume, her long brown hair falling on her shoulders, contrasted sharply with the gorgeous glitter of her courtiers. She was pale with emotion and her dark eyes stood out wide and awed on her face.

The rite proceeded smoothly, according to a tradition that dated back to the Capetian ancestors of the Valois. The Archbishop Rouen and the

Abbott of St. Denis performed the ceremony, and the "Te Deum" filled the vaults with its solemn notes. The words of the liturgy compared the Queen to the greatest women of the Jewish tradition, to Sara and Rebecca, Leah and Rachel, and the prelate invoked the blessing and protection of the Almighty on her.

On the altar, the insignia of royalty had been placed—the ring, the scepter, the hand of Justice, the crown held by a headdress of scarlet velvet adorned with gems.

Isabelle knelt in front of the Archbishop, who anointed her forehead and chest and put the ring on her finger, following each act with the solemn words of the ancient rite. Then she received the scepter and the hand of Justice and at last, the crown was handed to the Archbishop.

The choir stopped singing and a deep silence filled the chapel. Placing the crown on the bent head of the Queen, the prelate pronounced the sacred words of the ritual: "Take this crown of glory and rejoicing, so that you may shine crowned with joy forever."

Deep emotions were stirring Isabelle, she could feel tears trickling down her cheeks. All kinds of thoughts were passing through her mind—love and gratitude for her husband, pride in her position of anointed, sacred Queen, loneliness because, truly, the holy ceremony set her apart from the rest of the court, nay, the world.

As a far-away echo, the words of the Letter of St. Paul that the priest was reading now, reached her. They were solemn, and disturbing. "Women should be submissive to their husbands..." it started.

Confusedly, she felt that those words were indeed true, and that on the very day of her coronation, when she was surrounded with all the paraphernalia of power, when all she heard was the cheers of her people, she had to be reminded of the unalterable truth that her power came from her husband, and that without the King's authority her will was null.

But soon her attitude of skepticism, uneasiness disappeared drowned in a phantasmagoria of music, lights, incense and gold. There was love and pride in the eyes of the man who knelt at her side to follow the High Mass, there was loyalty on the faces of the courtiers that thronged the cathedral—there was no time or reason to dwell on anything unpleasant on that golden August day.

Later that day a superb banquet was held in the Great Hall

of the Palais, to which a huge crowd of citizens was allowed to assist, separated from the marble table of the Sovereigns by an oak barrier.

The people stood with wide eyes, wondering at the scene of luxury and beauty displayed in front of them, pointing at the various personages, recognizing the King, his brother, the Duke of Berry, the Duchess of Touraine. Isabelle could overhear them commenting on the elegance of the tables, the richness of the gold and silver platters heaped on the sideboards, the elaborate food being served.

Minstrels were playing their instruments, singing their songs, reciting their poems and a pageant of the War of Troy was performed in the middle of the Hall. It was very cleverly done, with castles and ships moving about on wheels, warriors in shiny armors with spears and spikes, and it captured everyone's attention. The crowd of onlookers was large, and they started pushing each other so hard to see the representation close by, that one table was overturned and the poor ladies sitting at it ran away screaming, scared but unhurt.

The noise and heat of the hall made Isabelle dizzy. The baby she was carrying became heavier with every breath, and waves of nausea tormented her. She rested her head on the back of her chair and took her husband's hand.

The King rose to his feet: "Open the windows, let some air in," he ordered. But the windows were tightly locked and the pages had to break them with their maces.

Splinters fell all over the floor, but little relief came in as it was still early afternoon and the day was hot.

"How do you feel, my dear?" Charles asked of a pale, perspiring Isabelle.

She smiled a wan smile. "I would like to go back to St. Pol," she said, "where it is always cooler than at the Palais."

"You are right, Isabelle, and the gardens there will allow you to take a peaceful walk, after you have rested a while. I am anxious to show you the latest addition to my zoo, a large lioness that I have called Isabelle in your honor."

"Your cages of wild animals do not please me too well, Charles, but I thank you for the honor. Why, I am looking forward to making the acquaintance of the other Isabelle."

Charles helped Isabelle out of her chair, and, leaning on his arm, she prepared to leave the hall. Everyone stood up, then, ready to follow their sovereigns' example.

Catherine stood up too. Her rank at court had kept her away from her mistress on this solemn day of her coronation, but now she could see that her services were required and she was hurrying to her side.

"Do not go yet, Catherine," Ludwig said.

She looked at him in wonder. "As you can certainly notice, your sister is not well, and my duty is with her, Ludwig," She hoped her tone had the right amount of reproach.

"I assure you that the King is very capable of assisting his wife. Why, he may even enjoy doing so." He winked at Catherine allusively.

She understood in a flash. "But the Queen is sick, and too far gone with child..."

"The baby is not due for many months and as for her sickness, it is just dizziness that the heat of the room has brought about, nothing more, I assure you."

You seem very eager to keep me here." She smiled at him, already yielding in spite of herself.

"Not here exactly, Catherine. Pierre de Craon has invited a few of his close friends to spend the rest of the afternoon at his lodgings, and I will not go unless you accompany me."

"Pierre de Craon?" Catherine was surprised. When she had first arrived at court, Pierre de Craon's name was never pronounced. Scandal surrounded him because he had embezzled funds destined to the Duke of Anjou's campaign in Naples and the Duke's widow was his implacable enemy. Soon after, and thanks mainly to his relative, the Duchess of Burgundy, Craon was restored to favor and had become a very close friend of Louis of Touraine.

"He is no friend of yours or the Queen's."

Ludwig shrugged. "My solemn Catherine, he does not have to be my bosom friend for me to accept his invitation. Besides, the gardens of his palace are cool and shady, and to spend an hour of my time in your company I would make friends with Beelzebub himself."

The blasphemy horrified and yet secretly flattered her. She could not deny it to herself—since Ludwig's arrival, the rhythm of her life had quickened its pace; there was an excitement inside her that she had not experienced since the days of Michel's courtship. The thought of her beloved dead husband sobered her down an instant. But her knight was gone, the protector that had fulfilled her dreams and aspirations of her soul and awakened her body to the sensual pleasures that it could yield and claim.

She looked at the man at her side, so strong and virile, so... alive. She felt desire for him, his arms around her body, his lips on hers, his body inside her. The wave of sensuality left her weak and trembling.

Ludwig sensed her languor and possessively pulled her to himself. "Come, Catherine," he whispered, and he led her to join Pierre de Craon and his group.

* * *

The shady corner of the garden looked peaceful and inviting. Multicolored cushions were spread on the grass and a table was set nearby with cups and jugs.

Catherine reclined on the soft silk and Ludwig sat at her side. Dizzy with excitement and longing for his embrace, she tried to compose herself and calm the pounding of her heart. She let her eyes wander around the park, taking in the lush vegetation, the bright patches that the ladies' dresses made against the green of the grass and trees, the graceful movements of a group of young girls dancing to the music of harps and flutes in a clearing of the park.

All of a sudden she started with surprise. Not far from the place where they lay, she saw a girl gently pushing herself to and fro on a swing. She was very young and graceful, dressed in a light gown of pink that the rhythmic motion of the swing lifted to reveal small feet and delicate ankles. She was bare headed, and her short dark curls danced freely around her oval face. A man approached her, young and swarthy looking, who smilingly pulled her hands away from the ropes of the swing and started pushing her. The man turned his face toward the pretty girl and said something that made her smile and Catherine recognized Louis of Touraine.

Ludwig had been observing her with loving, pensive eyes, and her surprise did not escape him.

"It is Louis of Touraine!" she exclaimed. "Why is he here? Where is his bride? Who is that girl?"

"Do you not remember her, Catherine? Apparently she was at court a few years ago and has been back with her mistress these past few days only. Her name is Mariette d'Enghien, and she is a lady-in-waiting to Valentina Visconti."

Catherine remembered. Mariette was hardly more than a child when she had been at court last, and had blossomed into a lovely young woman she would not have recognized.

"Where is the Duchess of Touraine?"

"My pretty cousin Valentina? I imagine she went back to St. Pol when the King and Queen left the Palais."

"You mean the Duke left his new bride alone to come to Pierre de Craon's lodgings and make love to another woman?"

"Louis and Valentina have been married two years now, remember?" he said jokingly, but then he saw the look of annoyance on Catherine's face and went on more seriously: "I will admit that I am surprised too. Valentina is a beautiful woman, and good and loving as well, according to everyone's reports and my brother-in-law could not have found a better and more deserving bride. He is a fool to jeopardize his happiness for the sake of little Mariette!"

For a few instants they observed the couple that, unaware of their stares, were whispering and smiling at each other, then Ludwig pulled Catherine gently to himself and caressed her face with delicate fingers.

"I want you to think about us, now, my Catherine," he said. "All these longs days, months we have been together, constant companions, and you have never allowed me to kiss you, nay touch more than your pretty hands. And yet you did love me, and your kisses were tender and passionate when I held you in my arms in the park of Ludwigsburg. Have you forgotten the past completely? I do not believe it; I cannot believe it. See, you have been wearing the brooch I brought you almost constantly," he finished triumphantly touching the gold pin that shone on her bosom.

She blushed, annoyed at him and herself. "Do not delude yourself, Ludwig. The brooch is pretty and the blue forget-me-nots go well with most of my gowns—that is why I wear it so often. But of course I have not forgotten the past; in fact it is the very memory of those years in Munich that hardens me against any weakness that I may feel."

"You are being too harsh. I was a very young boy then. What did I know about love, tenderness, loyalty? Will you reproach me forever for the sins of a Ludwig that does not exist anymore?"

"I know about love and tenderness now. I was married, and very happy. I felt secure in my husband's embrace, certain that no harm would ever come to me as long as he was with me."

"You were married but a few months, had known him for such a short while before your wedding. Life did not test the strength of your love for him; he remained for you the young knight in shiny armor of your first meeting. I am different, Catherine, and you are aware of my faults—of some at least...", he added with a smile. "But you are also aware of how attracted I am to you," he went on. "All these years the memory of you has never completely abandoned me. I always felt that I would see you again and that you cared for me too."

He looked at her intensely. She lay close to him, her eyes half-closed, lulled by the sound of his voice, caressed by the tenderness of his words.

When he bent over her and touched her body and kissed her lips, he-knew that she would respond to his love with the same ardor. She was soft and docile in his arms and her mouth was like fire on his.

He felt a surge of love for the woman in his embrace—she was giving up her dreams, hopes, for him.

"I will tell you what you want to hear, Catherine," he murmured. "I love you and will ask my father and the King for their permission to marry you."

Chapter IX

Intrigue At Court

Catherine did not like Pierre de Craon. He was a short man, with a florid face and head of tight auburn curls, always extravagantly dressed and bejeweled. He had a dry, caustic wit, a quick temper and ingratiating manners that had long made him a favorite at the French court. Hardly a ceremony, a ball, a tournament, took place that he was not at the center of it, a little smile on his mouth, a light of scorn in his eyes, a quick repartee on his lips. The King liked him too, and the Queen would often laugh at his retorts or admire some pretty jewel that adorned his person, but she had never found him particularly charming or attractive.

She was very surprised, therefore, when she saw him standing next to the Queen, eagerly recounting something that seemed to arouse her interest and curiosity.

It was a chilly March evening, and big braziers were burning in the great hall of Isabelle's apartment in the palace of St. Pol. The day had been sunny though, with a clear blue sky and a. shiver of spring in the air. Tiny buds were starting to show in the fruit trees that filled the gardens. Soon the cages that held the wild animals of which King Charles was-fond, and the large aviaries where hundreds of multi-colored birds flew noisily to the delight of Isabelle and the whole court, would be reinstalled in the park.

Spring was a lovely season, when every day brought a ride through the woods, a hunt in the forest, a banquet at tables set under the trees, a stroll among the pretty flowers and bushes that adorned the royal residences. This Spring promised to be an enchanting one for Catherine, and she was looking forward to the balmy evenings of April and May, and to solitary walks and meetings with the man who had come back to haunt her mind and senses.

That night in March, Ludwig was not in Paris; he was among the lords that had accompanied the King to Amiens where he was to meet the Duke of Lancaster. Pierre de Craon had not been of that number, and there he was, resplendent in his bright yellow costume lined with beaver fur, a high-crowned hat on his auburn hair, for once absorbing the full attention of the Queen.

Isabelle did not look her best that night; a month before she had been delivered of her fifth child, the longed-for Dauphin, and her body had lost slenderness and elasticity. She was a matron of twenty-two, even if the sparkle and vivacity of her dark eyes sometimes belied the sluggishness of her body.

A few later, Pierre de Craon bowed profoundly and left the Queen. Isabelle beckoned to Catherine impatiently and she had hardly sat down when the Queen started talking, brimming with mischievousness and delight.

"It is about my sister-in-law, Catherine. I have just learned something that will take that smug smile of hers off Valentina's face," she started. "You know I have always resented her 'holier-than-thou' attitude. The daughter of Giangaleazzo Visconti has absolutely no reason to give herself airs. Anyway, Pierre de

Craon tells me that Louis, who has been devotedly playing the loving husband, does have a mistress, a long-standing relationship with one of his wife's ladies-in-waiting."

She did not notice surprise in Catherine's face. "Why, Catherine, you too know about it, do you not," she exclaimed with annoyance.

"I imagine you are referring to Mariette d'Enghien," Catherine answered. "Yes, your Majesty, I have heard this rumor, but at the same time, I have heard so many rumors about the adventures that the Duke is supposed to have with any woman in sight that I wonder whether or not this may be just another piece of gossip that Craon or somebody else has picked up somewhere and relates to everyone as gospel...truth," she lied.

"My dear Catherine, how like you never to believe anything bad of anybody," shrugged Isabelle. "You are wrong, this time. Craon assures me of the story authenticity, as Louis was imprudent enough to choose him as his messenger."

Catherine felt a pang of pain for the Duchess of Turaine. "I have always had the impression that the Duke's love for his wife is sincere, your Majesty," she answered truly.

"An affair with a lady-in-waiting of his wife does not reveal great feelings for her, does it, Catherine?" she laughed. "It is high time my cousin realized that she too has to bear with the infidelities of her husband, that no magic shield protects her from the hurt they inflict."

There was an edge of bitterness in her voice and Catherine felt sure that gossips had not spared her either, that an echo of the countless adventures of her beloved husband had reached the proud Queen, and wounded her.

"But, your Majesty," she objected, "the Duchess has only recently lost her second child, and her sorrow for his death seems to linger forever in her eyes...". Her sentence trailed off. How inconsiderate of her to remind her beloved friend of the painful loss that the death of two of her own babies had caused her.

But today Isabelle seemed insensitive to the memory of her suffering. "You are certainly aware , my friend," she said ironically, " that Valentina Visconti is not the first mother that loses her infants, and as for that lingering sorrow you talk so emotionally about, that does not prevent her from gathering poets and musicians in her rooms, listening to their flattering words, accompanying their songs with her harp."

As the Duke and Duchess of Orleans lived in another part of the vast palace of St. Pol, obviously the two sisters-in-law saw each other very frequently, and no event at one of the cousins' private apartments went unnoticed at the other's.

Isabelle had tried in vain to prevent the marriage between her brother-in-law and her cousin. Her hatred of the branch of the Visconti that had ousted her mother's family was deeply rooted, and all the many accomplishments of Valentina had made her resent the intimacy that their ranks and kinship imposed upon them even more.

Valentina was prettier, her elegance more sophisticated, the dowry she had brought from Pavia had dazzled the court; nobody had ever seen such magnificent jewels, exquisite tapestries, richly illuminated books, beautifully carved chests and chairs. Poets and musicians wrote verses for her, composed songs in her honor, lovingly painted her pretty face, and were forever extolling her beauty and virtue.

But Isabelle was the Queen, the first lady of the land, and she would rarely let Valentina forget it—it was her only weapon against the seemingly invincibility of her cousin. Now Pierre de Craon had given her another arrow; she was going to use it, no matter what the consequences might be.

Pierre de Craon's inconsiderate gossip unchained a series of events that were to have catastrophic consequences for Isabelle and indeed France. The amorous passion of Louis of Touraine became one of the many pawns in the struggle for power that was being waged between the royal uncles on one side, and the King's counselors, the "Marmousets", led by the Constable of Clisson, and the Duke of Touraine on the other. They were all aware of the King's weakness and volatility, they knew that there was a vacuum and that power was up for grabs.

Until then, the faction headed by the Constable had been the more influential, but the Duke of Berry and the wily Duke of Burgundy had not resigned themselves to a secondary role and were waiting for a chance to regain the upper hand. The Queen's jealousy of her cousin unwittingly offered them their opportunity.

The Duchess of Burgundy had always befriended Isabelle, subtly reminding the Queen on occasions that her own husband had been the promoter of her exalted marriage. Isabelle had been long aware her love story was indeed a real one, but that powerful pressures had been at work for Charles to fall in love and marry a German princess. She knew where her loyalty lay and, notwithstanding her diffidence towards the Duke of Burgundy, looked upon his wife with great partiality.

The Duchess of Burgundy relished her role of confidant of the Queen and had always disliked Valentina, whose position of sister-in-law of the reigning King relegated her to a lesser rank. Isabelle was eager to tell her cousin the truth about Louis, and the Duchess of Burgundy did nothing to dissuade her.

"But why, why Your Majesty, tell the Duchess of her husband's disloyalty?" Catherine in vain pleaded with her friend. "Nothing good can come out of it."

"Perhaps not, but I think that Valentina ought to know the truth about her husband at last. I have also been informed that Mariette d'Enghien is with child, and a bastard brother of her own child may one day advance claims with the family that it will be impossible to ignore."

Of course Isabelle had no real reason to inform her sister-in-law of the Duke's affair but her malevolence against her. Catherine was aware of Isabelle's feelings and also knew that it was impossible to dissuade her from her purpose.

* * *

Kneeling in front of a beloved painting of the Virgin, Valentina mechanically repeated the prayer she had learned as a child in her nurse's lap. "Holy Mary, Mother of God..."

But in her great sorrow the words had no meaning, did not express the anguish of her heart. Why, Holy Mother, why, she wanted to ask over and over, and wait for an answer that would explain everything and console her.

Through her tears she looked at Mary's face, trying to find her answer in Mary's smile and compassionate eyes—but the image was blurred and confused, a bright spot of color from which no solace could come.

She got up and went to the window, looking unseeingly at the courtyard and the windows of the Queen's apartments. In front of her swollen eyes danced the figures of Louis and Mariette holding each other in a passionate embrace, Isabelle's revengeful look, the sneering men and women of the court.

She was not naive; she knew that princes and kings, more than the common mortals, have mistresses and concubines. Her own father had had scores of love affairs and so had Uncle Barnabo, and King Charles. But Louis was different. The audacious young man who had braved the Alps to steal a secret kiss of his unknown bride, the passionate husband who had awakened her heart and body to love, the tender father who had dried her tears when their child had passed away... How could he fall as low as to take his wife's lady as paramour? And Mariette, the girl she had loved like a sister, the young lively friend of Pavia and Paris, the promised bride of another man...

Sobbing, Valentina sank to the marble seat in the window–space and covered her eyes with trembling hands.

She did not hear when Louis entered the room and started with a cry when he put a hand on her shoulder.

"My dearest Valentina, do not make this moment even more unbearable than it already is," he said with a pained voice.

She raised her eyes, trying to compose herself and face the man she loved and who had betrayed her with dignity. His face was ashen, and his eyes avoided hers.

"I have banished Craon from this court," he said, "and I promise you that he will never set foot in Paris again. As for the Queen, I cannot obviously banish her, but my brother will see to it that she asks for your forgiveness."

"Craon and Isabelle have not hurt me, Louis. You have," she replied, "and from you I expect words of repentance and promises for the future."

He blushed—her eyes were so cold and unfriendly.

"I love you, Valentina," he said. "I have since the day I met you and always will. I also consider you the best of wives, a most loving mother, a perfect princess. You are dearer to me than any other person in the world, you are my conscience and guide. I need you, because I am not as strong and noble as you, and I need your compassion and piety because at times temptation is a siren whose voice I cannot resist. I have sinned against you, and hurt you—I ask your forgiveness. I have loved a woman who is unworthy of your friendship, and yet, on her behalf and mine, I have to beg you to grant her a last grace."

"A grace?" she repeated, anguish gripping her again.

"Mariette is with child, my child. She is to marry the Sire de Cany in a few months and if he knew of her pregnancy he would reject and humiliate her. We ask you, we beg of you, to be magnanimous and promise that you will raise my bastard child among your own."

For a minute, surprise left her speechless. How dared he? How could he and his paramour have the effrontery of asking such a thing of her, the wife whose feelings had been hurt so badly? Outraged, Valentina looked at Louis.

He was crying quietly now, and the skin of his face and hands was like wax. Dejection was written all over his proud body, in the sloping lines of his shoulders, hunching back, bent down head, nervous legs.

She felt a wave of pity for him. She, the wounded one, was sorry for the man who had wounded her. She wanted to take him in her arms, cradle him the way she cradled her baby, and kiss away his pain. She was the stronger, as he had always felt, and it was up to her to forgive and forget.

She stroked his hair gently, in a maternal gesture of which she became immediately aware now and whispered: "I will raise Mariette's child with mine, Louis, and love him as I love mine."

He covered her with kisses, thanking her and promising his eternal gratitude and fidelity. Then he was gone, his step once more firm and self-confident, his tears dried and forgotten, his smile joyous.

Was he rushing to tell Mariette the good news? Valentina did not care—not any longer. She knew the truth now, and had no weapons against it.

To Louis she was no longer a woman of passions and feelings—he had put her on a pedestal and endowed her with the attributes of a Saint—goodness, forgiveness, compassion. He would run to her in times of need and despair, but other women would charm and attract him, and to them he would rush because they were like him, of blood and flesh, and in their weakness he would find his strength.

* * *

The letter that the Duke of Brittany had sent him was brief and to the point: your enemies are becoming too powerful, the King is a puppet that they can move to their pleasure.

The Duke of Burgundy sighed. Of course his cousin of Brittany was right, and this last episode, which had seen Craon exiled by order of the Duke of Touraine, was just another example of Louis's influence on the King. His nephew Louis—here was a man that worried the

Duke of Burgundy. He knew him as a capable, ambitious man, and one of whom the King was extremely fond.

The Duke of Brittany was not too concerned about Louis -Philip of Burgundy was well aware that his wife's cousin resented the influence that the Constable Clisson, the chief advisor of the King, exerted on Charles—but in this case, Burgundy's and Brittany's interests coincided and Philip was ready to listen to his cousin.

Brittany resented Clisson as a vassal who had defied him in the past, and had become too powerful to be punished; Burgundy disliked Clisson because he had taken the place that was once his and his brother Berry's at the King's side.

But Louis of Touraine was the real menace. His matrimony to the daughter of Giangaleazzo Visconti had rendered him even more ambitious. The Duke of Burgundy had been informed that his nephew was scheming with his Italian father-in-law and the Pope to establish a Kingdom of Adria in central Italy, and bitterly regretted to have been the promoter of the Visconti alliance.

But how could he have guessed that the King would one day take an interest in the affairs of state and ask him to go back to his lands of Burgundy? His charming nephew, who, since childhood had loved weapons and war above anything else, pretty women, jousting and jewels? It was so easy to guide him, when the premature death of his father had made him a King at age twelve, persuade him to fall in love, wage a war, exile an enemy. Charles could not say no to his uncles—or to anyone else for that matter—he was as lightheaded, still as frivolous as when, on his death-bed, his father had entrusted him to his uncles' protection. "My son is so young and light-minded," Charles had said. "Please, brothers, stay by him and guide him with a strong hand. He can be so easily swayed."

They had done their best, he and his brother Berry, and what had been their reward? Clisson and his gang had been chosen as Charles' trusted advisors, and the fun-loving youth, had decided to be King, after all.

Philip of Burgundy read his relative's letter again. The Duke of Brittany informed him that Craon had been welcomed at his court and hinted obscurely at a dangerous mission on which Craon may soon embark. "Your protection may be required on his behalf, Cousin," he wrote. "I am sure I can count on your friendship and on the ties that already exist between the noble families of Burgundy and Brittany."

The Duke of Burgundy paced the room uneasily. What did that intriguer have in mind? He would have to recommend him the utmost caution. After all, Louis and the Marmousets were still the strongest, and the time had not come for Philip of Burgundy to make his move.

Chapter X

The Bubble Bursts Up

"Her majesty commands you to her room at once."

The voice of the maid woke Catherine from a late sleep. She instinctively reached for Ludwig, only to realize that of course he was already gone, as he always did when the first morning light woke him from the night of love he had spent at her side.

So many nights of love, and mornings, and days, since that first time when he had revealed her his passion in the garden of Pierre de Craon. So many promises too, and not one fulfilled. "I will marry you." "My father will have to accept you as my bride." "I will tell the king of our love." She had stopped pressuring him, reminding him of his pledge. But she had not stopped loving him, enjoying the sexual excitement that she discovered in his arms every time they made love, dreaming that one day his love for her would be stronger than his ambition.

As she hurriedly dressed to answer the Queen's summon, Catherine's memory lingered on the night spent with Ludwig.

After long hours of lovemaking had appeased the cravings of their bodies, they had lain exhausted on the silk sheets of her bed. Catherine enjoyed those moments, when her body felt calm and fulfilled, her mind keen and lucid. Then she liked to tease her lover for his fascination with life at court. No piece of gossip, rumor, seemed trivial to him, nothing going on there could take him unprepared.

"When one depends on one's sister or friend for his position," Ludwig would retort when she pointed out his appetite for the most insignificant details of the life at court, "one never knows what might turn out to be useful in the future."

She would put her head on his chest, loving his strong body, the smell of his skin, the hardness of his muscles, and listen while he bared his soul to her. The courtier mask was gone, the polished manners he had quickly learned in France, and the German prince surfaced, who had to scheme and plot for his future, ingratiate himself with those who had more power than he.

She loved him even more when he was like that, weak and anxious, ambitious and ruthless. She loved him so much that she accepted to be his mistress, while she only wanted to be his wife.

There was great commotion in Isabelle's room. The Queen was sitting on her bed, her hair disheveled, eyes red with crying, her ladies coming and going aimlessly. Catherine rushed to Isabelle. She was full of apprehension and had a hundred questions on her lips.

"Pierre de Craon has murdered the Constable!" Isabelle cried.

"Pierre de Craon?! But he left Paris two months ago!"

"He came back last night, waited in ambush for Clisson, and when the Constable appeared, Craon and his party of assassins attacked him. He defended himself valiantly with his dagger, fell from his horse and, almost lifeless, found shelter in a baker's shop. Craon and his band have escaped."

"Is he dead?"

"Not yet. The King saw him last night and reports that the surgeons are confident that he will survive. He has more than sixty blows and cuts on his body and it is a miracle he is still alive. But the King is so upset, so furious at Craon and Brittany, that I am afraid he will fall ill. Oh, why did I listen to Craon, why did I not keep silent with Valentina?"

She burst into tears and Catherine sat next to her, cradling her, trying to calm her desperation.

"Your Majesty, this does not have anything to do with you or the Duchess of Touraine," she lied. "The Duke of Brittany has long been an implacable enemy of the Constable and this murder is the result of their private feud."

The animosity between those two personages was a well-known fact, and it was easy for Isabelle to persuade herself that she had no part in the whole scheme. But, of course, why would Craon have become Brittany's accomplice, had he not been banished from Paris?

Later that day, the King visited Isabelle in her apartment. He was in a state of great agitation and his words were at times disconnected.

"The Constable made a will in my favor, Isabelle," he announced. "He is leaving me a fortune in gold, lands, buildings, jewels. He must-be the wealthiest man in this land, I swear. My uncles will not like this, I am sure," he added maliciously. "It will not make his memory more popular with them than his person was."

Had the rumor already reached him that the royal uncles were behind Brittany in arming Craon's hand against the King's influential minister, or had he been aware all along of the animosity that divided the two factions? Isabelle wondered.

"But the Constable is not yet dead," he continued, "and with God's help my doctors will keep him in life. I have summoned both Berry and Burgundy to Paris, my dear, and sent envoys to Brittany to order that the scoundrel be removed from his sanctuary and summoned to Paris. If the Duke does not comply with my request, it will be war on him!"

"War, Charles? Surely the Duke of Brittany will surrender Craon immediately."

"I am not so sure, Isabelle. He has always been a shaky ally and I am afraid that his hatred of the Constable is stronger than his loyalty to me."

As everyone had predicted, the Duke of Brittany refused to betray his friend and the royal uncles tried in vain to dissuade the King from waging war. They pointed out that Clisson was going to live, the Duke of Brittany could switch his important allegiance to England, one of the King's daughters was to marry Brittany's heir.

Charles, feverish and excited, would not listen to words of restraint, he wanted war and his council approved the campaign.

The King and his army left at the beginning of July; Ludwig went with them.

"It has all the appearances of an endless expedition," he announced the night before their departure. "The King's health is very poor; this will require short daily marches and frequent stops. The dukes of Berry and Burgundy are not starting with us; they have been delaying their departures for weeks, in the hope, no doubt, that the King will change his mind and desist from his plan. It is ironical, of course, that those gentlemen, not to give themselves completely away, will eventually be compelled to fight against their very own secret ally."

The court had frequent news of the expedition, as envoys and messengers were sent weekly by the King to his Queen and council.

His health was not improving, the heat made him restless and insomniac. His uncles did join the campaign but against their wishes. Their knights were forever arguing the rights and wrongs of the expedition, Brittany had again refused to hand Craon to the King's ambassador—the tone of his messages was querulous and impatient, and every time Isabelle received them she felt uneasy.

It was lonely without the King, and his escort, and the court spent most of the summer months moving from Paris to Vincennes, from Vincennes to St. Germain-en-Laye, from there to Creil.

Then for over two weeks, no messenger was sent from the campaign. The Queen started having forebodings of great misfortunes gathering around her family, and would spend days on end on her knees, begging the Virgin and all the saints to protect her husband and the Dauphin.

The day had been too hot to induce the ladies from the cool rooms of the Queen's apartment. The thick walls of St. Pol kept the warm rays at bay and the closed shutters at the windows enhanced the freshness of the chambers.

Marguerite de Gremonville and Catherine were playing chess. She had always found that game too complicated to be enjoyable, and particularly on that afternoon her thoughts kept straying from the board and the pretty ivory pieces, and wondering where Ludwig was, whether he was being faithful to her.

"Checkmate, Catherine!" exclaimed her opponent, lifting her last pawn from the board, and she roused herself from her reverie.

"You certainly are not a fun companion today, my dear," Marguerite complained, "nor have you been for the last couple of months, if truth has to be known. I can understand you miss your lover, but is it wise to let everybody notice it so plainly?"

"You are right, Marguerite," Catherine said. "I have been rather absent-minded and crabby lately but it is getting so depressing here with all the men gone, the Queen unhappy, no news from the campaign."

Marguerite sighed. Both her husband and lover, the Sire de Villiers, were absent too, and, according to the rumors that the little group of bored courtiers were spreading, she had found consolation in the robust but coarse arms of one of the Queen's equerries.

Marguerite was no longer the simple dark-haired girl whose worldly ways had impressed the even simpler Elizabeth of Wittelsbach during her visit in Brussels. She had become a dashing, sophisticated lady with refined tastes and a light of impudence in her eyes; had married a wealthy nobleman and taken her first lover soon after her wedding. She and Catherine had remained friends through the years, and their similar duties to their sovereign made them more intimate than they might have chosen to be otherwise.

"Do not remind me, my dear," Marguerite started, when all of a sudden a piercing scream came from the room where the Queen was resting.

They got up, rushed to her chamber, and found her apartment in a turmoil.

The Queen was laying on her bed, her head hidden under pillows, her body shaking with frantic sobs, Ludwig of Bavaria—how, why was he back?-was kneeling beside her, in vain trying to calm her, pull her to himself. One of her doctors was there too, her maid, Femmette, and the Countess of Eu.

What had happened? The ladies were looking at one another in dismay, absolutely at a loss. The doctor had a vial with some greenish liquid in his hands, which he seemingly wanted the Queen to drink; the Countess of Eu was whispering something to Femmette.

When Ludwig noticed the people filling the room, he quickly got up and approached them, gravely: "My friends, I have had the very sad task to inform the Sovereign that his Majesty's health has rapidly deteriorated and that his life is in danger. The news upset the Queen's noble and loving heart to such a degree that her doctor had to be called for. He thinks that the Queen should rest awhile and I ask you all to trust us with her caring and resume your pursuits. Madame de Campremy, would you please stay behind; your presence is required here."

For the next few minutes, everybody in the room was busy with the Queen and at last she was able to control her shaking and sobbing. They helped her to sit up and dry her poor swollen face, while the doctor administered his potion. She looked calmer and more composed, thanked them kindly, and requested to be left alone. They complied with her wishes and Catherine followed Ludwig in the little study adjoining the bedroom.

Ludwig's face was ashen, his hair and mantle dusty, his hands shaking. He took Catherine in his arms and held her tenderly, his lips gently caressing her face. Clearly he was not seeing his mistress, but his old friend and confidant, his natural ally in that foreign court.

"My Catherine," he started, "the King was lying in a coma when I left him, he might be dead by now, and the Kingdom in the hands of his uncles."

"But what happened? I know he had not fully recovered from the fever he caught in Amiens. Is this the cause of his disease?"

"I do not know, nobody knows, it may even be the work of sorcery."

"Sorcery!" she cried, frightened by that horrible word. "Certainly you can't be right!"

"You would not have thought so if you had seen him that day near Mans, rushing around madly on his horse, trying to hit whomever happened to be in front of him, and killing four of his men."

"My God!" she exclaimed in horror. "Ludwig, do tell me in detail whatever happened."

"It was a terribly hot and stuffy morning. The daylight had an unusual brightness and the rays of the sun were merciless. Notwithstanding the heat, the King was dressed in heavy black velvet and wore a furred hat. We had hardly left the dusty road we had been following from Mans, and entered a dense forest of oak trees and firs, when a strange apparition presented itself to our amazed eyes.

It was an old man, tall and emaciated, with long white hair falling on his shoulders and a thin body scantily covered with rags, who cried in a terrible voice, 'Do not ride any further, noble King, because you are betrayed!'

We stood petrified a few seconds, then the Duke of Orleans, his sword drawn, rushed to his brother, ready to defend him. But we soon realized that the old man was not dangerous, he had no weapons on him, nor was he threatening the King. So he was let go, and soon disappeared among the trees, as suddenly and mysteriously as he had appeared.

Charles was noticeably shaken and alarmed and his uncles tried in vain to reassure him, pointing out that it was just an old crazy beggar and his words were meaningless. I was riding next to Charles and I could see sweat falling copiously from his forehead, and his hands clutching his reins spasmodically.

"Fairly soon we left the shady coolness of the forest and were once again at the mercy of that pitiless hot sun. The march was slow and monotonous. We were absorbed in our thoughts, revolving in our minds the strange incident and its most likely meaning, when a loud clang shook us from our torpor.

"A lance had fallen on a steel helmet and that abrupt noise acted as a spur on the King, who drew out his sword and charged wildly crying: 'Forward against these traitors!'

"He tried to strike Orleans, while Burgundy was crying for someone to hold the King who was obviously out of his mind. He was thrashing around, wild words coming from his mouth, which betrayed a mind full of nightmares and obsessions.

"We could not defend ourselves without running the risk of hitting him and that crazy carousel lasted until his chamberlain, seeing that Charles was close to collapse, seized him from behind and helped him lie on the ground.

"My poor brother-in–law was motionless by now, his eyes closed, he was hardly breathing. The Duke of Burgundy did not let a chance pass by of asserting his authority—he had the King taken back to Mans, called a halt to the expedition and dispatched me to Paris to notify the Queen."

Catherine was too troubled and scared to think coherently. The King might die, may already be dead. What would happen to Isabelle then? The dauphin was six months old and in poor health, who would become the regent—Burgundy or Orleans? Was this the end of Isabelle's fairy tale life? As a dowager queen, her position would be uncertain and precarious; her life dominated by the necessity of pleasing whomever was in power, finding a balance among the different currents and intrigues at court.

But Ludwig had more to tell.

"My equerry and I had hardly started for Paris," he continued, "when his horse lost a shoe and we had to stop at a blacksmith's. There was a tavern adjacent to the shop and I decided to wait there while the horse was being shod. To my utter surprise I recognized, sitting at a corner table drinking from a tankard, the old man that had so scared the King a few hours ago. He kept touching a purse hanging from his belt, mumbling and smiling to himself. Nobody seemed to know him, or be interested in him, and he not once lifted his eyes from his tankard. In a flash I understood what had happened and who was behind the plot."

"The plot?" she asked, uncomprehending. "What plot? What do you mean?"

"But do not you understand, Catherine? Obviously, the old beggar was paid by somebody who wanted to scare the King and put thoughts of treason in his mind. Their plan went beyond their wildest hopes—the King became crazy!"

"But who would have wanted such a thing, Ludwig? And what kind of assurance did they have that the apparition of the old man would make the King lose his wits?"

"They certainly could not count on the King getting crazy, I will grant you that. No, they wanted Charles to feel surrounded by enemies and traitors, scared and ready to give up the campaign against Brittany. They know how excitable the King is, and given to impulsive decisions. As for who is behind this scheme, Catherine, you just have to ask-yourself who would benefit from Clisson's death, who is related to Brittany, who has lost influence at court and is I patiently waiting to regain it."

"The Dukes of Burgundy and Berry," she murmured. Of course it did make sense, it was so clear that they resented both the Marmousets with Clisson at their head, and Louis of Orleans as the ones that held the reins of power in the King's name.

"Exactly, Catherine, even if it is more accurate to think only of Burgundy as the real leader of the opposition to the King's advisors. Berry is too busy with his collections and his young wife to plot and scheme. As long as money runs freely in his hands and he can acquire more jewels, build palaces, amass books and coins, he does not mind who is in power. But Burgundy is different. He and Louis of Orleans are the real powers behind the throne.

"To finish the story, I followed the old wretch when he left the tavern, put my sword to his throat and asked him to reveal who he was working for, if he held his life dear. The poor imbecile was shaking with terror; it turned out he was half mute and could only stammer that a man of the Duke of Brittany, whom he had never seen before, had given him a gold coin and promised him another one if he would follow the King and tell him over and over again that he was betrayed and should go no farther. Obviously, the beggar did not know a thing, so I let him go unharmed.

"I did not expect that the Duke of Burgundy would put his signature to such an act of treason, obviously, but the fact that Brittany is involved is one more proof that the conspiracy is wide-spread and has the Duke of Burgundy as its promoter."

"What are we to do, Ludwig? How can we protect Isabelle?"

"Not a word of what I told you must escape these walls, Catherine. As far as anyone knows, the King is sick, very sick, and everybody's prayers must be directed to God to spare his life. If, God willing, he recovers, this mad spell of his will be just a brief episode soon forgotten; if he dies, then the struggle between the two rivals to the throne, Burgundy and Orleans, will become very fierce, and the Queen and her children will need the help and protection of all their friends."

The King did not die.

Isabelle's desperate prayers were answered and a month later, accompanied by his brother Orleans, Charles visited his Queen at the palace of St. Pol.

Choking with emotion, Isabelle ran to meet her husband, but at his sight she had to force herself not to recoil in fear but instead embrace him with anxious tenderness.

It was a different man from the one with whom she had fallen in love at first sight, whose looks and kindness had won her heart and mind, whose loving sensuality had fulfilled the needs of her passionate nature.

Charles's face had become thin and gaunt; his eyes were shiny with feverish impatience, his hands ceaselessly clasping and unclasping, his body frail under his ample jacket and mantle.

At his side Louis, who had recently become Duke of Orleans, looked healthier and stronger than before, and sparkling with the gems that as usual adorned his doublet and cape.

Charles pulled Isabelle to his chest and gently kissed her cheeks.

"My dearest wife," he whispered, "I am back at last and happy to see you. How are my children, have they missed me?"

Isabelle answered mechanically, trying to remember her beloved husband in the stranger in front of her. Mortal fear was gripping her heart — would she love this man again, go beyond the piety and condescension she felt for him, forget the absent look in those eyes she had loved so much?

She desperately hoped so and she returned his kisses with a tenderness and ardor that she did not feel.

Chapter XI

The Firebrands' Ball

We will not be able to meet for a while," he said, and the tone of his voice made her heart sink.

"But why not Ludwig? Are you leaving Paris?" she asked, trying to sound calm and composed.

The hand that was caressing her breast trembled an instant, stopped, then resumed its leisurely exploration.

"My father has given his consent to my marriage to Anne of Bourbon," he said quietly, avoiding her eyes.

Wildly, Catherine pushed him away from her and sat up without really understanding the words, her blonde hair tumbling all over her naked shoulders, her hands suddenly as cold as ice.

"How dare you? You must have known it for days, months, perhaps, and never a word to me, never a hint that would make me aware that the end of our love affair was in sight!"

Ludwig sat up too. He took his hands away from her body but put a protective arm around her shoulders that were now shaking with the sobs she could not suppress.

"I did make promises to you, Catherine," he said, "and for breaking them I ask your forgiveness. But you have always known how my father felt about my marriage, how opposed to you he has been all these years."

"But the King and the Queen had promised their help!"

"The Duke of Bavaria cannot be bought as cheaply as the Campremy were," he said cruelly. "No dowry can make up for the fact that a future Duke of Bavaria needs a wife of high standing, noble ancestors."

"Nobody will ever love you as much as I do," she whispered, hating herself for the confession that was escaping her lips.

"And I love you too, Catherine. I love you as much as I can love, and I do not want to lose you."

"What do you mean?"—an absurd hope was in her voice.

"We can still continue to see each other, my darling. I will be at court, and only spend brief periods at my wife's castle in `the country; therefore, there is no reason for us to stop a relationship that, I dare say, makes us both happy."

Catherine recoiled from him in horror. His coldness and selfishness made her look at him with different eyes—was this the man she had loved for so long, whose sight still made her jump as if it were the first time, whose caresses could excite her into ecstasy? Yes, he had not changed. She had deluded herself into believing that Ludwig was a man who could forget his ambition, love of money and power for her sake but of course that had never been true and he had promised her marriage only because he wanted her in his bed. He had been blinded by his passion for a while, perhaps, but soon enough his pride in his name, his calculating nature, had won over his love for Catherine.

"You had better go now, Ludwig," she said as calmly as she could. "It is the end of our relationship, as I have only contempt and disgust for you. May you be happy with your-new bride—I have heard Anne of Bourbon is a pretty and very wealthy princess—if ever you can be happy, which I doubt."

With dry eyes, Catherine watched him dress for the last time—his body so strong and lean, his long legs, a blond shock of hair-falling over his blue eyes.

Without looking back he quietly closed the door behind him and was gone—from her life.

* * *

It was Ludwig's and Anne of Bourbon's wedding day and great festivities had been planned in their honor. A banquet and ball were to follow the ceremony, and an elaborate masquerade had been organized by the Queen to end the evening.

The snow was falling down in large flakes and the sky was lead-grey. Isabelle was sitting at a window looking onto St. Pol's courtyard. Contrasting feelings were agitating her—she was happy for her brother, whose marriage to one of the noblest princesses of France fulfilled his every ambition and dream, and at the same time disappointed that Catherine, the girl she had loved as a sister as long as she could remember, would never become her real sister, and was spending lonely days of desperation.

Her handsome, ambitious brother—he had always refused a match with Catherine. Isabelle thought that the Visconti streak was dominant in him, he was forever scheming and calculating, the way their grandfather Barnabo must have been. No little German lady-in-waiting for the descendant of the Emperor Ludwig, love her as much as he may!

It was a great comfort to have him at the court, she must confess. Those last few months had been so unsettling, confused. Her beautiful, glamorous world had lost its foundation; nothing around her was secure anymore, nobody trustworthy.

Her own feelings towards Charles were confused, too. She loved him, of course, but sometimes her love was overcome by the pity that his state inspired and she did not see the handsome blond prince she had married, but the poor hallucinated sick man that pushed her away.

Most of the time, Isabelle was sure that he would recover, that in a few months she would remember this period as a nightmare that would not come back, but she could not keep doubt from insinuating itself into her soul, taking her unaware and throwing her into an abyss of despair.

What would happen if Charles died? What kind of influence would she have to protect her children and herself? His uncles were so ambitious and greedy for power and wealth; Charles's brother had wanted to be King since the day he had understood that he was destined to be second.

As always, Charles was generous with his gifts to Isabelle and she owned extensive fertile lands, well-fortified castles surrounded by vast fields, all of which yielded rich revenues. She knew that the French people murmured against her wealth; they accused her of covetousness, they complained that because of her greediness their taxes were inexorable, their poverty extreme. They would complain, would not they; and yet the Paris bourgeois' luxury and display of wealth was such that they could not be distinguished from the nobility at court, so richly they dressed, so sparkling were they with gems and diamonds.

The French even accused Isabelle of not loving her children, of being in charge of their households only to be able to strengthen her influence over them and increase her own fortune—she, who still pined for the death of two of her precious babies, who lived in fear that her Charles, her Dauphin, would follow them to the grave; she, who felt yet another life stirring inside her.

Her only way to survive was to have wealth, lands, revenues-she did not have power, that she knew. She had to assist impotent to the rivalry and struggles between the royal uncles and Louis of Orleans while all her being, all the Visconti and Wittelsbach in her, revolted at this passivity,

As long as her fortune was large and undisputed, as long as her coffers were full of gold and gems, as long as her children recognized her authority, she would not perish.

Isabelle's thoughts kept going back to Charles; He had been acting very secretly those past few days, walking around and whispering with Huguet de Guisay, who was fast becoming his closest friend. She did not like it when her husband behaved in that way—he had a sly look in his eyes, and almost twitched with excitement. It reminded her of that day in August, when she had seen him for the first time after his folly attack at Le Mans.

She did not want to think about that day; Charles had been well for months, now. She remembered what that wise old doctor that healed him, William of Harselly, had told her before he left the court: "Your Majesty, the King should not be too intensely absorbed in the cares of government. Distractions and amusements will be more profitable to his health than any serious session with his counselors."

For once, it was an easy prescription to follow. Charles loved festivities and tournaments, hunting and dancing, and with the help of Louis of Orleans, Isabelle was able to organize magnificent pastimes for him. The Marmousets were gone, and the government was once again in the hands of the royal uncles, while Louis impatiently waited in the sidelines for a chance to regain the upper hand.

Louis, Valentina…and Mariette, all three would be present at the banquet in honor of the newlyweds. Haughty and aloof Valentina, tender and frail-looking Mariette, handsome Louis, divided between the love for his wife and passion for his mistress.

Isabelle disliked Valentina even more now, her delicate beauty, moral rigidity, unyielding ways—Louis's bastard was raised in her apartments, she knew of her husband's countless adventures with this lady and that, but not a breath of scandal surrounded her—protected by a magic shield of purity and goodness, she lived her life in the lascivious and scandal-ridden court of France.

It was ironic the way Fate had played with Isabelle and Valentina. They were destined to hate each other, their families had seen to it, and they had become the two greatest ladies of France, living in the same palaces, their blood ties made closer by their marriages.

Isabelle could not like her, she would not even try, and the sickness of her husband had made their proximity even more uneasy.

When the dark cloud of folly descended upon Charles, when he shouted and recoiled from Isabelle, his wife and the mother of his children, it was Valentina's name that he implored, it was her face he wanted to see, her hands he wanted to hold—how could Isabelle love her cousin? How could she?

"Deliver me from that woman! The sight of her is unbearable to me! Valentina, sister, come, come to me!" That was what her husband shrieked, that was what she had to listen to and forget afterwards. But when he was calm again he came close to her, his hands trembled at the touch of her body, his mouth never had enough of kisses—then Valentina was forgotten, and Charles was hers again, and more than ever.

She did not want to dwell on that nightmare, not on a merry wedding day, when everything should be joy and amusement.

Her dress was splendid. Isabelle liked red, and velvet did wonders for her skin. Her "hennin" was too tall perhaps, but it went beautifully with the dress, and she loved the way its veil fell and shimmered around her forehead and shoulders. She would also wear the necklace that the Duke of Berry had just given her.

The best artisans seemed to be working full-time for him alone. Everything he owned or gave away was always superb in taste and executed wondrously well.

"Niece," he had said gallantly when she thanked him for his gift, "you inspired the artist that carved the pretty lady in "houppelande" and "hennin" on the pendant, but he confessed that, while his enamels could well reproduce the silks and damask of your attire, his art was too poor to do justice to the delicate nuances of your skin, and the shiny jet of your eyes. And, I must say, I agree with him!"

Dear old Berry! His taste had always been impeccable and marriage to that child, Jeanne, had rendered him so gay and full of buoyancy that he looked younger than his own son!

The evening was progressing splendidly.

Anne of Bourbon, a plain girl with dark hair and a sallow complexion, splendidly attired in cloth of gold, shone with glittering gems and happiness at the side of her handsome bridegroom.

Catherine had taken the utmost care to make herself beautiful, and there she stood, among the other ladies, tall and graceful in her dark green dress, her pretty shoulders framed with ermine, her candid bosom, emphasized by-the low cut, attracting the gentlemen's eyes. One man was by her most of the evening, an older-gentleman severely clothed in black velvet, whose eyes lingered admiringly on her face and figure. She seemed to enjoy his company and pay attention to his words, but Isabelle noticed that her eyes would continually stray to the newlyweds, and her laughter was too shrill and amused to be sincere. Catherine was putting up the best facade she could, and Isabelle admired her pluck.

Soft silks, rich damasks, iridescent velvet adorned men and women alike, precious furs lined their mantles and hats, tall "hennins" held shimmering gauzes around the women's faces, dark sapphires and rubies, snowy pearls and sky-blue turquoises shone on every bosom, glittered on belts and rings, sparkled on dresses and doublets.

The dukes of Berry and Burgundy had come with their wives. Little Jeanne of Berry was all giggles and smiles and her old husband could never take his eyes off her slim and graceful body. Margaret of Burgundy, by contrast, looked even more stern and severe, her dark blue dress emphasizing the pallor of her face and the sharp outline of her features. Louis of Orleans had promised to join the festivities later in the night, while Charles had mischievously hinted that "they might all see him later, if they could go beyond appearance."

The food was elaborate and tasty and strange new implements called 'forks' were used, which Valentina had brought from Italy to eat pieces of fruit. Cupbearers kept passing gold goblets of spiced wine, light ale, cider, and the noise and laughter grew in intensity.

When the tables were removed, musicians came in and for a while the roguish rhythms of their songs echoed in the hall. They sang of love and lust, of wine and marriage, of unfaithful lovers and cuckold husbands. The atmosphere became more relaxed, the eyes of the ladies shone impudently, hands touched other hands, the whispers became more intimate, the jokes more daring. An aura of sensuality seemed to envelop the men and women present.

Isabelle was sitting a little aside on a high carved chair covered with a gold canopy, surrounded by the royal uncles and Margaret of Burgundy. At the last moment, Valentina had declined to attend the festivities—she was close to her confinement now and hardly left her apartments—but Isabelle suspected that her cousin's wedding to a noble and wealthy French lady had annoyed the Duchess of Orleans, and that was the real reason behind Valentina's polite words of regret.

Isabelle felt older than twenty-three years, not a part of the merry group of her courtiers, almost a symbol of the duties and responsibilities that are a sovereign's lot, which was foolish, as by rank and inclination, she was very much the center of everything gay and amusing that went on at court.

With the help of her ladies, Isabelle had planned a very extravagant masquerade to follow the dancing. Each of them would don the costume of a wild animal, and tease the men to recognize them.

Isabelle's mask was the most splendid, she had chosen a tiger head made of fur and cloth of gold, with two enormous emeralds for eyes and topped by a turban adorned with purple ostrich feathers. Catherine was to be a crocodile; Jeanne of Berry, a deer with gold antlers; Mariette d'Enghien a bird of paradise. The costumes were very original and precious and the palace cutters and seamstresses had worked at them for weeks.

Isabelle loved masquerades, she found disguise very exciting. Under a mask she could become all the women she did not dare to be in the open, say the words she would blush to whisper to anyone, tease and provoke men that would be in awe of the Queen.

The dancing had started; the fast tempo of the "carole" music tempted Isabelle to the floor. Stephen de Semihier approached and invited her to join him in the dance. She ignored the look of disapproval of her uncles and was soon enjoying the quick steps, the rounds and swings of the "carole".

Stephen's wife, Anne, had recently joined Isabelle's household. She was a pretty woman, very quiet and sweet, and Isabelle had liked her immediately. She was devoted to her husband and the Queen hoped that she might set an example of fidelity among her ladies. Yet she doubted it—they all seemed lost in a whirl of frivolity and pleasures that made them forgetful of any pledge they gave.

Isabelle could not, would not reproach her friends, though. She understood their frailty too well—she still did not yield to temptation but was aware of its insinuating voice, enticing ways.

Stephen was talking about Provence, the beautiful land where his estate lay, where the sun shone in January and the sea was perpetually blue.' His country was never far from his thoughts and words and he seemed forever homesick for the bushes of oleanders that bloomed among the Roman ruins, and the scent of the mimosas and roses that climbed over the stones of his palace.

"At dawn when the bright-colored boats of the fishermen sail back with their catch, the ocean is alive with a thousand shimmering dots of gold, the sand is white, and the little villages nestling on the hills nearby look clean and sparkling under the new sun," he said.

"You are quite a poet, Stephen," Isabelle joked.

"Eustache Deschamps might yet get jealous of you, I am sure."

"You should come to Provence, your Majesty. I know you would then understand my enthusiasm."

The picture he painted of his country sounded enchanting, but the long trip to reach the South, the dusty, roads, the bad food, uncomfortable castles one had to stop at, darkened that vision considerably in her eyes. She was perfectly happy with her yearly pilgrimages to Chartres and the other shrines in Northern France, and completely comfortable in the royal residences that lay within a few miles from the capital. Still, it was pleasant to hear Stephen talk of Provence and watch enthusiasm make him vibrant and attractive.

It was getting late. The Duke and Duchess of Burgundy decided to leave, followed a little later by the Duke of Berry. He was far from delighted that he had to leave Jeanne behind, but she had asked him so graciously that he could not refuse her request to stay.

His massive figure majestically wrapped in a blue cape had barely left the hall, when a sudden apparition left all agape and speechless.

Six men, disguised as savages, entered the room and started capering in front of the ladies. They wore costumes made of some material covered with frazzled hemp, and dark tow covered their faces also, so that they were unrecognizable. The musicians accompanied their dancing and somersaults with a fast tune, which incited those buffoons even more. They started howling like wolves, making obscene gestures, moving their arms and legs crazily.

Isabelle recognized Charles immediately under his disguise. She knew his tall, lean body too well to be fooled for long, and a shock of his fair hair would show through the wild fuzz on his forehead, when he capered and jumped.

"Who am I, pretty lady?" the savages would tease this woman and that, their hairy hands touching her bosom, caressing her cheeks. "Do you want to see if we hairy men are like the others? Are you afraid of me? Do not be, I can be very tender!"

The ladies giggled and gave out little shouts of amazement and wonder, while the more audacious among them touched those monsters, and one or two even allowed themselves to be embraced and kissed.

Then the events happened in quick succession.

The Prince Louis entered the hall accompanied by Philippe de Bar. For a minute he stood there, a look of surprise and curiosity on his face, then he did something foolish: he took a torch and approached it to one of the monsters to identify him.

Immediately a flame leaped from the torch and flickered on the hair of one of the revelers. In a flash all his body was afire.

A moment later, the flames had spread to a second dancer, then to a third—it was Charles!

"The King is on fire!" shrieked Isabelle, then she fainted.

The last thing she remembered was Jeanne of Berry covering Charles's body in the folds of her dress.

When she came to she was in her room, lying on her bed, surrounded by her ladies and the strange figure of a half-burned savage that was her husband and the King of France.

"You are alive, Charles!" she sobbed, and he took her in his arms and held her close.

Isabelle could smell burnt hemp, the pungent scent of pitch, the sour odor of sweat. It almost suffocated her, but her relief was so immense that she did not mind.

"Your brother wanted to kill you!" she whispered.

"That is not true, Isabelle. It was ill-considered of him, but he meant no harm. Now he is absolutely devastated and remorseful."

"Who were your companions, Charles?" she asked, too weary to pursue the subject of Louis's guilt. "And how are they?"

A look of despair filled his eyes. "Joigny is dead," he murmured, "and there are few hopes for Foix, Poitiers, and Guisay. The Sire de Nantouillet is all right, though. He threw himself in a cooler full of water and thus saved his life."

"I will be eternally grateful to Jeanne of Berry," she whispered, in his embrace again. "I don't want to think of what would have happened without her."

She felt Charles shiver. "You are right, my love, but I will never be able to forgive myself for being so inconsiderate as to have allowed myself to be part of that silly masquerade!"

She agreed with him silently. His health was too frail to withstand terrors of that kind without suffering irremediably. The thought kept filling her with fright—what would then happen to her children and herself?

The night's tragedy had shown Isabelle she could not trust anybody; even the closest and dearest relatives of her husband were bent on his destruction, on the ruin of the Valois.

The following day she called for Catherine.

When her friend joined her, Isabelle was still too upset and troubled to notice how tired and worn out Catherine looked. The fictitious mask of gaiety she had worn during the night was gone, and the pale and dejected woman who had been crying for days over her shattered dreams did not hide herself any more.

"Sit by me, my friend," Isabelle beckoned her. "I need your friendship more than ever now. I have been thinking through the events of last night and I have reached a decision that goes against my instincts, perhaps, but is the only one I can contemplate without feeling anxiety and fear. They think that I am just a woman, too interested in my life of leisure and pomp to entertain my ambition, to be of any danger. How little do they understand me! I will be shrewd and attentive, choose my allies carefully, learn to distinguish between real power and its hollow appearance, faithful friends and disguised foes."

"Foes? You do not have any enemies, your Majesty!"

"I do. Anyone that resents the King and tries to take his place is my enemy, and those I will crush. You see, Catherine, if I play my game well I will be a survivor, a winner, but if I lose sight of my objective, nobody will have pity on my weakness and I will be trampled upon."

"What do you propose to do?"

"I will go see Arnaud Guillaume, and you must accompany me."

"Oh, your Majesty, I am afraid of that man and his powers."

"I am in awe of him too, Catherine, but his spells and herbs soothe the King more than all the medicines his doctors administer to him and I owe Arnaud gratitude for that."

"But why go to him, now, when the King has been well for so long?"

"I want to know who is behind my husband's attempted murder. Arnaud Guillaume can see in the future, he can tell me who my enemies are, who wants the King dead."

Both Isabelle and Catherine felt uneasy climbing the stairs that led to the apartment inhabited by Arnaud Guillaume. The room they entered was dark and the air stifling with the stench of sulphur and other substances. In one corner, a small fire smoldered under retorts and stills, and two candles were lit at the sides of a high bookstand, in front of which stood a tall, thin man.

At the noise the women made entering the room, the magician turned, and a sly smile crossed his face when he saw the Queen.

"Your Majesty," he said eagerly, bowing in front of Isabelle, "it is a great and rare honor to have you in my lodgings."

Catherine looked at him intently, her curiosity greater than the anxiety she felt in front of a man who was said to communicate with spirits and devils at will.

His appearance was forbidding—a white gaunt face on which dark eyes shone like pieces of burning coal, a thin yellowish beard reaching to his bony chest, long slender fingers stained by the minerals and herbs he handled. He wore a loose black robe on which strange signs and numbers were painted, tightened at the waist with a belt from which a small skull, a horn and a few keys dangled.

Catherine had heard so many stories about Arnaud Guillaume. They said he was French by birth, but since his youth his love of adventure and thirst for knowledge had made him roam the world. He had visited Spain and Italy, Persia and Syria, Arabia and Portugal. From those distant lands he had brought back to France secrets of magic and medicine, spells and potions that enslaved men and women, forbidden powers granted to him by the god of darkness.

The two ladies sat on hard stools that the magician had produced from the darkness behind him.

"My Queen," started Guillaume in a most ingratiating tone, "I trust that the potion I concocted for his Majesty is still effective and the cruel demons that inhabit his mind are still in the hell where I chased them."

"Yes, Guillaume, thanks to you and your magic powers, the King is well, and the devils that teased and tormented him have ceased their cruel work."

She shivered involuntarily, remembering Charles's vacant eyes, the horror with which he pulled away from him, the contortions of his body. Later, when his body wanted hers with the ardor of the first years of their marriage, it was hard to forget, and let herself be touched and loved.

Her words of gratitude rendered the man even more humble and smiling. "How can I further serve my Queen?" he asked eagerly, bending his back in a gesture that was almost a prayer.

"I want to know whether the Duke of Orleans is plotting to assassinate the King," Isabelle said imperiously. "I know that you have informers and spies—it should not be too difficult for you to find out the truth. Remember, Wizard, not a word of this to anyone. You will be generously rewarded for your work, but I want complete secrecy."

Isabelle got up and left the room followed by Catherine.

A horrible grin lit up the magician's face, and soon became an irrepressible scornful sneer.

"Ahmed," he called to somebody hidden by the darkness of the den, "it will be easiest gold that I have ever earned. Why, I already have my answers here!"

* * *

Deep sobs were racking the man's body and tears trickling down his cheeks.

"Father," he murmured to the priest, "I am guilty. I could not resist temptation. There was my brother, my beloved brother, the only obstacle between me and the throne of my fathers, and I willingly tried to destroy him."

"Merciful is the Lord, who spared him."

"But the other men died at my hand, innocent men, friends, among atrocious sufferings."

"You have sinned against God and your brothers, and only His clemency can forgive you. But God sees your heart, knows how sincerely you repent of your sin, and God forgives you, my son."

Louis of Orleans stood up. The priest's word, the forgiveness that God granted him through his minister, failed to console him. He had sinned so horribly that it seemed to him that the sin that had blackened his soul was invading his body too and making him as repulsive as a leper.

He could not tell the truth to anyone, not even his wife. "I want to be king so badly that not even the brother I love is safe with me." Could he confess that to anybody but a priest, his intermediary to God?

The people of Paris and France forgave Louis of Orleans for his imprudence. They loved the handsome, dashing prince. Besides, the King was alive, and if some courtiers had perished because Orleans had been ill-advised, that was too bad, but there were so many eager to take their place that their loss was not going to be felt by ordinary citizens.

In fact, Louis of Orleans became even more popular with his people when they watched him, barefoot and in drab clothing, follow a procession of expiation to Notre Dame, and initiate the building of a chapel in the Convent of the Celestins that was destined to receive his mortal remains, and Valentina's.

Chapter XII

Life In Brittany

The sea waves broke monotonously on the shore, the sand was gray and wet, the gray boulders slimy with weeds and barnacles. The sea gulls rested there briefly, then darted to the water, their piercing cries drowned by the incessant rolling of the ocean.

Catherine always ended her solitary walks sitting on a huge rock that the wind had shaped into a hallow nest, her shoulders leaning against the firm support of the stone, her feet hidden under the heavy cloth of her dress, her eyes lazily following the appearance and disappearance of far away waves. Sometimes the white sails of a ship stood out wanly against the gray background, or a long line of fishing boats formed a brilliant rainbow on the gray water, but usually both the land and the sea were deserted and she could evoke the events of her past, dream the dreams of her future undisturbed.

Catherine had never seen the ocean until the day she had followed her husband to that lonely spot of Brittany.

She had grown up in a city framed by mountains, followed her friend to a country of rolling hills and meadows. The snow-capped peaks of the Alps had awed her with their distant majesty; she knew they were the abode of eagles and chamoises, mischievous elves and cruel Snow Queens. One day a page had stolen a kiss from her and put an edelweiss in her hand. She had hidden the velvet star among her gowns, marveling at its softness and beauty. When the luminous whiteness of its petals had turned the page and his kiss had long been forgotten.

Nothing had prepared her to the furious majesty of the sea forever pounding on the coast, the beauty of the foaming breakers, the grace of the flitting birds. The howling wind talked to her in mysterious voices, the tortured shapes of the rocks reminded her of the gargoyles on the cathedral walls.

Philip of Vermandois, her husband, was enchanted at her love for the ocean. His castle stood on a low elevation overlooking the shore, and when full tide was in one could almost believe to be on an island, surrounded by gray billows.

Catherine loved walking to the beach before sunset, watch the tide roll in impetuously and the beach receive it like a woman submitting to the embrace of a lover. There was an instant of perfect silence before the deafening roar of the water started and soon the endlessly-stretching beach, with its treasures of shells, plants, rocks, disappeared under the on-rushing waves. It was an awesome scene and she never tired of it.

Sometimes her husband accompanied her and, holding hands, they walked side by side, not saying much, glad to be together, the wind strong on their faces, the horizon without end in front of them.

Her past did not matter, then, and she only wanted her present life to continue forever according to the same simple pattern.

"I was afraid you would feel lonely and bored, after the gaiety and luxury of your life at court," Philip once confessed. "This is a solitary spot, but I do not plan to spend too much time in Paris, unless you insist on it."

She took his hand smiling: "Your doubts were completely unfounded, Philip. I have never been more content and have no wish to go back to the court oftener than it is necessary."

She was being completely honest. Her last months in Paris had been so full of pain and disappointments, her heart and spirit, had been so completely broken, that she regarded Philip's firm embrace as her only bulwark against anguish and unhappiness.

They had met on the night of Ludwig's wedding to Anne of Bourbon. Her mind and heart were full of Ludwig, it was an effort for her to talk and smile at the people around her, and the older man, whose hair had already turned completely gray, had made no impression on her at all. She had talked to him, and laughed at his words, but she had not seen him—or anybody else—because Ludwig, her handsome, cruel, beloved lover, was the only man that was real to her. The others were just shadows, ghosts whose gestures had no meaning.

But Philip of Vermandois had come back, had not accepted her rejection.

He was a tall man with broad shoulders and a thick waist.

The sober way in which he dressed, the dark colors of his hoses and capes, the simplicity of his hats, bespoke a life spent away from the court, but the heavy gold chain that fell to his chest, the soft fur that lined his mantles, the straightforwardness of his attitude among younger and more refined courtiers, witnessed to a man of wealth and standing. He had vast holds in Brittany, where his ancestors had been conspicuous in their fights against the pirates that infested the coast and for their loyalty to France, even when their lord, the Duke of Brittany, would yield to the English lure.

Ludwig and his bride had left Paris. Visions of the days and nights that the newlyweds spent together in the bucolic refuge of Anne's castle tormented Catherine, memories of Ludwig's sensuality and experienced love making left her sleepless and agitated in her lonely bed.

"So many men are attracted to you, Catherine," Isabelle would try to console her, "your stubborn loyalty to a man that jilted you is not realistic. You are young, beautiful, free—do not let these precious moments go by, enjoy them as much as you can."

Strange, new words for Isabelle. But the King's insanity had brought about a change in her—there was restlessness in Isabelle, a feverish desire to enjoy every minute to the utmost, a love of wealth and ostentation so pronounced, that sometimes Catherine became uneasy in her presence.

She did listen to Isabelle, though, and engaged in brief romances that meant nothing and left her body and soul soiled. Alone and wounded, she looked around, and Philip of Vermandois was there, his hands stretched, his smile loving, not a word of reproach on his lips.

The King's attacks of folly had a deep impact on Catherine. Charles was a kind man, generous husband, powerful king. He owned lands, castles, wealth, his words were law to millions, his subjects considered him anointed by God and were ready to die for him.

"Then God played with him, Philip," she would tell her patient listener, “and one of the greatest lords of Christendom became a raving imbecile.”

“Perhaps we forget sometimes that God is our master,” he would answer, “and a life of indulgence and sin turns us away from his benevolence.”

“Are we lost without his forgiveness?”

“But God forgives, my dear, he reads our souls and hearts better than we ourselves can, and his goodness is infinite.”

Philip was so very patient and understanding. Catherine would kneel in the half-light of the chapel and pour out her confused fears, yearnings, hopes, to God and his Blessed Mother, trying to find the answers in their static smiles and open arms.

When Philip of Vermandois asked for her hand, Catherine felt that she had been listened to, her heart read, her hopes fulfilled.

“I will marry Philip of Vermandois, Isabelle,” she told the Queen, and she felt more at peace and content than she had been in years.

“But the man is too old for you, Catherine! Why, his only son is married too and has children of his own.”

“I know, but it does not seem to matter now. I want to be completely honest with you, your Majesty—as much as I have enjoyed my years in Paris and as grateful as I am to you and the King for your friendship and affection, I feel that I do not belong here any more. Intrigues, envies, petty gossips, the whirlwind of my life at court have tired me. I long for the peace of the country, the remoteness of Philip’s estate in Brittany.”

“But what will happen when you are healed of your sickness over Ludwig and realize that you are married to an old man that you do not love?” Isabelle asked shrewdly. She was sure that her friend was making a mistake—her young, passionate Catherine would never be happy with that old man Vermandois!

“You have told me many times that love does not matter in a marriage. I had love when I was married to Michel, I will content myself with security and safety now.”

“I wish you happiness, Catherine. But I will miss you terribly after all these years. I hope you have thought everything over and I pray that you will not repent of your decision.”

Isabelle felt sad and yet slightly irritated at Catherine—how inconsiderate of her to leave now, when more than ever the Queen needed her sympathy and support. Ludwig was no longer at court, the King might suddenly relapse into madness, the royal Dukes were preparing to jump at each other's throats, and her hatred of Valentina of Orleans had reached new depth. Still, if that was what Catherine wanted... Fortunately, she had Anne of Semihier in her entourage now. Such a nice, quiet girl...But her Catherine, her sister...

"Remember, dear Catherine," she said emotionally, "that your place at court will never be taken by anybody else. You will have

to come back as often as you can, and if you ever feel that you belong here, that Philip and Brittany do not live up to your expectations, your friend Isabelle will be happy to welcome you back."

Catherine took the Queen's hand and kissed it, too moved to talk. Then the two women kissed and weeping took leave of each other.

Catherine and Philip of Vermandois started for Brittany in March.

"When my son Morel came of age and was knighted," Philip had told Catherine, "I decided that the time had come for him to become the head of the Vermandois, and I took up my residence in a smaller manor near Mont. St. Michel, while Morel and his family inhabit the ancestral Vermandois castle. I hope you will not be disappointed by the castle, my beloved; it is certainly modest compared to the palaces you are used to, and even the castle of Vermandois is more magnificent, but I trust that you will find it comfortable and dignified."

Anxiety transpired from his words—she was so much younger and more worldly than he—and, in a rush of tenderness, Catherine put his hands to her lips.

"Do not worry, Philip, I will be very happy," she whispered gently.

When they reached the manor the countryside was still barren and a light mist blanketed the landscape. It was a small chateau, built in gray stone, square and solid. Four towers stood at its corners, their roofs covered with dark slate, and small windows opening on three tiers. It had been built for comfort and pleasure, and, not— withstanding its dull color, no menacing dungeon marred its symmetry, no drawbridge had to be lowered to let them in.

A massive door opened onto a vast hall where a cheerful fire was burning in the fireplace, wreaths of pine and fir hung on the walls, torches and candles were alight, and the faces of the servants who ran to their welcome looked smiling and honest.

Later, after they had partaken of a huge meal of roast pork and jellied fish washed down by strong cider, Philip showed Catherine around her new home, pointing out a silk tapestry, a carved cupboard, the intricate tracery of the chapel, delighting in her joy and admiration.

Their apartments were on different wings and Philip had had Catherine's rooms redecorated after the wedding.

"I always think of you in green, Catherine. Your beautiful eyes have the color of emerald, and the first time I ever saw you, you were dressed in green and your golden hair made a halo around your face. I thought you were as beautiful as the angels that the Limbourg brothers illuminate on the books-of-hours of the Duke of Berry, as frail as a golden butterfly on a green meadow."

Green and gold were everywhere in her rooms, billowed in the curtains in around her poster bed, lined chests and cupboards, covered the floor, softened the hardness of the prie-dieu. Fantastic golden birds, delicate flowers and butterflies glittered in the silky softness of cushions and drapes and, when Catherine looked at herself in the polished metal of a silver mirror, her reflection seemed undistinguishable from the figures that adorned the curtains of her bed.

With love and gratitude Catherine looked at the man, old enough to be her father, whose only desire seemed to be her welfare and happiness. She felt neither passion nor physical attraction for him—those sensations were no longer hers to experience—but tenderness and respect, which were to be her lucky lot from then on.

Catherine took pride in her role of mistress of her own house in the rows of scented linens heaping in closets and chests, the well-supplied pantry, the vats of wine and cider aging in the cellars, the ring of keys dangling from her belt. A host of servants were at her service, but her eagerness for the new part she was playing would not allow her any slackness or idleness.

A lady-in-waiting, Madame Bernardine d'Orgemonte, had been selected for Catherine by Philip. She was a woman slightly older than Catherine, whom war and poverty had deprived of family and means of subsistence, and she disapproved of the way Catherine ran her household, which she considered befitting a bourgeois' wife more than a Vermandois lady. Her people had been in the service of the Vermandois family for many generations and, as Catherine knew that her reaction was dictated by the high esteem in which she held all the Vermandois, she bore her no grudge.

Sometimes Philip would absent himself for a few weeks, to visit either the court of the Duke of Brittany's in Nantes or his son at the castle in the southern part of the country. Catherine did not accompany him on these occasions, as she had no interest for the court of Brittany, which she imagined as a modest copy of the more sumptuous royal one she knew so well.

Catherine was not very anxious to meet her son-in-law and his wife, who came from a very noble lineage and had not been overjoyed at her father's marriage with a German woman of the lesser nobility.

But if the ducal court had no attraction for Catherine, nor the ancestral home of her husband's, her deeply felt religious emotions made her wish to visit the Abbey that stood atop the islet of Mont St. Michel, just off the coast of Brittany.

A few hours' ride along the sandy beaches brought the little party in view of the island, which appeared like a cone-shaped rock culminating in sharp spires and belfries. The causeway that linked the Mont to the coast was thronged with pilgrims of every sort, some astride their horses, others riding mules, a few carried in their litters, most of them on foot, stepping on the whitish sand carefully to avoid them treacherous spots that the river currents, flowing beneath them, made shifty and dangerous. They were quick sands and more than one eager pilgrim had lost his life drowning in that mud. The sea could only be crossed at low tide, when vast expanses of sand were uncovered and the sides of the Mont dry. Tall walls encircled the islet, beyond which a little town nestled, half-timbered houses crowded against one another, a narrow cobbled street wound to the top.

The legend spoke of St. Michel appearing to a holy bishop of the region and exhorting him to erect a building in his honor. That was done, and soon the isolated crag was covered by a cluster of other structures, cloisters, crypts, dungeons, abbatial buildings, inns, shops, unassailable ramparts. The beautiful Abbey church, built in the light-colored granite of Brittany, crowned the summit. A gold cross and a statue of St. Michel shone atop its tallest spire.

It was a picturesque sight; light blue roofs luminous under the sun, heavy buttresses supporting the walls, white silver sand stretching for miles, the small island of Tombelaine appearing faintly in the distance.

Inside the church, the darkness was interrupted here and there, by the flickering of votive candles, the smell of incense mingled with that of the flowers adorning the holy images, the shuffling of the pilgrims echoed among the massive pillars.

Catherine knelt in prayer in front of the statue of St. Michel slaying the dragon. Against the dark background, his halo and gold sword shone dimly while the red open jaws of the monster suggested all the frightening fierceness of evil.

Later, the Benedictine Abbot of Mont St. Michel entertained Philip and Catherine lavishly in the Hall of Guests. He illustrated a multitude of miracles that had taken place on the island and described the life led by his monks, divided as it was between work and prayer, according to their founder's rule.

It was a relaxed and busy existence, and Catherine wondered aloud whether that part of the country, so flat and tranquil, so much dominated by the presence of the sea, was not in itself conducive to meditation and work.

"You may be right, Madame," nodded the Abbot approvingly. "A long time ago, when this island and the coast were still covered by thick forests, men from across the sea lived here, and they meditated in front of the ocean and worshipped among the trees. They were heathens, of course, and to free the place from their evil influence, the blessed St. Michel had his church built here, but, nonetheless, even those pagans must have felt the majesty and serenity of the spot."

* * *

One day at last, Morel of Vermandois and his wife came to visit Philip and Catherine. As no child had been born from their own marriage—and Catherine had no children marriage of her own—it seemed likely that Morel would remain Philip's only heir of their family. If Philip was disappointed by her bareness, he never expressed any regrets, but Catherine did notice that he seemed to grow even fonder of his son and very proud of his grandchildren.

It was a pregnant woman that a solicitous husband helped to alight from her litter one Fall afternoon, and Catherine felt a little pang of jealousy at the sight of the heavy creature that was carrying yet another Vermandois in her womb.

Eliane de Vermandois must have been a pretty woman, but her clumsy body, lackluster blond hair, inquisitive dark eyes fringed by very pale eyelashes and especially her mouth, small and perennially pouting, rendered her very unattractive to Catherine. The man at her side was very similar to Philip, slightly taller, his dark hair only touched with gray, the same vigorous body starting to thicken at the waist.

He bowed to Catherine deeply, then looked at her with a frank curiosity that became surprise and then admiration as his eyes lingered on her mouth, followed the curve of her breasts. Catherine was glad that the delicate colors of her dress enhanced her complexion and golden hair and its embroidered belt showed off the thinness of her waist. She felt like a slender willow next to the turgid oak that was Eliane, and very confident of her charm.

"God's blood, Father," laughed Morel, "you have chosen a dainty little wife for yourself, and given us quite a pretty new mother, has he not, Eliane?"

A dry smile crossed her lips; it is hard to hear another woman's beauty praised while we ourselves feel heavy and ugly, it is true, but Eliane did not take her husband's compliment kindly.

"You are right, husband, my new mother is very pretty. I am afraid though, that her slenderness will make it very hard for her to carry the children that undoubtedly Father expects from so young a wife."

The rest of their visit followed the same pattern. Morel was charming and attentive to Catherine, his eyes belying the respectful "Mother" that he pronounced perhaps too often, Eliane almost rude and flippant. She chose to hurt Catherine on the subject of her childlessness as often as she could, bragging about her fecundity, pitying Catherine because she did not know what it felt like to hold a baby of her own and see the proud look on her husband's face at the sight of a son.

Catherine could understand that Eliane was displeased when her father-in-law married a young woman—the birth of new sons would have deprived her husband and children of their inheritance—but when she realized that her fear was unfounded she should have relented. She did not, the woman in her took over, and she disliked Catherine because she was pretty, her husband admired her, the Queen was her friend.

Eliane was happy to report the rumors that floated around the court and from her Catherine learned, for the first time, that Isabelle was very unpopular in the country.

They reproached her the taxes with which they were burdened and that went to pay for her luxury and the presents she showered on her German family. She was accused of growing indifferent to the King and having affairs with that man or the other, her friendship with her brother-in-law had become too close and she was mounting a campaign against the Duchess of Orleans because she was afraid of Valentina's influence on the King. She was called "the German" and considered greedy and avaricious.

Catherine did not know what to make of Eliane's words because she was aware of her antipathy towards the Queen, a German like her, who had always ignored the Vermandois lady when she had accompanied her husband to the court. Catherine still remembered the enthusiasm that had received Isabelle at the time of her entry into Paris and the memory of that triumphal day made it unbelievable that the same people that had wildly cheered their Queen could revile her so a few years later.

Eliane's spiteful nature rendered her jealous and discontent and her weak character had not prepared her to withstand the blows that fate had aside for her.

Within a few months from their visit, Morel was killed at the battle of Nicopolis, Eliane was delivered of a daughter that lived but briefly and had to resign herself to the role of dowager when the new head of the family, her son Jean, brought his young bride to Vermandois.

Morel's death broke Philip's spirit—he felt guilty to be alive while his son's body was rotting in a distant land, where no prayers were said on his tomb, no cross marked the spot where he had fallen.

Chapter XIII

Valentina Must Leave The Court

The wizard was scared. His hope of curing the King permanently was getting weaker and the Queen was growing impatient. He knew that if he failed in his task he would be thrown out and other sorcerers, magicians, quacks, would take his place. Arnaud Guillaume could not allow that.

He was growing old, and increasingly fond of his life at court, where an apartment in the Palace was at his disposal and heavy bags of gold came his way any time a filter he concocted brought a lover to the bed of a love-sick lady, or a pin he speared through the heart of a wax image rid a man of a wealthy relative that took too long dying.

The Queen was the most generous of his clients, but she could be very unpleasant when her wishes were thwarted. Arnaud was aware of this, and felt relieved that at last he had come up with a plan that would buy him some time.

A little satisfied grin was on his face as he hurried towards the Queen's rooms, and for the occasion he had donned his most elegant robe of gray velvet, and a bejeweled black hat.

Little Isabelle, the Queen's daughter, was with her mother when Arnaud Guillaume was announced. The young princess had been sobbing desperately, clinging to her mother, one hand holding her favorite rag doll.

"But I do not want to leave you and Father, and my brother and sisters," she whined.

The Queen smiled at her but her eyes were ebbing with tears too and her voice trembled when she comforted her daughter. "My little

Isabelle, imagine, you will be a very great lady, the Queen of a beautiful country and the beloved wife of a handsome prince."

Isabelle had never met Richard, King of England, but she had seen a portrait of him. The young monarch looked handsome and resplendent in his court costume, with yellow curly hair framed by the massive crown, symbol of his power, delicate long fingers holding the gold scepter and globe, a slender figure draped in the folds of a sumptuous red mantle lined with ermine.

Looking at those perfect features, the dark serious eyes, the smiling mouth Isabelle noticed how similar Richard was to the handsome prince she herself had married and how different from the young, princess that was to be his second bride, her plump, dark-haired Isabelle.

Her daughter was only seven, and so much like Isabelle in appearance and temperament that sometimes it was like looking at a living portrait of herself as a child. The Queen loved having Isabelle magnificently dressed, and often her cutters and seamstresses would make their dresses from the same piece of material and embroider them with the same pearls and precious stones. Red, scarlet, purple were the colors that enhanced the little princess's skin and eyes the most, turquoises and sapphires, Isabelle's favorite stones, adorned the countless chaplets, belts, pendants her mother had given her.

"But, Mother, the English are bad people, you know that. They have been threatening our country for so long and kept Great-grandfather prisoner in England until he died."

The Queen smiled at her. "Isabelle, you will learn that our enemies can become our best friends, if the circumstances change and faith is kept. The war with England is over, my pet, and King Richard wants to be a friend of France. Your marriage to him will strengthen the ties between the two countries and make the idea of another war obsolete."

The words she was uttering sounded empty and trite to her own ears. Isabelle did not particularly like or trust the English, but her father was favorable to that alliance and the Duke of Burgundy had been very quick to point out the advantages of the union between her daughter and King Richard.

Her mother hated to have Isabelle leave her so soon. She treasured her company, loved to listen to her childish prattle, watch her play with the Dauphin and her younger sisters. A new baby girl had increased her brood to five children and little Isabelle was particularly fond of newly-born Michelle, a name that had been chosen because Charles felt a particular devotion for the Archangel and both he and Isabelle hoped that through his blessed intercession and that of the Virgin, God would be moved to pity and deliver him from his horrible sickness.

Isabelle's thoughts had strayed away from her little daughter and she gave a start when Anne entered the room and announced that Arnaud Guillaume asked for the honor of an interview with her.

"Isabelle, you have to leave me now," she said. "I have important matters to discuss."

The little girl looked disappointed, and in a rush of love and guilt, Isabelle gathered her in her arms and held her tightly.

"Darling," she said, her cheek close to the rounder, softer one, you will be a great and wonderful queen. I will come and visit you in England, I promise, and you will return often too, because your father and brothers would never forgive you otherwise. Besides, you will not be leaving France for a long time yet, so let us be cheerful today and think of what you would like to wear to receive the King of England's ambassadors. They will tell their sovereign how pretty you are and what a noble queen you will make. I will join you in your apartment presently."

Young Isabelle smiled happily, her fears forgotten; her instinctively feminine nature absorbed by the thought of the costume she was going to wear, and left her mother.

A stern-looking Queen acknowledged the magician's low bow and Guillaume shivered internally—he would need all his shrewdness to placate the Sovereign!

"Arnaud Guillaume," said Isabelle, "for many months you have been promising me that the medicine you are preparing for the King will cure him definitely, but I am still waiting for this miraculous potion. In the meantime, his Majesty is often unwell, does not recognize me or his children, is haunted by nightmares and obsessions!"

"I crave your Majesty's forgiveness," pleaded the man, "but the spell that was cast over the King is so powerful that I need the rarest herbs and metals to prepare the potions that will heal him. I have sent my servant to the Orient with precise orders. He knows where to find these precious ingredients, and how to obtain them, and my books promise me that once I have them, I will be able to concoct such a powerful medicine that it will destroy the King's demons forever.

"When do you expect your servant back?" asked Isabelle, slightly mollified.

"He has been gone these past six months," answered Arnaud. "He will be here before the winter sets in, I assure you, your Majesty. But I have other news, which I hope, will make your Majesty glad."

"Tell me what is on your mind, Wizard," Isabelle said imperiously, noticing the sly smile on his face and the satisfaction with which he rubbed his hands.

"Is your Majesty aware of the trial that is taking place at the Chatelet?"

"Of course, the court is buzzing with it like a mad beehive, but I do not see how relevant the interrogation and torture of two prostitutes turned witches can be to the matters that I have at heart."

"If your Majesty allows me, I will try to explain in what way I think we can use the trial to our ends.

"Marion la Droituriere and Margot du Coignet are on trial because they evoked the Devil. He appeared to Margot, talked with her and taught her how to make magic wreaths that would cause the impotency of the man that Marion loved and the death of his bride."

"Please spare me the details, Wizard," commanded the Queen. "I have heard of these wreaths, and how the bridegroom and bride danced on them at their wedding party, unaware that they were a gift from Satan, and that they both became horribly sick and the bride died. But I still fail to see the importance of the trial."

"Perhaps a certain small detail has not reached your Majesty's ears, though."

"A small detail? Out with it, Arnaud!"

"When Marion went to the place where the party for the newlyweds was being held, she was carrying her wreaths hidden under her dress. They say that she looked very upset and could not keep her eyes off her lover. But she had to pretend indifference, or her presence at the gathering would seem suspicious, so she accepted to dance with one of the men who asked her. His name was Thomas le Borgne, and is one of the Duke of Orleans' servants."

"And you think that through the Duke's servant you can link my cousin Valentina's name to those of the two sorcerers!" the Queen finished triumphantly.

"Your Majesty is as usual quick and perceptive," said Arnaud unctuously. "I have already approached the man, in fact, and bought a confession from him that Marion confided to him that her accomplice Margot had sometimes visited the Duchess of Orleans and evoked the Devil for her."

"But will the people believe it? Do not forget that the Duchess is popular among the Parisians, her charities are generous and her piety well known.

"She is not very popular any longer, your Majesty. Not after we started our campaign of rumors and gossips." He looked at Isabelle with a smile of complicity.

Isabelle felt a pang of remorse, and looked at the magician with distaste. She understood his smile, and also knew that he was right, that she, the Queen of France, was indeed the accomplice of that horrible man in planning the downfall of the Orleans, or more especially Valentina of Orleans.

She clearly remembered the day when Arnaud Guillaume had come back with the information she had requested about a plot to kill the king. He had not been able to tell her much.

"The Duke of Orleans seems to have acted on the spur of the moment, your Majesty," he had said, "or, if he did not, he did not confide in anyone."

He had seen the look of annoyance on the Queen's face and had added quickly, "But, of course, his desire to conquer a kingdom for himself, and the help that his father-in-law is willing to give him, must be taken into account. As long as the King is alive, the Duke knows that his plans will be thwarted. The Duke of Burgundy will not allow him to embark on any adventure that will jeopardize France."

"Why, Wizard," she had exclaimed surprised, "you are quite a politician!" He was right, of course. Isabelle too understood how ambitious Louis of Orleans was, how badly he wanted to be first and how bitter he felt faced with the madness of a brother to whom now more than ever he felt superior. He could not have France, he was trying to build the Kingdom of Adria for himself. To that purpose Louis would use any means, and the confused state of the Church offered him a most favorable chance.

For many years now, there had been two Popes—one in Avignon and one in Rome—and the unity of the Church was divided into two separate sections at strife with each other. Louis of Orleans supported and protected the French Pope, Clement, who in turn, was favorable to his designs because he hoped to end the schism to his own advantage and be installed in Rome. He had lured Louis with the promise of lands that belonged to the Church of Rome, but before he could give away the elusive "Kingdom of Adria", he must own it, and Giangaleazzo Visconti was ready to fight to help his son-in-law and his ally in their pursuit.

An Italian campaign would, in the Visconti plan, draw France into an alliance against Florence and any other city that opposed Giangaleazzo's rule, but would be of no benefit to the Kingdom. Why start another war when, at last, there was peace with England? Only to foster Louis of Orleans' ambition?

The Duke of Burgundy was against the Italian adventure—his Flemish subjects were loyal to the Roman pope and did not want Clement in Rome—and Isabelle knew that behind the utopia of a Kingdom of Adria lay the malicious intelligence of Giangaleazzo Visconti, his burning desire to become master of Northern Italy, to destroy Florence and the other independent cities that were an obstacle to his plans. He thought that France would be his dupe and he was using his daughter and her influence over the King to bring about his design.

Isabelle had been pensive for a while and the magician had never taken his eyes off her face—his livelihood depended on the Queen's moods and he had become a shrewd reader of her character.

"It is a well-known fact," she had finally resumed, "that the Duke of Milan hoped that his daughter would become Queen of France. He instilled that ambition in her, and when my children were born and their dream shattered, he started deluding her with visions of a kingdom in Italy and a splendid court of which she would be Queen and a source of inspiration. I do not understand how people can be taken by the sweetness and gentleness of Valentina's appearance, and ignore the steel in her eyes and the thin line of her lips."

"I agree with your Majesty," said the Wizard. "She is the evil spirit behind the Duke of Orleans' ambition. He can have countless paramours, lavish gold and presents on them as long as she is his counselor and he listens to her advice, and works through her for Giangaleazzo's further glory."

"And now the Duchess of Orleans is poisoning the King's mind against me! She spends long hours with my husband teaching him new card games, playing her harp to him...and weaving dark intrigues against me. When the King sees me, he is afraid of me, he shuns me, his wife, and calls for Valentina!"

She sounded outraged and sorrowful and Arnaud had immediately taken advantage of it.

"Perhaps, for your peace of mind, for the King's, your Majesty, the Duchess-should leave the court."

"Neither the King nor the Duke will ever allow that,"

"They might," he suggested, "if it is for her own good. As your Majesty knows, Milan is a land famous for its magicians and Giangaleazzo Visconti has astrologers and sorcerers in his service, whose arts and tools he uses to get rid of his enemies. The people of France ignore that, of course, but perhaps vague gossips, accusations of obscure origin spread by pilgrims and beggars and becoming more convincing as more people listen to them and swell them in their turn, could be spread all over the country. The people would understand then that the daughter of such a man should not be the constant companion of their King and ask to have the daughter of the murderer removed from the royal palace. I feel that the devils that have the King in their power are growing weaker and less resilient. If only the Duchess of Orleans and her witchcraft would leave the court, I could promise his complete recovery."

Isabelle had approved Guillaume's plan and soon a net of spies and informers in his employ had started rumors of witchcraft and spells. People had whispered secrets to their drinking companions in the hundred taverns of Paris, beggars wrapped in rags had thanked their benefactors and promised to pray so that the King would be delivered from the evil influence of his sister—in—law. Voices of sorcery had spread to the four corners-of France.

As Arnaud pointed out, Valentina of Orleans had lost most of her popularity. The people of Paris were getting angry. They loved their

King and wanted him to recover his health. But if he was a prisoner of demons, if the Evil one had him in his clutches, what hope was there for the sovereign? They knew now that his arrogant brother wanted to be king, and that a foreign prince was plotting to make his own daughter Queen of France and his descendants take the place of the Dauphin.

"You might be right, Arnaud, the Duchess is not very popular any longer, and an association with the witches at the Chatelet should bring about her downfall. I have heard that some shops kept by Italian merchants were smashed and their contents looted."

"Yes, it happened a few nights ago, but their owners did not protest too loudly—they want to remain in Paris where business is good and know that the Duchess' protection of her fellow countrymen makes them unpopular too."

The Queen looked at her accomplice. She hated to be tied to him, the net of dependence that he had woven around her, but for the time being she needed him. Later, perhaps, when Valentina had gone and Charles recovered his health, she would get rid of him....

In the weeks to come, Isabelle had to congratulate herself for having such a man in her service.

Paris was buzzing with the rumors that the Duchess of Orleans was the witches' secret evil partner and their association dated back years ago, when Valentina had tried to poison little prince Charles, the Dauphin. Margot du Coignet had put poison in an apple that the Duchess had tossed to the Dauphin. But his Guardian Angel was protecting the little boy, because he did not grasp the apple and it fell. His cousin Orleans, Valentina's son, picked up the fruit, bit it, and instantly died in atrocious pain, while his mother looked on helplessly.

By the time the process of the two witches was over and they were dragged from the Chatelet to the Halles, the vast market of Paris, to be burned among a huge multitude of people, the city's rage and indignation against the Duchess had been worked up to such a frenzy by able informers and spies in their midst, that the crowd had hardly finished watching the writhing bodies at the stake that they had run, with shouts and raised fists, to the Palace of St. Pol.

"Death to Valentina of Orleans! Death to the sorceress!" Their screams had reached Valentina in her apartments, and she had shivered in terror; they had reached Isabelle, and she had smiled in triumph.

The Duke of Orleans rushed to his wife's help, and tried to placate the self-righteous fury of the mob—in vain, stones and rocks had been hurled at him, and shouts of "the witch to the stake" had drowned his words of calm and peace.

"I am afraid that you will have to leave the court for a while at least, my dear," Louis told a frantic Valentina.

"But why, why, how can such a rumor have originated? I never lay my eyes on those unfortunate women, how could I be their accomplice? How can I be accused of poisoning the Dauphin, I who love all the children and cherish your nephews as much as my little ones?"

"I know this only too well, darling," murmured her husband. Was not Valentina raising his bastard, and being as devoted and motherly to him as she was to their own children? He could answer her questions—he knew why she was being accused of sorcery, and by whom—but if she learned who her enemy was she would want to stay and fight, and that he could not allow. He feared for her safety but he also had a feeling that if his wife was away from Paris his chances of playing a major role in the politics of the kingdom would be much greater. Isabelle was a woman, after all, and very few women had ever been immune to his charm!

"I suggest that you and the children reside at the Castle of Asnieres for the time being. I will do everything in my power to try to find who is at the origin of this calumny, and confront him with his lies. But the mobs are unreasonable, wild animals that listen only to their instincts, and it is not prudent to excite them more, right now. You do not know the castle of Asniere, yet. It is very pleasant, I assure you, and so close to Paris that I will be a constant visitor there."

Valentina acquiesced—she did not have any choice, really—and with a heavy heart she started the preparations for her departure.

* * *

Nobody would have guessed a link of consanguinity between the two ladies who stood facing each other. One was a tall, slender blonde woman, with delicate features and a gracious bearing. There was gentleness about her, a languor that gave an impression of weakness, and contrasted sharply with the vitality and self-assurance of the other, a shorter, stouter woman.

"I came to take my leave of you, Isabelle," said Valentina of Orleans. The tone of her voice was firm and proud, yet her eyes were sad, uncertain, and her lips trembled slightly.

"I think your decision to leave Paris was wise," answered the Queen.

"Wise, perhaps, but certainly a tormented one," replied the Duchess simply. "Louis will not have the freedom of leaving Paris as often as he might wish, and our separation will add tremendously to the burden we carry, although we are completely innocent."

"My dear Valentina, certainly no doubt has been cast upon your husband's reputation," said the Queen.

"My reputation is as dear to him as his own, Isabelle. Seeing the Parisian populace surround our lodgings, accuse me of sorcery, ask for my exile, is hurting him as much as me."

"It is indeed amazing how quickly and widely rumors of your supposed magic arts have spread," added Isabelle. "You know, Valentina, I sometimes wish that those gossips were true, that you had acquired some kind of witchcraft in your country of birth, by which you could help the King recover his sanity. But alas, the powers of your father have not been inherited!"

The Duchess paled. With a voice strained by emotion and indignation, she could only answer, "Pray, Isabelle, do not repeat these calumnies to me. My father is not, has never been a magician and I resent that you, my sister-in-law and cousin, who have such close blood ties to my family, choose to believe this horrible slander."

"Blood ties!" laughed Isabelle. "They were forgotten, were they not, when your father attacked and murdered my grandfather and had my uncles banished from Milan. But now, in your hour of trouble, you decide to remind me of them, me, a victim of your father's cruelty!"

"You never did forget or forgive, did you, Isabelle?" whispered Valentina, as if to herself. "That is why I am being exiled, is it not; that is why the people of Paris, who used to be so warm and partial to me, now hate me and accuse me of black magic!"

The Queen did not answer, but looked at her implacably.

"Yet, you know that I am innocent," went on the Duchess of Orleans. "I am innocent of any of my father's deeds that caused you sorrow, I am innocent of any spell cast on the King. Still you want to believe in my guilt, do you not? Why, Isabelle, why?"

"I think your influence at court is nefarious, Valentina. I consider you but a puppet on a string. The string is in your father's hands, and he pulls and twists it at will. The Duke of Burgundy and I want peace for France; we do not want to be entangled in yet another war to satisfy the ambitions of your husband and father."

"My exile will bring peace and prosperity to the country," Valentina said with a little smile. "I am glad to go then, if it is to serve such a noble purpose."

Isabelle did not detect the irony in her words. She looked her rival, saw the prettier woman, tall and erect in her traveling costume, her face flushed by the contrasting emotions agitating her. Once more she thought she discerned self-righteousness and pride in the delicate traits, of her cousin, and the pent-up anger at the woman she recognized more beautiful, elegant, cultivated than herself, the woman who, alone, could soothe the tormented spirit of the King, burst out in a torrent of words.

"Hatred is our inheritance, Valentina Visconti. Your father assassinated my grandfather, deprived my relatives of their dominion, wounded my family in Germany in their love and pride.

"You came to the court of which I am the Queen and the center, and tried to dispossess me of my prerogatives, to set yourself up as an example of virtue and beauty. As a last resort, you poisoned the spirit of my husband against me. I do not know whether you are a sorceress, but after he has been with you, the King, who has always passionately loved me, recoils from me in fear and horror, does not recognize me, his Queen, the mother of his children!"

"I have never uttered a word against you, Isabelle; the Blessed Virgin is my witness to this. I feel so much sympathy and compassion for my poor brother—in—law, I want so much to calm his tortured mind, that, perhaps instinctively, I find the right words that soothe him, the smiles that help him to forget his unhappy state. If you hold him dear, as I hope you do, you should not begrudge him the little comfort that perhaps my presence affords him."

"I do not begrudge him anything," Isabelle interrupted her furiously, "but explain to me why he shouts at me, does not know who I am, believes I am persecuting him!"

"This I cannot do, Isabelle," Valentina said with a quiet smile. "I am not a witch. You must ask yourself, interrogate your heart and perhaps you will find your answer there. But I do see plainly enough that where you are, I cannot be. You are the Queen, Charles's wife, your rights are foremost. I will haunt you no longer; the castle of Asnieres will offer a shelter to my children and me until the time when the truth is known. Farewell, Isabelle of Valois."

Valentina bowed her head lightly and left the room, followed by the triumphant gaze of the Queen.

Chapter XIV

An Arbiter Among The Princes

As the Duke of Burgundy had taught Isabelle, or better, as her life as Queen of France had been teaching her, power was the only decisive element in the life of a sovereign.

The King's sickness had divided and weakened both the monarchy and the country. Charles was alive, but all of a sudden he could snap into a world of ghosts and terrors and leave the see of power vacant.

Burgundy and Orleans, those two supreme egoists, did not think of the good of France but only of their private interests and tried to make themselves masters of the kingdom.

Isabelle understood their plans—their ambition was no secret to her—and decided then that she wanted a share of that power. Her Visconti blood helped her, it became almost a game played against two skilled opponents who did not mistrust a simple woman, a Queen interested more in the height of her hennin than in the election of an Emperor favorable to the House of France.

The climax was reached in 1401, when the enmity between uncle and nephew came to a showdown.

The Duke of Burgundy lived in the palace of Artois, while his army—made up mainly of Flemish crossbowmen and archers—was more or less camping in the streets nearby. Meanwhile, the Duke of Orleans and his army from Brittany and Normandy were directly on the opposite side of the palace of St. Pol where the court was staying at the time.

The news of the imminent confrontation that her counselors were reporting depressed and saddened Isabelle. A few days before her daughter Catherine had been born and the memory of the pain she had suffered still lingered in her mind and filled her with morbid thoughts. Charles was prey to one of his attacks and ignored the fact that his two close relatives were plotting to destroy the kingdom. Isabelle felt completely powerless, confronted by events that were going to be catastrophic for her and her children, but which she could not prevent.

When the Duke of Berry was announced and started to speak, a ray of hope dawned for her and made her listen to his words intently. The old gentleman looked upset, divided as he must have been between loyalty to his brother and duty to his nephew and King. His round face was paler than usual and the elegance of his attire could not disguise his extreme agitation.

"Niece, you must talk to them and make them return to their senses," he pleaded. "Our brother, the late King, depended upon us to advise and help his son; this quarrel between my brother and Louis threatens to plunge France into chaos and anarchy."

"But, Uncle, what can I do? I am so weak and in so much pain that I cannot even leave my rooms."

"Summon them to your presence immediately, plead with them, use your authority and charm, but convince them to stop this dangerous dispute."

A flicker of excitement stirred in Isabelle. What a victory it would be if she did indeed stop those two proud men, made them see the light.

The Duke of Burgundy had been close to Isabelle since the day when she had arrived in Amiens—at times she had resented him and his ambition but eventually her misgivings had been dissolved and she had come to share most of his views. Louis of Orleans had not conquered his Kingdom of Aria, after all. Isabelle and Burgundy had convinced the King of the futility of an Italian expedition, and Charles had withdrawn his help. Burgundy had congratulated Isabelle and professed himself an admirer of her intelligence and diplomacy.

Louis had seen his dream shattered, and had vehemently protested against what he termed "her partiality for the Duke of Burgundy." But Valentina was not at his side any longer, her influence had weakened, and their common love for pomp and pageantry made them soon resume a very fond friendship. Better than anybody else, Louis understood Isabelle's need for money, jewels, lands, and never begrudged the liberality with which Isabelle drew from the treasury.

Perhaps the links of friendship and respect that tied the Queen to the protagonists of the impending fight did make her the ideal arbiter of their conflict.

Louis of Orleans was the first to arrive in her apartment. Isabelle received him in her study, sitting on a high carved chair resembling a throne and wrapped in a soft ermine fur that protected her from the cold November day.

He came in smiling, took off his hat in an ample gesture, bowed deeply and kissed her hand. "Isabelle, you look radiant," he whispered and she smiled in return. Louis always made her feel beautiful and desirable.

"Motherhood suits you, my dear," he continued. "They tell me your little Catherine is almost as beautiful as you, which of course I will not believe until I see your daughter myself. Valentina sends her love and rejoices with you in the birth of your daughter."

"How is your wife, Louis? And your children? I wish so much that they could leave the beautiful Blois castle and visit their cousins from time to time," she lied.

"Valentina loves the country, and is perfectly delighted with her life there, Isabelle. She has her books, music, the care of the children. She receives a fair number of visitors, too, and her dear poets and friends, Christine de Pisan and Eustache Deschamps, are almost her permanent guests. As for the children, my three little boys are fine and growing up healthy and robust. Charles is especially handsome and bright, Isabelle, a worthy husband to any princess in Europe."

There was pride and expectations in his words and Isabelle smiled at him. "Perhaps, Louis, one of my daughters would make him a good wife and tie the Orleans more closely to the Valois' fortune."

"How can you doubt my loyalty to my brother, Isabelle," he protested, and his words rang with sincerity. "I would never do anything that could endanger him and his children."

"You do not mention me, Louis, are you not loyal to me also?" she said teasingly.

"You know how devoted I am to you, Sister. We had dissensions, I know, but France comes first in both our hearts."

"How can you say that and have an army mustered in Paris ready to start hostilities against your own uncles?"

"But my uncle puts his Burgundian and Flemish interests above my brother's. His policy is constantly inspired by what is good for his dominions and even in the question of the schism he allies himself with the enemies of the French pope."

"Louis, it sometimes appears to me that the supreme good of France is forgotten by everybody," she started.

Just then the Duke of Burgundy was announced and Isabelle slowly got up and advanced towards him, her arms outstretched. He bowed slightly and took her hands, holding her to himself while he kissed her cheeks. He looked old and tired, his beaked nose more prominent than ever on his emaciated face. When he saw Louis he frowned, but ignored him and helped the Queen back to her seat.

"Pray, sit down, Uncle Burgundy, and you too, Louis, and let us forget for a while that two armies are camped outside the palace, bent on the destruction of France, not of her enemies."

"Now, Niece, I will not let you accuse me of treason. You know my friendship for you and my devotion to the King, your husband."

Louis did not utter a word but was paying close attention.

"Uncle, what should I think of this terrible situation, when foreign soldiers from your lands are ravaging the outskirts of Paris and no worthy inhabitant of the city can go about his business lest he should be robbed or killed by your troops? The King's palace itself seems to have become a pawn between you and Louis of Orleans and there is so much hatred in your heart that you do not even acknowledge his presence here."

"I have not forgotten that Louis is my beloved brother's son, Niece, and I assure you that my feelings for him are those of an affectionate uncle. But I am anxious about the future of France, and I am afraid that the King's sickness is making the country so weak that it will be only too easy for the English to invade again, if they so choose."

"My uncle, my brother, do remember the words of the Gospel: 'A Kingdom divided against itself will be grieved.' France is enjoying peace and prosperity; do not start a fight that will tear her apart. Think of the late King Charles, how he found France humiliated and robbed of her lands, and left her proud and whole again. He was your brother,

Uncle; he was your father, Brother. You both loved him; do not undo the work of his life."

Isabelle spoke for a long time, getting more confident in her power of persuasion as she saw the effect that her words were having on those men. They were moved, she could feel it; the more so, she knew, as neither of them really wanted confrontation just then. They were prisoners of their pride and stubbornness, but could be persuaded with tact and patience.

At the end of the interview, the two princes embraced each other and swore eternal friendship. They had let the Queen convince them and each of them had given up his just cause to spare their beloved France the horrors of a civil war, or so they wanted to believe.

After the Duke of Burgundy had left, Louis lingered behind.

"Dearest Isabelle," he said caressingly, "how could I ever imagine that a woman as pretty as you are is also as intelligent and astute. France is indeed in your debt and so are my uncle and myself."

His words flattered her. She looked at him. The handsome man was smiling and she liked the admiration she could read in his eyes. Such a charming man, Louis, so different from the repulsive person Charles was changing into. How could Valentina ever bear to be separated from him?

Once alone, Isabelle felt suddenly empty and lonely and thoughts of him filled her mind for a long time.

CHAPTER XV

A CONCUBINE FOR CHARLES

Accompanied by the Sire of Savoisy, Isabelle made her way to the King's apartment in St. Pol. She did not live there any longer, and the mere sight of its somber walls, narrow windows, was enough to make her feel uneasy and somewhat guilty.

Charles had never recovered from his madness; in fact, his spells of insanity had become so frequent to be almost permanent, and to free herself from the terrors that his proximity aroused in her, Isabelle had purchased a new official residence, the Hotel Barbette.

The Palace of Barbette was the first house she owned that she felt was exclusively hers. She loved the square shape of the building, the mellow color of its thick walls, the grotesque grimaces of its gargoyles, the brightness of its stained windows. It had taken her months of care to have the interiors as splendid and refined as she wanted them, its garden redesigned.

Carpenters and wood carvers, bricklayers and tile makers and a hundred more artisans had worked miracles of ingenuity to please her. Her uncle of Burgundy had sent the most precious tapestries from his town of Arras and from Reims come the sumptuous hangings for the beds and walls had come. From the Orient she had received scented supplies of spices and perfumes that now filled the ceramic jars in the bathrooms.

From the various royal residences she had chosen the best platters, most fragile glasses, the priceless objects of silver and gold that the Kings of France had accumulated for centuries, and with those she had adorned the furniture, walls, floors ofher home.

Long years at the court of France and the reports of her informers and spies had left Isabelle with few illusions. She knew that the people resented the heavy taxations, the limitless expenditures with which she "bled" the treasury, that they grumbled against her, calling her the "foreigner"—which they usually did with all their non-French queens—and that her name had been changed to Isabeau, and uttered with hatred and contempt.

Still, Isabelle did not care—as long as she could leave St. Pol and its horrors for good.

Charles, the beautiful young prince that had made her the greatest princess on earth, had become an imbecile, whose gaunt figure, thin beard, scrawny hands revolted her.

Never again would he appear in her rooms in his soiled rags, his limbs twitching, his mouth uttering obscenities, his feverish hands touching her everywhere, fouling her body, violating her whole being.

Away, away from St. Pol, removed from his loathesome presence.

Away to St. Ouen, and its countryside of rolling hills and sunny woods. There the farm house was surrounded by stables for horses, oxen and cows, sheep-folds, pigeon-houses, barns. There, in the month of September, when the grapes were gathered and the new wine was made, she could spend delightful days, forgetting the court formality and pretending to be a simple shepherdess. There she would help the farmers pick up the golden grapes, sit on rough stools milking cows, bite sour apples hanging from trees, try to catch the fat fish swimming in the ponds. There the air was fresh, and one did not have to listen to the howling of a crazy husband, and watch the state of abjection to which he was reduced—covered with blisters and ulcers, a horrible stench emanating from his clothes—the King of France.

Barbette, St. Ouen...refuges, paradise.

But no act of magic had made St. Pol disappear (magic—she did not believe in magic any longer, and had had Arnaud Guillaume, who had failed her so badly, quietly murdered) and once in a while Isabelle had to enter those walls, walk along the courtyard, climb the stairs, enter the chambers where her husband and children dwelt.

The thought of her children brought a smile on her face, and happy thoughts to her heart. God had blessed Isabelle in her body, made it fertile and ripe, able to bear the sons and daughters of France. She hoped that the Wittelsbach blood in them would overcome the weakness and disease that their Valois inheritance entailed, and render them sturdy and resilient, cunning and forceful.

She was aware of the lies that her enemies had been circulating for years—the little princes were neglected, their clothes in rags, their food scarce, their attendants indifferent to their well-being." They should see the accounts that my treasurer submits monthly for the expenses of their households," she would think sarcastically. The state of her finances was chronically low, but the money necessary to the princes' upkeep was regularly sent to St. Pol.

Isabelle thought of Marie, the little daughter that had been consecrated to the Blessed Virgin at birth and had lived in the convent of Poissy since her fourth birthday. She had taken the veil on a luminous September day, surrounded by all the pomp and ceremonies belonging to a royal princess. The autumn sun had been shining warmly on the old stones of the cloister, the bright asters and roses of the courtyard, and the perfume of incense had mingled heavily with that of the flowers in the chapel, when Marie, in her childish voice, had made her solemn vows.

Looking at the small figure in white, with curly hair already hidden under a wimple, Isabelle had felt a pang of misgiving. Would Marie be happy, never knowing the love of a man, the kisses of her children, the pageantry of life at court? But since that day all her doubts had vanished—the quiet, regulated life Marie led in the convent, where she was treated according to her rank but at the same time protected from the intrigues of the court, had made her as happy and cheerful as Isabelle wished all her children were.

But not all her children were as content, alas.

Little Isabelle, the Queen of England, was back after a dramatic escape from the country that had murdered her husband and kept her a prisoner.

Isabelle remembered the radiant child that had left home eager to meet her bridegroom, learn the ways of her new country, be loved by her subjects. The messages she had sent to France were glowing: King Richard was as good and generous as he was handsome; Windsor Castle, where she was lodged, was not as sumptuous as the royal residences of France, but she loved walking its beautiful gardens or riding under the majestic oak trees of its park. She had English lessons and that language was becoming more familiar to her; she was learning to play the lute and loved listening to the King who was a skilled musician. Richard was getting increasingly fond of her and liked her magnificently dressed and adorned with gems.

Then, all of a sudden, catastrophic news reached the court—Richard had been deposed and imprisoned and his cousin, Henry of Bolingbroke had had himself crowned King, while the little Queen had been removed to Sunning Hill Manor where she was virtually a prisoner.

Isabelle had been desperate. Charles was prey to an attack of his malady and, as usual in such days, the important decisions rested with Philip of Burgundy.

"Can we do anything to help Isabelle?"

"Very little, I am afraid, my dear. We signed a treaty with England which the new King has not yet renounced. I am sorry to say that peace will not last very long with Henry as King because what made Richard unpopular with his barons was his desire for peace and the shrewd Lancaster will not repeat the same mistake. But be of good cheer, Isabelle. Henry is in no position to antagonize France right now and I am sure that no harm will come to my niece. Why, Henry himself might consider her for his own Queen because I am afraid that Richard will not live very long, now that he has been dispossessed.

He was almost a prophet, but then the Duke was an attentive and shrewd politician. Richard was indeed murdered in the castle where he was held prisoner and, if Henry did not intend to make Isabelle his wife, his son, another Henry, fell deeply in love with her and tried to win her affection. In vain, though, as the young Queen, who was then only about twelve, despised and hated the members of the House of Lancaster and was to remain for many years faithful to the memory of the handsome bridegroom who had first awakened her heart to love.

The widowed queen that had returned to France was a tall, thin young woman, with lustrous black hair and a milky complexion. The look of sadness and longing on her face added a mysterious attractiveness to her features and made everyone want to put a smile on her lips. But the little queen's heart was broken—she could not forget her life in England and the trauma she had suffered when her world crashed around her.

Little Isabelle was her mother's favorite—she would see her today, after her dreaded, hateful visit to Charles was over. She would stay with Charles only a few minutes, she promised herself, and plead her desire to visit with her children to justify running away from his apartment. She had not seen her daughters Joanna and Michelle in a while, and they would both soon leave Paris to join their betrotheds, the heirs of Brittany and Burgundy. Isabelle longed to see Louis, the Dauphin, whom the death of two brothers had made heir to the crown, and in whose features she recognized her own father's bright eyes and blond beauty. Her two babies lived in St. Pol as well, John and Catherine, and Isabelle sometimes felt guilty for leaving them completely in the hands of their nurses. But there was so little time for young children at Barbette, St. Ouen....They were certainly happier in St. Pol, where they could play with their brothers and sisters.

Isabelle and Savoisy had reached the King's apartment. A page opened the door, and her companion bowed his leave of the Queen.

The first thing that hit Isabelle when she entered the room was its darkness and stench. It was a warm Spring day but all the windows were tightly locked and the curtains drawn. A ghost-like figure was seated on the bed, wrapped in a torn-up blanket while his hands clutched at the soiled sheets that half-covered the mattress.

She remembered that beautifully gilded and painted bed, its blue silk canopy adorned with gold fleurs-de-lis, but now the gilt had become dirty and opaque, the delicately painted figures were smudged; the canopy was torn in a few places.

More than his surroundings, though, the man that was still her husband aroused her horror and disgust. "How can you allow his Majesty to be reduced to this state?" she inquired of an equerry standing near the door.

The man looked at her pleadingly, "Your Majesty, please believe me, there is nothing any of us can do to alleviate his misery. The King has refused to wash these past five months, and if approached by a servant with a basin of water, cringes away in terror and starts screaming. His nails are so long that his face and body are scratched all over, but he will not have them cut. One of the wounds he inflicted on himself is infected and a rash is spreading on his arms but no doctor is permitted close by. When his food is served, he oftentimes throws the dishes on the floor, then walks barefoot on the shards. He will go days without drinking, then empty a keg of water."

Charles noticed the woman and got up from his bed, limping slowly towards her. No light of recognition showed on his face when he looked at Isabelle. At a close distance the stench emanating from his person was stifling. Pieces of food and excrement were hanging from his rags, lice and vermin showed on his skin and among his hair. He stretched a bony arm eaten up by a rash and touched the shining stones around her neck. "Pretty!" he murmured in an alien, throaty voice.

Isabelle pulled back instinctively, but his hand lingered on her skin, an imbecile smile started on his face and he came closer. "Do you want to stay with me tonight, my sweet?" he asked, his grin widening. "Savoisy brought me a pretty woman at last, and plump and shiny as I like them!" His long, sharp nails cut through the cloth of her dress, reached to the skin of her breast.

She tried to wrench herself free from those claws and run away from the den and its horrible inhabitant. But his fingers were strong, a metal trap from which there was no escape.

The imbecile smile still lighting his face, Charles dragged her to the bed and threw her on the dirty mattress.

"Let me go!" she cried, trying to push him away from her and looking for help. But the equerry was swiftly leaving the room, and his leer of complicity made her realize the hopelessness of her protest.

Pinned down to the bed, unable to move, Isabelle saw the man rip her clothes, tear the "hennin" from her head, pull away the jewels around her neck and arms. A string of gold and pearls broke under his steely fingers, and the beads rolled noisily on the wood floor.

"It is a present from my grandfather in Italy, do not break it," she murmured incongruously to the man crushing her, but he did not hear—a perverse boy maiming a multi-colored butterfly and leaving it quivering in an agony of pain.

His hands were everywhere on her body, exploring the softness of her thighs, squeezing the breasts that so many maternities had made fuller and heavy, while his foul mouth breathed horridly on her face and his lips and tongue pressed against hers.

She tried hard not to inhale the stench emanating from his body and rags, but when he interlocked his bony legs with hers, she closed her eyes and gave in to his strength in a silence full of hatred.

The man was groaning and perspiring profusely and his long nails, digging into her soft flesh, left long scarlet marks on her shoulders and legs. The bed creaked and moved under their bodies and, lifting her eyes, Isabelle could see the torn up canopy swing grotesquely atop the peeling posts.

When it was over, and the man had fallen into an agitated slumber, Isabelle looked at him. If there had still been pity left in her for her husband when she had entered the room, the brutal rape had killed it forever. Never again, she promised herself, would she come to St. Pol and be subjected to his loathsome attacks, never again would that monster dare touch her flesh and defile her body.

Sitting on a stone bench, she tried to compose herself and calm her agitated spirit. The equerry and Savoisy must be aware of what had happened, and that brought blushes of humiliation to her cheeks. Still, Savoisy at least was a friend, a courtier that used to share Charles' adventures and campaigns and on whose loyalty she could count. She would have to confide in him and ask for his help.

Outside the massive door, the Sire de Savoisy was waiting for his Queen.

"Savoisy," Isabelle said, acknowledging with silent gratitude that he did not seem to take any notice of her torn dress, disheveled hair, "I know your love and friendship for the King, and I will be frank with you. His Majesty is reduced to an animal state, when only animal instincts are alive in him. Do you remember how sensitive he was to women's graces, how ardently his passions manifested themselves? He cannot have changed completely from the man he was before his attacks."

A little sad smile curved Savoisy's lips, a glimmer of merriment shone in his eyes. "No," he answered, "his Majesty has not changed in this respect. Fortunately there are houses in Paris whose inhabitants still consider it an honor and privilege to be in the King's service."

"This is a delicate way of putting it, Savoisy," she smiled. "It is a remedy, I must agree, even if not the perfect one, because the King is thus at the mercy of any unscrupulous woman and his very life may be in jeopardy. I will think about the situation, my friend, and I hope we will come up with a better solution. In the meantime, I ask you to continue to be for the King the friend you have shown to be so far. I am very grateful to you and please know that your attachment to our House will not go without reward."

The Lord of Savoisy bowed deeply and accompanied the Queen to the gates.

Isabelle left St. Pol determined never again to set foot there. If the children wanted to see her, let them come to Barbette. As for Charles, the germ of an idea was taking shape in her mind to solve the problem of his loneliness and her own reluctance, or better, her firm resolution never again to submit herself to the wild passion of the mad king.

A few days later, all the pieces came together, and a perfect plan was put into effect.

One evening, while her hair was being dressed for a ball,

Anne de Semihier, her favorite lady, sat by Isabelle and started gossiping idly, as was her wont. She commented on the poor taste of one of her friends, the frivolity of another, the handsomeness of a knight recently arrived at court.

Her silly prattle annoyed the Queen, and she interrupted the young lady rather testily.

"Anne, Louis de Bosredon is a good-looking youth, I agree, but I do not see why you, who have a handsome healthy man of your own, should be attracted to that effeminate knight. Do not tell me that your husband's short absence already makes you restless in your bed."

Of course, her words were unfair to Anne, who was one of the very few ladies at court whose loyalty to her husband had never been doubted, and the poor girl blushed. Isabelle had a pang of remorse.

"Come on, Anne, think nothing of my words, but do tell me whether anything else interesting is going on of which I am unaware."

"Your First Secretary, your Majesty," she answered, "Guy de Champdivers, seems very upset by a letter that he received from his nephew in Burgundy. Apparently one of his nieces, a pretty girl called Odette, who was destined to the convent, was raped by a son of one of her father's friends, who is already married. Champdivers, the nephew,

I mean, is quite desperate because Odette is pregnant and the Abbess will not have her take her vows in that condition."

"That-is unfortunate, Anne, and I am sure poor Champdivers is upset. The Duke of Burgundy recommended him to me years ago and he has always been a loyal servant. I wonder whether there is anything I can do. Contact the convent, perhaps...." She stopped in the middle of her sentence because an idea had just struck her.

"Anne, dear," Isabelle said, "do send for Champdivers, I want to talk to him immediately."

Shortly afterwards, the First Secretary was admitted to the Queen's presence. He was a middle-aged man, always dressed in somber colors, whose reddish hair had turned almost completely gray. He looked perplexed and uneasy in her presence and Isabelle asked him to sit down while one of her attendants offered him a cup of spiced wine.

"Champdivers," she started, "You have been in my service since my arrival in France and have always served the King and me loyally. I hope I can show you now that your Queen is not ungrateful."

He stammered an answer, still uncertain about the direction and outcome of their conversation.

"I have, learned that dishonor has visited your family, and I am touched by it because I know how proud you are of your noble Burgundian stock and how fond of your relatives. I am happy to say that I think I have the perfect way out for your nephew's difficulty. As the King is very sick, the cares of government are in my hands and I cannot devote to him the time and attentions that I should and would like to. I am afraid that, without my supervision, his household is in disarray, his servants steal from him, cheat him, starve him and deprive him of clothing. His doctors are not constantly at his side and the disease does not progress in the way in which we all wish it would. In short, my dear Champdivers, I want a woman in charge at the palace of St. Pol, a woman who will have the King's well-being at heart and will respond to all his needs. I am told that your niece, Odette, is a gentle and pious girl. Her future was destroyed by a brute, her family's reputation is at stake and I have decided to help her and you. She will have her child at St. Pol and she will fulfill her life's calling taking care of her unfortunate monarch instead of shutting herself in a convent."

Whether or not the man understood the full implications of Isabelle's generosity, he was pleased with that solution to his family's problems, and easily persuaded his nephew to send the girl to Paris.

Odette de Champdivers was a delicate blonde with blue eyes and a thin body disfigured by a very advanced maternity. She stood timidly in front of the Queen, keeping her eyes lowered and answered her questions in a childish and frightened voice. She was grateful to her Majesty, she said, and promised to do her best to look after the King's person and persuade him to lead a more orderly life.

Isabelle liked her—a timid, grateful girl who would bring Charles some solace and whose presence would be her own protection against her husband and blot out forever the memory of her last visit to St. Pol.

Yet Destiny had etched out the days of the King's violence with indelible clarity on her body.

Slowly and inexorably Isabelle's figure started to thicken, her breasts became heavy, her gate slow and on a winter day, when the snow was falling from the sky in large flakes and a bright fire smelling of pine was lit in her fireplace, the Queen was delivered of a boy.

It was a puny baby, with a big nose and sensuous lips. His nurse presented him to the mother proudly. He had been washed and wrapped in silk and laces, a wooly bonnet on his head, little fists opening and closing furiously.

Isabelle looked with distaste at the wrinkled reddish skin, the fissures of the eyes. She was bound never to forget the day of her humiliation, and forever see in her son's features those of the man who had fathered him. Another Charles, she thought, another Charles that I will not love.

In the flesh and blood of this loathsome creature, she recognized the curse that had been pronounced against her— he was a living proof of God's ire towards the Valois.

When a name had to be chosen for the little boy, Isabelle had no doubts.

"It will be Charles," she decided—she really had no choice.

Chapter XVI

An Outsider At Court

Catherine had been back at court before, but it was only during her visit there in the autumn of 1403 that she became fully aware, for the first time, of how everything and everybody surrounding the Queen had changed.

It was as if for years her mind had obstinately refused to recognize the subtle changes that were taking place and had brought back to Brittany the mendacious image of a Queen and a court that no longer existed. Now, all of a sudden, the thin veil of falsity was torn apart, and reality stood in front of her eyes in colors that were the brighter for having been ignored for too long.

The Queen that welcomed her with a fond embrace had grown into a stout middle-aged woman. The neck of her dress was cut very low, half-exposing her breasts and massive shoulders, and the great height of her "hennin" could not dissimulate her fleshy cheeks and chin. She was magnificently dressed, more so than Catherine remembered, and the precious silk of her red dress was heavily embroidered with pearls, and more pearls and gems were around her neck and on her fingers.

As if by magic, the ladies and gentlemen hovering around the Queen had remained as young, nay younger, than they were when Catherine of Fastavarin lived among them. But of course they were not the same people, just younger and livelier reflections of the courtiers of yore. They showered the Queen with compliments, laughed at her words, flattered her constantly. The qualifications for service of most of the gorgeously attired young men seemed vague, and the pretty ladies attending Isabelle were too busy organizing pastimes to fulfill the requirements of their services.

The King never appeared in the Queen's palace and his name was hardly if ever mentioned, while his brother, the Duke of Orleans was seldom absent from her side. Louis, Catherine had to admit, still radiated the indefinable charm that was his own, and still made great use of it, enchanting any woman with whom he was. But Valentina was gone; she had never come back from her exile, and lived with her children at the castle of Blois.

A new personage had made his appearance, and the impact of his presence was felt by all.

It was a short, squat man, with reddish hair, spotted skin, a bulbous nose. His blue eyes had a chilly look in them that belied his ingratiating manners and unctuous smile. His name was John of Nevers, Duke of Burgundy.

The duke, who at the death of his father Philip had become the head of the House of Burgundy, preferred to be called by the nickname he had earned at the siege of Nicopolis—John the Fearless. The flower of Burgundian and French knighthood had been defeated by the forces of the Sultan Beyazit and John himself, who had covered himself with glory at the siege, was captured and had to be ransomed.

The campaign against the Sultan, who threatened the destruction of the Byzantine Empire, was considered another, if different, crusade against the Moslem invaders, and John of Nevers had come back surrounded by a great fame of valor and nobility of soul.

"I am afraid of him," Isabelle confided to her friend. "I consider him a hypocrite bent on the destruction of those opposing him."

"Still you consented to the marriage of two of your children to his son and daughter," remarked Catherine.

"As much as I dislike him, I know that his power is immense, even greater than his father's, my poor beloved Uncle Philip. Good relations with John of Nevers are of paramount importance and even my brother-in-law Louis had to agree and recognize the soundness of my judgment, when the matches between the Dauphin, and Michelle, and the princess of Burgundy were arranged."

"And he promptly obtained your approval for the marriage of his own son to your daughter Isabelle," Catherine observed. "It was a shrewd move on his part, to counterbalance Burgundy's influence."

"What, pray, do you mean by that?" frowned the Queen." Louis's son Charles is a gentle, darling boy, in love with music and poetry. If anybody can make my Isabelle happy again, Charles of Orleans is the one. He writes exquisite verses in her honor and in many ways he is so much like King Richard that I am sure that he was the perfect choice for Isabelle."

"I beg your Majesty's pardon," said Catherine, "if I have been too bold in my comments. If you allow me one more impertinence, though, I could not help noticing the Duke of Orleans seems to have become more influential and powerful than he used to be."

"He is a good friend, I will not deny it. Now that his wife resides elsewhere, and the death of his father-in-law has crushed all hopes of an Italian kingdom, Louis and I have no conflicting interests. We both work for the good of France and our House and you will have to admit that he makes a much more charming ally than that brute, John of Nevers."

"Yet that monster is your daughter's father-in-law, and you allowed Michelle to live at the court of Burgundy and be under his family's influence."

"My dear Catherine, your comprehension of affairs of state and international policy feels the effects of your long stay in the wilderness of Brittany! Of course I allowed Michelle's matrimony to Philip of Burgundy, and I consider it a most enviable match. Why, the court at Brussels is already rivaling ours in splendor and wealth, and by the time Philip becomes its Duke, Burgundy will stretch over a huge part of Northern Europe. The Burgundians will inherit Holland, Flanders, Brabant, Luxembourg—my daughter's dukedom will be larger than my own kingdom of France.

"I am ambitious for all my children, Do you remember that for years, poor as I was, I kept the young Duke of Brittany and his brother at court—another drain for my finances that I could ill afford. But John of Brittany was then my daughter Joanna's fiancé, and I was afraid that, once the Duke's mother married the King of England, he would be under England's influence. Therefore, to keep that province in the hands of a ruler friend to our House, my son-in-law, and give my plain Joanna a handsome husband, I had to support the two youths in Paris until John was old enough to succeed his father and return to Brittany with his bride."

"And now Joanna is Duchess of Brittany, and one day Michelle will be Duchess of Burgundy, and Isabelle Duchess of Orleans. Yes, my Queen, you have been ambitious and successful for your children!" said Catherine with admiration.

She did admire Isabelle, the energy with which she had thrown herself into the perilous sea of France's politics, grabbed the power for herself and, when she could not hold it alone, tried to strike a balance between the rival forces of Orleans and Burgundy. France was at peace, and if the taxes levied on the population were heavy, they were infinitely less so than they had been during the long years of war.

But Queen Isabelle—Isabeau—was extremely unpopular in France.

Her subjects attributed to her the most infamous passions and reproached her for every ill that befell them. License and vice reigned supreme at court, they would say, and at the center of them stood the Queen and her paramours.

Paramours...Isabelle laughed at the word with disdain. She revealed to Catherine that she had taken a lover, but only after years of loyalty to a husband who had become a madman, when any hope of healing had died down and only disgust and fear were left in her.

She noticed disapproval in her friend's face. "I beg of you, Catherine," she said, "not to confront me with that holier—than—thou attitude. I was alone in my bed for long years, when my body craved the embrace of a man, and my dreams left me frustrated and depressed in the morning. I knew that Charles's malady had alienated me from him forever, but I still remembered the pleasures that his experienced love-making gave me. My physical union to Charles was one of the most satisfying aspects of my marriage and I was not ready to give up love altogether. Also, you may have noticed that chastity is not a virtue at my court, and the relaxed customs, the daring styles of clothing, the freedom of the relations between men and women, made my situation of 'virgin queen' very hard to maintain."

"I am certainly not blaming you, your Majesty. I too can remember how lonely it is not to have a man to love and protect you, but I wonder how a man like Louis de Bosredon, young and selfish as he is, can satisfy your needs for love and be a support for you."

Isabelle broke into an amused, ironical laughter. "My dearest

Catherine, Louis may not fulfill my spiritual needs, I agree, but he certainly satisfies my body, I assure you!"

Catherine felt her dislike for Louis de Bosredon increase. He was young, arrogant, with the graceful body of an adolescent and the sensuous mouth of a man that knows himself irresistible. The Queen's favor, the presents she showered on him, the gusto with which the young man enjoyed his new role, had made him very unpopular among the courtiers, men and women alike.

"I have heard that Louis was found in a 'compromising situation' with another youth, Pierre de Giac, in a secluded part of the park," she could not help saying, knowing perfectly well that her words would infuriate the Queen.

"A vile rumor, a piece of gossip spread by those who are jealous of him and resent my protection. Louis is man enough, let me assure you, as ardent a lover as any woman may wish, and that you, my friend, my sister, can believe a lie that is said to discredit me, that hurts and surprises me."

Catherine blushed and apologized with sincere remorse. She realized that her sheltered, isolated, perhaps self-centered life in Brittany had reinforced her inborn characteristics of self-righteousness and felt that she, of all people, was in no position to judge or accuse Isabelle.

A few days later, Catherine's love for her friend acquired a new dimension of comprehension, which Isabelle sensed and to which she responded with gratitude.

"I will go to St. Pol to visit the children today," she announced to Catherine, "and you will come with me. I have not seen them for a long while now, and I am sure you would enjoy talking to my handsome Dauphin and meeting little Catherine."

Catherine was surprised. She knew that the Queen never went to St. Pol—she wanted to avoid meeting the King, now completely left to the cares of Odette de Champdivers—and the little princes were occasionally accompanied to the palace of Barbette by their nurses. Isabelle's maternal love seemed to have become more superficial through the years, a duty she had to perform as if her disgust and fear of her husband had carried over to their children.

Catherine hardly remembered the little princes, and her recollections of the King went back to previous visits in Paris, when Charles of

Valois was still a handsome, if gaunt and absent-looking man, whose shrill uncommunicative laughter had sent a chill to her bones.

The wing of St. Pol where the princes lived offered a marked contrast to the sumptuous lodgings of the Queen. The furniture was shabby and scanty, the floors hardly swept, the window panes dirty and grimy.

Catherine had never met the little girl that bore her name, who was the only royal princess that still lived at court. She was very young, almost a baby, and very similar to her mother in the fresh color of her skin and dark eyes, but her nose was too long and protruding, her face lacked the roundness and dimples that are the prerogative of beautiful children. Her pink gown embroidered in silver was slightly threadbare and too short, her long brown hair fell limply on her thin shoulders.

The two children with her were older boys, Louis the Dauphin and John of Touraine, and the same air of carelessness and apathy hung around the young princes like a dull cloud. The three of them were sucking rose sugar and candied orange peels, taking them from a silver bowl that a servant had brought in. They were not a bunch of joyous children happy to see their mother, eager to share the events of their lives with her, curious about the strange lady who accompanied her, but three sullen solemn creatures anxious to go back to whatever their occupations had been.

Isabelle seemed taken aback by the situation that, apparently, confronted her but seldom, and, after a few vague questions about their health, studies, and horses, and even vaguer answers, she asked that her youngest child, Charles, be brought to her presence.

The prince's nurse was just coming, holding little Charles by the hand, when another door opened and the King entered the room followed by a couple of men.

Catherine instinctively knew that it was the King, but never in her wildest dreams would she have recognized the handsome man of her memories in the gaunt, dirty, malodorous ghost that crossed the threshold. His emaciated aspect excited her pity, but his long scrawny face half-covered by a greasy graying beard, his claw-like hands feverishly twitching and untwitching, the torn and soiled costume he was wearing, everything in him filled her with invincible repulsion.

The traits that had made Charles of France a human being had been completely obliterated and it would have taken an exceptional woman to feel pity and not disgust, love and not repugnance for the "thing" that he had become.

Catherine knew that Isabelle was not strong enough for the new part in which Fate had cast her, but it was enough to see Charles' crazy eyes, to listen to his idiotic laughter and disconnected words, for Catherine to understand her friend better than she had done until then.

Everything became clear to Catherine—Isabelle's greediness and extravagance, her lover and favorites, the level of immorality and licentiousness to which the court had sunk—anything was justifiable to survive the nightmare into which she had fallen.

Philip of Vermandois had always encouraged his wife's trips to the capital. He had foreseen the rivalry between the two powerful houses of Burgundy and Orleans, and understood the Queen's desire for the presence of her dear devoted friend at her side.

Catherine had never seen Ludwig again. The prince was often at the court of the Emperor or resided for long months in his wife's estates. She had dreaded and secretly wished to see him again. Content as she was, and secure in her husband's love, her heart still skipped a beat when a tall, blond man with arrogant blue eyes bowed in front of her, or the self-assured stride of another man reminded her of Ludwig.

"Do you ever think of Ludwig?" Isabelle had inquired of her more than once through the years. "How can a passionate, impetuous woman like you be happy with a man almost twice her age, whose ardor was burnt long ago?"

Catherine had denied any feelings of nostalgia for her life at court, regret for marrying the Sire of Vermandois, but she had had to admit to her friend—and herself—that she had not forgotten the handsome prince of Bavaria.

"There are so many kinds of love," mused the Queen one day. They were slowly strolling along a path in the garden of Barbette. The day was mild and a light breeze played with the leaves and flowers of the beautifully tended garden. "For a long time I thought that love can only strike you suddenly, and fill you so entirely with the image of the loved one that it soon becomes all-consuming. Thus it happened in Amiens for me, when I curtsied in front of Charles and our eyes met for the first time."

"I think," said Catherine, "that we are prepared to fall in love in such a way. Countless songs and poems describe the delights of love at first sight. You 'fall' in love, it is an irresistible force that takes you unaware, frightening in its intensity, and against which no resistance is possible. I had these feelings when I first met your brother, and then again with Michel I felt the same emotions."

"Then you discover that your body wants love too, and nothing is sweeter than the embrace of a man, or the pressure of his body against yours. Poetry did not reveal you that!"

"Perhaps it did, Isabelle, under allegories that our naiveté could not penetrate."

"Perhaps. I know now that that love is as strong and rewarding as the love of my poems and I cannot live without it."

Was she justifying her passion for Louis de Bosredon? Catherine wondered, but she also had a feeling that Isabelle did not believe she needed any justification—she had suffered for years, young Louis was the reward Destiny owed her.

"Can you 'grow' to love somebody, Catherine?"

"Indeed you can," she answered, thinking with fondness of the man that she had married to forget another, and whose life was devoted to her happiness.

"What I mean is that you have seen a man for years, danced, spoken, laughed with him. His charms are well known to you, but they leave you unmoved and you can praise him without blushing, flirt with him with a light heart. Then, one day, when he enters the room your heart skips a beat, when he looks at you, you feel yourself blush, you find excuses to touch him as if by hazard, and when he leaves gloominess sets in."

Catherine looked at the Queen in amazement. Certainly that was not a description of how Isabelle had "grown" to love Louis de Bosredon!

Isabelle saw her surprise. "My dearest Catherine," she said, "I want to confide to you my sweetest secret—I love again, and with so much tenderness, passion and understanding that it is as if I were in love for the first time and had not known its meaning until now."

"My lady," she answered, moved by the Queen's sincerity. "I am surprised, I must confess, but thrilled for your sake and I wish you complete happiness. But who is the man that has aroused your feelings with such intensity? He must reciprocate your love with the same passion and he is lucky, because you are the most devoted and loving woman."

"The man I love," she said quietly, "is in the dark about my feelings, and considers me only a sister, a political ally. It is Louis of Orleans."

Chapter XVII

A New Kind Of Love

The Queen from her palace of Barbette to the Lady of Vermandois on the Day of the Exaltation of the Cross.

Dearest Catherine:

As always your return to Brittany leaves me sad and forlorn. Everybody—Anne especially, of course—notices my melancholy and comments on the gloominess that falls upon the palace as soon as the sound of the horseshoes beating on the stones of the courtyard vanishes and I catch the last glimpse of the carriage hiding you and taking you away from me.

You were here yesterday—or is it two months ago, already?— to share my thoughts, listen to my confession rejoice in my happiness. In short, a devoted sister was with me, and now I am alone again....

No, it is not true any longer, I am not alone, Catherine, my dearest wish has become true, and I love and am loved as I have always dreamed that it might be.

But let me tell you all from the beginning—one more confession that your patient ears will receive from your friend.

You know my feelings about John of Nevers, and agree with me that never a more ruthless and ambitious man lived. I must say for him that he is highly intelligent and plays the mobs masterfully, championing their grievances, opposing any new taxation, allying himself with the Sorbonne and defending its privileges. He has been accusing Louis of Orleans and me of squandering the country's finances and plunging the kingdom into an abyss of ruin, while preferring to forget the luxury and dissipation that prevail at his own court.

The people of Paris and the University have finally found in John of Burgundy the leader they wanted.

A month ago, to protest new taxes that the Royal Council had to levy, a huge mob marched against St. Pol with stones and sticks, shouting obscenities, calling for Orleans' downfall and mine. I was frightened. A stream of shouting populace was rushing towards Barbette as well and I knew that Burgundy would not, perhaps could not, disperse them the mobs for once seemed to be ruling him.

Then Louis appeared. He quickly and efficiently organized my flight from Paris, gathered my children together, found horses and carriages for my ladies and me. He was so capable, unselfish, risking his own life to save mine and my children's. Surely, to love a man as noble and generous as Louis was not a sin, the Virgin Mary could not frown upon my love for him!

We were traveling west, towards Brittany, where I knew that my friend and her noble husband would give us shelter, but we did not go very far. John of Burgundy, accompanied by a large army, overtook our little group and, overpowered, we had no choice but to follow our captors back to the now-hated city, hear the shouts of triumph of the rabble, look at their distorted faces, menacing gestures.

All through this ordeal Louis bore himself with the nobility and grace that are so much part of his charm. Still, I could notice that he was controlling himself with the utmost effort and the humiliating return to Paris escorted by the army of his rival could not be easily forgotten by that proud man.

John of Burgundy tried to justify the outrage he had committed against his Queen—the people could not suffer to have the Dauphin taken away from Paris...their loyalty to the Valois was firm and devoted, but they wanted both the King and his heir to reside in the capital, etc., etc. Fortunately, though, he succeeded in calming the mobs, and very soon the people of Paris started going about their business in peace again. The howling crowds surrounding the palace disappeared and their place was once more taken by vendors, beggars, prostitutes and idlers. Louis and John swore eternal friendship, took the holy bread and wine together in Notre Dame, and gave each other the kiss of reconciliation.

A happy surprise did much to put me in a joyous frame of mind again—my dearest father announced his visit to Paris, his first in so many years, and you can well imagine the turmoil of excitement and happiness the news caused me.

My father...I would celebrate our reunion with extraordinary magnificence, give the most splendid and elaborate balls and receptions for him, choose the most exquisite food and wine for his dinners. I would have the ceiling of the palace Great Hall painted to represent the sky, with white fluffy clouds dotting its blue surface and golden-haired maidens riding multi-colored birds and butterflies. The artificers would make the sky open up and a rain of rose petals, lilies and carnations descend on the guests. I would present him with a beautiful black horse from Damascus, and a gold casket full of jewels and precious stones.

Catherine, I tell you all these details because these were the thoughts that were filling my mind on the afternoon that marks the beginning of my new, happiest life.

Do you remember how fond I have always been of the beautiful gardens that surround the Convent of the Celestins? I find walking under the ancient trees soothing and I often stroll to the adjoining cloister and its dark and silent church.

On that day too my walk took me to the Church of Celestins, and its solemn tranquility invited me to enter. My eyes soon got used to the darkness of the interior and I directed myself to the Chapel of the Blessed Virgin. It is the chapel that Louis of Orleans has had erected as a penance for the danger to which he exposed the King on the night of that tragic ball, you remember, and its magnificence, gleaming marbles, precious statues contrast with the somber interior and the deep shadows cast by the pointed arches of the vault.

I knelt in front of Mary's statue and let my eyes rest on her calm, smiling features, on the plump baby reaching for the golden apple she held in her hand. A crown was placed on her blonde hair and her dress was trimmed in gold. Louis had had the chapel built, the statue carved. I wondered whether he had asked the artist to model the Virgin after Valentina, or Mariette, or any of the women he had loved. His love was like a will-of-the-whisp, no woman could hold his attention for more than a fleeting instant. What hope did I have to arouse his passion, when for years he had considered me only a sister?

I let my thoughts wander back through the many years Louis and I had known each other, when our different political interests had made us enemies, when the same love for gaiety, brilliancy, extravagance, had approached us. Did I ever detect a sign of more than brotherly affection in him; did physical attraction to me ever transpire in his attitude? Alas, I had to answer in the negative. Louis had always enjoyed the greatest popularity at court, where his brilliant qualities had won him the admiration of men and women alike. He was liberal and generous, skilled in the use of weapons, refined in his taste for books and music, a devoted and irresistible follower of Venus. His love for his brother had never been doubted and was yet another obstacle to the fulfillment of my desire. Could he ever forget that I was married to his brother, and a brother that a terrible disease had rendered defenseless? Would he consider my virtue too formidable an impediment even for such a philander?

My relationship with Louis of Bosredon was satisfying, but I did not love him, and while I knew that just to love again was a blessing, I also knew that to love a man that did not love you was agony. I felt tears of disappointment trickling down my cheeks and I reproached myself for my childish emotions.

I rose slowly and started for the door. A shadow stood out from a group of columns and, with a small cry of disbelief, recognized the man that had been filling my thoughts.

"Louis, what are you doing here?" I exclaimed rather foolishly.

"I followed you," he answered simply. "You are always surrounded by your people at court," he added, "and it is impossible to talk to you alone."

I chose to ignore that, every day, he was offered innumerable chances for a private interview, as I rather liked his following me and our secret meeting under the soaring vaults of the church. I tried to keep an indifferent face and retorted ironically: "And what do you have to tell me that needs so secluded a recess to be revealed?"

"I have a word of warning for you, Isabelle," he replied gently, "and one that my love for you and your honor makes me bold enough to say without, I hope, incurring your anger."

Disappointment made me silent. Was this the reason he had followed me then, to reproach me my affair with Bosredon? How dared he?

"Ugly rumors are circulating beyond the palace walls. One of the gentlemen at court, and of the lesser ones, for that matter, has been distinguished by you and favored with your generous friendship. The people feel that they are being 'fleeced' so that this upstart can enjoy royal presents and privileges. They pity 'poor' King Charles and consider the 'foreigner' responsible for France's misfortunes. Of course, there is no truth in this, Isabelle," he added quickly, probably sensing my tenseness and incredulity, "but when a preacher like Jacques Legrand has the temerity of addressing you from his pulpit and declaring that Venus alone reigns in your heart, all your friends must come to you and shield you with their advice."

Wrath was choking me and prevented me from answering for a long time. I sat down and he sat next to me, then gently took my hand and held it in his. My mind was in a turmoil of indignant answers, but I was aware of the softness of his touch and warmth of his presence.

"I am appalled at the audacity of that monk," I said at last, "and even more so as the King did not think it fitting to punish him exemplarily, but the preacher is, at least, a man of good morals, while I am afraid that your reputation is not unblemished. You have always been the darling of a court of loose and free customs, your example has been followed by countless young men, your luck with the ladies has become a by-word. Yet, you have the audacity to warn your Queen and, by implication, set yourself as a paragon of virtue to a woman who spent years in loneliness and desperation. That you can do so is a proof of your hypocrisy and selfishness."

He felt the sincerity of my indignation and did not defend himself. "Isabelle, do not see me as an enemy, but consider me your best friend, because your well-being and happiness are as dear to me as those of my children."

"Nothing is as dear to you but your ambition, Louis," I replied, "and only a kingdom would satisfy that!"

He got up and started pacing the chapel. My presence was forgotten and the words were rushing from his lips. "Yes, I have been ambitious all of my life, but it is hard to be the second-born of a noble King and know from infancy that you will always be second to a beloved brother. I do love my brother, Isabelle, of this at least you can be sure! My qualities of intelligence and culture have been extolled by admiring teachers and friends since I was a child, the ladies have always been generous to me, my wife faithful and devoted. My gifts destined me to be first, but I was born second. I deluded myself with visions of a kingdom of my own, at last, and it was hard to reconcile myself to the end of that dream. All though the years, though, my love for France has never subsided, and my main object now is to have her prosperous and at peace. My brother's malady renders the kingdom weak, and one has to be more than ever aware of the ambition that aims at the destruction of the country."

Of course, Louis had not forgotten the humiliation inflicted on him by his rival, and I knew that the reconciliation between the two men was only an expedient.

"We should be wary of John of Never," continued Louis. "He considers himself Burgundian and Flemish, but uses the French people, the popularity he has won with them, to reach his own end, which is the establishment of a huge kingdom, stretching from the Netherlands to the Pyrenees. His father's foreign policy was so far-sighted that, one day, all the Flemish lands will be unified under the House of Burgundy, and Bruxelles or Dijon will compete with Paris as the capital of civilization."

I had to agree with Louis. It was enough to think of the ugly face of John the Fearless, his icy eyes, to know that only war and destruction would come from him. "Is there anything we can do?" I asked timidly, afraid that the sound of my voice would bring him back to the reality of our meeting and ashamed of my outburst of accusations.

Again he sat down next to me; again he took my hands in his. "You and I must be united against him, Isabelle, and make him see that France is our supreme interest. If he wants war, he will find the Queen and the Duke of Orleans ruthless in their country's defense. You are with me, Isabelle, are you not? You know how much I need your friendship, help...love."

He took my hands to his lips and kissed them passionately, then his expert mouth was on mine and his strong arms tightened around my body. It was a moment of supreme happiness and one that tied me to Louis forever.

Dusk was falling when we left the church. Clasping each other's hands, we advanced into the monastery gardens, smelling the sweet perfumes of roses and lilies, honeysuckles and lilacs. His tender voice whispered words of love, promises of loyalty, vows of faithfulness. I opened my heart to him, searching my inner self and confessing my feelings of disgust for my husband, sexual attraction for Bosredon. Louis understood. He is a wise mature man, who knows the frailty of the flesh, the weakness of the spirit, and has no wish to fight against human inclinations. Our spirits were at a unison, our bodies wanted each other, our minds had recognized that we belonged together.

From that afternoon on we have been inseparable, our passion deepening, our fear of John of Burgundy making our alliance firmer. Our relationship is frowned upon by many; the "scandalous life" we lead is the subject of countless pamphlets and sermons. In Louis I have found my kindred soul. His generosity more than matches mine; my caskets are filling with the beautiful jewels he acquires for me. I share his love for precious books and paintings, extravagant and refined entertainment.

The cares of the government are in our hands, but on the horizon looms the ever-present threat of John the Fearless. The horrid man humiliated us and made us flee Paris; he is like a spider spinning a web of destruction around us. I am baffled by the popularity that John has acquired in Paris but, then, I never trusted the mobs. They always follow the one that shouts the loudest and promises the most, they always dream of a future when streets are paved with gold and life is an eternal May Day.

My father's visit is a great success. He is bedazzled by the magnificence of our court, impressed with the amount of power that is in his daughter's hands, charmed with the beauty of the ladies. Louis and I are seriously considering finding him a wife in one of the great families of France. He would thus be able to visit me often—a delightful thought—and forget awhile the bitter disputes that divide him from his nephews when he is in Germany. We shall see.

Ludwig has announced his arrival in Paris. I will endeavor to have the two of you meet again next time that you are at court. Has Isabelle turned matchmaker? Not quite, I assure you, but I am so completely happy in my love for Louis that I want to share my happiness with the world, and you, my dearest friend, are-always present in my heart and mind.

Take care, Catherine, and remember that your visits are always treasured and looked forward to by your friend, Isabelle.

Chapter XVIII

The Last Meeting

The rain had been interminably falling from a leaden sky. The drops drummed monotonously on the grey roofs, the stones of the courtyard, the withered leaves that still lingered on the trees of the garden. A bright fire was crackling in the marble fireplace of her chamber, and the air smelled of pine and resin.

Soon her attendants would bring in a small table, set a damask cloth on it, gold cups and plates gleaming in the glare of the flames. A sideboard would be loaded with her favorite food, jugs and decanters filled with the ruby-colored wine she enjoyed, and by her hand, ready to be picked up, would stand her goblet of sapphire-blue glass where the carved figures of a love pageant revelers danced merrily. Then her ladies would curtsy deeply and leave her waiting for the companion that Anne would usher in presently.

Similar scenes had occurred many times before, and Isabelle knew their procedure by heart. But tonight she did not feel any excitement or expectation; the sight of her soft bed draped in silk and heaped with furs did not conjure up visions of voluptuous embraces and ecstatic raptures.

In that room, her little son was born, in that bed she held him in her arms for the first time, looked at his face, trying to recognize his father's features in his closed eyes, delicately penciled mouth, tuft of dark hair.

It was her twelfth child, but cherished by her more than his brothers and sisters, the token of a love that all thought sinful, the symbol of her youth and attractiveness. He only lived a few hours and she had never seen his eyes, she wondered what color they were.

Isabelle still remembered the frown of contrariety that had creased Louis of Orleans' face when she had told him that she was with child again, his child.

"Isabelle, have you considered that if this child is a boy, he stands in the line of succession after my brother's children?"

"I do not see why this worries you, my love. He will be a Valois, like my other boys, and the son on the throne of France would make up for the father who never obtained what he deserved. Unless you would rather have Valentina's son become King!"

He had smiled at her words and stroked her hair. "Still jealous of your cousin, are you Isabelle? And what does Valentina have to be jealous of? She is exiled from the court, has no influence on politics now that her father is dead, devotes herself to the upbringing of her children, or better, my children, to her books and music. But you, Isabelle, you have everything—power, wealth, influence. You have my love, too, if this is any great prize," he had added ironically.

"This is the most important thing in my life, Louis, but I know that, if you love me, you do admire and respect Valentina more."

"She has been a good and faithful wife, Isabelle. Perhaps too perfect for me; I am no saint and it is hard to live with a woman who is irreproachable. I have wronged her many times, but never a word of protest has come to her lips. Perhaps this is the reason I stopped loving her—I never cared for patient Griselda.

"But enough of this, dear. Come to my arms and tell me all about this new child that makes you so happy."

He should not have worried about the succession to the throne of France, their little boy was never to be a threat to his half-brothers.

She sighed. Life was unfair, at times. Why should little Charles be alive and well, who was conceived in hatred, the fruit of the rotten seed of a crazy father, and this baby die, the son of the man she loved, the living pledge of their belonging to each other?

She could never look at Charles without remembering his father, the man that had raped her and closed her heart to compassion. She wondered how Odette could willingly submit herself to his embraces, bear his daughters, wash his wounds, cut his hair and nails, caress his shivering body. Odette's love for the King—a miracle itself—had produced a miracle. Charles of Valois had become a man again, a sad, gaunt man with empty eyes and a vague smile, that is true, but no longer the howling beast that had haunted St. Pol for years.

But it was too late for Isabelle. Her love for her husband was dead forever, and her relationships with Louis de Bosredon and Louis of Orleans had awakened her senses with an intensity that she could not, would not ignore and wanted continuously satisfied.

A tall dark man entered the room and interrupted her daydreaming. A black cape lined with brown sable covered him from neck to foot; a ruby-colored hat in the form of a cock's comb emphasized his swarthy skin and long nose. His face showed a great handsomeness, but the small chin had lost its sharp contour and the cheeks had a hint of flabbiness in them. With a rapid gesture he tossed away his mantle and revealed a compact muscular figure attired in a blue jerkin and blue and violet hose. Fantastic animals, unicorns, narvals, were woven in the material of his doublet and his soft red boots sported extremely, pointed shoes.

Isabelle started at his arrival and a joyous smile of welcome dispelled the melancholy of her expression. She stretched out her hands to his kisses and motioned him to sit beside her on the low couch where she was lying. She was cuddling under a white ermine fur, red stones sparkled around her neck and a sold chaplet adorned with precious butter-flies shone in her dark, abundant hair.

She was a short plump woman with large dark eyes and a generous mouth. Her strong nose and chin were softened by her fleshy cheeks and her thick shoulders and ample bosom announced surrender to the advance of corpulence. The sluggishness of her body was belied by the vivacity of her eyes and movements and, while she lay indolently on the couch, a dormant energy ready to spring out at the first provocation emanated from her.

Strong, heady perfumes of rose and jasmine permeated the room, count-less trinkets of gold and gems adorned the furniture, silk tapestries were hung on the walls.

The beautiful, feminine room, the warm fire, the ostentation of wealth and luxury surrounding them struck the man, as they contrasted so sharply with the cold rainy night he had left outside, the dark malodorous streets he had ridden, the poorly-clothed men whom he had glimpsed as they entered taverns and brothels.

"I share your grief, my dear Isabelle," he murmured, kissing the pudgy be-ringed hand of the queen again.

"Louis, I have been waiting for you," she complained in a low throaty voice that still betrayed the harsh sounds of her mother tongue. "You know how much that child meant to me, and it is unfair that he was taken away from us."

"Poor little mite. Perhaps it is better this way, my dear, rather than having him known as a bastard, frowned upon by his brothers and sneered at by the whole court."

"I would have defended him," she cried passionately, "and nobody would have dared to slight him. He would have been one of the King's

Sons and the word "bastard" would not have been uttered in the same breath as his name. That role was filled when your son with Mariette son was born."

The rancorous tone of her words did not upset him. Louis shrugged his shoulders and did not pursue the subject.

"How do you feel, Isabelle?" he inquired. "I see sadness in your eyes, my love, and I want to dispel it. I am planning great celebrations to welcome you back after your confinement, but do not ask me for details, not another word will pass my lips!"

He got up and reached for a gold goblet, filled it with wine and greedily drank the spiced liquid. He looked restless; his hands kept fidgeting with the small dagger that hung from his belt.

She did not fail to notice his mood:"What is on your mind, Louis? I am sure that it is not the death of our son that has thrown such a pall of gloom on your countenance," she remarked bitterly. "Perhaps some gossip about us, more scurrilous than the ones that the good citizens of Paris have been able to fabricate until now, has reached and upset you, or is John of Burgundy's presence in Paris that worries you?"

He sat down heavily on a massive chair at the other side of the fireplace. "Neither," he answered. "But I want to share with you some pretty lines of a new pamphlet that is now the rage among our friends and enemies alike. You, my dear, have become a shepherdess, Belligere, while I am afraid that the name that they have chosen for me, Tristifer (mischief maker) is not very flattering. It is a long poem and I will have it copied and sent to you, as I can only remember a few verses, and these imperfectly, too.

"'Belligere a tout abandonne' Son coeur et sans parler donne,' (Belligere has left everything, and given her heart silently) while Tristifer 'Un pensement malvois avoit d'aimer ce qu'amer ne debvoit..' (Had an evil thought, to love the one he should not).

"According to the poem, our first meeting went more or less thus: 'Mais, ains que passe la nuitie sera tele choise exploitie tant seront d'amours'echaudes que Florentin sera fraudes.' (But before the night is through the deed will be consummated. They are so inflamed by love that Florentin will be cheated.)

"The story goes on endlessly in the same pastoral accents. It has long been the people's privilege to make fun of their rulers, harp on the imperfections of their betters, and I do not resent it. Let them gossip about us, invent calumnies, slander the court. Their lot is not very fortunate, Isabelle, and every day more I realize how privileged we are, we that the chance of birth has put above human considerations and every day's needs. Let them call me Tristifer, as long as the taxes they pay allow me to gamble, dance, own beautiful residences, priceless jewels. Let them sneer at Belligere, as long as you have absolute control over their lives. 'They know your power and their pamphlets are not strong enough to shake off their shackles."

Louis had got up and was pacing the room, absorbed in thoughts that he was trying to shape into words. The Queen was paying close attention to his words but she never interrupted him. "I am not afraid of my cousin of Burgundy," he said. "I dislike and despise him because I can see through the game that he is playing to win over the love of the Parisian populace, but I am not afraid of him. It is my great delight to thwart his plans of expansion in the Northeast, as I was able to do when I acquired the Barony of Coucy, or when the Duchy of Guelders became my fief. But, my lady, is this the aim of my life, the destiny I was sent on earth to fulfill? My thirty-fifth birthday is past, I have lived most of my life already, and what do I have to show for it? Great wealth, a splendid existence surrounded by beautiful things but, Isabelle, they were mine at birth, I did not fight for them, I did not earn them."

"You forget your children," she interrupted him at last, a note of impatience in her voice.

"My children?" he faced her angrily. "I could not even secure a kingdom for them, all my attempts were in vain and my

Children, the descendants of kings and rulers will have to content themselves, as I have, with the empty existence of the courtier, showing off their precious costumes, perhaps writing graceful verses, winning the favors of women, squandering money on gambling and betting. I wanted more for them. My life is an endless splendid pageant, but its meaning is lost to me. Isabelle, do you not sometimes hate this vacuous life that we lead, this eternal dance of balls, hunts, banquets, the petty rivalries and jealousies that haunt us?-"

He was not waiting for an answer and did not notice her silence.

"Our people do not love us," he went on, "and why should they when all we want is for them to work and sweat, suffer and die, while we continue on our merry-go-round of pleasures and luxury? Look at this beautiful room, Isabelle, at the precious objects that adorn it, at the glimmer of gold and silver that surrounds us. The goblet that you are holding is worth more than its skilled craftsman ever earned in all his life, and the same is true of everything touching our lips and covering our bodies."

Swiftly he picked up a cup lying on the sideboard and threw it against the carved mantelpiece. The metal gave out a hollow sound and its echo reverberated as the object rebounded on the tile floor.

The noise snapped him back to reality. An ironic smile curved his lips and he stepped quickly towards the Queen's couch. "I do apologize, Isabelle. Could you ever forgive me my gloominess and outburst? I came here to comfort you, my dear, and I only upset and saddened you more."

"Sometimes I cannot follow you, Louis," she answered. "I do not have misgivings about our lives. Power, real power, is in our hands, and if you do not have the name of King, the title is all you lack. Are you reduced to envying John of Burgundy, that ugly twisted man who cannot enjoy life but is forever plotting to increase his power and obtain more lands?"

"To create one's empire is a noble aim, my Queen. I do envy John his boundless ambition because it gives all his actions coherence, a direction that mine do not have. But enough of this. Let us be cheerful tonight, Isabelle. Have your ladies bring me some food, I beg you, I am getting famished."

Isabelle rang a gold bell at her side and the door opened immediately.

Anne de Semihier entered the room, followed by a young page in the King's livery.

"Thomas Courtehouse, what brings you here?" exclaimed a surprised Louis.

"My lord, his Majesty requires your presence immediately. He wants to discuss with you a matter concerning him and yourself."

"Thank you, Thomas. I will go to the King without delay. Alert my escort to be ready to leave in a few minutes."

The valet withdrew and Louis approached the Queen. "I am afraid I must bid you good night already, my Queen. I wonder what urgent message my brother has to share with me so late in the evening," he added uneasily. "The cards have warned me against a tall dark man with a red-hood, but I doubt whether Charles answers this description!"

"Be of good cheer, Louis. A dark woman is on your side and she will thwart the tall man's intrigues!" she laughed.

He kissed her hand and touched her lips lightly. "I will come back tomorrow, Isabelle. Have a good night."

The door closed behind him.

Chapter XIX

The Assassination Of Louis Of Orleans

It had stopped raining but large puddles had formed among the disjoined stones of the pavement and a light fog was descending on the sleepy streets of Paris. Not a soul to be seen, a few dim lights filtering through tightly closed windows. A shutter opened a crack, a woman leaned out an instant, anxious for her husband, who was late coming home. The massive door of a house adorned with an image of the Blessed. Virgin opened too, but no light could be discerned, no noise heard. Still, a group of ten, twelve men left the house and silently took their positions near a tall building that stood higher than most of the houses in the Rue Vieille-du Temple.

A few minutes later the quiet of the misty November night was interrupted by the arrival of a small procession of riders, the darkness pierced by the flicker of a few torches. Louis of Orleans had left the Hotel Barbette and was riding towards St. Pol. His escort accompanied him, two of his pages riding on the same horse. He felt cheerful and relieved, he was glad he had opened his soul to the Queen. He took off one of his gloves, he liked to feel the reins in his hands, and some of the verses of the new pamphlet came to his lips: "M'en sui au joli bois venus. Ou l'on celebrait a Venus.."

The verse died on his lips. Menacing shadows stood out from the darkness of the buildings, naked swords and hatchets gleamed in the pale light of the torches, an abrupt muffled order resounded: "Kill him! Kill him!" Sharp blades penetrated his body, wounded his flesh.

That is the end then, Louis thought. I do not want to die; I have so much to live for. "I am the Duke of Orleans," he shouted with his last breath, and never heard the answer: " You are the very one we want!" because his poor lacerated body was torn from the saddle and hammered with clubs, cut with axes, slashed open. A tall man with a red hood, the point of which covered his face, held a torch up high, giving his companions light to finish their task. He was observing the scene with steady eyes and did not flinch when a piece of the Duke's brain splashed on his mantle.

The night was pierced by screams: "Murder! Murder!" The frenzied horse carrying two of Louis' pages had galloped away from the scene of the assassination and the young men's shouts echoed in the darkness. The torch bearers had fled too and only a young page, Jacob van Melkeren, had remained by his Lord. To no avail, alas; his body had been too frail a shield against the fury of the assailants and now it lay, crouched next to Louis', scarlet blood gushing from countless wounds and fast clotting in the cold air.

"I think we have finished him," exclaimed the man with the red hood. "Quick, take the Rue des Blancs—Manteaux; there are horses waiting for you there. You, Jean Lormois, Pierre Baillet and the others, before you flee, start a fire in the house where you were lodged. That will keep these street dwellers busy for a while and give us more time to escape. Be of good cheer. You did a good job and the Duke will reward you handsomely. We shall meet at the palace of Artois."

"So be it, Raoul d'Auquetonville," answered Thomas Courteheuse. The young man felt no remorse. On the contrary, he was highly satisfied with his part in the ambush and confident that the Duke would be particularly generous to him for bringing the false message to the Prince.

Raoul's words were obeyed and a few instants later the assassins had left the street, while smoke started billowing from the house and screams of "Fire! Fire!" resounded along the Rue Vieille-du-Temple. The dark maze of streets engulfed them; the pawing of their horses alone broke the silence of the night. Here and there the yellow light of a candle was still burning; a barber was cutting a late customer's hair, a saddle-maker was sitting at his bench. Orders were shouted by the murderers in flight: "Extinguish your candles! Put out any light! Close your shops!' Their voices were menacing, their weapons still in their hands, their sticks ready to hit anyone who resisted their commands. Their passage left a trail of fear and obedience.

By then the Rue Vieille-du-Temple swarmed with people, doors and windows opening and closing incessantly, questions and answers shouted from one side to the other, incitements to fetch pails of water to quench the fire urged by frightened voices.

A crowd had gathered around the mutilated body of Louis of Orleans. They were horrified at the sight of the blood still gushing out and forming dark puddles in the mud, of a hand without glove severed from its wrist and lying on the pavement with distended fingers.

"Who is he? A man of quality, no doubt; look at the fur of his cape, the jewels shining on his jacket. And his horse, too, how beautifully harnessed. Poor animal, they did not spare it either!"

"Must be one of the Queen's lovers, one of those she squanders our money on, one of her young paramours" volunteered the shrill voice of a woman.

"There certainly has been a lot of movement in this street since the Queen bought Barbette," interposed a third voice. "Remember how quiet it was before, Amelot? Now horses and carriages are coming and going at all times of day and night and the music and noise coming from the palace do not let a poor Christian get his night's rest as he should."

"That is why I did not come out to help when I heard all the ruckus," a fat, older man justified himself. "I thought it was some pages of the Queen's household fighting as it is their wont, and I certainly did not want to meddle in their dispute!"

"Oh, yes, we know what a brave man you are, Simon, sneered another curious bystander. "Always first to raise the price of your bread, are you not?"

Some witnesses to the murder had run to the palace of Barbette in the meantime, and members of the Queen's and the Duke's households were rushing to the spot where Louis of France's body lay in the mud.

Gently they lifted the body and carried it to the house opposite the place of the murder, the dwelling of the Marshal de Rieux. The Marshal himself and some house guests were waiting at the door, and directed the sad procession to a large room where the body was laid on a table. Nobody could have recognized the handsome prince in that heap of maimed flesh: his head was split almost completely in two and a large gash went from his right eye to his left ear. It was as if he had been prey to a pack of wild animals. They had torn him to pieces, broken his bones, scattered his brain. The women who washed him of his blood and wrapped his body in fresh linen were crying at the sight of such cruelty, at the memory of the dashing man that had charmed so many.

* * *

Paris and the country had not loved Louis of Orleans as he had deluded himself they had. At the beginning they had admired the charming young prince, been proud of his good looks, recklessness, luck with women. Years of greedy taxation to gratify his love of luxury and pleasure, rumors of his unfaithfulness to his perfect wife, accounts of his immense gambling debts, dabbling in sorcery and necromancy, the women he had seduced and discarded— had destroyed his popularity. The King's insanity had prevented the people from bringing the same charges against their monarch, nay his malady had rendered Charles dearer and closer to them. They had not forgiven Louis his affair with' his brother's wife, the money he had exacted from them to purchase his dreams of glory outside the kingdom.

A man had been their champion against the exploitations of the King's brother and the Queen; a man had raised his voice against the inequities they suffered at the hands of the courtiers—John of Burgundy. He became their idol. They forgave him everything, even the murder of his cousin and rival, Louis of Orleans. John the Fearless, as he was called, had armed the men that had stricken Louis, paid the rewards of the murderers, sheltered them.

When his deed became known, his guilt certain, he was so sure his power, his sway over the Parisian populace, that not once did he deny his part in the murder which, with perfect arrogance, he vindicated as an act of justice that had delivered the country from a dangerous enemy.

The tragic chain of events that was to find its bitter end in the proclamation of an English prince as king of France knew a ludicrous beginning the day when the King allowed an advocate of the Duke of Burgundy to justify and even praise the murder of his own brother.

* * *

The Great Hall of the Hotel St. Pol was full to capacity when Jean Petit started his defense of his master. Daises and benches had been erected to seat the Queen, the Dauphin, the Royal Council, the Parliament, the great lords of the country. The bright reds and crimsons of the robes of honor they wore, the dark hues of their blacks and violets contrasted with the pale countenances of the people assembled, because all, from the young Dauphin to the humblest of the sergeants, were aware that the day's proceedings were of an extraordinary nature.

Surrounded by some of her attendants, the Queen sat motionless, her face bloated, her eyes red and swollen. Her hands, the color of wax, tormented the ivory beads of her rosary, her lips trembled slightly. A long shiver shook her when John of Burgundy made his entry, proud and disdainful, aware of his power, contemptuous of the assembly's condemnation. Her eyes focused on his face, the ugly coarse face framed by a red velvet hat, and she kept looking at him during Petit's oration. She hated the man and would never forgive him the death of her beloved, he had better be aware of her feelings. Her gaze shifted briefly to the side where the Orleans clan was gathered, their faces grim, their eyes full of the outrage. The new Duke of Orleans, handsome Charles, sat a little apart from his younger brothers. He was so similar to his father, yet so different, more delicate and fair, with fine features and dreamy eyes.

Jean Petit's voice went on incessantly, now high-pitched with indignation, now soft with pleading, as he heaped accusations on the dead man's memory. Louis of Orleans had been a bad influence at court, Petit said, he had burdened the people of France with taxes the revenues of which he had squandered for his pleasures, and his name had been cursed by high and low. Thanks should be rendered, therefore, to the man that had planned his assassination, because he had freed France of a criminal.

The audience sat stone-faced, speechless at such audacity. Even the representatives of the University and the bourgeoisie, those staunch paladins of Burgundy, looked stunned. A tear glistened on Charles of Orleans' cheek, rolled down quietly. A little triumphant smile played on the thick lips of John the Fearless and his hands relaxed their grip on his silver sword. He had won the day.

The King absolved his cousin of his murder, his uncles, the Duke of Berry and the King of Sicily bowed their heads in frightened agreement. Undaunted but powerless, only the Duke of Bourbon swore never again to set foot in that nest of inequity, the French court, which had let the criminal go free.

* * *

The children of Orleans, though, could not forgive and forget. On her deathbed, Valentina, their mother pledged them to revenge, begged them never to give the assassins of their father respite and, when the young Charles of Orleans married Bonne d'Armagnac, his party, made up of some of the noblest families of France, found its natural leader in the Count, Bonne's father, who picked up the torch of revenge against the Duke of Burgundy. Around Bernard of Armagnac rallied the noblemen who had loved Louis, the people of the southwestern and central parts of the country, who looked with growing concern at the ever increasing predominance of Burgundy and his allies in the Northeast.

Thus started the plundering and killing, the besieging of towns, the countryside put to fire and sword, the terrible waste of a kingdom. Everybody donned the liveries of the party they favored and soon towns and countryside swarmed with the red hoods and white crosses of the Armagnac and green hoods and St. Andrew's crosses of their rivals.

Truces and peaces would from time to time delude the people into thinking that the parties had reached an agreement, there was going to be a stop to the slaughter, but soon enough the civil war would start again, more bloody than ever… Paris, and with it the heart of the country, was at stake and the supreme power was within the easy reach of anyone brave and willing enough to try for it.

The capital was nominally in the hands of John of Burgundy, but little by little the powerful Corporation of Butchers had become the master of the city. Its leader was a wealthy skinner by the name of Simon le Coutelier, nicknamed Caboche. He and his followers, tanners, butchers, tripe sellers, people used to blood and slaughter, spread terror and violence all through Paris. Their symbol was a white hood and soon everyone was wearing it, forcing family and friends to do likewise, wrapping it around the heads of the saints at crossroads and in churches. Even the Dauphin, sickly, bony Louis, who loved festivities and dances, pretty ladies and boys, was made to wear the hated symbol, after that the butchers had had the effrontery of reproaching him for his dissolute way of living.

Eventually the Hotel Barbette itself was surrounded by the screaming mobs led by the skinner's son, and they were eager for massacre, plunder, death. The Duke of Burgundy rushed to its defense from the Hotel Artois where he lodged, for once afraid that the mobs would give in to their worst instincts and let out their rage against the royal family. They threw stones, broke window-panes, hacked the massive doors, shouted insults, demanded hostages. The Duke's presence, his persuasive words saved the Queen—she was a Regent, a God-appointed Queen; the King of England, perhaps even the Emperor would intervene if she were seized—but Ludwig of Bavaria, the detested leader of the "German party" was handed to the rioters, who beat him mercilessly and threw him to prison.

The Barbette episode was by no means the end of the excesses, the blood of hundreds of citizens reddened the gutters of Paris, the stench of slaughtered bodies poisoned the air, the lives of men and women lost their value. When slaughter and massacre subsided for a while, if famine and disease halted their harvest of death, and the gates of the city were reopened, the people of Paris, their senses sharpened by the horrors of the past and the uncertainty of the future, gave themselves wildly to the few pleasures that life still held for them. Taverns were crowded then, and brothels and baths, people danced in the streets and lit bonfires, organized processions and plays, swarmed the countryside. They deluded themselves, again and again, that peace had come at last, and the disappointment caused by yet another renewal of the war only intensified their rage and violence.

Chapter XX

The Queen's Secret Nights

The postern leading onto Rue de la Perle opened quietly and two figures wrapped in dark mantles and hoods slipped out quickly and were soon lost in the maze of streets surrounding the Hotel Barbette.

The April evening was mild. Soon they slackened their pace, loosened their capes and tossing their hoods away impatiently, revealed the faces of two women. They were heavily made up faces, to which the red of the mouth and cheeks and the dark shades around the eyes gave the aspect of grotesque masks. Although the masks were strangely similar, an attentive observer would have noticed the bright, jet-like eyes of one of the women, the sensual curve of her lips, the liveliness of her face, the proud bearing of her stout body. The other woman was smaller and much thinner, with gray tired eyes that contrasted sadly with the vivid colors she had applied to her face.

Lost in their thoughts, the two women walked in silence, the younger one a few steps behind her companion. Night was falling; the passers-by were few and hurried and nobody paid them attention.

They crossed the rue Vieille-du-Temple, the rue du Temple and directed themselves towards the rue St. Martin and the Halles quarter. On their left loomed the massive shadow of the perimeter walls built by Philippe Auguste, their ramparts and towers still intact, although a more recent, wider wall had been erected to encircle the ever-growing city.

The side streets joining the main thoroughfares—rue Trousse-vache, rue aux Oies, rue des Lombards, rue de la Ferronnerie—were dark and silent because, as their names revealed, they were the realm of shopkeepers and artisans that the late hour had hurried home.

The two women, though, walked on assuredly, as if the dimly-lit area was very well known to them and presented no danger. Eventually the torches lighting the streets became more frequent, while people of every description started appearing from the dark lanes and cobbled alleys converging onto rue St. Denis.

The attraction point was obviously the Halles, the covered market quarter-where day and night goods of all kinds were bought and sold, dishonest merchants publicly exposed on the pillory, prostitutes sold their favors, pimps, thieves, beggars worked at their trades.

The short, thin woman quickened her pace and addressed the other: "Your Majesty..." she started, and was interrupted by an angry sound of protest.

"For heaven's sake, Anne, cannot you take hold of yourself and try to remember to call me by my first name? After all, it is not the first time you have accompanied me and used it."

"I am sorry, Isabelle," murmured Anne de Semihier. "It takes me a while to get accustomed to this familiarity, but you know that I have not betrayed you yet and I will not tonight either."

"You have been a good companion, my dear," agreed an appeased Queen with a smile. "I promise you we will have a merry time tonight, and you will not regret that I have chosen you to accompany me in these little escapades. I think we should go to the 'Innocents' tavern, the one by the cemetery. Their wine is not worse than anywhere else and students and clerics seem to congregate at the 'Innocents' more than at the 'Mule' or the 'Heaume'."

Anne assented quietly and they directed themselves towards the rue des Innocents, leaving behind the menacing machicolated tower built by John the Fearless in the Artois palace.

The tavern that-Isabelle had chosen stood in the small square opening up in front of the cemetery church and a few dwellings of humble appearance. It was housed in a tall narrow building, and the sign dangling above the door represented chubby children being slaughtered by a sword held by an invisible hand.

The Queen and her attendant pushed open the worm-eaten creaking door, and the smell, smoke, and noise of a rather small room enveloped them. Thick gusts of smoke escaped from the brick fireplace and added layers of soot to the grayish walls against which a few wobbly tables and benches were set.

The people patronizing that tavern obviously belonged to the poorer strata of the population—their ragged clothing, emaciated faces, unkempt hair attested to that, although here and there a tonsured head could be noticed, suggesting a cleric or priest, or the colorful garb of a member of one of the guilds. The women sitting at the tables were few=-poor creatures with shrill laughters and hostile eyes, old tired bodies, and haggard faces.

The inn keeper, an old, thin man whose left arm was only a stump wrapped in a dingy rag and hanging from his neck, was deftly filling mugs and tankards from a row of kegs lined behind him, while his wife was taking a platter of strong smelling herrings out of the fire.

The two women's entrance was saluted by raucous voices and eager invitations by some of the tavern clients to join them. Isabelle took off her mantle revealing a full voluptuous figure that the low-cut dress bared at the neck and shoulders, and advanced boldly towards a table in a corner, followed by the more timid Anne.

Four men sat on a long bench in front of the table, on the surface of which tin and earthenware mugs had left wet red marks. Two of the men had tonsured hair, but neither wore the canonical dress, while the other two, rough and coarse looking, sported the white hoods that were the symbol of the Corporation of Butchers.

Impatient hands touched the women, lingered on their soft flesh, while each man claimed his own right to have them sit next to him. The blood rushed to Isabelle's cheeks, her eyes were shining, her mouth curved in a provocative smile. She willingly acquiesced to the men's caresses, readily consented to listen to and laugh at their obscene jokes. Anne de Semihier had followed her example and was tightly held in one of the butchers' embrace.

Presently the tavern keeper's daughter shuffled to their table carrying two more cups full of a vile looking red wine, and the youngest of the men, a thin, point-nosed youth of about twenty, paid with a silver coin. "You are in money tonight, Francois," marveled the man who was sitting at the other side of Isabelle. "Have you been picking pockets, or robbed the College of Navarre, at last?"

"Shut up, Dom Nicholas, or you will scare these ladies," Francois answered mockingly, squeezing Isabelle closer to him. "They are too refined to accept the company of thieves and-priests. I am a student, my chubby Isabelle, not a robber as this defrocked priest would like you to believe. I have traveled all over Europe, studied law at Bologna and Prague, philosophy at Oxford, and now the Sorbonne has me amongst its most devoted theology students."

"And the Prevost is looking for you to lock you up because you and your fellow students have been swiping house signs all over Paris," sneered Dom Nicholas.

"Bah! The Prevost can do nothing against a student that is protected by the University, ergo the Church. Is it not so, Philippe Cayeux?" asked Francois, addressing the butcher who was busy untying Anne's corset. The fourth man was noisily snoring, his head resting on the table and covered by his arms.

"What? Oh, yes, of course. Nobody can do anything against the orders of the defender of the Church, John of Burgundy, and his loyal Caboche. Long live the Corporation of Butchers! Long live Burgundy!" mumbled'a tipsy Caboche's follower intent on his lusty pursuit.

"I am not here to listen to arguments about Burgundy and Caboche and his skinners and tripe-sellers," complained Isabelle, but the priest interrupted her.

"Be careful of what you say, Isabelle," he whispered. "It is not wise to talk lightly of Caboche and his people. You know that John the Fearless is their friend, and they have promised to defend him and restore law and order to Paris."

"Law and order, whatever that means," Francois scoffed at him. "I have heard that the Cabochiens plan to lecture the Queen and the Dauphin on their dissolute lives, and if this is the kind of rule we can expect from our new masters, I, for one, can do without it. Reproaching an old woman and an effeminate youth will not help, let me tell you, unless the reforms—and we at the University are working on them—cut deeply into what is rotten and debased in our political system."

Isabelle was bored. She had heard similar words many times before, and lost her delusions a long time ago. She did not come to the Halles to listen to political discussions. She was eager for strong arms to hold her, and powerful bodies to possess her; coarse accents, acrid smells to obliterate voices and perfumes that had become too refined and languid.

Disguised as a woman of little virtue and means, free from the luxury that surrounded every act of her life, for a few hours she could give vent to her instincts, fulfill her sexual desires away from the structures of the court and the demands of her rank. Nowhere as in the quarter of the Halles was the contrast between the two worlds as marked; nowhere else did she enjoy her different personalities as much.

Perhaps, at the beginning, she had felt something akin to remorse when she had persuaded Anne de Semihier to accompany her in her night adventure, because Anne loved her husband and was faithful to him. But Isabelle was aware, as was everyone else at court, that Stephen had long before broken his matrimonial vows, and had a concubine and several children in Provence, whom he visited for long months every year. Anne, who had no suspicion of her husband's double life, was always ready to extol his virtues to the skeptical courtiers and had never noticed the leers and sneers with which her words were received.

When Isabelle had told her the truth, all color had drained from her face, but she had neither fainted nor shed a tear. After that, of course, it had been much easier to convince her to take part in her mistress' escapades. Anne had come to enjoy them, too. She looked happy and relaxed, with Philippe's head lost between her breasts and his hands busy under her skirts.

Isabelle supposed she would eventually end the night with Francois, when he and that boring priest stopped discussing the state of the country. She rather fancied Philippe Cayeux, though; Francois was too thin and verbose. Dress him in an elegant houppelande cape and pointed shoes; put a jeweled hat on his head and he would be undistinguishable from the languid youths that populated her court. Philippe looked lost to her tonight. He seemed completely taken by Anne's more delicate body, high pointed breasts, the reluctance that still lingered on the soul of the dame de Semihier.

Francois felt Isabelle's boredom and impatience. He embraced her possessively and bit her neck playfully, his breath heavy with the smell of onions and herrings. "Come on, my pretty, let us go to the baths on rue des Etuves. I need a better wine than this to wash my mouth of the taste of the sour rotten herrings Mere Tabary cooked tonight. Are you coming with your girl, too, Philippe?" he asked addressing the other couple. Philippe assented grudgingly and got up slowly, the wine and excitement making him uncertain on his feet.

The priest looked annoyed and dispirited at being left alone with a sleeping drunkard as a companion, and shouted a few obscenities while hurrying the servant to bring him more wine.

It felt good to be out of the smoky inn and breathe the fresh night air. The two couples proceeded slowly across the square, stopping from time to time to exchange kisses or whisper promises of future pleasures. The rue des Etuves was presently reached and they stopped in front of a wide, low-roofed house.

At their knocking, the door opened quickly and an old woman, barefooted and scantily dressed, ushered them into a small vestibule. Francois seemed to know the hag, and a few words were whispered and assented to, while shining coins changed hand, and were adroitly hidden in the folds of her dress. The old woman clapped her hands loudly and a girl, hardly more than a child, naked but for a short tunic that fell from under her breasts to her thighs, appeared and beckoned them to follow.

The hall they entered was wide and bright, with blue tiles on the floor and columned arches leading to side chambers. It was occupied by a number of tin or wooden tubs, each one surmounted by canopies of different colors falling on either side and making it similar to a small, private room. In front of some of the tubs long narrow tables had been placed, covered with white cloths and set with plates and cups.

The girl directed Isabelle and Francois to a tin tub covered with green drapes and invited them to undress while more hot water was being added to the tub and a table moved in front of it.

Isabelle undressed slowly, taking pleasure in the stares that her full body attracted, casting secretive glances at Francois' figure, judging his muscles, his thin, well-shaped legs.

As soon as they were in the tepid water, the man started caressing her, playing with her breasts, running water through her hair. He was in a buoyant mood; perhaps, as the priest had hinted at, he had robbed a college, after all. Unfortunately, she did not care for his thin, angular face, short bristly hair, small piercing eyes. His body was not unattractive, though, with well-developed muscles and a long thick member that excitement had swollen and hardened.

She glanced in the direction where Anne and her butcher were bathing; what a strong powerful body he had. She liked the way his muscles sculpted his chest, found even his stomach swelling in a little paunch attractive. Some other time, perhaps, she would meet Philippe Cayeux and he would take her to bed and give her the pleasures of which his potent body must be capable.

She turned to Francois only to meet his eyes staring at her quizzically. "Too bad, Isabelle, your skinny friend has got the prize, and you must make do with poor Francois de Loches!"

She smiled, deciding to forget about the butcher and enjoy the cleric's company. She had seen Francois before, and never alone. He might be a good lover, after all.

As if reading her thoughts, he bragged: "You will not be too unhappy with your lot, tonight, Isabelle! But let us eat and drink first. I will need all my strength to judge from that fat body of yours!"

The young attendant that had filled the tub, a boy of about ten, was coming back holding a jug and two cups. He was followed by the girl with the short tunic, who carried a tray loaded with plates containing chicken parts, broad-beans, cheese, and bread.

Isabelle felt famished and attacked her food with great gusto. Her companion was doing likewise, but kept observing her with an attention that did not escape the Queen. "Can you not wait until we have finished eating?" she asked, pretending to equivocate his stare.

"I do not know why your face is so familiar to me," he wondered aloud.

"I have seen you before, too," she answered, "if not at the 'Innocents' perhaps at 'La Biche' or 'Le Cheval Blanc'."

"I know that," he said, "but it is not exactly what I mean.

Your face is as well known to me as any of the holy images that stand at the crossroads or hang on the walls of the churches. Where do you live, Isabelle?"

"I live in the quarter of Marais, and that is all you will learn about me, my handsome. We did not come here, either of us, to answer questions about our past or our lives!"

"You are right, Isabelle. Whoever you are, wherever you come from, you suit me fine tonight. Hurry up with your food, though, I want to take you to one of the chambers and show you what I have learned traveling across Europe!"

They were not going to be the only occupants of that room. From two of the beds, big bulky affairs barely protected by thin curtains, came groans and whispers, sighs and grunts that excited the couple even more.

Quickly, they got rid of the towels draped around them and plunged into the soft warmth of the assigned bed. Francois did indeed reveal himself as an ardent, imaginative lover, who could awaken new sensations in her sated body, and the noises coming from the other alcoves, the acrid smells of their bedding, only sharpened the intensity of Isabelle's sexual enjoyment.

Much later, when the Queen and her lady-in-waiting met again alone outside the Public Baths and started on their way to Barbette, each could read in the other's face a similar languid appeasement.

Chapter XXI

A France Divided

Brittany had chosen the Armagnac camp and Philip of Vermandois was wholeheartedly convinced that, God and Justice sided with the heirs of the slain Duke of Orleans. When the more moderate citizens of Paris decided to put a halt to the horrors that had made a hellish place out of the once beautiful city and the Armagnacs were called in to bring peace and order, Philip was overjoyed and decided that the time had come for Catherine and himself to go back to the court.

Caboche and his accomplices had fled the city and joined John of Burgundy in Flanders, where the Duke, who had not resigned himself to the loss of the capital, was biding his time to make an offensive reentry. Very soon Armagnac showed himself a ruler as pitiless and authoritarian as his predecessors, though, and a new reign of-terror started for the unhappy city.

It was then that the new King of England, Henry the Fifth, decided to wage war against the divided, rudderless country, claiming inalienable rights to his French inheritance.

The first phase of the perennial war between the two countries dated back almost a hundred years, when Edward of England, a grandson of Philip the Fair through his mother, had claimed his superior right to the French crown, held by a prince that was not a direct descendant of the French monarchs. In the bloody years that followed, France had suffered crushing defeats and lost large portions of her territory and only the wise policy and acumen of Charles V had rescued her from anarchy and regained most of her lost provinces.

Henry's right to the French throne was even weaker than his

grandfather Edward's, as he himself was only the son of a prince who had usurped the crown, but the young king had decided on the conquest of France, both to serve his ambition and enhance his popularity at home.

Henry's bellicosity was immediately echoed by the eager French nobility and even Philip of Vermandois, who was then sixty-eight years old, decided that it was his duty and privilege to throw his lot with the Armagnacs, who, more than ever now, stood for France, and left his home to join the powerful army that was being assembled against the English.

It was a long but uneventful trip from the breezy coast of Brittany to Paris, across endless miles of countryside where the ripe wheat, golden under the sun, was waiting for the sickles of the harvesters, and green meadows **of** hay were being cut by scantily-clad peasants. The trees had lost their blossoms and not acquired their fruits yet, and the emerald of their leaves shone brightly against the red of the poppies and the yellow of the buttercups covering the grass. The peaceful countryside belied the fights that had been tearing apart the country for so long, but the closer Catherine and Philip got to Paris, the more desolate the landscape became, the more sullen and scarce the peasants in the fields, the more dilapidated the aspect of houses and farms.

Once in the city, they separated; he to join the King's and Dauphin's people at St. Pol, she with Bernardine and a couple of her maids, to go to Barbette, ready to accompany Isabelle to Vincennes in the next few days.

The Queen looked sad and crestfallen. The news had reached Paris that the King of England had assembled a mighty force and was ready to cross the Channel. Every French nobleman wanted a part in what they saw as a triumphant campaign, in which the son of the usurper would be thrown out of the country he claimed his own in shame and blood.

"Louis de Bosredon wants to go too," she complained, "and Pierre de Giac and even Jean de La Tremoille. Of course I will not allow it. What would we poor women do, left without any friends and companions?"

"I do not see how you can prevent them from following their noble instincts, your Majesty," Noble instincts in those three dissolute rascals! Catherine hoped Isabelle would notice the irony of her tone. "Even my husband wants a part in this glorious adventure and he so old and tried by life. The Constable d'Albret, who will be the supreme commander, is not much younger either."

"You are such a comfort to me, Catherine!" Isabelle exclaimed ironically. "You always seem to find the words that will hurt me and enjoy being sarcastic. Do not look so surprised, my dear, that is exactly what you do, time and again! Unfortunately, I am used to you by now," she added with a quick smile, "and I still like you well enough to have prepared a surprise for you, which, I hope, will sweeten your disposition and render you a more agreeable companion. I hope the surprise I have for Louis de Bosredon will make him as happy and convince him that he would be making a serious mistake if he joined the campaign against my wishes!"

An uneasy laughter accompanied her words and she reclined more comfortably in the soft chair with wheels where she sat most of the time.

Isabelle had become very fat, her legs ached; she found walking painful and used that ingenious chair as often as her vanity permitted her to. She did not age well, and the young men and women with whom she loved to surround herself, agile and slender as they were, with fresh complexions and shining hair, emphasized the tired lines of her face, the flabbiness of her flesh. The courtiers pretended not to notice that their once charming Queen had, grown into an ugly old woman, and lavished the same compliments, fawned on her in the same way as they had been wont to do for so long. Isabelle loved her people and was extremely generous to them. She loved flattery also, and naturally enough, she would get crossed at Catherine sometimes because, try as she might, nothing could induce her to deceive the Queen.

Louis of Orleans' assassination, like the ugly madness of the King before that, had been a turning point in Isabelle's life—to neither event she had teen able to react rationally and compassionately, and both had unleashed her worst instincts. The pious, loving Queen, wife and mother, had become an unfaithful wife, an indifferent mother and eventually a woman whose only ambition seemed the satisfaction of her sexual instincts—she had innumerable lovers at court and often stooped to picking up men from the street, the tavern, the market, wherever and whenever her lust demanded it.

She did not justify herself any longer. Fate (and John of Burgundy) had deprived her of the man she had loved above others. Her life was empty and useless, she felt like a boat tossed in a sea of stormy waters, her anchor gone, her sails ripped to rags. Power had slipped away too, and rested now in the hands of Burgundy and Armagnac, who used her as a pawn in their endless war.

And Catherine, who had loved her since their childhood, only seldom let her impatience at the Queen's behavior show through. Isabelle did not need criticism, she knew, but love and patience because, not withstanding, her paramours and flatterers, the Queen was indeed lonely and abandoned, and had hardly anybody on whom she could count.

That night, when once again Catherine went to Isabelle's apartment, the rooms were bright with torches and sweet-smelling candles, the music of harps and flutes, lutes and viols filled the air. Beautifully dressed men and women were everywhere, sitting on chairs or cushions on the floor, dancing, talking, embracing in the shade of the columns. A huge table covered in red damask was in a corner, groaning under silver plates full of delicacies, tankards and goblets of intricate design.

The Queen sat on her chair, magnificently attired in blue damask, her graying hair covered by a cone-shaped hat embroidered in gold and turquoises. At her feet, on a velvet cushion, reclined Louis de Bosredon, as handsome as ever, the sparkle of his jewels attesting to the Queen's favor that had made him the most detested man at court for years. Not far from his mother, the center of an admiring group of men and women, was the Dauphin, Louis.

He was a young man of medium height, very thin and small boned, with a long narrow face dominated by the pendulous nose of the Valois, and dark eyes, dull and indifferent. He was married to one of the Burgundian princesses, but no issue had come from that union and widespread rumors hinted that he was more attracted to the young men that made up his mother's and bride's entourages than to the pretty ladies of the court. That night, Louis of Guyenne's body seemed to be racked by an insistent cough that made the eyes of the people present turn to him again and again.

Laughter and words floated in the air, and the sweet sound of the music played by a group of young girls, scantily dressed in the colors of the rainbow.

A woman wearing a gold circlet around her head from which a thin silver gauze descended to veil her naked shoulders, approached Catherine.

"We have not seen each other for many years, Catherine the German," she said, and with a start Catherine recognized Anne of Bourbon.

She blushed at the appellation, which the woman had not pronounced in kindness. "My name is Catherine of Vermandois, my Lady," she corrected her and Anne smiled ironically.

"Of course, the Queen did mention that you had married the old Sire of Vermandois. I beg your forgiveness."

Catherine looked at the woman that Ludwig had married, the wealthy lady of great family for whom he had carelessly discarded his loving mistress, and noticed, with satisfaction, her thick lips and yellow teeth, the dark skin and brown frizzly hair that the low cut of a dark green gown emphasized to great disadvantage.

Catherine smiled and curtsied lightly to the princess, and rising from her curtsy she stood tall and erect, proud of her slim body, high round breasts, golden hair that white had not touched, and let her rival examine her at her pleasure. She understood from the poisonous scrutinizing glance encircling her that Anne knew of her relationship with her husband, and was perhaps still jealous of the pretty woman that Ludwig had loved.

"The Duke of Bavaria must have mentioned your name because I understand that you were children together at his father's court," said Anne, "and I am sure that he would love to reminisce with you."

"Is his Highness in France?" asked Catherine, and she tried to mask the eagerness of her voice and calm the sudden flutter of her heart.

"He is in France, yes, but unfortunately not in Paris," Anne announced with indifference. "He is at the court of his nephew the Duke of Brittany, and not due back for a few weeks."

Catherine's heart sank. Ludwig in Brittany and she in Paris! Were they destined never to meet again? Her uneventful, calm life with Philip, so far away from the atmosphere of the court, the slow passage of time, had made her forget how much that man had meant to her. But once back in Paris, confronted by the woman who held the place that she had coveted years before, Catherine felt agitated and nervous, wishing to be away, safe in her Brittany manor and, at the same time, terribly disappointed that, once again, she would not see Ludwig.

Anne of Bavaria left her, nodding her head briefly, and took the hand of a man who had been standing next to her during her short exchange of words with Catherine.

His wife is probably not faithful to him, after all, thought Catherine, and the knowledge left her strangely elated.

The Queen's voice roused her from her thoughts.

"My dear friends," Isabelle started, "Louis de Bosredon has long been of invaluable help to your Queen. I know that I owe him more than I can ever repay him for, but to show him how highly he is regarded by those who have him dear, and especially the King and myself, I am presenting him with the castle of St. Ouen and all the lands adjoining **it."**

'So that is how you won over his wish of going to fight the English,' Catherine thought, looking at Louis de Bosredon's face.

He was surprised, no doubt about it, and extraordinarily pleased, as the prize he had been granted was regal indeed.

St. Ouen was the place where Isabelle liked to play shepherdess kept her pigeons, sheep, grew her favorite flowers, where, as she was fond of saying, she could pretend she was back in Bavaria, a shy young princess unaware of her high destiny. It was, besides, an extraordinarily profitable property, very large and well endowed with stables, fields, and vineyards. The castle that stood amidst a vast park rivaled in beauty with that of Vincennes, the most exquisite furniture adorning it, splendid tapestries and carpets hanging on its walls, refined objects of gold, silver, ivory and precious stones having been collected there since the days of John the Good.

A hushed whisper of wonder rippled among the courtiers, while Louis de Bosredon got up to his feet quickly, took Isabelle's hand and covered it with kisses. She beamed at him, a doting older woman lost in the wonders of a young love, Catherine could not help thinking even if she knew that their relationship dated back many years and Louis de Bosredon had long ago lost the fresh appeal of first youth.

The music started again, and a group of girls, barely veiled by thin gauzes, started a lascivious dance, their hair shiny mantles of gold and ebony, their voluptuous breasts showing high and firm, their nipples painted a bright red. The eyes of the men focused on the pliant bodies, slender legs, the pubic hairs covered by diamond nets, the enticing movements of the dancers, but the wonder and jealousy that Isabelle's gift to her favorite had aroused were still palpable in the air. Pierre de Giac, another of her favorites, wore a sour little smile and there was spite on the countenances of most men, a mixture of contempt and envy on those of the women.

Apparently unaware of the complex feelings that she had aroused among her people, the Queen had reclined on her chair and followed attentively the movements of the dancers. Bosredon's hand was on her breast and from time to time he would whisper something to her that made her smile, or kiss her throat and neck.

Soon a couple started dancing, then another, while a few looked for the compliant privacy of a dark corner or a side chamber. The big hall was very warm, and a host of young pages were gently shaking huge multicolored feather fans to cool the air.

Catherine was soon surrounded by attentive gentlemen, eager to hand her a cup of spiced wine, a sugared almond, a sweetmeat, teach her the latest steps of a dance.

Pierre de Giac, especially, was very solicitous, proclaiming time and again that it was very selfish of the Queen to allow Catherine to stay in the country, while her grace and beauty would be a prize ornament to the court of France. More than ever, the golden of her hair was praised, her emerald eyes, the shapeliness of her breasts, the slenderness of her neck.

Little by little, the long years spent in the solitude of Brittany with Philip as her only companion were forgotten; the wisdom she had acquired living with that good man quickly slipped away, as the matron of forty-five, the lady of Vermandois, became once more the girl of twenty, the pretty flirty German friend of the Queen. The spicy wine was heady, the room smelled sweetly of thyme and violet.

Catherine found herself reclining on soft cushions, felt eager hands touch her breasts, caress her skin, demanding lips press hers. Her body was yielding and responding, eager for the acts of love that she had not known for so long.

All of a sudden, the golden shimmering glow cast by bronze candleholders was shattered; she opened her eyes and with a shock recognized the shadow in front of her. It was Ludwig!

Catherine got up with a start, pushing away the man (what was his name?) her mind repeating dully: 'He can't be here, even his wife said he is not in Paris.' Her heart was dancing wildly, though, and the sheer happiness of seeing him again brought her back to her senses quickly.

Her partner was gone and Ludwig sat next to her, watching her intently as she tried to recover from the passionate encounter with her admirer.

While arranging her hair and dress, Catherine stole a glance at him. Time had dealt kindly with Ludwig of Bavaria. He was stouter than she remembered, but not fat. With a pang of nostalgia she recognized the gold of his hair and beard, now streaked with silver; his blue eyes had remained as bright as they were in her memory, the fine traits of his face as clean-cut and harmonious as when he was a young man.

A sense of triumphant excitement invaded Catherine. "He came here for me! Isabelle must have told him I was back, and he came. His wife is here, but he does not care. He has not forgotten me, after all!"

As if he had read her thoughts—but then, her mind had always been transparent to him—"It has been too long, Catherine," he said. "The court was not the same place for me once you were gone and I am overjoyed to see you again, as splendid and passionate as you were when we parted."

"Our separation did not break your heart," she answered, pretending to believe his lie, "and you married the woman of your dreams after all. Anne de Bourbon is one of the noblest ladies of the kingdom, and of the wealthiest. She gave you sons and daughters and made you even more influential at court, if I have to believe the rumors that you will be made Constable of France."

A complacent smile lit up his face, "Anne has been the right wife for the Duke of Bavaria, it is true. My sons are healthy, my daughters pretty. They are the closest friends of their cousins Valois, and I know that I will be able to arrange the most satisfactory marriages for them. Isabelle has rewarded me generously for my services to her and her children and I may indeed become Constable of France.

"Isabelle does not like or trust Armagnac; he is a vulgar and coarse soldier without either pity or nobility in his breast, but now that Orleans is dead, he must be her natural ally against Burgundy. Paris was a nightmare for us, when the Cabochiens ruled the mob. They stole, plundered, started fires, massacred innocents. As you know, they resented my influence at court, could not wait to lay their hands on me and they would have killed me if Burgundy had not intervened. He understood that murdering the Queen's brother would be going too far, and prevented the early demise of your faithful servant," he ended with a sneer. "But I did have a taste of prison, and I assure you that never again will I allow anyone to throw me there.

"But enough of me, Catherine. Do tell me about your life in detail, and how is that good old gentleman with whom you forgot me."

By then she had completely regained control of herself and launched into a long description of her life in Brittany and occupations there.

Ludwig interrupted her. "But you are relating the tedious life of a sexagenarian, my dear, and I can well understand how, after so dull a diet, even a lackluster man as Robert de la Ferte must have looked as brilliant as a peacock." He was referring to the courtier with whom he had found her, and Catherine's sense of guilt made her resent his implications.

"Vermandois may well be a monotonous man, Ludwig, but even the most dazzling gentleman sometimes knows the pains of infidelity and neglect."

He followed her glance. Anne was locked in the arms of the gentleman in green, and seemed completely oblivious to the people surrounding them.

He did not wince. He sounded perfectly indifferent when he answered. "Your ideas about fidelity sound very outmoded, my friend. I do not begrudge Anne her admirers, and she is friendly with the ladies that honor me with their benevolence. In Paris, things are done differently, as you may remember, if you care to go back to the days when you were good enough to make me the happiest of men."

"The happiest of men! How can you be so smooth-tongued and false, Ludwig!" she cried. "You know very well I was no more than a pastime to you, and you never thought of marrying me, even if Isabelle and the King had given me the most attractive dowry and looked with favor to our union, which I know they were going to do. You liked me well enough in your bed, did you not, and I enjoyed it too! But please do not use this courtier's language with me, Ludwig, because we have known each other too long to put a mask of hollow politeness on our faces when we talk."

"You have not changed that much, after all, my impetuous Catherine. Yes, you are right; I liked you in my bed. More than that, I always loved you or, at least, you are the woman for whom I have cared the most. But I never intended to marry you and I realize now that I was right, for both my sake and yours. Our lives have been happy, even if we went our separate ways, and it is sweet to find each other again now, when the Autumn of our lives has come.

"It is the autumn, Catherine, fruit-bearing and mild, with sudden explosions of hot days and the calm languor of serene evenings, it is not the chilly winter, when snows cover the earth and the trees are barren. We can still enjoy each other, my Catherine, and rekindle the flames that were ours one day!"

She closed her eyes. The familiar voice sounded as enticing and passionate as she had remembered it in her dreams, and his words found an echo in her heart. He was right—it was not winter yet, for either of them, and in his arms she would find the pleasures of her youth once more, in his kisses the happiness that was hers when he had loved her

Ludwig, she thought. I know your selfish, arrogant nature. You used me and threw me away, held my body and soul, and only played with them. Your love debased me, caused me tears and pain. Still, it is as if a part of me perversely enjoyed your cruelty so much that I long to be in your arms again, and feel your mouth on mine and be possessed by you more than anything else in the world.

She yielded to his embrace, and her body rediscovered his with exquisite pleasure -the long legs, taut muscles, the soft texture of his skin, his never-forgotten scent.

His passion matched hers, as if the love-making of one night had to make up for the long years of their separation, the words of a few hours reveal all the feelings that had been buried deep in their souls.

It was easy to forget then that she belonged to another man, the sacred vows she had pronounced when she had become his wife, the trust Philip had in her. When Ludwig's arms encircled her, and his body pressed hers, Catherine could easily forget the past, her duties, and give herself up completely to her passion for the man. Chilly winter loomed on the horizon; she wanted to enjoy her autumn to the full, gather in her arms all the fruits and flowers of the season.

In the days to come, Catherine seldom saw Philip, busy with war preparations.

Feeling guilty and remorseful, she would look at him and discover how old and tired he had become—or perhaps, surrounded as she was by the young people of the court and sharing the bed of a vigorous man, she was now more aware of her husband's age. She hoped that court gossip would not reach him, and he would never realize that she had changed, betrayed him and the better part of herself.

Chapter XXII

Agincourt

Catherine saw Philip for the last time in September, when the long siege of Harfleur by Henry of England and his men had ended and the decimated English army was headed north.

Her husband was confident of victory, sure that the French knights would force the English to battle and destroy them. The Constable d'Albret, the supreme commander of the French, was a wise general, the princes and knights were valiant, and their number, five times that of the enemy, made the outcome of the fight certain. The safety of the Kingdom required that the King and his heir remain behind, but all the other great lords were anxiously waiting for the signal to go—the Dukes of' Orleans, Bourbon, Alencon, Bar, the Counts of Nevers, Eu, Richemont, the Marshal Boucicault, Master Jean de Craon. While the shrewd John of Burgundy, friendly with the English and unwilling to strengthen the Armagnac camp, had not offered his help, his two brothers, Nevers and Brabant, had been among the first to join the French army.

Philip held Catherine in his arms lovingly, caressing her hair and looking into her eyes anxiously, as if afraid, yet desirous, that sorrow and dismay for his departure would be reflected in them.

"Do not fear, my little wife," he said, "I will come back; we will return to our home together and our life will resume its placid course. Once the threat of an invasion has been thwarted, peaceful and prosperous years await the country. An English defeat will also mean a less arrogant and belligerent Duke of Burgundy, I would surmise, and, free of his menacing presence, the Count of Armagnac will be able at last to restore the order and peace that the country craves."

"Why do you feel you have to go, Philip?" she asked, sick with guilt end remorse. "So many younger men are staying behind; even the Queen's brother has chosen to remain at his sister's side. Do you not think I need your protection?"

"My dear," he answered sadly, "when his King called, my son left his family and lands without hesitation, knowing what was asked of a Breton lord and ready to do his duty and die if necessary. Do you want me to be less than my own son, and so attached to life that the thought of danger is enough to make a coward out of an old man who has always tried to behave honorably? No, Catherine, you would not want that from the man you promised to love and respect. As for the young courtiers, here at Vincennes, or Barbette, their attitude is despicable, but not unexpected in men that have chosen to betray their King and do so shamelessly."

His words, the mournful tone in which they were uttered, sent shivers of shame and pain through her body. Her poor old Philip, who had been such a considerate, affectionate husband, betrayed by one of the very men he deeply despised.

"God," she promised silently, "if you allow him to come back safe to me, I will break my relationship with Ludwig, I will again be the chaste, loyal wife I once was."

But God did not hear her words or perhaps he did not believe her and did not want to enter into a compact with Catherine, the sinner. Philip was among the thousands of knights slain at Agincourt, on that October day, 1415.

The rain had made the fighting ground into a slimy mire, where the French knights, encumbered by their heavy armors, were an easy target for the skillful English archers, while their horses, hit by the missiles, tried in vain to save themselves and their masters, but instead, stumbled and slid in the mud.

Was Philip killed by a hatchet handled by one of those invincible bowmen, in the heat of the battle, or was he murdered in cold blood later on, when the implacable English king ordered no prisoners to be taken, and had thousands upon thousands of French slaughtered by his men? Philip's equerries were massacred too, and Catherine never knew the truth about the death of her noble husband.

Only the great lords of the Kingdom had their lives spared because of the ransom they would bring to King Henry, and they followed the conqueror to Calais and thence to England.

Seven thousand Frenchmen remained in the plain of Agincourt;

poor, naked, maimed bodies that the peasants of the neighboring villages and farms stripped of anything valuable they still wore, poor brave swash-bucklers to whom the lessons of Crecy and Poitiers had taught nothing, who still believed that only gentlemen knew the art of war, and were butchered by English peasants.

The court at Vincennes was in shock. Everybody had lost a friend or relative in the massacre, everybody had a friend or relative languishing in England, captive of the greedy king who had set enormous ransoms on their heads.

Unbearable remorse filled Catherine's heart, but it was mixed with a sense of relief too—at least, Philip had died doing what he thought was his duty, still unaware of her betrayal and certain of the rightness of his cause.

For a few days, after the news of the disaster reached Paris, the mere sight of Ludwig would render her shameful and desperate. Her feelings towards him were complex—she did despise the man that had chosen the relaxed role of counselor and advisor to the Queen, while so many of his friends and comrades were being massacred by the enemy, yet, as she loved him, she was thrilled and grateful that Ludwig was alive and close to her.

Catherine did not have much time to grieve over her husband's death or to listen to her tortured conscience, though, because her first duty lay with Queen Isabelle, who was in a state of deep despondency. Many of her friends had been killed and she especially mourned the death of Pierre de Giac and Louis de la Tremoille, her lovers of many years, who had redeemed their useless lives at court with a glorious death in the mud of Agincourt.

Her face swollen with tears, her eyes reddened, Isabelle would lean on Louis de Bosredon's shoulder and beg him to cheer her up, to sweep away her sad thoughts. She wanted her ladies around her too, expecting a serene countenance from women who had just heard of the death of a husband, lover, brother, son. She seemed to rely on Bosredon more than before, he was the only one who had been left to her, and that upstart was giving himself the airs of an absolute master.

The disaster of Agincourt had affected Ludwig too; he admitted to a feeling of guilt for being alive and free while most of his friends were dead, and it seemed to Catherine that the election of the Count of Armagnac to Constable of France, a position he had coveted, did not upset him as much as it would have before Agincourt.

Before...after...Agincourt. It seemed then that life could be divided into two long periods, one of which, filled with joy and laughter, amusements, and happiness, had ended on that October day, while the second one, gloomy, tearful and somber, had just started but was stretching to infinity.

* * *

Winter soon set in, a long, cold winter that brought with it more death and dismay. The Duke of Berry died and was buried in the beautiful cathedral of Bourges, next to the body of his beloved wife, Jeanne, the young Duchess that had saved the King's life on Ludwig's wedding day, so long ago. The Dauphin of France, Louis, was carried by the cough that had racked his frail body for so many months, and his younger brother, John, left the court of Valenciennes, where he lived with his bride, for Paris, to assume his new title of heir to the throne.

Terror reigned in Paris, as Armagnac and his men were just as cruel and oppressive as the Burgundians had been before them. A shadow of blood and death seemed to accompany the Constable wherever he went, and everyone was afraid of him, even Louis de Bosredon, whom Armagnac pointedly ignored when he visited the Queen. Once or twice Catherine overheard the Count reproach Isabelle for the extravagance of her life and the consistent presence of Bosredon at her side.

"The people of France will tolerate no scandal surrounding their Queen, your Majesty," he would say angrily, "and while they will accept a less than perfect behavior from a King, no breath of gossip should touch his wife. Our enemies confront me with examples of your generosity to your courtiers, and any gift or trinket you give to your favorites further discredits our cause."

The proud Queen would remain silent, smarting under the injustice of the man's words—if there was a time when life at court was decorous and gloomy it was then, in the aftermath of Agincourt—but too afraid to contradict him.

Armagnac also resented Ludwig's presence, the Queen's brother that he considered the leader of a German party favorable to his enemies. This hostile group included even Catherine, the "German friend of the Queen" and she had to remind herself of the little importance of her role at court to dispel the anxiety that the opposition of such a formidable personage caused.

Apparently, though, nobody and nothing were of too little consequence for the master of the Kingdom, and a letter that reached Catherine from Brittany emphasized the complete control that the Constable exerted over the country.

One of the men that she had left in charge of the estate wrote imploring her to use her influence with the Queen because Jean of Vermandois, the young grandson of her husband, had been granted the manor of Vermandois and all its surrounding lands, farms, cottages and had already sent his people to take possession of them.

Unfortunately, Catherine knew she could do nothing against somebody protected by the all-powerful Armagnac, and when she sought Isabelle's help, her friend sadly confessed her own impotence.

Another letter reached Catherine, signed by the unknown Jean of Vermandois, and tears of commotion rose to her eyes when she read it, because the young lord "in consideration of the love that my lamented grandfather bore you," kindly allowed her to return to the castle that she had called home for so many years and select the objects that were most dear to her.

Catherine went back to Brittany with a heavy heart. She knew full well that it was the last time she was to see the familiar landscape, the fascinating, ever-changing ocean, the solid building of which she had been the happy mistress.

She went back because she wanted to see those places once more; she had no desire to hoard plates or furniture.

She would take solitary walks along the wind-swept beach and, silently, another woman would join her. She would look at the intruder curiously, noticing her blonde hair, green eyes, delicate features. The stranger was so similar to her, yet different, as if her limpid eyes had only gazed upon scenes of goodness and generosity; her serene brow only entertained thoughts of loyalty and friendship.

Many of the objects that filled the castle rooms were dear to Catherine. Innumerable times she had touched the polished wood of tables and chests, walked on the soft carpets, caressed the intricate patterns of the tapestries.

She felt the weight of memories and regrets more keenly than anywhere else in her bedroom, where her wide, curtained four-poster stood, massive and yet graceful in the folds of its green silk and golden brocade. There every object had been carefully, lovingly chosen by her or Philip. The sheets and blankets on the bed still retained the shape of her body and the perfume of her skin. From those windows her eyes had roved over the sea and her lungs filled with the pungent scent of the waves.

To select one thing instead of another, choose this article and discard that, would have meant choosing and selecting memories, remembering an incident and forgetting another—she would not do it. Her life in Brittany as the Lady of Vermandois belonged to her past, and her past did not have claim on her present—once again she had become Catherine of Fastavarin, the German friend of the Queen.

Chapter XXIII

Respect The King's Justice

Isabelle felt nervous and agitated. Louis of Bosredon was nowhere to be seen and she was so used to his company that she missed him sorely. He alone was left to her, of the young men that she had loved, the merry courtiers that had filled her life and made her feel young and attractive, before Agincourt and night had descended over France.

Louis of Bosredon, always at her side, ready to hand her a cup of wine, a sweetmeat, eager to listen to her words, laugh at her jokes, admire her costumes and jewels. And at night, his young strong body, his impetuous love-making, which would give her the physical fulfillment that her body craved.

Louis...a fateful name in her life. Louis of Orleans, her great love; Louis, the beloved Dauphin that death had implacably snatched away from her; and Louis of Bosredon, the faithful lover of so many years.

But where was he? She impatiently had his valet summoned and started pacing the room slowly, ready to berate the man for his master's negligence. But when the servant entered the room, her heart sank and she had to steady herself on the back of a chair.

The valet, Le Clerc, was panting, blood oozing from wounds on his face and arms, and dust on his clothes.

He threw himself to Isabelle's feet. "Your Majesty, the Sire of Bosredon was seized by a group of armed men led by the Constable and dragged away. I was able to hide and flee the scene of the ambush, and so save my life, but I am afraid that I will never see my good lord again!"

He started sobbing loudly, covering his face with his hands.

"You coward!" cried the Queen. "Did you not have a sword, a knife with which to defend your master? You only thought of your precious life, did you not, but let me assure you that you will live to repent and pay for your pusillanimity."

"Oh, your Majesty, I beseech you to believe me! I did defend my lord, killed one of our attackers, wounded a few more, but what could I do against such a host, and when the King and the Dauphin were among the assailants?"

"The King?! You fool, the King is in Paris, and too sick to move from his apartments. How dare you!"

"I implore your forgiveness, your Majesty, but the King was there, with the Dauphin and the Constable. It seemed that they were waiting for us, midway between Paris and Vincennes, and with them was a group of men armed to their teeth. The Sire of Bosredon saw them first, he bowed his head deeply when he passed the King and we continued our ride towards Vincennes. The Constable's voice stopped us dead a few moments later.

"'You felon, dismount and pay homage to your Sovereign!' My lord was proceeding to do so, when another order sounded:

'Men, take him!'"

"At these words my master spurred his horse and I followed him at full speed, but we were soon overtaken by the soldiers who had drawn their swords.

"'Take him alive!' cried the Dauphin, and, in fact, they-seemed to want to capture rather than to kill him.

"My lord left a few dead on the ground and surrendered only when he saw that there was no way out of it."

The man sounded sincere and deeply afflicted.

Isabelle dismissed him graciously enough, but she was terribly upset and frightened.

It was May and the evening was mild, but a chilly wind of terror had entered the room with Le Clerc, and nothing could dispel the anxiety that invaded Isabelle.

She called Catherine. "This is the end for me, my friend," she wailed. "The Count of Armagnac has become my implacable enemy and is determined to destroy me."

"But why should he, your Majesty?" Catherine asked, pretending a surprise that she did not feel. "I am well aware that he dislikes the Sire of Bosredon and resents his presence at your side, but why should he try to hurt and harm you through him? The Count knows that you are no friend of the Duke of Burgundy and he is his real enemy."

"The Count of Armagnac is a fool," said Isabelle contemptuously. "Why, he has always greatly exaggerated my friendship for my cousins of Hainault, opposed the marriage of the Dauphin John to Jacqueline of Hainault, perhaps even caused my son's death, and all because the Hainault are friendly with the Duke of Burgundy. He thought that the Duke would exert his influence on the Dauphin through his wife's family, and I remember how furious he was every time Burgundy visited Valenciennes and was honored by that family."

"You do not really believe that the Duke of Burgundy has to be suspected for the death of the Dauphin John?" asked Catherine.

"Perhaps not, but his demise was sudden was it not, and the Count was constantly at his side when John came back from Valenciennes after his brother's death."

"But the doctors assured you that the Dauphin, like his brother before him, died of the terrible cough that was forever racking his chest. There was no suspicion of poison or foul play at the time," said. Catherine soothingly.

"The doctors?! I am sure that Armagnac pays them to tell me whatever he thinks I should hear! The truth is that the Count wants to continue to rule the country and both my boys, Louis and John, were strong-willed, independent young men who resented his power."

Catherine raised her eyebrows in disbelief—there was more than a shade of maternal pride and bias in Isabelle's description of the two boys that in quick succession had been briefly called "Dauphin". They were both dull, effeminate young men whose lackluster personalities nobody missed. But Isabelle had loved them both, and recognized in them the best characters of the Wittelsbach and Valois.

The Queen had not noticed her friend's expression of skepticism and went on agitatedly: "Armagnac needs a weak Dauphin, whom he can direct at his will. He has found him, at last."

Once more, thought Catherine, her words betrayed her dislike for her son Charles, a thin, pale youth with thick lips and downcast eyes. It was as if the death of all the young princes had been planned so that he, the ugly unloved fruit of Isabelle's marriage to Charles, could at last inherit the throne of his ancestors.

Isabelle had told her repeatedly that she was not fond of her son, that every time she looked at him, the memory stood clear and vivid in front of her eyes of the day when her husband, the ugly, demented man of her nightmares, had raped her and filled her womb with his rotten seed. She had seldom visited the child at St. Pol, where he was left in the hands of servants and nurses, and had been only too glad when the marriage of Charles to Marie d'Anjou, the daughter of the King of Sicily, had taken the Prince away from Paris and to the various castles where the Anjous resided. Charles had become extremely fond of his mother-in-law, in whom he found the love and maternal cares of which his own mother had deprived him, and was also greatly under the influence of the strong-willed and politically acute King of Sicily.

All this had left Isabelle supremely indifferent at the time, but then Fate had played a trick on her, and her unloved son had come back as heir presumptive to the crown.

Catherine had to agree with Isabelle that, if Armagnac wanted a tool against the Queen or John of Burgundy, he had found the perfect one in Charles, Dauphin of France. "Prince Charles is your son, after all," she said trying to assuage her fears, "he will not forget this and will restrain Bernard d'Armagnac if he ever has plans against you."

"If he ever has plans against me! How naive can you be, Catherine, after all these years at court. What do you consider the attack against Louis, if not an attempt to get rid of me?"

Her indignation at the outrage she had suffered, perhaps more than her pain, was choking her. She rose slowly and paced the room, lost in her thoughts.

Isabelle spent a sleepless night. When she closed her eyes, she saw the face of Louis of Bosredon, and he had tears in his eyes and blood on his face. "Isabelle, my Queen, protect me," he would moan, and his hands were joined in a gesture of prayer.

"I cannot protect you, my poor Louis," she would cry and tears rolled slowly down her cheeks.

She welcomed the first rays of the new day and tried to laugh away her forebodings of doom. Catherine, Anne, all her ladies were soon around her, helping her to choose her dress, jewels, brushing her hair, setting a little table for her breakfast. But Isabelle could feel a current of uneasiness beneath the everyday's rituals, discern the anxiety in her ladies' eyes that belied the smiles of their lips.

A few hours later a messenger sent by the Constable, the Count of Armagnac, was announced to the Queen. With a shiver of fear, Isabelle admitted the man to her presence.

The Armagnac servant wore the black and red hood that proclaimed his allegiance, and had the impudent smile of the winner.

"My master begs your Majesty to accept this token of his respect," he said. Was-there irony in his tone and was his mouth curved in a cruel leer?

He was holding a plain black sack, embroidered with the silver coat-of-arms of Armagnac, and he handed it to the Queen. The sack looked heavy, though, and one of Isabelle's ladies stepped out to take it. The man bowed deeply and left the room. This time the look of abject contempt on his face was unmistakable.

Holding the sack with both hands—it was heavy indeed—the lady approached the Queen and handed it to her. With trembling hands, Isabelle untied its silk rope and started taking out the object it contained.

Her screams of horror pierced the thickness of the ancient walls, echoed through the dark vaults of the corridors, reverberated on the glass windows. The sack fell from her hands and its contents rolled out, twirled around and came to a stop on the carpet.

There it lay, ghastly and terrifying, its mouth still contorted in the final scream of agony, its dark blood coagulated in fantastic patterns on its cheeks.

It was the severed head of Louis of Bosredon.

A scrap of paper was still attached to the sack. Fighting against the waves of nausea gripping her, holding to the arm of a chair, Catherine bent and picked up the paper. On it an unknown scribe had penned a few words: "Respect the King's justice."

Isabelle had fainted.

* * *

The following day the Dauphin Charles begged leave to see his mother. Isabelle paled at the announcement, quickly dismissed all her ladies but asked Catherine to remain at her side. The morning was sunny but in her hands she held a gold hollow ball filled with hot embers, and large braziers burned at the corners of the room. Isabelle's blood was slow and pale, the doctors had said, and she needed heat even on such a mild day.

The young prince entered the room unescorted, quietly and yet hurriedly, as if urgent questions were burning his lips but at the same time, he did not want to know their answers. He was dressed in black damask and wore a coat lined with gold tissue. His thin legs were emphasized by the black silk of his tight hose and by the richly embroidered "poulins" ending in long upturned points. He slowly took off his hat, revealing a wide-domed forehead, the color of wax, and his pale blue eyes stared dispassionately at the Queen. The corners of his mouth were down-turned, which gave him a perpetual air of sadness and indecision.

He bowed to his mother and raised his eyes to her. For once she looked...austere, he thought. Her pale face was framed by a dark wimple and the fleshy contours of her body were hidden in the soft folds of her black dress. She is mourning her lover, Charles realized with distaste, and, if he had felt a flicker of sympathy for his mother, it was soon dispelled by his aversion for the adulteress.

"Please have a seat my son," she smiled graciously at him, trying to hide her apprehension and actual dislike of him under a veil of maternal solicitude.

The Dauphin sat rigidly in the carved chair in front of his mother, and the primness and self-righteousness on his face were unmistakable.

"Milady," he started slowly, painfully searching for the words, "I am sure that you must have been wondering these past days what happened to that gentleman of your household you especially favor, the Sire of Bosredon and..."

She interrupted him violently, caution swept away by the intensity of her rage. "And you were kind enough not to let me in the dark for too long, were you not, Charles?"

He looked puzzled. "What do you mean? How can you know that he was interrogated, found guilty and executed? It was decided that I should bring you this announcement, and nobody else was dispatched before me."

"Do not lie to me, Charles," she cried. "You and Armagnac are responsible for Bosredon's death and you sent his severed head to me. Was it supposed to be a warning, or did you just do it to hurt me even more?"

The Dauphin's face was chalky. "I certainly did not authorize such a cruel act," he said with a certain kind of dignity. "I am sorry if this added to your grief, but his judges, not I, found him guilty, and his execution makes up for years of arrogance, greediness. He died because he was disrespectful of the King, ambitious, coward..."

"He died because he was my lover. Armagnac resents my role and influence at court, and, through him, the Constable wanted to strike me," she finished calmly.

The Dauphin blushed. "Mother, how can you avow your infidelity to the King so shamelessly?" he wondered indignantly.

"Was it a secret to you?" she inquired ironically. "At least I did not present the King with children born out of wedlock, which is what your father did to me, or is this a secret too? Poor Charles, I thought that the Queen of Sicily would see to your worldly education more thoroughly."

Isabelle resented Yolande d'Anjou, the widowed wife of the King of Sicily, whose beauty, intelligence, wisdom, were extolled by poets and religious people alike. She was idolized by her son-in-law too, who immediately rose to her defense.

"The Duchess of Anjou, Mother, has taught me to consider the qualities of virtue and nobility of the soul more important than any worldly riches, and if she left me in the ignorance of the ways and customs prevailing at court, I only wish that this ignorance had lasted forever because what I have witnessed has filled me with disgust and contempt."

His tone was peevish and angry and, strangely enough, moved Catherine to a feeling of indulgence for the prince that she had not experienced before. Poor young man, she thought, how soon is life going to teach you to compromise and forget your high principles!

No tenderness was in his mother's voice when she retorted: "Certainly the new advisor that you have chosen cannot be approved by your saintly mother-in-law, Charles. The Count, of Armagnac is a vicious, aggressive man, who wants to rule the country through oppression, taxations of all kinds..."

It was his turn not to let her finish her sentence. "How can you talk of taxations and oppressions, Mother, when the people of this unhappy country live in poverty and misery so that-you can grant favors and luxuries to your lovers and protégés. There is no bread on their tables, no coins in their purses, but pomp and extravagance surround you and your courtiers."

His look swept across the room, took in the silk tapestries, the glistening gold of cups and platters, the crimson hangings on the windows, the ornate torches flaring from every corner.

"Walk along the mud—clogged streets of Paris, the narrow lanes filthy with refuse and garbage, where scrawny dogs look in vain for a bone, enter any of the poor dwellings that open onto them, compare their furnishings, their worn domestic accoutrements with the splendor around you, and you will understand why you are so unpopular among the people of the kingdom. Preachers and monks talk of the goddess Venus that only reigns in your heart, and only a base death can be in store for those that you protect."

The vehemence of his invective crushed Isabelle. She seemed to cringe in her chair, pale, impotent, and furious, while painfully. The Dauphin regained control of himself.

"Madam," he said more calmly, "the Council has decided that it was not in your power to dispose of the lands and properties that the King had granted you. They are, therefore, returned to his Majesty's treasury, together with the jewels of the crown and the precious objects of gold and gems that are part of the royal residences."

She raised her head swiftly, looking at him with hatred, forgetting that he was her son, the heir to the throne. He was her enemy; he had taken away her beloved palaces, lands, precious jewels, way of life, security. "Murderer," she hissed, "what did you do to Louis?"

"Your paramour was beheaded, his body tied in a leather sack and thrown into the Seine. May God have pity on his sinful soul," he finished primly.

Catherine shivered. She could imagine that poor, tortured body, broken by the instruments of the executioners and reduced to a heap of bleeding flesh, hear his screams of pain, smell the stench of his burned flesh. A similar picture must have formed in Isabelle's mind, because a moan escaped from her lips and she reached for her friend's hand, which she pressed spasmodically.

No feeling of pity for the desperate woman in front of him seemed to touch the Dauphin, and he went on mercilessly. "We are aware that the people around you, the foreigners who crowd the court of France, are friends of the Duke of Burgundy, that implacable foe of the Valois, and, as we have reason to believe that you are turning a favorable ear to their pleas, we have decided to exile you from Paris and fix your residence in Tours. You will be accompanied by a small retinue, but will have no contact with the outside world or any emissaries that the Duke of Burgundy might care to send you. You will not be a prisoner, Mother, and you will live in dignity if not luxury, because we have not forgotten that you are the Queen of France, even if you seem to have."

Isabelle forgot her dignity, her hatred for her son; she forgot her clumsy, heavy body, her diseased legs. She threw herself to the knees of the Dauphin, and tears were streaming down her cheeks, sobs shaking her body.

"Please, Charles, do not let them exile me," she cried, trying to move the hardened heart of her unloved son. "They have taken everything away from me; do not let them deprive me of liberty too!" She was clinging to his legs now, a grotesque yet pitiful figure of helplessness and fear.

The sight of her dear friend, so proud and arrogant but a few hours before, so broken up and convulsed now, hardened Catherine forever against Charles of Valois. Had he relented then, further blood and misery would perhaps have been spared to France, and a grateful mother would have been on his side.

He did not, but only helped the Queen to her feet politely, obviously ill at ease, but determined not to yield to her prayers.

"I am sorry, Madame, but the Council's decision is irrevocable.

You are to start for Tours tomorrow. Madame de Vermandois can accompany you, and the Duchess of Bavaria, and a few chambermaids also. You will find other servants in Tours."

Catherine helped the Queen to her chair. She sat down heavily, drying her cheeks with her hands. She had taken hold of herself, and looked dignified and regal once more. Then she spoke, and her words had the chill of ice, the poison of a snake.

"I understand that you can do nothing without Armagnnac's consent. You are only a puppet, Charles of Valois. But I will never forget your behavior and I will harm you in return. From this moment on you have your most implacable enemy in your mother. Do not misjudge my power and influence, Dauphin."

Charles did not answer; he bowed slightly and started for the door. All of a sudden, he turned, a ghost-like figure in black, and his voice sounded scared and childish. "Mother, am I the King's son?" he asked.

The Queen laughed disdainfully. "If I were you," she said, "I would wish I were the son of anybody but a fool's. Reassure yourself, Charles, the mad Sovereign is your father."

Chapter XXIV

Tours

The Dauphin had hurriedly left after his interview with his mother and the prostrate queen had given herself up to an agony of misery and rage. When her tears had subsided she had started making plans for her departure for Tours, already thinking of ways to escape from the prison where her enemies were going to lock her.

"Armagnac and my son are my mortal foes, Catherine," she said, "and as the King is a complete imbecile, without any will of his own, there is only one person on whom I can rely for my safety, the Duke of Burgundy. There is no love lost between us, to be sure, but if he thinks that he can use me to his own advantage, he will come to my rescue."

"How can you bear to ally yourself to the murderer of the man you loved above another?" Catherine inquired, horrified at the thought of the queen's befriending the Monster, John the Fearless.

"Do I have any other choice? Have they left me with any alternative? My son has become my worst enemy, but I am not afraid of him. I despise him too much for that, as I know how spineless and weak Charles is. But Armagnac! Oh, Catherine, how much I hate the man! No wonder he is so unpopular in Paris that he never dares going out unescorted. He murdered thousand of innocents, had their houses looted and burned, their women raped, filled Paris with the stench of bodies rotting on the gallows yet I, the foreign queen, I have become the villain. It is because of me and my extravagances that the French are reduced to utter poverty; it is because I gave St. Ouen to Louis that the French starve. But I will show him yet. And my son, too, who dared to reproach me and who thinks Yolande d'Anjou is a paragon of virtue and moral excellence, his real mother. He murdered the man I loved, my Louis—my revenge will be terrible.

"Run to my brother, Catherine, and let him know of our departure for Tours. Tell him to reach John of Burgundy in the North and inform him that the Queen is on his side and will be his ally in his just struggle against the Armagnac. John is an acute politician, he will not under estimate the importance of having the Regent in his camp and will act accordingly, I have no doubts."

Catherine did as she was asked and, soon, she was in Ludwig's arms, happy to be with him for a few hours but desperate at the thought of leaving him and everything that was familiar and dear, for the unknown that Tours represented.

To her surprise, Ludwig agreed immediately to his sister's plan.

"She is right, Catherine, only harm can come to her from Armagnac, or that weakling son of hers and their accomplices. John of Burgundy is by far more intelligent and popular in the country; it will be advantageous for us to have him on our side. Paris is in the hands of the Armagnac, they dominate the royal Council, but the capital yearns for John, the hero of the people and the University alike, and the Council has no real power, but only follows Armagnac's directions."

"How can you talk so, when the Burgundians threw you to jail and almost murdered you, Ludwig?"

"In politics, my love, one has to learn to forget and forgive, until it becomes beneficial to remember and take revenge. I bear no grudge against John of Burgundy for what happened to me. He allowed the Cabochiens to take control and they, not he, hated me. But I am sure that he has learned a great deal since then, and no butcher will ever be permitted again to dictate to the proud Duke. Tell my sister that this very night I will leave Vincennes for Dijon. She shall obey the Dauphin's order and go to Tours accordingly. Once you are there, do not raise anybody's suspicions, either by words or actions. Help will come, you can be sure of that, but the utmost prudence is required of the Queen's and her friends."

"Give me something that belongs to you, Catherine," he added, "a ring, a pin. When the time comes to move to your rescue I will secretly send you back your token, and you will know that everything has been arranged for your escape."

Slowly Catherine unpinned her brooch. Time and wear had dulled the shining of the gold and blue enamel, but that pin was still her favorite jewel, a gift she was given by Ludwig on his arrival from Germany and which she had started wearing again only when she had become his mistress once more.

Ludwig took the jewel lightly from her hand, kissed it and put it in his in his pocket. "You will wear this pin again soon, darling, I promise you. Be hopeful, Catherine. Next time we see each other, it will be under more cheerful circumstances."

* * *

The Dauphin had lied, in Tours Isabelle and her companions were virtually prisoners.

The gloomy, massive castle dominated by a huge dungeon had received them on a rainy night, when humidity seemed to be seeping through the old stones and impregnate pillows and sheets, hangings and carpets with its chilly moistness.

The lodgings that had been assigned to the Queen and her retinue were modest and sparsely furnished. Gone was the silver and gold glitter of arrases and tapestries covering the walls of Isabelle's palaces, the soft perfumes burning sweetly to purify the air of her rooms, the bunches of flowers filling vases and faience containers that brightened every corner of her homes. The large flagstones of the floor were bare and cold, the tapestries hanging on the walls were woven in plain wool and depicted crude scenes of war and hunting. The furniture of their apartments was simply made and carved, and no inviting silk cushion softened the hardness of the chairs, no gold-framed painting adorned the little chapel adjacent to the Queen's chamber. Century-old trees surrounded the building and screened any glimpse of the beautiful Loire River that could be obtained through the narrow, tall windows opening at regular intervals on the facade of the manor.

A gloomy place indeed, which still resounded with the echoes of past days, when life was dominated by war and every castle was built like a fortress to withstand the attacks of the enemies.

If it reminded Isabelle and Catherine of Ludwigsburg, the castle of their youth, the long years gone by, the genteel, refined ways of the French court, had rendered them immune to the sad attraction that places and times of our past hold when we grow older.

Isabelle missed her life at court terribly, the luxury of her surroundings, the splendor of her dresses and jewels, the company of the gentlemen and ladies of her escort, the power she had once held. Armagnac and the Dauphin her son had deprived her of everything that made her life worth living.

She, who loved parties and festivities so much, was relegated to an obscure castle in the country, alone but for her lady-in-waiting and sister-in-law; she, who loved flirting and the pleasures of the flesh, was reduced to the company of her three jailors, men of humble extraction and less charm, She would spend many a sleepless night crying and raging, her hatred of her son getting deeper with every day of captivity, her helplessness and frustration making her physically and mentally sick.

It was hard for Catherine to be a cheerful companion for her friend. Ironically, Fate had thrown her lot with that of her lover's wife, and the proximity of Anne of Bavaria did nothing to lighten the burden of Catherine's days. The mutual dislike they had felt from the beginning had deepened now, when the monotonous life they led in the Queen's service made avoiding each other impossible.

Yet, Catherine could understand and justify Anne's aversion. Just whispering Ludwig's name made her blood stir, her body quicken. She longed for their reunion and felt all along that they were destined to be together again, while Anne's lover had been killed at Agincourt and she had no hope to give her strength and courage, no future to look forward to, when her beloved would be with her. Days, weeks, then months went by, but no help had come. The prisoners spent their monotonous hours embroidering, reading, playing chess, going for walks or rides in the forest, followed by the vigilant eyes of their wardens.

No news from the outside world filtered through the thick walls of their prison and this ignorance made Isabelle even more despondent and restless. She had entered Tours with plans and purposes of revenge but the long months of solitude had taken their toll and the queen had become an old woman, in poor health, who found solace only in prayer and religious observances.

Then one day in mid-October everything changed. They had not seen one of their jailors for a few days but had given little thought to his absence when a new warden appeared. He was a middle-aged man, thin, with long grayish hair and an air of refinement that made him stand out among his more vulgar colleagues. Like the other two men he seemed to be keeping a close watch on their activities, but their excitement at his arrival and speculations on the reasons for the sudden substitution, made them read kindness and devotion in his eyes, deference in his behavior.

"He must be the means that the Duke has devised to favor our escape," Isabelle would convince herself and her companions. "Let us act with the utmost care and prudence, so that the other wardens will have no suspicion."

The hopeful thought of her imminent liberation roused the Queen's spirits once more. She was perpetually alert, waiting for a sign or word that would confirm her expectations.

The "word" was whispered to Catherine one afternoon, when she slipped out of the castle yard, for once alone, to take a walk under the tall trees that were just then changing their colors. Golden and russet chrysanthemums grew in profusion in the garden; Catherine gathered a big bunch of them and breathed their pungent, bitter-sweet perfume with delight. She loved the flowers, but she knew that they were the harbingers of yet another autumn of their captivity, of a winter that loomed ahead with grey endless days of rain and snow and chilly rooms where the meager fires in the high chimneys could not warm their cold bodies and bored spirits.

All of a sudden, the new warden materialized in front of her, and handed her two yellow flowers that must have fallen from her bouquet. Her thanks were curtly interrupted by his hurried, secretive words.

"It is to be on All Souls' Day, at the Monastery of Marmoutiers."

He retreated swiftly, before she had time to answer or ask for further elucidation, and Catherine stood there, in a turmoil of emotions, squeezing the flowers, crushing their delicate petals and leaves. Something pricked her finger, and with a sense of relief and happiness, she saw her brooch pinned through the flowers the man had handed her. She gently freed it from the chrysanthemums and lovingly caressed the object that Ludwig had touched and held it tightly in her hand.

When she repeated the man's words to Isabelle, she could see triumphant vindictiveness in her eyes and, shedding any last trace of apathy, the Queen went into a flurry of preparations. The main obstacle was to obtain permission to go to Marmoutiers, because the monastery stood a few miles from the castle and beyond the range of their allowed excursions.

Isabelle loved plotting and scheming, and this time, when there was so much at stake, she used all her powers of persuasion and charm to extract the permission from her custodians to go and listen to Mass at that venerable convent. The Queen's piety, the long hours spent kneeling in front of the holy images, the constant fingering of the ivory beads of her rosary were well known among her jailors, and they lent a favorable ear to her entreaties to be allowed to go and pray for her dead children and parents on the day that the Church consecrated to the memory of the Defunct.

She decided that only the Duchess of Bavaria and Catherine would accompany her, surreptitiously emptied her casket of her most valuable gems and handed them to her friends asking them to hide them under their ample skirts and in the folds of the mantles protecting them against the chilly fog of the November morning.

The Queen's body was so heavy and full of aches and pains that she could not ride any more, and had to be helped to her carriage, drawn by an old, docile horse. Anne of Bavaria and Catherine rode on two mules at her side, while their wardens, heavily armed, opened and closed the small procession.

The fresh air smelled cool and pungent, the grey folds of the fog blurred the contours of trees and dwellings, the excitement and danger of what lay ahead made Catherine more alert and alive than she had been in months.

It was not long before the dark mass of the monastery appeared before them. The moment was coming! Catherine bent to the carriage, drew open one of the curtains and nodded cheerfully at Isabelle.

The Queen was pale, her eyes feverish with anxiety. How she hated her big body, her lack of agility, how she was yearning to join her liberators, a sword in her hand!

The place was deserted. A grove of hazel-trees and oaks grew on one side of the convent and their branches looked barren against the leaden sky, yellow and brown leaves heaping at their feet among the bushes and tangles of the underwood. Not a sound to be heard but the quiet clip-clop of their mounts; yet Catherine was sure she glimpsed a flash of steel amidst the trees, heard the neigh of a distant horse.

One of the wardens dismounted and helped the Queen out of her carriage. Anne and Catherine followed his example, left their horses and a few minutes later the little group entered the dark vaults of the church, which the voices of invisible nuns filled with mournful chanting.

The office of the Dead, so solemn and sad, the nasal voice of the priest, the gloomy surroundings, the ordeal ahead, all contributed to Catherine's dejected mood, and she found herself crying silently. Her lips repeated the words of the priest, her heart was filled with thoughts of the people she had loved and who had left her—Michel, her mother, whose face she could not remember, Philip of Vermandois, whose faith and trust she had betrayed. Isabelle and Anne too seemed extraordinarily moved—she heard Anne's sobs, saw that the Queen's face was wet with tears.

They were the only people present in the church. The nuns were hidden behind the high stalls of the choir and, by design or chance, none of the villagers farming the countryside around the monastery were in attendance.

When they left the church, the massive oak door creaked on its hinges with a plaintive noise. Outside, the sun had broken through the thin veil of the fog and was shining brightly on the steel of tens of soldiers circling the building.

There was nothing their jailors could do. Two of them cringed in fear and begged for mercy, while the third one knelt in front of the Queen, who smiled graciously at him and thanked him for his services

A man stepped out boldly from the group of soldiers lined in front of the convent. He was tall and strikingly handsome in a dark, rugged way, with a strong aquiline nose and a large, sensual mouth. He did not wear an armor but held the helmet that he had just taken off in his hands. He advanced towards the Queen proudly while she exclaimed with delighted surprise, "Why, it is you, Jean de Villiers de l'Isle Adam! I thought you were a faithful friend of the Count of Armagnac!"

The man smiled scornfully, "Like you, your Majesty," he replied, "I had allied myself to that man for the good of the King. Time and time again Armagnac proved himself a false and brutal friend, and his insults and rapacity have convinced me that the good of France lies with the Duke of Burgundy, that valiant soldier, John the Fearless, to whom I have sworn my allegiance. Armagnac is the worst tyrant France has ever known and I will not rest until I have carved the red cross of St. Andrew on his corpse!"

"What a fierce purpose this is, my friend," laughed the Queen. "I must admit though, that the Constable and his party deserve the hatred of mankind. But I am delighted to see you who, I presume, come here as an envoy of my cousin of Burgundy."

"Indeed I do, your Majesty. His highness requests the honor of your company and these noble ladies' at his headquarters in Chartres. But he sent a much better ambassador than myself, to whom he is certain you will listen favorably."

He bowed deeply and rejoined his maniple, while Ludwig of Bavaria eagerly came forward and embraced his sister fondly.

With a pang of disappointment, Catherine saw him ignore her and go smilingly to his wife, bow to Anne and kiss her on both cheeks. She realized, of course, that he had to behave according to the rules of their world—Anne was his wife, a lady of the noblest lineage, the mother of his heir—he could not, would not insult her before hundreds of witnesses, but she could not help a blush of humiliation.

Later that day, when they had reached the castle of a lord loyal to the Duke of Burgundy where they were to rest before the last leg of the journey to Chartres, Ludwig joined Catherine in her room and the ardor of his kisses and caresses reassured her once more of the love and attraction he felt for her. Politics, the reality of their situation, were very far from her head then, and she only wanted to be held tightly and loved by the man who had captured her heart so long ago.

But Ludwig was restless and brooding. She sensed it. He knew that the Queen had no alternative but Burgundy's friendship; still, the memory of Paris in the hands of the Cabochiens, the arrogance of the mobs that took their orders from John, the humiliating imprisonment he had suffered, everything had left a layer of bitterness and distrust that he could not overcome.

"Do not forget, Catherine, that it is true that Burgundy freed the Queen, but he needs her more than Isabelle needs him. She is the

Regent, after all, and without her authority his acts or reforms have no value. The King declared the Dauphin Lieutenant General of the Kingdom; therefore Burgundy has to cover himself with her name, so to speak, if he wants to exert any authority. But what is Isabelle to gain from this alliance, besides a freedom that, I am sure, the Dauphin would eventually have granted her, anyway?"

"Revenge, Ludwig," Catherine answered. "You know your sister little indeed, if you think that she will ever forgive the Constable and her son for killing her lover, depriving her of her riches, humiliating her in front of the whole world, condemning her to months of exile and boredom. I understand your words, my dear, and I agree with you that she will be just a tool in the hands of that ambitious man, but she has no real alternative. With Burgundy at her side, she will have revenge, at least."

He nodded in agreement. "I am sure that you are right, and I must confess that it is sad for me to think how terribly the tragic events of her life have affected my sister. I keep remembering the sweet, carefree girl of Munich, the devoted wife and mother I found on the throne of France when I first arrived, the loving sister and daughter Isabelle has always been, and I suffer to see how changed she is. Sometimes I wonder whether I should not go back to Germany, take the reins of the Duchy in my hands again, and forget about the Kingdom of France."

"You would not leave your sister and me now, when we need you so badly, would you Ludwig?" she exclaimed in panic and her anxiety made him smile tenderly at her.

"Of course not, Catherine. It is just that so often I think I am a burden more than a help to my sister—you know how the French hate the so-called German party and are wary of foreigners in periods of crisis."

"That is true, but Isabelle depends on you too much to let you return to Bavaria," she said. "And, as for myself, you know my feelings well enough!"

"And I reciprocate your love, Catherine dearest, and want you by me forever," he murmured tenderly, taking her in his arms once again.

Chapter XXV

Revenge!

Revenge! That word seemed to dominate France for the years to come. Revenge of the Burgundians against the Armagnacs, the Queen against her son, England against the country that stubbornly refused its King as her own, one side of France against the other.

Hardly ever leaving the Queen's side, Catherine witnessed, first with horror, then with the acquiescence that comes from habit, the bath of blood, hatred and revenge that covered France.

As one of the many ladies of her escort, she was with the Queen when she entered Paris in July 1418, sitting in a gilded carriage next to the Duke of Burgundy, among the enthusiastic rejoicings of the same good people of Paris who had cursed her name a few months previously.

Close to Isabelle rode Jean de Villiers de l'Isle Adam. His black palfrey was richly trapped in black velvet embroidered with St. Andrew's crosses, his gloves glittered with the gold and stones that Isabelle had started showering on him, the most recent of her lovers.

His handsomeness had enslaved her senses; his fierceness filled her heart with admiration. True to his words, when the gates of Paris had been opened to the Burgundians by a traitor, and the city was flooded by the Duke's mobs, thirsty for blood, Jean de Villiers had dragged the body of Armagnac from the prison where he had found shelter, and on the Constable's quivering breast carved the red mark of the victorious Duke. John of Burgundy had gratefully rewarded Villiers with the dignity of Marshal of France, and the proud baron had dared to raise his eyes to the Queen and gain her love.

From the darkness of a past almost forgotten, the memories of another procession through the city filled Catherine's mind, when she and the Queen were both young, and life seemed to have only smiles for the German princess elected to be Queen of France. Now their bodies and spirits were tired and disappointed, and if Isabelle still gave herself to the pleasures of the flesh, she did so with a sort of sad rage—the fulfillment of her senses seemed to be the only firm anchor of a life on which she had no control.

"Noel! Noel!" shouted the people gathered along the sides of the streets, and they waved branches and flowers cheerfully, calling the names of the Duke and the Queen. Their houses were hung with tapestries and multicolored cloths; men, women, children wore their fineries; the fountains poured wine; stalls for the sale of drinks and fruits had sprung everywhere; pickpockets were busier than usual.

Still, the scene was not festive; an invisible cloud of sadness that no joyous shouts could dispel seemed to hang on the brilliant summer sky.

The city had witnessed too much death and destruction, famine and plague, too many neighbors had turned against one another, too many promises had been broken, for the people of Paris to give themselves wholeheartedly to what seemed the beginning of a peaceful era.

Catherine wondered whether Isabelle was aware of this lack of hope and buoyancy in her people, or if her absorption in her new lover made her insensitive to her surroundings. She sometimes found Isabelle's total surrender to the delights of love trying and slightly ludicrous in a woman of her age, fat, almost unable to move, and whose yellowing skin and teeth had long deprived her of the enticements of beauty. Strangely enough, men still thought her attractive. Perhaps it was her openness to love, the never-ending enchantments it had for her that drew men to the obese, aging Queen, and made them sense the lost grace of her youth.

The malaise that the people had felt even on the triumphal day of their hero's return turned out to be justified—peace was a distant chimera that neither party pursued too actively.

Soon, the King of England crossed the Channel again, once more bringing death and destruction to the land of France, conquering Normandy, murdering the inhabitants of Pontoise, finding an ally now in the Duke of Burgundy, now in the Dauphin.

Isabelle had not forgiven her son's part in her lover Bosredon's death and her exile. Her trust now lay entirely in the Duke of Burgundy and Villiers de l'Isle Adam—they favored a reconciliation with England and were ready to sacrifice half of the Kingdom to obtain peace. Her daughter, Catherine, would become Henry's Queen and Isabelle's pride was flattered by the thought of her favorite daughter acquiring such a splendid state.

"Catherine is so much like me," she would reminisce fondly. "She has the same dark looks, my energy and strong will. She is not as pretty as my poor Isabelle, though. Do you remember how beautiful she looked when she left for England? But as soon as Catherine's face and body fill up slightly she will be enchanting. Unfortunately, she does have the Valois nose, so long and unbecoming. Perhaps she should wear her hair falling down her shoulders, the hennin only emphasizes her nose, do you not agree?"

Young Catherine was often with her mother now, and she was very aware of the high destiny awaiting her, and eager to meet the handsome King who was becoming the master of France. The shabby dresses that she had worn during her long years of neglect and poverty at St. Pol had been replaced by the luxury and richness of the gowns and capes that her mother favored and indeed, with her bright dark eyes and lustrous hair, she was very similar to the Queen although taller and thinner than Isabelle.

King Charles had been an absent ghost for years, his malady gave him almost no respite, and Isabelle was aware that his death would mean the accession of young Charles to the throne. The new King would be an enemy, and harm her in any way possible. She knew it and her links to the Burgundians and the English became even tighter. She still loved to delude herself—as beloved mother of the Queen of England, she had visions of influence and high rank at that court and, when the Dauphin had John of Burgundy murdered during an interview that they were holding on the bridge of Montereau to decide on a common cause against England, only her hopes in King Henry enabled her to survive her overwhelming grief and terror.

"That monster will have me murdered next," she cried. "His lust for power is all-encompassing and he will get rid of any obstacle on his path mercilessly."

Isabelle wrote anxious letters to her daughter, Michelle, who was married to the new Duke of Burgundy, Philip, begging her not to let her husband forget so treacherous a murder, asking her on bended knees not to allow the torch of revenge to flicker and die down.

Philip the Good, as the young Duke was called, was a generous, sweet-tempered young man, very different from the shrewd, hard politicians that his father and grandfather had been. More than Isabelle's tears and Michelle's prayers, though, the interests of his regions of Burgundy and Flanders dictated his policy, and, with those uppermost in his mind, he met Isabelle in Troyes to discuss the conditions for peace with England.

King Henry reached Troyes a few days later, glowing with the radiance of victory, smiling the smile of a man whom the gods have kissed.

Like the other ladies of the Queen's escort, Catherine was eager to see the young warrior who had inflicted the terrible defeat of Agincourt on the French knights and, like most of them, resentful of the brutal way in which their men had been murdered in the mud of the fatal plain.

Isabelle did not share their feelings, though. She was in a flurry of excitement and hope, and would remain closeted for hours with her daughter, discussing dowry, clothes, jewels, because an agreement had finally been reached, and Catherine of Valois was going to marry the King of England. The princess herself was ecstatic—she had met Henry and had immediately fallen in love with the handsome man, who was tall and slender, with blue eyes, dark hair and a captivating smile.

The King of France was in Troyes, too. Odette de Champdivers' tender solicitude had worked wonders on the monarch, and he was no longer the demented, dirty madman that filled St. Pol with his howls, but a calm, sedate man who still looked quite regal in the handsome doublets and coats he wore. His hair was almost completely grey now but neatly cut and adorned with a simple circlet of gold. He had never recovered from his malady, and his mind was as feeble as a child's, but his presence was indispensable to the Duke of Burgundy and the Queen, his name essential to the agreement between France and England that was to be signed before the wedding of Henry and Catherine would take place.

The Treaty of Troyes...the French people, some of them at least, called it the Treaty of Shame, and would never abide by it because it recognized the King of England as heir and successor to King Charles and renounced Normandy and the other French provinces conquered by Henry. Both the thrones of France and England were to belong to Henry and his heirs after him, while the "so-called Dauphin" was denied any right and had to be fought against until his complete submission and that of his party.

The "so-called Dauphin"—was Isabelle letting her son be proclaimed a bastard, and herself unfaithful in front of the whole world?

She shrugged her shoulders impatiently at her friend's dismay. "Do you not see, Catherine? It is only a technicality, but necessary, because if Charles is the legitimate heir, his right to the throne is inalienable, and not even the King can deprive him of his inheritance. But if he is not a prince of the fleur-de-lis, a descendant of St. Louis, then the King has no natural heir, and Henry can become his adopted son and successor."

"But how can you admit your unfaithfulness to your husband, how can the King accept this statement, which makes a laughing stock of him?"

"The King! You know as well as I do that he has no contact with reality, is completely wrapped in the folds of his folly and will agree to anything or with anybody. As for the "so-called Dauphin", the doubts of his legitimacy will destroy his peace of mind, render him even more vacillating. To be proclaimed a bastard in front of friends and supporters will weaken his cause, cast doubts even among his most faithful allies. Henry of Lancaster is jubilant and grateful, he will be a generous son to me, will not forget how much he owes me. What a handsome man, he looks so ardent too. He does not hide his admiration for his bride-to-be, you can see that he cannot wait to take her to his bed!" She laughed bawdily, mightily pleased with herself, and Catherine had to admit that she had played the few cards she had in her hands very skillfully.

The day of June in which the ceremonial wedding of her daughter Catherine to the King of England was celebrated was a triumphant one for Isabelle. The church of St. John in Troyes that the bridegroom had chosen for the ceremony was filled with princes and nobility, town people and bourgeois, while, close to the high altar where the Archbishop was celebrating the nuptial Mass, the King and Queen of France knelt in isolated splendor, their crowns glittering with gold and precious stones, the velvet of their mantles shimmering under the lights of hundreds of candles in gilded sconces.

Once more, and perhaps for the last time, Isabelle basked in the cheers and welcomes of her people, as she made her entry into Paris accompanied by her husband, and the King and Queen of England. Once more she heard the "Noels!" of the crowd, enjoyed the bright colors of the house decorations, and marveled at the mystery plays performed by the people in honor of their sovereigns.

Months of poverty and unhappiness followed then, when her daughter Catherine left for her new country, her lover abandoned her for another mistress, the destruction of the Hotel Barbette by partisans of the Dauphin brought her back to the hated St. Pol.

Peace was still very elusive; the Dauphin had not been subdued yet, but instead his popularity increased, as more and more parts of the country rallied to his side and people started saying the word "France" with a new feeling of love and unity.

The Queen and her court were tied to the English, come what may; they depended on the generosity of the foreign King for their survival, on the pension he bestowed on his mother-in-law for their food and clothing.

Isabelle had become poor. The eternal wars ravaging the country had ruined farmers and peasants, lands and fields had been wasted, harvests were scarce, taxes could not be paid. Isabelle had recovered some of the properties that her son had taken away from her, but to little advantage. Plunder and spoliations had reduced the once prosperous farmers to poverty—now they swelled the ranks of the beggars and thieves swarming the towns. She had to sell her jewels then, her plates, cups, precious tapestries; she had to borrow money from bankers and Jews, pawn her crown.

The large rooms of St. Pol looked immense now, when the best furniture was gone, the silk carpets had been sold to rich bourgeois, the icy winter winds blew down the high fireplaces, creating more drafts in a palace where cracked window-panes could not be replaced, cold brick walls could not be covered.

Every day brought new defections among the thinning ranks of the sovereigns' courtiers—the pleasant, luxurious life of the court was only a memory, and it took a steadfast heart and great loyalty to remain in the gloominess that was now St. Pol, suffer the poverty to which the King and Queen were reduced. The empty rooms sounded hollow with the echoes of the survivors' steps and voices, the silence around them could become unbearable.

Where were the pretty, vivacious ladies that had surrounded their fair Queen, the dashing gentlemen that had vied for her favors? Marguerite, Blanche, Jeanne...Even Anne de Semihier had abandoned Isabelle and, haunted by the image of her still beloved, oblivious husband, had taken the long road South to Provence. She soon disappeared in the desolate winter countryside, where rapacious soldiers and famished wolves roamed, both bent on destruction and death, and strong-beaked crows feasted on rotting carcasses.

Isabelle bore her new unhappiness bravely. Jean de Villiers' desertion had wounded her deeply and made her look inside herself with more courage than was her wont. Did she at last see the old, fat woman that had given up her son to revenge herself, the greedy, avaricious Queen who had bled her country dry to enrich her favorites, the unfaithful wife who had rejected a sick, defenseless husband? She did not say. She never mentioned Villiers again, but never forgave the Dauphin; she did not take any new lover, but never showed any empathy for her husband.

One last blow was in store for Isabelle and Catherine—and then the winter of their lives would set in—one last blow that would hit them differently, but with the same cruelty, and make them crouch quietly like wounded animals—and reach for each other's hand.

When Ludwig joined her in her room that night, Catherine immediately felt his nervousness. Tightly wrapped in his warm mantle, the man sat silent and dejected, and his eyes did not want to meet hers.

Catherine was invaded by fear. She stretched her chilly hands to him and touched him gently: "What is on your mind, Ludwig?" she asked, trying to control her anxiety.

He looked at her. "I know that what I am going to say will be a blow to you, Catherine, but it need not be, I assure you, because it will not really affect you if you care for me."

He was stumbling for words, and his nervousness had brought color to his face.

"What do you mean? Talk more clearly, if you please, I cannot stand this incertitude."

"I have decided to go back to Munich, Catherine, where the people still love and want me, and my sons will learn how to become German princes."

"It seems strange that you thought of this gap in their education only now, when the forces of the Dauphin are getting stronger and your sister can rely only on the English for her survival!"

She was in a turmoil of sorrow and disappointment but hoped that her tone was cool and controlled.

"But what can I do for Isabelle? How can I fill her coffers, give her prosperous farms, faithful lovers? The time of my usefulness in France has run out; I am nothing but a hindrance to the Queen..."

"A hindrance!" she cried indignantly, "You did not think so, Ludwig, when your sister was all-powerful and you dreamt of being a royal official of the same country where you feel like an alien now. For years you have profited by the queen's position—everything you have, everything you are, you owe your sister and now when she needs you desperately, and has only me as a friend, now at last you remember that, after all, you and your children are German. I had underestimated the depth of your selfishness, I admit it."

He winced at her words and blushed.

"I love you Catherine," he said, "and I do not want to be without you. You will come to Bavaria with me, nothing in our relationship will change. Anne has known about you for years and she is too intelligent and wise to make a fuss about it now. I know that you are devoted to my sister but, remember, you left her before, and for a man for whom you had no strong feelings…"

"But those of respect and trust." she finished. His lack of fairness struck her more deeply than ever. How could he compare the two situations, how could he compare the Isabelle of to-day to the woman, the queen she was when Catherine had left her for Brittany? How could he protest that he loved her, and urge her to leave the person that needed her the most?

Catherine was silent for a while. She understood that her words would not make him flinch from his decision, but she could no longer pretend to be blind to his selfishness and cowardice.

"You are betraying your sister," she said, "and a sister that has been the most generous and loving person in your life. For the first time in our relationship, Ludwig, I feel that I am the stronger. I cannot, I will not betray a woman that has been my family for as long as I can remember, and I will never follow you."

"But you love me, Catherine, your desperation shows it more clearly than any words," he pleaded.

"To my shame. I will confess my love for you, and it will be the last time. I love you, Ludwig, I will forever miss your kisses, your body, the sense of security that you gave me just being near. But I do not love your soul, its selfish callousness, the weakness that I see today in its entirety for the first time.

As badly as I may want to leave the sinking ship too, my self-respect, my love for my friend will not allow me to do it. I want to be able to live with my conscience, and I do not know how you will be able to live with yours."

Ludwig stood up and tried to gather her in his arms, but she slipped away from him, and it was painful for her to do so, because her whole being wanted to be embraced and protected by the very man she rejected.

"Think of Munich, Catherine, and the castle where we first discovered love," he pleaded once again. "Together, as when we were both young, we will climb the highest mountain, gather flowers and edelweiss. You will be respected and honored at my court, I promise you, and not a word of gossip will dare touch the woman loved by the Duke of Bavaria."

She smiled at him, against her will. As she had told him, she was indeed the stronger, the one that could look towards the future and not delude herself with visions of a life that was not to be.

"The Autumn of our lives has passed, Ludwig," she said, echoing his words of long ago, "and chilly Winter is setting in. I have realized this truth and I accept it. I hope you will do the same."

Her tone was sad and had an edge of finality in it that Ludwig did not fail to notice.

"Then, this is our good-bye, Catherine," he whispered.

"Yes, it is," she answered. "I hope that your sister will forgive you as I do."

A few days later, when Ludwig and Anne took their official leave from the Queen, he bowed to Catherine deeply, and she thought she saw longing and regret in his cold, bright blue eyes. He did not express any feelings, only the hope, ironical as it sounded, of a peaceful future in the country where she had elected to remain.

Isabelle was crying spasmodically parting from a brother she deeply loved and knew she was never to see again, and her tears seemed to move him for a minute. But that emotion soon passed and Ludwig was again the controlled, aloof man he had always been.

Holding to each other, the two women followed longingly the tall erect figure of the brother and lover that was leaving the room and their lives forever, and when the door closed behind him with a last, final bang, they embraced each other and cried bitterly.

Chapter XXVI

Winter Sets In

Isabelle and Catherine were left alone; each had the other as only companion and support. The ghost-like figure of the King made his appearance from time to time, but he had sunk into such a state of imbecility that he hardly spoke, and what he said made no sense at all.

Joyous news came one day from England, accompanied by rich presents for the Queen: a boy had been born to Catherine and Henry and the infant, whom the Treaty of Troves destined to the crowns of England and France, had been christened Henry. The Duke of Exeter, the English Governor of Paris, came to St. Pol. in full regalia to bring the announcement of the birth.

The youthful duke, a renown warrior, bowed to the Queen and handed her a parchment from Catherine of England. Soldiers of his escort had brought a large chest into the room, which was opened end, to the ladies' delighted eyes, revealed a treasure of soft silk bolts, damask cloths, gold cups, precious jewels.

"The Queen of England begs your Majesty to accept these as New Years' gifts and tokens of her affection for her mother on the joyful occasion of Prince Henry's birth," said the Duke.

The presents thrilled the Queen. Deprivation had only intensified her love of luxury and elegance, and she caressed the precious cloths, ran her hands through the glitter of gold and gems with sensuous delight. A new year had started and, even if the war against the Dauphin raged as fierce as before, the birth of a little prince, the generosity of her daughter, the renewed respect of the English rulers of Paris, seemed to augur a new era for Isabelle, a time brightened by Catherine and

Henry's long visits, and enlivened by sojourns in Vincennes and the other royal residences that were dear to her.

Catherine of England joined her parents in Vincennes in June. Her child had been left behind, but she had a pretty miniature of him, which showed a solemn-looking baby with dark hair and very blue eyes. The young Queen herself had become a beautiful woman, with the luminous creamy skin of her mother, and a figure that maternity had ripened and made sensuous. The splendor of her attires and jewels was a proof of the love that the King bore her, but she was restless and nervous.

"My lord is sick, Mother," she confided weeping. "He makes light of it and says it is only a temporary disease that campaigning and worries have brought about, but I cannot believe him. He has become very thin, his skin has lost his bright colors, he hardly eats at all and is so weak that even standing is a feat for him. Do you remember how handsome and strong he looked on our wedding day? Oh, Mother, I have terrible forebodings. What will become of my little Henry if his father dies, when he is only an infant? What will become of me?"

Ironically, the situation she dreaded was so reminiscent of the one that Isabelle had had to face when the King's malady had left the realm rudderless and prey to the ambitions of the royal dukes, that her helpless mother could only take Catherine in her arms and fervently pray that the noble and generous King would be restored to health.

King Charles was in Vincennes, too, but his health, always robust, had started declining lately and he did not recognize his wife and daughter any longer. They sometimes caught a glimpse of his thin figure, leaning on the arms of gentlemen of his escort—Odette had recently died—walking slowly about the park, but his rare visits to the Queen's apartments had ceased altogether.

It was a hot summer, and the coolness of the palace was more inviting than the scorched meadows surrounding it. News of illness was reaching the Queen from Dijon too, where Michelle, Philip of Burgundy's wife, was fighting for her life, stricken by a mysterious disease that the doctors could not cure. Death, indeed, seemed to be reaping her sad harvest with renewed vigor, and Isabelle was destined to lament the death of yet another child before the end of that Summer.

One day, when the litter carrying the sick King of England arrived at the castle, Catherine's forebodings and grief could be well understood because there lay a man that was clearly not long for this world. His emaciated body, hollow cheeks, the burnt-out look of his eyes, bespoke an unforgiving malady—he knew it, and his thoughts kept going back to the little son he hardly knew, his words betrayed the anxiety he felt for the future of his heir and his wife.

King Henry died on the last day of the month of August, when black clouds in the sky announced the welcome relief of a long-awaited-for storm, and time seemed to stand still, as it always does when en event of magnitude takes place.

Isabelle's grief over the death of a man upon whom she looked as her protector was intensified by the departure of her daughter, because a tearful and pale Catherine accompanied her lord's body in the long trip that was taking him back to England and Westminster Abbey, to be buried among his ancestors.

The castle of Vincennes looked so empty and silent after the departure of the English that the Queen decided to go back to St. Pol. Philip of Burgundy had just announced the death of his beloved wife, Michelle, and Isabelle felt more lonely and unhappy than usual.

"Death has spared only three of my children," she would say tearfully, "and Catherine's departure leaves me bereft of filial affection. Marie has been in her monastery too long to have any feelings for me or the things of the world, and as for Joanna, she and her husband John of Monfort are siding with her brother and against me. I am grateful, though, that I have you, Catherine. You are as dear and close to me as any member of my family and only death can separate us."

Catherine nodded silently, too moved to answer, but full aware of the truth of her words. Their mutual affection had lasted a life time, and resisted absence, criticism, disapproval, to become as strong as any blood tie.

It is one of the privileges of old age—is there any other?—to remember the past, and the mind is so beautifully trained that, out of the thousands of episodes that sum up a life, it selects and brings forth from its files those that made one happy, neglecting the moments of despair, humiliation, and gloom that constitute most of human destiny. Thus, Isabelle saw the dark castle of Vincennes, the cold palace of St. Pol fill up with a happy host of people that had disappeared long before. She heard the voices of the little princes call loving names to an attentive and devoted mother, an enamored and faithful husband declare her the only woman in his life, a dashing Duke of Orleans proclaim his undying passion. The ghosts from Isabelle's past were all young and beautiful, gifted with pure feelings and noble motives.

Catherine was caught in the web of her memories—they shared so many—and walked with her in the gardens at Ludwigsburg, gazed at the beautiful buildings of Brussels marveled et the wonders of the court of France, basked in the admiration of en entire country.

On a September evening of the year 1422 a small silent procession of horses and litters halted on front of the massive gate of S. Pol. Few people seemed to pay any attention to it, when an incident occurred that threw Isabelle into a fit of superstitious terror.

A page of the escort was helping the Queen out of her carriage, when an old woman approached. She was poorly dressed and a few gray hairs escaped from her coif, her body was thin and bent, but her face looked almost miraculously unlined. Her clear blue eyes looked intently at Isabelle and she said distinctly:

"Queen of France, an old prophecy says that our land will be lost by a foreign woman and saved by a virgin from the Marches of Lorraine. Beware, Isabeau of Bavaria, the time of its fulfillment is approaching!"

The group stood frozen in their places, while the woman turned her back and was gone in the maze of little streets surrounding the royal palace.

The tone of her voice had not been menacing, but she had pronounced her words as if they were articles of faith that admitted no doubt. The self-assurance of a beggar in front of her Queen and her lack of awe were in themselves frightening. The devil must have inspired her and the ladies touched their rosaries and holy images for protection. Nobody in the Queen's group had ever heard of such a prophecy, but the sudden apparition of that hag and those Satan-inspired words made them shiver with uneasiness.

Once again they were in St. Pol, and again the life of the

Queen and her attendants followed the monotonous, gloomy pattern that the arrival of her daughter, Queen Catherine, had interrupted during their stay in Vincennes.

As before, poverty haunted Isabelle, because the new ruler of France, the Duke of Bedford, who governed in his nephew's name, was illiberal and inconsiderate of her needs—she was absolutely of no consequence in the realm of politics now. Once again jewels and gold objects were sold or pawned, and the bright colors of the cloths that Catherine had sent to her mother became faded.

When Catherine of Vermandois looked at herself in her silver mirror, she saw a thin and tired face that she did not like. She did not mind the myriad of tiny lines surrounding her eyes, the flabbiness around her chin, but the contours of her lips were pinched in an obstinate curve, and despair was in her eyes.

"Is this you, Catherine of Fastavarin?" she would wonder at her image. "Is this the vivacious happy girl who came to France a life time ago, is this the woman who stirred up the emotions of brave, generous men, and gave her heart sincerely and without conditions?"

Bitter tears would fall then, and her heart would ache with nostalgia for her youth.

Isabelle's feelings were similar to Catherine's, but tinged with a sense of remorse and rage that her friend did not experience.

If, like Catherine, she wept over her lost youth, the men she had loved, the pleasures she had enjoyed, Isabelle also wept over her broken marriage vows, lack of compassion for a man who had given her honor and riches and whose bed she had left for his brother's, over the indifference she had shown towards her children, the hatred she felt for one of them.

It was too late to make up for the wrongs she had done, take words and actions back, and Isabelle felt her impotence more acutely than ever when King Charles' death was announced.

He had been ailing for a while, but his end was quite sudden and death came to the tortured monarch swiftly, as when the faint light of a candle, which has been burning dimly for a long time, is blown out by an unexpected breath.

With dry, vacant eyes, Isabelle and Catherine watched the King's attendants, pale and solemn in their black gowns and hoods, carry the bier where his body lay and place it on a vermilion stretcher. From St. Pol the coffin was to be taken to Notre Dame to be blessed, and from there to St. Denis Cathedral for the final rest, but custom did not allow the Queen to follow her husband's funeral.

The short procession quickly disappeared from the palace courtyard and the same thought struck the two friends with sudden intensity: with the King's death, their last, tenuous link to life was also broken. Long, empty years stretched ahead of them, filled with poverty, humiliation, oblivion. They would perhaps be alive, but dead inside, as no friends, no children, love, would warm up their lonely days, no grateful people would remember their Queen, no loving sovereign would share his honors with his mother.

With a silent sob Isabelle, Queen Dowager of France, took her friend's hand and in her eyes Catherine read the desperation that filled her heart and the horror of their future.

EPILOGUE

The Burial Of Charles VI

On St. Martin's Day, the King of France was buried in St. Denis, in a white marble sepulcher erected next to those of his parents, Charles the Wise and Good Queen Jeanne. A great multitude of people filled the Abbey, many with tears in their eyes and memories of the King's past splendor in their minds.

Not a prince of the blood was present at the funeral rites, and only the Duke of Bedford and his English escort had followed Charles' coffin from Notre Dame to the Abbey of the Kings of France.

The bier was open and his body, clothed in a mantle of vermilion lined with ermine, a crown on his head, a scepter in his hand, lay on a bed of blue velvet embroidered with fleurs-de-lis. Four attendants held the poles of a gold cloth canopy suspended over the coffin, and as the slow procession progressed towards the place of his eternal rest, his people could once more gaze upon his countenance and whisper that their good King looked as if he were only asleep. His features were calm and composed, the ravages that the malady had wrought on his face pacified by the gentle, soothing hand of death.

When the rites were over, a herald stepped forward and proclaimed: "Pray for the soul of our sovereign Lord, Charles of Valois, good people. May God protect the Duke Henry of Lancaster, King of France and England!"

King Charles's servants, then, repeated the herald's words, holding their maces and swords upside down—their service to their King was over.

In the meantime, in the village of Domremy, in the Marches of Lorraine, a young girl was readying herself for her mission.

Her name was Joan, and she could neither write nor read, but angels and saints were sent to her by God because she had been deemed worthy to perform the miracle that France needed—unify the country under the leadership of the Dauphin Charles, the son Isabelle had hated and rejected.

And Charles, the future King Charles VII of France, who had doubted his legitimacy all his life, and been ashamed of his promiscuous cruel mother, could believe the words of the pure maiden, who assured him, her "gentle Dauphin" that he was indeed son of King and true heir of France.

Isabelle never met Joan of Arc, but she knew of the maid's glorious exploits, the deliverance of the city of Orleans, the coronation of the Dauphin at Reims—she understood then that the prophecy had come true and that the Maid of Orleans had saved the country that the German Queen had betrayed.

Did she also understand that, when the flames to which the English had condemned her charred Joan of Arc's body, they only delivered her from history and consecrated her to divinity?

CPSIA information can be obtained at www.ICGtesting.com
Printed in the USA
BVOW05s1751040614

355387BV00002B/222/P

9 781595 945259